GARY McMAHON

DEAD BAD THINGS

A THOMAS USHER NOVEL

**ANGRY
ROBOT**

ANGRY ROBOT

A member of the Osprey Group
Midland House, West Way
Botley, Oxford
OX2 0PH
UK

www.angryrobotbooks.com
Pilgrim's progress

An Angry Robot paperback original 2011
1

A catalogue record for this book is available
from the British Library.

ISBN: 978-0-85766-126-5
EBook ISBN: 978-0-87566-128-9

Set in Meridien by THL Design.

Printed in the UK by CPI Mackays, Chatham, ME5 8TD.

Dedicated to Gary Fry:
here are some bits of my mind!

AUTHOR'S NOTE

I have taken certain liberties with the geography of Leeds.
Let's just call it artistic licence. For instance, the LGI in Leeds
doesn't, to my knowledge, have a Cancer Care Unit, and
even if it does I couldn't tell you what floor it's on. The city
in this novel is the Leeds of my imagination – part fact, part
fiction, wholly extraordinary. I hope keen-eyed readers will
forgive me for transforming the place in these subtle ways,
and that they enjoy the haunted landscape I've created.

The angel came to him again, a few years later, but this time what it brought was something real, something tangible. Not some vague insight, but a *thing* – a lovely little thing, in fact.

It never arrived when he expected, this angel; it always turned up when he had almost forgotten about it. Or when he had somehow managed to convince himself that it was not real – that it was nothing but a dream or an illusion.

The angel. The beautiful bald-headed angel.

He was sitting by the hole in the ground he'd just filled with soil, wondering how long it would take for the remains to begin to rot. Down there, beneath the packed earth, lay a small boy he'd taken from a street in Birmingham three days ago. A small, underfed boy with not much to say for himself; he was maybe three or four years old.

He had kept the boy in the back of his van, tied up and gagged with old rags, until it was time to deal with him. By then the boy was weak, half-starved and almost unconscious. The rest had been easy, a mere trifle.

It had been simple to let the bad things out. Even now, relatively early in his career, he had perfected the technique.

The boy was his seventh victim. Which wasn't bad going, all

things considered – he'd only been killing them for five years, since the first time the angel had visited him. The angel had told him what to look for and how to identify it. The angel had given him the gift of insight, of *knowing*, and nothing had looked the same since.

"Hush now," he said, stroking the small mound of earth as if it were a downy little head. "Time to sleep. You can't cause any trouble now – not now or ever." The moon was almost full; it lit his actions, putting him under a celestial spotlight. "The dead bad things are gone." He glanced up, at the moon and the stars, and wondered if the God he had come to know and love was watching him, judging him. If so, would he be found wanting, or was he in fact carrying out the will of God, as he hoped?

The angel had told him what God wanted, back during that first visitation. The angel told him, and then it touched him, granting him vision. Gifting him insight.

"Hush now…" His words flowed between his lips like blood – the blood that had been shed by the boy, from his smashed lips and the holes in his head. "Sleep well."

"Having fun?"

He looked up, and saw the angel standing in the shadows by a clump of trees. Shadows gathered like oil in water around the angel, cloaking it in a soft, gelid darkness.

"Well, are you? Having fun, I mean?" The angel's smile was a broad slice in the flesh of its cold, hard face. The angel's eyes were large and dark and glassy, devoid of anything that even resembled humanity. It was not of this world; it was of somewhere else, somewhere distant and untouchable. It was an angel.

"I don't think that's the right word," he said, staring at the angel but losing sight of it, despite the short distance between them. It was as if the angel were receding, floating away or retreating into darkness. "I mean, fun implies that this is some kind of entertainment rather than work. The work of the Lord."

"Ah," said the angel. "Him." It smiled again, but this time it was a thin black thing that squirmed across the lower half of its face. In the dark, in the shadows, it looked like a tentacle of darkness was reaching out of the angel's mouth to grope around on its hairless chin.

"Isn't that what you told me before? That I was doing God's work?"

The angel nodded. "Of course. That's right. I did, didn't I? And I have more work for you. Another important task."

The man stood at the side of the grave, brushing down his jeans, and then walked forward to stand in the tiny clearing in the middle of the woodland glade he'd thought would hide his deeds so well. But one can never hide from angels: they see everything, through the Lord's gaze. He knew that; it was a truth he could not deny. "What is it?"

The angel moved to the side. Just one step: a dainty little shimmy. Resting behind it, small and strange on the hard ground, was a bundle of blankets. The bundle moved. Then it began to mewl, like a kitten. But he knew it wasn't a kitten the angel had brought him. It was a baby. A human baby.

Of course it was.

"I want to you do something for me. Something... *vital*. You might not even know how important it is until after you die... but that doesn't matter. What does matter is the fact that I'm asking you, and you're going to do it. For me." The angel blinked, but the gesture looked false, faked, as if it didn't really need to moisten its eyes. Like it was a little act, a deliberate gesture calculated to emulate humanity. "*Capiche?*"

"It's a baby."

"Oh, how observant," said the angel. "Looks like all my time and effort isn't being wasted on you." The angel opened its mouth slightly, but not in a smile. It looked hungry. Ravenous.

"Ok." He nodded his head.

"Like you really had a choice anyway, eh?" The angel tilted its head.

Tha man said nothing.

The angel reached behind without turning around. Its arms stretched unnaturally, the knuckles of its small white hands scraping the ground and the fingers scrabbling in the dirt like pale insects. The angel picked up the baby and lifted it, then pushed it away from its body. "Take it," said the angel.

The baby was sleeping. Its eyes were closed.

"It's a girl," said the angel. "A little cunt." The angel laughed – a hard, bitter sound with far too many edges. "A breeder."

He was curiously offended by the angel's words, but knew enough not to voice how he felt. He took the baby and held it close, feeling its warmth bleed through the thin blankets and creep towards his heart.

"Guard this baby. Care for it. You can do what you want with it – sniff it, cut it, bite it, beat it, fuck it if you like. I don't care. Just don't kill it. The baby needs to live. That's all I ask. Make sure it lives. Or you die." Then the angel was gone. It didn't walk away, or float or fly; it just wasn't there anymore.

The baby squirmed in his hands, making those same mewling noises. Then, suddenly, it opened its eyes and smiled up at him, gobbets of dribble running down its chin.

It opened its mouth and it grinned at him.

At him: a killer of infants.

The baby smiled again.

He smiled back, and thought about how easy it would be to break the baby's neck.

PART ONE
GIVING IT ALL AWAY

"Give sorrow words: the grief that does not speak
Whispers the o'er-fraught heart and bids it break."

William Shakespeare, *Macbeth*, Act IV, Scene III

ONE

Police Constable Sarah Doherty watched the rain as it slid like a horde of transparent slugs down the car windows, wishing desperately that the sun would come out some day soon. A little sunshine, she thought, always made things look better, even if they were dead bad...

Dead bad: that was one of *his* terms, her father. He'd used it often, usually to describe his mood before turning on her, and she hated herself for even thinking the words. Hated herself for using his phrasing, even in the relative safety of her head.

She stared at one particular trickle of rain, following the smeared trail as it wound an uneven line down the glass. Held within that single drop she saw the entire world and her inconsequential place within it. She felt small, tiny really, like a speck on the finger of a giant. One flick of that finger and she would be gone – nothing but a cosmic crumb thrown into the void.

"You OK?"

Sarah blinked and turned her head, staring at her partner. For a second she failed to recognise his familiar battered features.

Benson smiled. It was not a pretty smile – not on *his* face – but it was something she had grown accustomed to. For such an ugly man, Benson possessed an abundance of compassion for his fellows, which somehow made him attractive. "You were miles away." He swivelled in the driver's seat, leaning forward slightly. The seat belt went taut across his broad chest. The springs in the seat creaked.

"I was. Miles away, that is. Miles away in the past, lost with the ghosts." She shrugged her shoulders, one side at a time, trying to reduce the tension. Her back ached; an old injury caused by her father in a particularly dark moment. Closing her eyes for a second, she said: "But I'm OK now. Don't worry about me." When she opened her eyes again Benson was still smiling, but now his face looked almost handsome – almost. Not bad at all, really, for a man with badly scarred cheeks and a large dent in his forehead.

The street outside was empty at this hour, even the most hardy of drunks and homeless people having found somewhere to curl up and sleep off whatever ailed them. The rain was heavy; it made a loud hissing sound as it pelted against the brickwork of the big Victorian terraces that lined both sides of the wide street. Not too far away, the urban greenery of Round-hay Park lay shrouded in darkness, and Sarah thought about how easy it might be for someone to slip away unseen across the grass and into the trees... someone who had been doing wrong on her watch.

The radio crackled – a sharp, staccato echo of the rain outside. Benson reached out and turned down the volume. "You ready?" he stared at her, as if he were looking for something – some sort of clue to her wellbeing – in her eyes.

Sarah nodded. "Let's go. It's probably a fucking hoax call. You know what they're like round here – I'll bet it's just some snotty accountant getting his own back on a neighbour who's in a higher tax bracket."

Benson laughed as he opened the door, but the sound of the rain drowned out his mirth. Sarah got out of the passenger side, hunching her shoulders in an instinctive protective gesture. It didn't work; she was soaked through in a few seconds. The rain was cold. The chill went right through her.

"Fuck," she said, tilting her checkerboard bowler down over her forehead. "I need a coffee."

"What's that?" Benson was leaning over the roof of the car, his head cocked to one side. He looked like an inquisitive rottweiler.

"Nothing," said Sarah, shaking her head. Then she walked around the car and joined him, resting one hand on her hip, near the ASP expandable baton which hung from her belt.

The moon was a smudge in the black sky, and there were very few stars clustered around it. The rain seemed to be in the process of erasing everything else from the sky, as if it were trying to drown the world. The thought chilled Sarah even more than the low temperature and she tried to bury it. The last thing she needed when she was out on patrol was to spook herself like this. It had been happening more and more lately, her mind creating phantoms from thin air, and she had to put a stop to it.

Nobody would trust a scared police constable, particularly a scared *female* police constable. It was something she had been forced to learn quickly, this type of casual prejudice: a simple harsh fact of life on the modern police force.

She followed Benson – who was the senior partner, despite having only three months more experience than Sarah – and watched the roll of his shoulders as he swaggered through the rain. Sometimes he seemed like an unstoppable force, a clenched fist on two legs.

The rain churned angrily in the gutters, forming foaming streams along both sides of the road. Litter swirled in the black water – a ripped cardboard coffee cup, a stained fast food carton floating like a little boat, and several sodden pages from a discarded newspaper. Sarah could just about make out the name Penny Royale printed in bold text at the top of one of the pages. It was a case she had not been directly involved with, but six months ago, when the torn and battered body of the young girl was found in bed at her parents' home on the Bestwick estate, the child's death had sent shockwaves through the entire community.

Sarah's Achilles heel was cases involving murdered children, and she found it particularly difficult to remain in control of her emotions when, as in the Royale case, it seemed like the parents (both still missing) had been responsible for the killing. She wished that someone would find them, preferably dead. The world would not miss such shoddy, murderous parents. The world mourned dead children, not scumbag adults. And it mourned them far too often.

Benson pulled up abruptly outside one of the terraced houses. He raised a big, knuckly fist and rapped briskly on the wide wooden door. Then, realising that the heavy rainfall might make it difficult to be heard, he knocked again but harder this time – like he really meant it, she thought.

Benson, Sarah knew, had his own weaknesses. She had no idea what they were, but had glimpsed them rising above the surface on a couple of occasions, like a shark's fin breaking water for a moment before vanishing again beneath the waves.

Slowly the door opened and a small, pale face peered out through the gap between door and frame. "Yes?"

"It's the police, madam. Did someone make an emergency call?" Benson took a step back, off the doorstep, as if aware of his naturally intimidating presence.

"Oh, yes. Yes." The door opened wider to reveal an elderly woman standing in a narrow hallway, her dressing gown pulled tight around her hefty frame. "I'm sorry… my husband works nights. I worry." She smiled, as if this explained everything.

"That's OK, madam. Was it you who made the call? Are you a Mrs Frances Booth?" Benson took out his notebook and flipped it open, ducking into the doorway to keep the paper dry.

"Yes. That's right. I was… well, this might sound a bit daft, but I'm concerned about the old dear next door. Mrs Johnson."

The woman stepped back, into the hallway. "Would you like to come in?"

"Thank you." Benson stepped inside and Sarah followed, remaining silent. She smiled and took off her hat, inspecting the interior of the house as she did so. Expensive wallpaper, quality carpets, framed prints of good quality art on the walls. It was a nice place; a place where money dwelled.

"I really hope I'm not wasting your time."

"Oh, I'm sure you're not – it is Mrs Booth, isn't it?" The woman nodded, almost eagerly. "We were in the area, anyway." Benson's tone was light, friendly. He excelled at putting people at their ease, despite his bulk and the scars on his cheeks. Sarah always found it strange that the public warmed to him so quickly and easily, but then she usually remembered that he had the same effect on her. Two days after meeting, they had jumped into bed together. The occasional sex was something they were both slightly wary of taking any further, but she always thought it a good example of how he was able to take a person off guard and slip in behind their defences. She frowned at the memory, but then suppressed it before Mrs Johnson noticed.

Business first; pleasure later. Much later – probably when she was all alone and relaxing in a nice hot bath. The kind of pleasure Benson offered would have to wait a bit longer.

"So, why are you so worried about your neighbour, Mrs Booth? Please tell us everything you can." Benson paused, letting the woman gather herself before telling her story.

"Well," she said, folding her arms across her large chest. "Mrs Johnson – Celia – goes out every day without fail. She takes a walk to the park and gets her shopping on the way back, you see. Every day. Since her husband died – he was a dentist. But I haven't seen her for two days, and so I started to be concerned. I started to worry." Again she smiled nervously, clearly afraid of coming across as a paranoid old hen or a timewaster.

"Please… continue. Be clear and concise, if you can." Benson wrote something in his notebook. Sarah nodded at the woman, urging her on.

"I didn't tell anyone in case Celia was ill or something, so I just went round there to check on her – you know, like a good neighbour. There was no answer. This was, oh, yesterday lunchtime. There was no answer when I knocked on the door, but I heard movement inside. Well, I say *heard*, but… it was more a sort of feeling that there was someone inside, watching me." Her slippered feet shuffled on the carpet. She bit her bottom lip. "I am being daft, aren't I? I am, I know I am. Daft."

"Of course not. You're being very sensible, Mrs Booth." Now it was Sarah's turn. She stepped forward, opening her arms and moving them away from her body – a gesture of trust, just like she'd been taught at university. "This isn't daft at all. You did the right thing. I only wish everyone could be as civil-minded as you. Our job would be a lot easier." Sarah smiled with her mouth shut, trying her best to be reassuring. She didn't like to smile; wasn't used to it.

"There's something else." The woman glanced at the floor, and then back up again, right into Sarah's eyes. "An hour ago I went outside. I don't sleep well when Charles isn't at home – Charles is my husband – and the cat wanted to be out. I was in the back garden and I popped my head over the fence. Just to check. To be sure. To see if there was anything…" She faltered, unsure of herself now that she had begun to get to the meat of her tale. "You know."

"Something not quite right? Is that it?" Sarah chose her words carefully; she was sensitive to the woman's anxiety.

Mrs Johnson nodded quickly, as if she hoped that nobody would notice. "Yes. That's exactly it." She blinked. Her eyes were large and moist.

"And what did you see over there?" Benson looked up from his notepad, trying his best to seem casual yet clearly on edge.

His hand gripped the cardboard cover. His large knuckles bled out to white.

"There's a window panel missing in the back door. Just the one, but it was definitely gone. Like someone had removed it. The only reason I noticed was because the damned cat leapt over the fence and started sniffing around the door. I had to call her back before she went inside."

The rain made swishing noises outside the door; inside, somewhere at the heart of the house, timbers gently creaked and popped.

"You just wait here, Mrs Johnson, and we'll check this out. Put the kettle on, we'll be back in a few minutes. I'm sure there's nothing wrong, but it's good that you called us. We can have this sorted in no time." Benson slipped the notepad back into his inside pocket. He zipped up his jacket and turned to Sarah, nodded, then waited for her to lead the way.

"Oh, I hope she's OK." Mrs Johnson seemed poised on the verge of panic.

"She'll be fine. Don't you worry, now. Put the kettle on and we can all sit down to a nice cup of tea. Two sugars for me, none for Constable Doherty." His diversion tactic was smooth; it always worked a treat. Mrs Johnson followed Sarah into the kitchen at the end of the hallway and began to fill a kettle from the tap. "Two for me," said Benson, smiling flatly. "None for my partner."

The key was in the back door – something Sarah hated to see. Didn't these people realise that a kid or a junky with a skinny arm could reach through a skilfully shattered window pane and grab them? She turned the key and opened the door, stepping back out into the rain. It seemed colder and lighter at the back of the house; the rain felt as if it were trying to turn into sleet. Or snow.

"Over the fence," said Benson, overtaking her and grabbing a timber upright. "You first – I'll get something to stand on, just in case I bring the thing down."

Sarah nodded, turned and hauled herself over the fence, bringing up her legs in a single swift movement and vaulting over the flimsy wooden panel. She heard Benson still on the other side, rooting around in the garden for something to aid his progress. Then, suddenly, his head and shoulders appeared above the lip of the fence. He climbed over slowly, trying to keep his weight off the panels as he used the step-ladder to clamber up and over the nearest support post. In seconds he was standing next to her, one hand resting on her shoulder.

"The window panel. See it?" She pointed down near the ground, at the missing panel. There was no broken glass to be seen; whoever had done this, they had done a professional job and cleaned up after themselves.

"Yeah." Benson moved towards the back door. His voice was low, almost a whisper. "Yeah, I see it."

There were no lights on at the rear of the house. The windows were dark, and covered with either heavy curtains or blinds. The door was old, the lower half consisting of a series of glass panels and the upper part made up of a grubby section of UPVC that looked so thin a child could have kicked it in. A dog was barking nearby, from another garden located somewhere over the back fence. The sound was harsh and incessant, and it began to unnerve Sarah. She hated dogs – they were stupid and vicious and in her opinion their owners were little better. *Dumb animals for dumb people*, she thought. *Everybody dumb together*.

Benson placed his fingers on the door handle. The door opened smoothly. He turned and looked at her, his eyes wide. He nodded. Just the once. His scars shone in the meagre light from the nightlights and security lights mounted on the external walls of neighbouring properties.

Sarah instinctively grabbed her baton, removed it from her belt, and flicked it up and out so that the weapon swiftly extended to its full length. The brief ratcheting sound was too loud in all that silence; even the dog's manic barking failed to mask it. But there was no movement, nor a single sound, from within the house. It *felt* empty.

Even after just a couple of years on the force, Sarah had developed the knack of sensing whenever potential danger was hiding nearby. It was one of the first skills you learned when you worked the beat, and possibly the most valuable.

There was no-one here, she was certain of it, but that didn't mean the house was safe. Far from it. Because she could sense something else in there, an altogether more unsettling presence: something still and quiet and so very wrong.

In that tense and drawn-out moment, standing there on the threshold and staring at the back of her partner's head, Sarah became convinced that somewhere in the house they were going to find a dead body.

TWO

The kitchen was dark. The only light in there was coming from outside – generated by the streetlights and the drizzly layer of neon pollution that hung above the city streets. There was not even a sliver of light showing beneath the internal door. Benson went in first, checking the area for intruders. It became immediately clear that there were none in the vicinity, so he relaxed his shoulders and dropped his hands to his sides.

Sarah entered behind him, making for the side wall, where a work bench was piled with dirty pans and crockery. Scanning the area, she noted that the kitchen was slightly grubby, as if the place had not been cleaned for several weeks. A layer of dust coated the benches and cupboard doors. Either shadows or dirt stained the benches. She could see it as she eased along the edge of the room, keeping away from the centre.

Benson slowly opened the inner door to reveal a narrow hallway. Most of these kinds of Victorian houses had a similar layout: a main hallway right through from front to back, lounge and reception or dining rooms at the front and a large kitchen at the back. Upstairs: the bedrooms. Below: the cellars.

Sarah took a deep breath and tried to compose herself. She was usually calm in these situations, but for some reason tonight her throat was dry and her chest was slowly tightening beneath her uniform tunic. She was wearing a lightweight stab vest – standard issue these days – and it felt two sizes too small.

Benson motioned for her to follow him as he went through the door. He held his baton at the ready; Sarah could see his fingers tighten around the shaft. She had seen him use the weapon on a few occasions. He was an expert in hand-to-hand combat. Sarah had also used her own baton more than once, and it felt good in her fist. Reassuring.

They moved slowly yet urgently through the hallway. The old boards creaked beneath their weight, announcing their presence inside the house to anyone who cared to listen for such subtle telltales and giveaways. If anyone were hiding in the shadows, waiting to pounce or bolt, they would be all too aware of the location of the two police officers within the building. These old houses spoke, slowly and quietly, and if you understood their language you could build up a wealth of information.

Sarah often thought that she might possess some kind of special insight. There was nothing physical to prove this, of course, just a sort of tingling of the senses, like a breeze ghosting through her mind. Old houses, dark places, anywhere that normal people might consider staying away from, spoke to her softly yet explicitly; the intimate whisper of that phantom breeze in her ear. Police training was responsible for some of it, along with a natural aptitude for the work... female intuition? Yes, all of those things could be used to explain away how she sometimes felt. But still... still... she could not rationalise the way she felt at times like this. All she could say, if pushed, was that these places, these situations, made her feel like she was home.

Up ahead, near the bottom of the stairs, something moved. Benson did not even notice – his gaze was fixed on the doorway to their left – but to Sarah it looked like a gentle fluttering. She thought of a small bird's wing in a dark room, or the movement of lips as they flapped lightly to expel a tired death rattle. The motion was there for less than a second, and then it was gone. Anyone else might have written it off as nothing – an illusion, or perhaps a manifestation of anxiety in a tense situation. But not Sarah. She knew what it was: a warning. She had seen something – *sensed* something – which would otherwise have gone unnoticed. It was all the confirmation she needed of her unswerving feeling that something was wrong here. Something was out of whack.

Benson ducked his head into the doorway, and then pulled it back out again. He glanced at Sarah and shook his head: nothing of interest in there. Move on. There were two other doors leading off the hallway, and he checked each one in turn. Benson made the same deft in-and-out manoeuvre, and gave Sarah the same signal. The rooms were empty – of perpetrators, of victims, of life, of death.

Sarah looked up at the stairs, peering through the gaps in the carved timber banisters. That subtle movement she had glimpsed moments before. Had it been going up or coming down? The walls looked damp, but it was only the darkness forming yet another illusion. The walls were not really rippling – it was the play of Sarah and Benson's shadows across their tall, flat surfaces. She knew that, yet the knowledge did not make the sight any less unnerving.

She followed Benson up the stairs, staying a few paces behind in case anything happened without warning. In cadet training they had been taught never to bunch up, always to leave room to manoeuvre – fighting space – between the separate members of a team as they entered a potentially hostile location. It was a matter of common sense, of course, yet still it was surprising how many trainee constables would walk directly behind the person in front, narrowing any space in which to act if things got out of hand.

Sarah's feet fell lightly upon the stair treads. She felt watched in the cramped space. Her grip on the baton tightened, and she was once again enveloped in a shroud of anxiety. Dust swam in the air before her eyes, creating random sketches in the stairwell.

Benson paused as he reached the first landing, turning slowly to examine each side of the area at the top of the stairs, first left and then right. He moved forward to allow Sarah to access the landing, and then placed his back against the wall opposite the top of the stairs. Sarah stood at the top of the stairs, still convinced that something was about to happen, or that they were going to encounter one of the many faces of death which waited inside this house, this place of dust and shadows.

"End of the landing." Benson's voice was low, his eyes were hard. He tipped his head towards the far end of the landing, where a single door stood open. The other doors were closed – five of them in all – and each one had a dark handprint near the handle. Sarah knew without having to check that the handprints were blood, and that they symbolised a locked door – if not a physical one, then certainly a notional one.

But how did she know that? There was no time to examine the thought; Benson's urgency pushed her on.

There was a patch of blood on the carpet across the threshold of the open door. It was a large stain, like a shadow far deeper than those she'd seen elsewhere within the house: a blood shadow.

"There's something in there." She stared at the open door. "Some *thing*."

"You don't say." Benson's voice was louder now; he had accepted that there was no longer a reason to remain quiet. Whatever was inside the house, and if it was still alive, it already knew of their presence.

Then, slowly, as if it were drifting towards her on the air, Sarah caught the smell. It was the stench of the charnel house: the odour of bloody death. She knew it, even after such a short time on the force. They both knew it.

"Back up required…" She heard the start of Benson's radio request, and the static from the two-way in his hand, but the rest of it was filtered out by whatever intuition she possessed and was even now jerking to life. Her senses were... *twitching*. That was the word she associated with the sensation. It was as good a word as any other, she supposed.

Twitching.

My twitch, she thought, imagining nervous tics and facial actions. *It's my fucking twitch*.

She was barely even aware of her legs moving as they carried her along the landing, past the blood-barred doors, and towards the open door at the end. It was automatic, as if some external engine were powering her. Even if she wanted to stop, she would have been unable to interrupt the motion of her legs, or stop the low whispering sound of her police-issue boots on the carpet.

She had to go there. Whatever was inside wanted to be seen by Sarah, and by her alone. They had business, these two, in that dark house on a dark street after midnight. The nature of that business was a mystery, and might remain so, but the very fact of its existence could not be denied.

Sarah moved slowly along the landing, her baton held loosely now in a hand that felt limp and boneless. It flopped at the wrist, that useless hand, and waggled like an animal against her thigh. The baton dropped to the floor but she didn't stop to pick it up – she knew that such a weapon was useless here, and against such things as whatever the hell was waiting for her inside the room.

"Doherty! Come back. Get back here!" Benson's voice was harsh, yet fading. It sounded miles away, as if he were calling to her from a distant cliff top. She could hear the words, even make out what they said, but their meaning was pointless. Useless. They did not touch her.

She stood above the blood-shadow, staring at it, seeing within its depth a face whose curves and edges were familiar. She knew that face, but couldn't quite grasp whose it was. It looked a bit like her, but then it didn't, not really. It belonged to someone else... and yet she and it were connected in some way.

She stepped over the threshold and entered a vision from her dreams, a scene pulled dripping from her nightmares.

The room was bare but for an unmade single bed pushed up against one wall, and an old-fashioned dentist's chair which took centre stage. Sitting in the chair, with its back to the door, was a figure. It was small: a small boy. His hair was messy; it looked wet. His arms hung loosely at his sides, the fingers not quite touching the floor. The posture of the body suggested that death had occurred some time ago: it was floppy and slouched, as if the muscle tone had gone and the effects of rigor mortis had faded.

Sarah moved up behind the boy. Her arms were held out, she noticed, and she stared at her hands. Her fingers flexed, and then opened. She was reaching for him. Reaching out to the boy. The poor dead boy.

The chair was mounted on a mechanism which allowed it to turn, to spin, so Sarah placed her hands upon the backrest and pulled the boy around to face her. In her mind's eye, like a trace of memory, she knew exactly what she would see before it spun around into view.

His legs shifted as he turned. One arm swung heavily, the hand open.

The boy, his skin as white as cotton and his eyes bulging wide, was strapped into the chair by thick leather braces. These, too, were old: the leather was frayed and the bonds were locked together like trouser belts, by a spike slotted into one of many holes and then the whole thing was pulled tight, tight, tight…

He was tied at the waist and at the throat. The boy. The small, small boy.

There were holes in his head. The front of his pate had been shaved – not quite down to the scalp, but very short; a fine blonde fuzz. Then someone had slowly and patiently drilled holes into his skull.

The boy's small, small skull.

Holes. In his skull.

Sarah knew that the killer had used an old-fashioned hand drill with a wooden handle. She just knew; she fucking *knew* it. The fact that the chair was an antique, and the care taken to prepare the victim, meant that whatever scenario had been created here would only have been sullied by the use of modern power tools.

And she just *knew*... Her twitch. It told her so.

So the boy's head had been drilled full of holes – slowly, methodically. Then – and this was the worst part – something narrow and red hot had been pushed into the holes, cauterising the wounds but also searing the brain matter beneath. It was awful – medieval. Like something the Spanish Inquisition might have dreamt up.

Sarah stared at the chair. At the dead boy. And at the small holes in his small head. There was very little blood, apart from a few drizzles that had run down onto the boy's face. The air smelled faintly of burning; the smoke from singed flesh and blood filled the corners of the room, painting them a muddy yellow colour.

"Oh, God." Sarah felt sick. Her hands were on the boy, grasping his shoulders, and she stared at his loose body wondering why this all looked and felt (and smelled) so familiar. It was like a dream she'd once had, or a film she'd seen. Second-hand memories scampered through her mind, fleeing before she could grab them and pin a name to their bristling hides.

"Oh, Jesus..."

A hand fell upon her shoulder. "Come on. Let's get out of here. Back-up's on the way." It took her several seconds to recognise Benson's voice. Everything was different now, after the discovery of the boy's body. Things had changed – doors had crashed open to release a darkness that she knew she must outrun, if only she could. The world had transformed – or perhaps it had simply taken on its true shape. "Come on, now."

It was all different now. This was something more, something else: she had been given access to a place she did not want to visit.

Sarah allowed herself to be guided away from the chair, across the bare room, and out of the door. She stood shaking on the landing, yet she didn't know why. There was fear, yes, and re-vulsion – but what else was churning through her system, what other nameless emotion was even now charging her body with a terrible energy?

Was it excitement? No, not that. Please, not that. Let it just be nausea.

The bloody handprints on the closed doors now looked like they were waving, but was it a farewell or a greeting? Sarah closed her eyes but she could still see the boy. His image was locked forever inside her mind: an unwelcome tenant in her subconscious. When she opened her eyes the red handprints were no longer there.

"You OK? What happened in there?" Benson leaned in close. His breath was stale; his cheap aftershave was a vulgar presence in her nostrils.

"I… I dunno. It was weird, like I was walking in a dream – a dream I'd had before. I couldn't stop myself. I knew that boy was in the room, and that he wanted me to see him. He wanted to meet me." The realisation did not help. It simply made things worse.

"I don't understand."

Nor did Sarah. She didn't understand this at all, not any of it. A murdered boy wanted to meet her; it was hardly a sane thought.

Hardly sane at all.

THREE

No matter how far I stray from the North, it always calls me back. It never stops. I can always feel its barbs in my flesh and hear its crude whisper in the depths of my ears. The place is in my blood; my bones are moulded from the dark ore of its loathsome hills and moors, the coal from its shut-down pits and collieries.

The North: it's where I'm from, the place where it all started, and the place where I knew it would all eventually come to an end.

London.

I've always enjoyed a love-hate relationship with London. The capital seems always to welcome me, when I feel nothing but loathing in return.

I'd been there for a few months, but wasn't sure exactly how many. After discovering Penny Royale's body in that bland little house on the Bestwick Estate in Leeds, I seemed to enter a sort of psychological gap where nothing made sense, not even my own flesh. The drink helped, of course; it always had in the past and I knew that I could rely on alcohol to blot out the immediate pain.

I had lost everything; lost them all. Rebecca, Ally, Ellen, and even the child Penny Royale – a girl I had not even met until she was dead.

I woke up that morning feeling like I'd swallowed a dead rat: my tongue was coated in a thin layer of fur and my mouth tasted like decay. Blinking into the gloom, I tried to remember where I was. When I was. *What* I was. I failed on all counts.

All I knew was that it was somewhere in London, and that I was hung over.

Flailing around on a soft mattress, I managed to establish that I was in a single bed, and it was situated low to the floor. It took me a few moments to realise that there was no bed at all, and the mattress had been set down directly onto bare floorboards.

The gloom, I realised, was mostly inside my head. The room was less dark than I'd suspected. There were no lights on, and the curtains were drawn tight across the single window, but weak light was filtering through from somewhere. Perhaps it was the first kiss of dawn, or simply the electric smog of streetlights.

I sat up. My head ached. As I moved, my right hand came into contact with an empty bottle. The bottle went rolling slowly across the room. It made a loud clanking sound as it hit the skirting board but it didn't shatter. Whisky: it had to be whisky. In the past, during near-forgotten days and nights spent wrestling with my demons, whisky had always been the worst. Or the best. The answer to a question I had not even asked.

I opened my mouth. Closed it again. It felt like there were rubbery strings – like cold pizza cheese – stretched between my lower and upper jaws. Jesus, I'd really tied one on. Things must be bad...

Oh, yes. They were. Of course they were. Always.

I had lost everyone I ever loved.

Wincing with pain, I managed to stand on my shaky feet. My lower back was on fire; the nerves there were either trapped as a result of bad sleep on a shitty mattress or else they were simply not in the mood for motion. I rolled my hips, closing my eyes and trying to clear my head. I was in a room, in a house. At least I was undercover; if I looked up I could see the ceiling. And it was almost daylight.

Before long I felt in control enough to walk to the window and twitch the curtain. I didn't open it all the way at first, because I knew instinctively that any kind of brightness would be bad – even a tiny amount of muted daylight might render me blind. It took me a long time to ease the curtains open, inch by inch, and to become accustomed to the dusty twilight I found on the other side of the window. Outside was a street perched at the edge of dawn: terraced houses stood shoulder-to-shoulder, faded white lines marked the road like old scars, and grubby wheelie bins lounged like surly teenagers in unkempt gardens.

I already knew that I wasn't in Leeds. I remembered that much at least. I had fled to London, searching for somewhere to lose myself. Going underground – deep underground: as deep as I could manage.

Then it came to me. Of course; I knew exactly where I was.

Number 14 Blanchford Street, Plaistow. It was one of *those* addresses, the ones I never seemed to forget no matter how hard I tried: a grey zone.

I backed away from the window and looked around the room. Bare floors. That limp mattress on the floor. A rickety wardrobe. A scuffed chest of drawers. A lopsided bookshelf, with several well-thumbed paperback books spread out along its length.

A door.

Outside that door, a landing. Stairs. More rooms downstairs, each of them similarly basic, decked out with minimal furniture and fittings. Nobody lived here. Nobody came here. Not ever.

It was a grey zone.

There was, at one time, a file held in some obscure government department of every nation in the civilised world – it's probably on a computer hard drive these days, but I'd like to bet that it's still in existence. This file consisted of a simple brown manila cover, with two words typed front-centre: *grey zones*. Then, beneath these words, there was the name of the city to which the folder belonged. Inside the folder was a list of addresses, at least one for each major city in the world. The one matching the name of the city on the front of the folder was usually highlighted, perhaps in red, sometimes (but rarely) in green.

As you might expect, one of those addresses was in London. It corresponded exactly with the building in which I was standing: Number 14 Blanchford Street, Plaistow.

These grey zones, one in each city, in each town of reasonable size and population, are places where you don't want to go. They are the most haunted places in the world. The most cursed locations we know. Over the course of time, each country's government used a combination of compulsory purchase orders and scare tactics to buy up their own nation's grey zones, just to ensure that the buildings remained empty. At least until someone figured out what to do with them.

As far as I know, they remain empty still.

Officially, the Dakota building is regarded as perhaps the most haunted or cursed building in New York City. The film *Rosemary's Baby* was filmed there. John Lennon was assassinated on the stone front steps. But the Dakota isn't in fact the most haunted building in New York – it doesn't even come close. I can name you perhaps a dozen others, each one more haunted than the last. More *cursed*. The final address I might mention is that of a tiny brownstone townhouse in Brooklyn Heights. In 1957 a serial killer named Theodore Wesley was secretly arrested there for the murder and cannibalisation of over thirty teenage runaways. As soon as he left the house his memory of the crimes was lost, as were the public records relating to the case. Even when they executed him in a bunker located deep underground, Theodore Wesley claimed no knowledge of what they said he'd done. He died in secret; he died in confusion. Less than a dozen people ever got to hear his name.

That small townhouse is the single most haunted or cursed place in New York. None of the guide books mention it. You'll not see it on the Holiday Show. Only a handful of people know it exists.

Number 14 Blanchford Street, Plaistow, is the equivalent location in London. Many things have happened there. None of them have been reported. The public, it seems, does not need to know.

In the grey zones there exist deep gouges in the fabric of reality, where another reality has ruptured forcefully into our own and the psychic bleeding has somehow been contained within the confines of the structure. Nobody knows why this has happened. Rites and hexes help seal the zones, but there is no substitute for simply keeping the buildings empty. People have energy, and whatever is trapped inside these places is often woken by the presence of such energy. And once they wake up, they sometimes try to escape.

I am one of the few people who can spend any amount of time inside a grey zone. Most other people – *normal* people – would go insane, if they even managed to get out. A grey zone is like a maze: once you open your mind to its wonders, you can get lost inside.

You can get lost forever in there…

There was something in the corner of the room, resting among the dusty shadows. I couldn't make out quite what it was, but there was a vaguely human aspect to its shape and the way that it was slouched there, head in its hands, knees pressed tightly together. It looked like the figure was wearing some kind of dark cowl or cape, but with a grey or white hood. The figure did not disturb me. It just sat there, unmoving, like a shop window mannequin.

I walked out of the room, sober at last. The figure still did not move. It just sat there, wrapped up in its own despair. I doubted that it even knew I was there.

Oddly, grey zones are the only places on earth where the dead don't bother me. If they even see me at all, I think they consider me one of their own. They accept my temporary residence in their prisons and allow me sanctuary within their walls.

I don't like to think too hard about why that might be.

Downstairs, in the sparsely furnished kitchen, I boiled a kettle and made some coffee. The electric and gas supplies were always kept connected to these otherwise ill-maintained places. I don't know why; perhaps they kept things in order just in case some-one dropped by from the other side.

It was all coming back to me now, through the slowly rising veil of a hangover. I had come to London to lay low for a while, until the heat died down. My old friend Detective Inspector Teb-bit had helped me. He had arranged a lift in a prison van at the dead of night, and nobody but Tebbit knew that I was down here. But even he didn't know my exact location; he had re-quested that I keep it to myself, just to be safe. Too much had happened for me to remain in Leeds while others cleaned up the mess.

The kettle boiled, giving me a start as the button suddenly popped out with a sound like a kids' cap gun going off. I poured the water into a cup, watching the instant coffee grounds clump together as I tried to stir them into the liquid. The coffee tasted bitter, like lies. But bitterness was something I was getting used to. So were lies.

Bitterness and lies formed part of my standard diet. They had done for quite some time. I was even beginning to enjoy their taste.

I went through into the lounge, where I flopped down onto the ratty sofa and stared at a television set which had probably not worked since the 1970s – that was certainly when the model had been manufactured. My reflection in the screen looked tiny, a pale and insignificant scrap of flesh. I watched as it sipped coffee from my cup. My hands were shaking, but the reflection's hands were steady. There was a stocky figure standing behind the sofa, both hands grasping the headrest. It was covered in what looked like a black sheet, with a white hood. I realised that whatever it was must have followed me downstairs.

I turned around, but knew that there would be no-one there. I was right: the room was deserted, but it was far from empty. When I looked back at the screen the figure was absent. Mine was, too: the screen was flat and dark and empty, reflecting nothing. I knew it was some kind of visual metaphor, but my head hurt far too much to think about it.

I got up and grabbed the threadbare rug from the floor, then threw it over the television set, obscuring the screen. I didn't want to see – I *never* wanted to see, but at least here, this time, I had a choice.

The lamp in the corner of the room was on. I must have forgotten to turn it off the night before, when I'd been so drunk that I still could not remember going to bed. I went to the lamp and extinguished it. The main light came on instantly; a bad joke in a lonely room.

"Please. Let's not get silly." My voice sounded too loud in the almost bare room. I clenched my teeth, cutting off any more words before they came.

The light went off. A snickering sound left the room and vanished up the stairs.

They like to play, some of them. Most of them just ignore me in places like the house in Plaistow, but a very few of them are occasionally keen to mess around, to mess with my head.

I wondered if it was the ghost of a dead child. Dead children seemed to follow me: my life was jam-packed with dead children, each of them wailing at me, but at a pitch that I was unable to hear.

When the phone rang I jerked so violently that I dropped my cup. It shattered on the floor, the spilled coffee creating a dark brown splatter-pattern. Like old blood. The phone kept ringing. It was the second time it had rang in as many days. Someone wanted to speak to me badly, but nobody knew that I was here.

I tried to ignore the phone, but the sound drilled into my skull, nudging my brain. This time the mystery was enough to make me walk across the room and pick up the receiver.

"Hello."

There was a short pause, as if someone were taking a long breath. And then a voice: "Hello, Thomas. I've been trying to reach you." The voice was female, but there was little about it that I could warm to. There was a tinny quality to the voice – not quite computer-generated, but somehow machine-like, as if whoever the voice belonged to was holding some sort of masking device against their lips as they spoke, perhaps as an aural disguise. The first word I thought of was: *clockwork*. It was a clockwork voice on an ancient phone, speaking to me across a line that should have been dead.

"So now you've found me," I said. I was scared, but for some reason my voice masked the fear. I had already gone through so much by now that even this strange turn of events failed to break through my armour. I stared at the pitted walls, the out-of-date wallpaper, the smeared, unidentifiable pictures held like specimens behind dirty glass in cheap plastic frames.

"Yes. I've found you." If I strained hard enough, I thought that I might hear the cogs and springs creaking.

"So what do you want?"

Another pause in the conversation, but this one was slightly longer. It contained the sound of gears shifting; a suggestion of mechanisms struggling to cope. I wasn't sure if I was actually hearing these things, or if I was simply aware of them at another level entirely.

"I want to hire you. To find someone."

I closed my eyes. "And who do you need me to find?" I wanted to open my eyes but found that I couldn't. Suddenly I no longer had any desire to look at the room, at the bland walls and the stained floorboards, at the flickering light of morning as it hovered like a killer outside the grubby windows.

"I don't know. That's what I want you to tell me." Then the line went dead. There was no dial tone; no sound at all. There had never been a connection in the first place – I had checked the phone when I arrived.

I opened my eyes. I was alone, all alone.

I was alone, as always, with the dead.

FOUR

Sarah sat up in bed. She glanced over at Benson, where he lay with his hands clutched tightly to his chest. He always slept like that. Curled against himself, as if seeking protection: warding off his demons. It looked uncomfortable, but he seemed to sleep soundly that way. Sarah stared at him for a while, wondering what his dreams were made of, and then she looked away, unable to stomach the sight any longer.

Sometimes, usually after sex, he repulsed her. She had never come to terms with her sexuality, not after what had happened in her past. It was part of her pain, a facet of her private damage. She glanced at the floor, at the handcuffs cast aside near the litter bin and the knotted scarves bunched up in the corner. Benson's wrists had been red when she'd taken them off, but this time there had been no swelling and the skin wasn't broken. They would be fine by morning, or late afternoon – when he would probably wake up with a raging hard-on and a craving for coffee. Last time she had not been so gentle, and he had been forced to wear sweatbands on his wrists for a week to hide the bruises.

She wished that she hadn't invited him back last night (or this morning, as their shift had ended at 4am). But after drying their uniforms as best they could on the station's crappy radiators and signing off duty, they'd both been shaken enough to desire the other's company. *Any* company, if she was honest – because it was better than being alone, especially after what they had discovered inside the house in Roundhay.

The poor broken thing they had found tied into the dentist's chair, with its small skull and the small holes.

Initial findings had revealed that the owner of the house – a Mrs Celia Johnson – was staying with her sister in Brighton. She had been away for a week, and knew nothing of the break-in and what had subsequently been done inside her home. The dead boy had not yet been identified, but the smart money was on him being a runaway – a lost or abandoned soul nobody would even miss. The woman's late husband had been a dentist, a fact which explained the antique dental chair and other related apparatus found in the same room. Explained it, but did nothing to render the scene harmless: it looked like something out of a pulp novel, or a scary movie.

"Fuck." Sarah whispered into the grey room, enjoying the way the word tasted. "Fuck." She slid out of bed and left the room, closing the door gently behind her so she did not disturb her lover. She smiled. *Is that what he is, my part-time lover*? *My battle-scarred paramour?*

The house lay in shadow. It was still early – just about dawn; she could see its first light at the landing windows – and sleep had somehow eluded her. All she'd managed was a brief nap before the nightmares had woken her. She never remembered the dreams, yet she always retained a sense that they were buried deep within her, plucking at her insides with terrible sharp claws made of glass and steel. They were a part of her, those dreams, and she would never be rid of them.

She padded down the stairs, feeling like a visitor in her own property. Since inheriting the place in her father's will, she had struggled to grow accustomed to the big draughty rooms and the old, creaking timbers. Even when she had lived here as a child, it had never felt like a home: just a house, a temporary shelter in which to stay until she was old enough to run away. A place where her childhood fears dwelled. Sometimes it even felt like a prison.

The living room was a mess. Her father had died over seven months ago of a sudden heart attack, but she was still trying to find the time to sort through his hoarded possessions, which were crammed into every inch of the place. Sarah had put off the job for as long as possible, feeling uneasy and guilty at the thought of rummaging among her father's things. She had never been allowed to touch his stuff when he was alive, and the strength of the man's personality still lingered, causing her to stay within those childhood boundaries. She had not seen him for five years until the day she viewed him in his open coffin, but the bastard continued to terrify her.

When she had stood over him, looking down into the cheap casket, she had expected his eyes to flicker open, his mouth to curl upwards into a sarcastic grin, and his body to sit up as he looked around in judgement at the gathered congregation. Whenever she played out this fantasy in her head, everyone at the funeral would laugh. They turned to her, their faces slick with sweat, pointed their bony fingers, and roared with a frightening humour, enjoying a joke from which she was excluded...

Sarah was a good copper – a promising young constable who was tipped by those who mattered to make detective when it came time for her to make her career choices – but an old and nagging fear held her back. She was courageous on the job, was even prepared to take on a man twice her size in a confrontation, but when it came to the memory of her father, something made her lose her nerve and revert to the little girl who hid in corners and kept watch for her daddy. The past, she thought, was like glue. No matter how far you thought you had moved on, it kept you stuck in one spot.

"Bastard," she said, raising her head to look at the ceiling. There were cobwebs gathered in the corners. The lampshades were filled with the tiny, hard sweet-shop cadavers of flies. "Can you hear me, you old shite?"

There was no reply. Of course there wasn't. The old man was dead. He was dead, but he was far from gone. That dry, throaty chuckle was just the sound of pipes clattering noisily behind the walls. The heavy tread of footsteps across the floor above was nothing but timbers settling as she stood in the cold room, warming it incrementally with her body heat. She knew this; it was obvious. Yet still she was unable to rid herself of the idea that he was standing in one of the upper rooms, rocking on his heels and enjoying yet another of his obscure jokes at her expense. Shaking in silent mirth.

"Stop it." She was speaking to herself, but it didn't feel that way.

There was nothing here to worry about. Nothing at all to fear.

He's gone, she thought. Long gone. I'm not scared anymore.

"You OK?"

So why the fuck did she flinch so violently when Benson called out behind her?

"Shit, man. You spooked me." Her voice was light but she did not smile as she turned around. She stared at him, her eyes narrowed to slits she could barely see out of. "Don't do that again." The silence which followed was uneasy and filled with too many unspoken questions. Her ears began to buzz.

Benson dropped his gaze. He looked nervous. He always did when he came to her place – perhaps he too felt the chill of her father's shadow. Because that's exactly where they were, standing in his shadow: the long, cold, dark shadow of Detective Inspector Emerson Doherty. He was a real legend, the old man; one of West Yorkshire Constabulary's finest sons. It was her father who had solved the famous "Bradford Bathnight Murders" back in 1972, and who had worked on almost every high profile case of the last thirty years – even that of the Ripper, as part of the main task force who had struggled so hard to find the killer until he'd been brought in by two ordinary beat coppers.

Her father was a legend.

He was a legend and a bastard.

Her father was a legend and a bastard and a pervert.

"I'm sorry," she said, moving quickly and lightly across the room towards Benson. Her bare feet slapped softly against the floorboards. "I'm just feeling a bit edgy. You know?" She slipped her arms around his waist, scratched gently at his muscled back, feeling him relax.

"It's OK. Last night was rough. We're both bound to feel a bit shitty about it." He pressed his body against her. His dick was hard. His scars glistened in the growing light. A halo of dust hung around his head. Sarah almost pulled away. "We're fine," he whispered in her ear, and she felt his damp breath against the side of her neck. The scar tissue was smooth and almost slick to the touch. "I promise."

"Fancy some breakfast?" Now she did pull away from him – but at least this time she had an excuse. "I have bacon. Maybe even a couple of eggs, if you're lucky." She edged towards the door.

Benson nodded. His mouth was smiling but his eyes were hard, like chips of coal. His teeth were very white. They made Sarah think of dentists... and of their hydraulic chairs. She felt suddenly short of breath.

"Come with me. You can talk to me as I cook." She left the room, knowing that he would follow close behind her. Sometimes, when his guard was down, he was like a loyal puppy. He would trail her, allowing her to manipulate him in small ways. Benson was strong, but she sensed that she was even stronger. She could probably break him with the flick of a wrist, if that was what she wanted. But she didn't know what she wanted. That was part of the problem.

At least the kitchen was clean. Her first job upon arriving at the house had been to make the room hygienic. She had scrubbed it for hours, and even moved in the pots and pans and appliances from her old flat. They looked out of place on the old work surfaces and in the rickety cupboards, but they provided an odd form of comfort. Bits and pieces of her new life making her old one seem less threatening. At least that was the plan.

Sarah grilled the bacon and fried the eggs. When the toast was ready she buttered it and sliced the rounds into triangles, which she then arranged on a large plate at the centre of the oval dining table. Benson sat at the table and watched her, his lips twitching. It was the closest he had come to a smile since they had found the dead boy. His shoulders were bunched, tension apparent in his posture.

"Do you miss him?" He kept staring at her as he spoke. It made her feel slightly uncomfortable, but she was unable to pinpoint why. Her legs were cold; she wished she'd put on her dressing gown over her flimsy Betty Boop nightshirt.

"Who?"

"Come on, you know who I mean. Your dad."

"He wasn't my dad," she said coolly, turning her attention back to the hissing frying pan. "He was just my father." She flipped the eggs, being careful not to burst the yokes. She hated it when that happened.

"You weren't close, then?" Benson's voice filled the room.

"Why all the questions? You've never asked about him before?" She turned down the gas on the hob. Checked the bacon; it wasn't quite crispy enough for her taste. She pushed the grill pan back under the heat. The skin of her hand tightened as it moved close to the flame.

"I know. I just thought, well. You know. I thought it was time we actually tried to get to know each other. We've been fucking for weeks now, and all I know about you is that your dad was the famous DI Doherty." He was attempting to keep his tone light, but there was an edge to it, an undercurrent she didn't like.

"Is that why you fuck me?" She closed her eyes. "Because I'm the daughter of a legend?" The hot oil in the pan spat at her. She felt it on her cheek. The pain was good; it was real.

"Don't talk shite. Of course that isn't why. I like you. We seem to work well together."

Sarah laughed. "Jesus, you sound like you're filling in a form, or something. Like a character reference: '*works well with others, likes to tie me up when she rides my dick.*'"

Benson laughed, breaking the moment of tension, but Sarah could tell that he was still unsure. Good: let him stay that way. Nobody got through her layers, not if she could help it. She liked to keep everyone off balance. The real Sarah Doherty was buried way too deep for a scar-faced journeyman like Benson to find. She regretted this thought instantly, but that didn't make it untrue.

"You want ketchup on this?" The bacon was ready. She put the food on the plates.

"What?"

"Ketchup. You know, red sauce. Or something else?" She turned and set down the plates on the table, taking the seat opposite. "I have some stuff in that cupboard over there." She motioned with her head but made no move to stand.

Benson seemed confused for a moment. He looked at her, then down at his plate, and then across towards the cupboard. "No," he said. "No, thanks." His eyes were dull, as if he'd just been beaten in a game whose rules he did not understand. There were dark circles under his eyes. His short, dark hair stuck out in little clumps.

"Suit yourself," said Sarah. Then she got up, went to the cupboard, and took out the ketchup.

They ate in silence. The smell of burnt bacon hung in the air. A puzzling sense of unfulfilled confrontation lay between them.

Afterwards, Benson washed the dishes while Sarah returned to the living room with a cup of coffee. She turned on the TV and watched the morning news. There was a brief report mentioning the dead boy, but not the state in which they had found him. Someone had been stabbed outside a nightclub in central Leeds. There had been a crash involving two coaches on the motorway, heading towards Manchester.

Sarah got up and went to the bureau. It was an old piece of furniture, possibly an antique. Sarah remembered it from her childhood. Once she'd watched her father slamming her mother's head repeatedly against it during an argument over shopping.

She opened the top drawer and began to riffle through the papers she'd found there, bored and restless, looking for something to distract her darkening thoughts. A few days ago she had noted a couple of envelopes stuffed with Polaroid photographs inside the bureau. At the time she had not been able to examine the photos – she was due at the station, and just nosing around as she finished her morning orange juice with no real aim in mind.

She dug deep and found two envelopes. They were slim, brown, and obviously old. One of them was badly torn and the contents were threatening to spill out.

"Come on, then," she whispered, juggling the envelopes as she took them out of the drawer. She almost dropped the torn one, and this was all the invitation the photos needed to wriggle free. They spilled to the floor like thrown playing cards, scattering at her feet.

Sarah bent down and grabbed them, creasing one or two but not really caring. She was certain they weren't important: just more of her father's shit. The same old stuff he had been hoarding for years. The house was filled with such items, and she was tempted to call in a house clearance company to have the lot taken away without even giving it another glance. Or was that just something she told herself to stop her from being afraid of what she might find?

Slowly, she fanned out the photos in her hands. The first one showed her father, much younger than when he had died. He was naked except for an old-fashioned bobby's custodian helmet and a avaricious smile. Sarah's mother was kneeling at his feet; her arms were trussed up tightly behind her back and bound by what looked like coils of nylon rope. Her father had an erection. Her mother was staring at it. Her lips were slightly apart. There was fear in her eyes. The image was slightly degraded, and nothing was too clear, but the look of absolute terror in her mother's eyes was unmistakable. Sarah had seen it before.

She always looked like that when she knew her husband was going to rape her.

"Jesus..." Sarah was hardly surprised. As a child, she had seen far too many examples of the man's abusive nature – had even experienced it first hand, several times. But this was something new. She had never known him to *photograph* any of his activities. The risk of the images getting into the wrong hands was too strong, and exposure would surely ruin his carefully-cultivated reputation as an officer of note.

The muscles in her jaw ached. She was grinding her teeth. A photograph like this meant nothing, of course; it was simply a kinky shot of two married people playing sex games. Hardly something new amongst the police, who tended to let off steam in all kinds of personal ways. *But...*

What if he had recorded other things. Bad things. *Dead bad things*, as the old bastard had called anything that did not fit into his fucked-up sense of right and wrong, his twisted world view.

Sarah carefully slipped the photographs back into the envelope, and then she replaced both envelopes inside the overstuffed drawer. She would examine these more closely later, when she was alone. She had a day off before rotating back onto the day shift; there was nowhere important she needed to be. She had even briefly considered cancelling her rest day and calling into the station, maybe to relieve someone who had better things to do, a family and friends to spend time with, a real life to lead. But not now: not any longer.

It seemed that she too had better things, more interesting things, to occupy her time. The old bastard must have been looking at these old photographs not long before he died. She could think of no other reason why they would be so easily found; surely he would usually have kept them under lock and key in his office space in the cellar?

Sarah returned to her seat and sipped her coffee. It was lukewarm, but it tasted good. Maybe she would brew up a fresh pot, just to keep her going as she went through her father's belongings. Because wasn't it about time she did that? Hadn't she been procrastinating for long enough?

The day stretched ahead of her, filled with potential. The secrets of the house beckoned. Beneath her feet the cellar swelled with darkness, forbidding her entry. The windows shone with burnished morning light. Now all she had to do was ditch Benson, so she could finally get down to business and reacquaint herself with her father.

FIVE

Trevor looked at the boy and frowned. What was his name again? Ah, yes: Derek. Not a very memorable name, but with a surname like Pumpkiss, Trevor could hardly be choosy. He much preferred his stage name, Dove, but that was all in the past now. He doubted he could ever go by the name Trevor Dove again – not after what had happened. Not since he had been exposed.

"You OK?" Derek was wearing a pair of skinny jeans and scuffed baseball boots. He'd taken off his shirt when he had accidentally-on-purpose spilled red wine on the sleeve. It was a lame move – far too obvious – but Trevor had pretended to fall for it. The boy was charming, in a low-rent kind of way, and he had a beautiful smile. Nice white teeth. The shapeless figure of an adolescent.

"Sorry… yes, I'm fine. Just thinking." He tried to grin, but his face refused to move in the right way and it probably looked more like he was having a stroke.

"Thinking?"

"Yes."

"I see. I like a man who thinks."

Trevor tried not to laugh. As seductions went, it was pathetic. The boy clearly read too many porn mag letters pages, spent too much time on internet forums. "Is that so?"

"Yes. It is. I like *you*… I like you a lot."

There you go: he'd moved into second gear.

Trevor took a step towards the boy, moving past the large sofa and standing near the polished oak coffee table. He'd already refilled their wine glasses but neither of them had taken a drink since the spillage incident. Trevor reached down and picked up his glass. He took a large mouthful of merlot. Nice. Like the boy and his bright white teeth. His soft white skin.

"Come here," said the boy. He had lowered his voice; his eyes were shining. He was trying to be the alpha dog. Once again, Trevor held back a surge of laughter.

"OK," said Trevor, moving forward until he was standing only inches away from the boy. "Here I am." Trevor towered above the boy; he was a head taller.

"Yes, there you are." The boy lunged. He was clumsy and graceless, but didn't even realise how inept his moves were. He thought he was being so smooth, so in-control. His mouth crawled across Trevor's face; his hand grabbed Trevor's crotch, rubbing it.

Trevor tried to throw himself into the act – he really did. Derek was wonderful to look at, and he had one of those cute little skinny-fat-boy pot-bellies. Yet he was narrow of build, and his skin was coloured a shade of white which took the breath away.

"What's wrong?" The boy pulled back, but he kept his hand pressed against Trevor's cheek; his other hand remained down there, stroking gently. "Don't you like me?"

This time Trevor did laugh. It was a small sound, and very brief. The boy removed his hands from Trevor and took a single backwards step, pretending to sulk.

"No. Really. I do like you. I'm sorry, friend… it's just that I've been through a bad time, a really shitty time. It's affected… well, you know. My responses." He held the boy's gaze, almost challenging him to react.

Derek sat down heavily in the armchair. He stared at his feet, and then picked up his glass. "So it isn't me, is that what you're saying?" He looked even more like a little boy and Trevor at last began to feel the beginnings of a red-rushing wave of desire.

But God, he was so fucking shallow. So self-obsessed. "No," said Trevor. "It's me. Really."

Derek smiled. "Well, how about we just take it slowly and see what happens. I've never failed yet, you know." His lips were red. It was the wine, of course, but Trevor kept thinking of blood. Fat lips covered in blood.

His desire fled; the red rush faded.

"I think that's a good idea," said Trevor. "How about I open another bottle?"

He went through into the kitchen and took a fresh bottle from the wine rack above the sink. The place was clinically clean – not a dish out of place or as much as a crumb visible on the work surfaces. Trevor had always been slightly obsessive, and these days those qualities were focused on his housekeeping. Back when he performed on the stage, speaking with the dead, he had been obsessed with his outfits, his hair, and his carefully crafted repertoire with the audience. Now that he had left the stage behind, he had turned to other, more prosaic obsessions.

He opened the wine and let it breath, staring at his face in the kitchen's many reflective surfaces – the stainless steel oven, the clean glass of the microwave door, and the highly polished side of the toaster. What he saw there saddened him: he had lost a lot of weight and was starting to look his age. The showman in him was disappointed that he'd let himself go, but the rest of him considered it a suitable punishment for what he had done. Why should he look good when his life had turned to shit?

Trevor felt like punching his reflection, but knew that he wouldn't bother. He didn't want to hurt his knuckles.

He heard the boy – Derek, damn it; his name was Derek – moving around in the lounge. Probably checking out the book-shelves (there were a lot of copies of Trevor's own book, *Heart of a Dove*, in the house, but they were stored in boxes; the publisher had allowed it to go out of print long before the rumours began and the book had ironically started selling again), or perhaps riffling through his CDs. There was no money lying around; Trevor was far too wise for that. He'd been turned over before, in a similar situation, so he no longer kept cash on the premises unless it was locked in the safe.

Sighing, he picked up the bottle and walked back through into the lounge.

Derek was standing looking at a poster. He had unrolled it and was holding it with both hands, reading the text. His thin fingers gripped the edges lightly, and his face was obscured by the big square of glossy paper.

Shit, thought Trevor. I thought I'd locked all of those away.

But did he really think that, or had he left one out for whoever he brought back from the club to discover? Like a test, just to see how far they would go.

Derek glanced up from the poster. He was smiling. "Oh my God. It's you, isn't it?" He turned the poster face-out, as if Trevor had no idea what was printed there.

But he did. Of course he did. It was one of the posters from his last tour – the one which had come to a disgraceful end in Bradford. He looked at the image of himself: a gaudy little queen in a pastel suit, with bouffant hair and a cheesy smile, motioning with his hands. He looked ridiculous, but he hadn't thought so back then, only six months ago. Back then he had thought he looked fucking great.

But that was then, when he could still contact the dead. Now that his gift had deserted him, he felt like he was no longer Trevor Dove, professional psychic. Indeed, that was why he now went by his loathsome, comical real name: Trevor Pumpkiss.

"Put that down," he said. "Please. Just put it away."

Derek, sensing that this was serious, rolled up the poster and placed it back on the shelf where he must have found it. "I'm sorry. It is you, though, isn't it? You're that psychic bloke, the one who…" A look of surprise crossed the boy's face, as if for the first time in his short life he had suddenly become self-aware.

"The one who they say raped his kid brother?" Trevor handed him the bottle. His hands were steady. The boy's hand, when he reached out to take the wine, was not.

"I… I didn't mean anything."

Trevor shook his head. "Don't believe everything you read in the gutter press, friend."

Derek put down the wine bottle and then returned to the armchair. When he sat down, his naked torso gleaming pale and delicious in the soft light, Trevor finally felt a twinge of genuine passion. "Let's start again," he said, smiling at the boy. "Like we've only just met. How does that sound?"

"I'd like that." Derek's smile was slight yet knowing; he licked his lips before sipping more wine, just as he'd done in the small basement club near Call Lane, where they'd met at the bar. "I'd like it a lot."

"So tell me about yourself." Trevor sat on the floor and crossed his legs, as if squatting at the feet of an idol.

"There's not much to tell." Derek's left eye twitched; it was a subtle movement, but a dead giveaway that there was indeed a lot to tell. "I left home at fifteen, after my dad beat the shit out of me for being gay. After that I drifted through a succession of empty relationships, taking on dead-end jobs to pay the bills. There was a brief time when I lived on the streets. Then, one cold winter evening, I was picked up by an older man who gave me a bed in return for a blowjob. That's when I realised my calling: that I was just a dirty little whore." A grin crawled across his mouth: sleazy, unpleasant, making him look old and used up. "I stayed there for a year, honing my skills." He smiled, but it lacked any real humour. There was a glistening darkness trapped behind his eyes, and for the first time Trevor thought the boy looked as if he had substance. "He taught me everything. Then I left him to make my own way, and much later I met you in the Crimson Club." This smile was more natural; it played at the edges of his mouth, making him look even cuter (and once again younger) than he actually was.

"I see."

"It's an old story," said Derek, shrugging his narrow shoulders. "The same one told by thousands of other lads my age. Nothing new. Nothing unique." There was such a sense of desperation behind the words; and a terrible hunger for recognition which made Trevor feel uneasy.

Derek looked down at his legs.

Trevor realised that he was stroking the boy's knee. He stared at his hand, and then glanced up at Derek's face. "How old are you, friend?"

Derek closed his eyes. "I'm twenty-one."

"Really?"

"Really." He opened his eyes again and they looked hard, like chunks of glass. In that moment Trevor would have believed that the boy was older even than him – older than anyone he had ever met. His eyes, anyway, were ancient.

Trevor struggled awkwardly to his feet and leaned across his guest. His hand brushed Derek's chest and as he lowered his mouth to the other's lips, he felt his own eyes close. Behind them, peering through the darkness, he saw his baby brother's small white face. Desire surged; he forced the game, needing to play it through to the last move.

They went to the bedroom, where the sheets were already turned down. "You were expecting to bring someone back here tonight?" Derek smiled. He kicked off his shoes and took off his jeans before lying down on the bed.

"Not just anyone," said Trevor. "Someone. Somebody like you."

They tussled for a while, jockeying for position: with a new partner, it was often difficult to judge who would be on top. It became a battle of wills, almost a genuine wrestling match, but finally the boy went loose and acquiescent and brought up his knees to accommodate Trevor.

The moment felt heavy, as if the air had turned to sludge. They moved slowly, their limbs heavy with tension. Trevor turned his head to the side, and when he glanced into the full-length mirror on the wall he saw what looked like the palm of a hand pressed against the other side of the glass…

It stayed there for a second, the tips of its fingers white against the glass, and then it pulled away, vanished.

Trevor blinked. There were tears in his eyes. He returned his attention to Derek, but already he was fading, becoming limp. "I'm sorry," he said, burying his head in his partner's naked shoulder. "I can't…"

This wasn't the one; it was not his brother. Never his brother.

He rolled off the boy and lay on his back, staring up at the ceiling. The circular light shade was an eye staring down at him; the white plaster on the ceiling was alabaster skin. It was a face. Something was up there, looking down at his vulgar contortions.

"It happens," said Derek, beside him, but Trevor could tell from his voice that the boy was angry.

"Get out." He turned back to the mirror. The hand was back, but this time there was another alongside it: there seemed to be an unseen figure leaning against the mirror with both hands. "Just go." The hands clenched, became fists. Then they began to silently batter at the glass.

"What the fuck are you talking about? Am I too old? Is that it? I can get you someone younger, if that's what you need."

Trevor sat up on the bed and stared at the boy. "I don't want you here. You're not him, not Michael. You're nobody. I can't do this." He was aware of the fists slamming against the glass behind him, but he could not hear them. They were a sign, a signal; they were telling him what to do. The owner of the fists wanted him to hurt the boy, to pummel him just as the fists were striking the inside of the mirror.

"Get out before I hurt you."

Perhaps it was something in Trevor's eyes, or the look on his face, but Derek suddenly moved from the bed and picked up his clothes. He pulled them on as he shuffled across the room, his dead eyes wide and fearful, his skin pale and thin so that the veins beneath made a fine blue tracery. "You're mad. Fucking crazy."

"Yes," said Trevor, grinning. "Yes, I am." He began to stand, but the boy turned around and ran down the hall. The sound of the door slamming was hilarious, but Trevor could not even begin to understand why it made him laugh.

Then, when his hysteria was under control, he turned back to look at the mirror.

There was a figure standing there, but its outline was vague, blurry, as if formed by smoke. He could still see the room reflected in the glass, but *behind* the image was this other, this man. It was like one reality being overlaid across another. The thought both terrified him and filled him with a sense of wonder.

Trevor watched the figure until it was gone from sight, as if that second reality had stepped back from the first – the weaker image supplanted by the stronger. But even though he could no longer see it, he knew that the figure was there, waiting. The man hovered just out of sight, out of reach, but he would not remain that way forever. And Trevor realised that the man was desperate to reach out to him through the glass.

He crossed the room and went to the built-in wardrobe, and then he reached up to open the upper door, the one close to the ceiling. Inside the compartment were assorted work clothes – old slacks and stained T Shirts he wore when he was gardening or pottering around the house doing chores. Buried underneath these things was a small lacquered wooden box. Trevor took out the box and shut the door. He turned and walked back to the bed, where he sat down and stared at the black box. Slowly, tenderly, he brushed his fingers against the lid. Then he opened the box.

Inside were photographs. Not many of them, just a few. Each

of them was of a small boy with thin legs and a sad face. The boy's hair was fair; his eyes were pale. He was beautiful.

"Michael," said Trevor, his eyes filling with tears. "I miss you." He picked out a picture which showed his brother standing in the shade of a high wall. The boy was wearing a pair of ice-blue shorts and a Disney T Shirt. He was not smiling. He had never smiled – not even before Trevor started doing those things… the things he was unable to stop.

Trevor was weeping now; his throat felt raw, his cheeks were damp. He had an erection. A gap opened up inside him. It was a place that he kept hidden, but it was always there, just beneath the surface. It never left him, this gap. It simply sat there inside him, waiting to be filled. But it could not be filled; it would be empty forever, because his brother Michael was dead. Trevor had killed him. He had not lifted a hand to deliver the final blow, but he had done it all the same – he had killed the thing he had loved.

When he was thirteen years old Michael had cut off his own genitalia and bled to death, all because of Trevor. To stop him from doing those things… those horrible, wonderful, treacherous fucking things that he did.

Those acts…

…oh, such acts… such amazing acts of love…

His shoulders hitching, his vision blurred by grief and shame and regret – and, yes, desire – Trevor looked at the mirror. He could see nothing in the glass but the reflection of his own sad world, a self-created prison in which he was punished over and over again by his unnatural passions.

"Help me," he whispered. "Please help me."

It occurred quickly, and if Trevor had not been staring at the correct spot on the glass he might have missed it. It happened fast, but it *happened*. It really did happen.

A small, thumb-sized graze appeared in the top right corner of the glass, like the sudden damage caused by a pebble hitting a car windscreen. It sounded like a gunshot. Trevor stopped crying. He stood and approached the mirror. The deformation did not vanish. It was there. It was real.

Then something else began to happen, and Trevor was held rapt, his attention focused completely on the mirror.

Slowly, as if put there by a steady, careful hand, a word appeared – backwards – on the glass. It was a name, and it seemed to be written in greyish water, or perhaps spittle. Semen? Certainly it was some kind of liquid.

The name was also a word, and it was one Trevor knew well; he had dreamed of it often, and none of the dreams ended well. They usually ended in a wash of Technicolor bloodshed, when he killed the owner of that name.

The name was: *Usher*.

He reached back inside the lacquered box and took out what was buried under the photographs: the small cellophane wrap of heroin and the drug workings sheathed in an old rag.

As Trevor unwrapped the burnt spoon and the clean hypodermic syringe all he thought about was that name. But soon his mind would be free and he'd think of nothing… nothing but flying. Soon he could fly close to that other reality, the one he had glimpsed behind – or within – the mirror.

SIX

Later that morning I was sitting in a small café beside Upton Park underground station, watching the ebb and flow of punters from a massage parlour located above a cheap-looking tanning salon across the road. The grotty red door of the walk-up massage parlour was shut tight to the frame, and a square of paper tacked below the buzzer drew many a casual glance. I imagined it had names like Karla or Kandy written upon it, along with the words "model for hire".

I sipped my milky coffee and stared at a tall man with bad acne scars as he walked past the door for perhaps the fifth time in a period of twenty minutes. He'd been in just about every shop along Green Street and bought a small selection of items: a newspaper, some breath mints which he kept popping into his mouth at the rate of one capsule each time he passed the red door, and what looked like a large plantain wrapped up in a torn brown paper bag. At least I assumed it was a plantain: its long, curved shape also suggested some kind of sex toy.

I tore my eyes from the street and took in my immediate surroundings. There were just a few people in the café at that time of day – a clutch of morose customers caught in the friendless gap between the breakfast and lunch crowds – and the place

seemed slightly melancholy. An old man read from a horserac-
ing paper at a table near the toilets, a stubby pencil gripped
loosely in one hand. Two tired-looking middle-aged women
(perhaps they worked across the road) argued quietly in a European language I could not recognise, waving their hands before
their thin, drawn faces as if trying to summon demons. A slim
young man in a smart suit sat at the counter and sipped orange
juice from a smeared glass. The man's briefcase was resting at his
feet like a loyal puppy; he had the side of one leg pressed against
the case, so that he would feel the disturbance if anyone tried to
take it. He was staring into space, a strange little half-smile on
his lips.

My coffee had gone cold. I caught the eye of the chubby waitress
and she hurried over, her meaty forearms pale against the dark
blue of her tabard. She wiped her hands on her skirt as she stood
beside me. Then she took out a small ring-bound notebook and a
stubby little betting shop pen from the front pocket of her tabard.

"What can I get you, deary?" She sounded like proper old
East End London stock: even her accent reminded me of ancient black and white films I'd seen as a lad. She probably lived
in Romford.

"Could I have another coffee, please? White. One sugar."

She scribbled the order down on her pad, snatched up my
cup, and turned away, clearly disappointed that I had not
wanted anything more than a drink. I considered ordering a list
of items from the dog-eared menu just to relieve her tedium but
then dismissed the idea as silly.

I came to this café every day, sometimes for breakfast and
other times just to sit in this same window seat and watch the
world go by. It was the farthest I'd ventured from the grey zone
since arriving in the area, and the proximity of the underground
station provided a strange kind of comfort. If I wanted to, I could
head into the city… or I could simply watch the commuters
going about their business. It was the illusion of movement, the

notion of travel rather than travel itself, which helped calm my nerves. I didn't really *want* to go anywhere, but if for some reason I changed my mind I could hop on a train any time I liked. Destinations beckoned; journeys promised options I would probably never take.

That was good: the promise of escape. It was something that had always been lacking in my life, so I grabbed hold of the illusion whenever I could.

The waitress brought my coffee and favoured me with a tired smile.

"Thanks," I said, nodding.

She raised a hand and moved slowly away, spinning almost daintily on her heels, her gaze drawn to the window and the people passing by on the other side of the dirty glass. The way she moved was like a slow, sad dance step and she kept her eyes on the window. I wondered if she was looking out for someone special or just watching for the sake of it – much like I was.

Watching; just watching. Waiting to be noticed.

"Excuse me."

The waitress turned around, her eyes now focused on me.

"Sorry, but I'm suddenly hungry. Could I order a bacon and egg roll? Lots of ketchup." It wasn't a lie; my appetite had returned and my stomach ached because it was so empty. "With a side order of fried tomatoes."

"Coming right up, deary." She seemed happier now that she had a proper order to fill, something to do with her time. "Be back in a tick." I wondered if she spoke that way at home, or if it was an extension of the uniform she put on for work. I watched the gentle swaying of her ample behind as she stepped briskly behind the counter and went into the kitchen to speak with the cook.

People: despite the urge to keep away from them, I could not help my fascination with how they lived, how they existed in such a world as this. It was part of my curse, I supposed. I wasn't sure if I'd been this way before my wife and daughter were killed or if it was something I'd picked up since then – a sort of displacement activity for my imagination. Either way, humanity became more and more like a drug to me. Maybe one of these days I'd suffer an overdose.

People.

They were easy, really: simple. It had taken me decades to understand this, but recently I had begun to realise what made my fellow human beings tick. Previously I'd struggled with them, being more comfortable with the motives of the dead. Perhaps it meant that I was moving on, leaving something behind. Or maybe I was moving *towards* something, and this was all part of some metaphysical growth experience.

Who knew? Not me, that was for certain. All I really knew was what I saw before me: the grubby, tragic, intriguing mess of the human race and the tattered reality they so desperately clung to – a reality that was as fragile as blown glass.

So was that it? Had I suddenly, after all these years, learned how to feel pity?

"There you go, deary. Enjoy." The waitress was back at my table already. She slid the plate in front of me, her chubby hand like a bloated claw. I blinked and it was just a hand again; reality deftly reasserted itself and I was able to look up and smile at the woman to express my gratitude. Then I looked back at my plate.

Those tomatoes looked grand, and all philosophical thoughts aside, I was fucking *starving*.

The man at the counter ordered another fruit juice. He had a low voice; quiet and dignified. The old man with the racing form guide folded up his paper, stuck it under his arm, and went to the bathroom. He left his pencil on the table, where it slowly rolled off the laminated surface and onto the floor. The European women left the premises, still arguing, but even quieter than before. Only their hands could be considered loud as they hacked at the air, shouting with aggressive strokes and slashes.

It struck me that I was very aware of what was going on around me, even more so than usual. It was my habit to fully engage with any situation in which I found myself. The fact that I saw ghosts everywhere, even when I wasn't looking, gave me a rather unique relationship to my surroundings. My knowledge of other states of existence, and other realities beyond the one we moved through, made me cling to earthly experiences like a child to the tit. The metaphor was crude, but it was effective: like mother's milk, the world I inhabited offered a kind of sustenance not available to me elsewhere.

All this went through my mind as I gobbled up my fried tomatoes and started on the roll. The tastes were intense; it might just have been the best bacon and egg sandwich I had ever eaten.

The room seemed to fill with breezy air, as if a silent wind had blown in from somewhere and settled over everything. No, that wasn't quite right. It was more like a layer of dust had drifted in through the door as the women had taken their leave and it now coated everything in a thin layer. The silence was almost unbearable. Previously there had been a radio playing at the rear of the café, but someone had switched it off. I could not even hear any conversation between the waitress and the cook. The air conditioner had gone silent. Passing traffic made no sound.

The man at the counter was motionless, like a stone statue. His hands rested on the countertop and his feet were perched on the footrest of his stool. He was still staring dead ahead, as if lost in thought. It was difficult to see from where I was sitting, but from what little I could make out of the side of his face he didn't seem to blink. I watched for a while, intrigued, and his features remained still and expressionless.

That was when I realised something was wrong.

I dropped my sandwich onto the plate and turned my attention to the window. The street outside was empty: no pedestrians passed by, the road was clear of traffic. It was impossible; that street was the main road through the area, passing

West Ham's football ground only a few hundred yards away, up the slight incline. Whatever the time of day or night, it was always jammed with vehicles.

Then, as if trying to summon my attention, a phone began to ring. The sound was one of those annoyingly catchy and inevitably terrible mobile ring tones. I hate things like that; they are instantly obsolete and often plain embarrassing.

The tune was coming from the counter – or, more precisely, from the man at the counter. The young man in the smart suit.

I turned to face him, but still he had not moved. His hands were limp; his body was hunched, the spine curved. He didn't look comfortable.

"Excuse me." My voice sounded thick, syrupy, like someone calling from a nightmare. I repeated the words: "Excuse me." Nothing. The young man did not move. "I'm sorry… your phone. It's ringing."

It was as if the world were holding its breath, but as soon as I made this observation commotion flooded back in, filling the cafe. Sound and motion from the window caught my eye; I turned to look and everything had returned to normal. When I turned back to the young man he was reaching into his jacket pocket to take out his mobile phone. I watched in a kind of stunned dread as he removed the phone and brought it to his ear, flipping the lid as he did so. He pressed the small rectangle to the side of his face and spoke: "Hello."

There was a moment then when I considered running. I knew the situation was wrong, that something weird was taking place, but what kept me there was the fact that I had not paid my bill. I'm nothing if not an honest customer. I didn't want the waitress to think I was a cheat.

"What? Who is this? You'll have to speak up – I can't make it out." The young man's cultured voice grew louder; he was becoming irritated. "Sorry? Listen, I have no idea – who? What? Who is it you want?"

I knew before he said it; to me, it was obvious. As certain as the seasons.

"Who? Usher? What is that? Oh… what? Oh, *Thomas* Usher? No, never heard of him. I think you have the wrong number."

I wish he had just hung up the phone, that he had put it back in his pocket and continued to drink his juice and think his idle thoughts. But he didn't. He kept on talking, expressing mild annoyance that someone was ringing him up to ask for a man whose name was unknown to him – a man who was, even now, standing and pushing back his chair.

That man:

Me.

The call was meant for me.

I walked away from the table, and from my delicious bacon roll, and approached the man at an angle. I could see his smooth, clean-shaven cheek, a white smear of soap caught in the bushy hair at his temple, the way the pulse in his neck beat wildly as he spoke.

"I'm sorry," I said, and I was. I really was. Sorry for everything, and to everyone. So very, very sorry for all of it. "I think they're asking for me."

He turned around on his stool, this vital young man in his expensive clothes and shoes, and with his flashy mobile phone clutched so tightly in his lovely manicured hand. "What? Who are you? What is this?" His eyes were huge; they looked at me with interest but they saw nothing, nothing at all. They never did, eyes like his. All they ever saw was the surface. They never peered beneath, even for a second.

Briefly, I envied him. Then I felt only pity.

I smiled. "I'm Thomas Usher. I don't know what's going on, but that's my name." I wasn't trying to confuse him; it was a genuine attempt to tell the truth, to get to the heart of the matter. Whatever the matter was.

Surprisingly, he held out his phone. He looked like he wanted to say something – perhaps to yell at me, or even to hit me as he screamed about the insanity of the situation. But all he did was hand me his fancy little phone.

I smiled again, trying to reassure him: *It's OK. None of this makes any sense, even to me. Just go with it. Go with the flow.*

I raised it to my ear. I could hear the hissing sound even before I held it in place.

Go with the flow.

"Hello."

The voice; that clockwork voice: "It's me again."

I nodded. "So it is."

"I have a name for you. It's not much, I know, but there are rules here that I am compelled to follow. I can't break those rules." There was a tiny, almost indiscernible click after every word, as if they were being put together by a machine.

The young man: "What the fuck is going on?"

Me: "Tell me."

The voice: "The name is…"

The young man: "Give me back my phone."

He was grabbing me, but I batted his hands aside. His protests were all for show; he was scared, at least as scared as I was. Probably more.

Me: "What's the name?"

The voice: "Immaculee Karuhmbi."

The young man: "I'll call the police–"

Me: "Who is that? Is that who you want me to find?"

The voice: "I can tell you nothing more. Just the name."

The line went dead.

I handed the young man his phone. "I'm sorry… I don't want any trouble. Here, have it back. It was nothing anyway. Nothing I can understand."

"Fucking psycho!" He snatched the phone and rose from his seat. I noticed that he was small, much shorter than me. I hadn't noted that fact when he was sitting down. He'd seemed bigger then, when he was seated. "Get out of my way." He stormed off, tugging open the door and almost diving onto the pavement outside in his haste, his eagerness to be out of my presence.

I didn't blame him at all.

"What was all that about?" The waitress had returned from the kitchen. She was holding a glass of orange juice. The sides of the glass were beaded with moisture. It looked delicious. "He left without his drink." It looked beautiful. It looked real.

"I'll take it." I sat down in the vacant stool. The old man with the racing paper emerged from the bathroom. He was humming a tune I knew – Nina Simone: an upbeat number about Feeling Good. Capital F. Capital G.

"He didn't even pay." The waitress looked shell-shocked: her eyes were wide, her mouth hung open. Sweat limned her hairline and followed the curve of her forehead, making it glisten like a corrupted halo. She was an earthbound angel, just like the rest of them. All of them but me: I had no idea what I was.

"I'll pay," I said, taking the drink, accepting it from this sweaty angel. "By the way, I don't suppose you've heard of anyone called Immaculee Karuhmbi." It was a long shot but I took it anyway. What did I have to lose?

"Immaculee? Why yes, deary. Everyone round here knows her."

I almost choked on the young man's orange juice. I'm sure he would have appreciated my discomfort. "Do you know where she is now?" It was too much to hope for, but still I hoped. This was becoming important to me. More than simply something to do, it was transforming into a task I could not refuse, a mystery I simply had to solve. A mission. The enigma was bigger than it seemed – larger than me – and I wanted to get to the heart of it.

The old man had stopped humming; now he was whistling. It was the same tune, but performed on a different instrument. He was another angel. I felt like kneeling before him to worship. My emotions were at breaking point; I had lost all sense of perspective. Every place I went, each second I spent there, was either a slice or heaven or of hell. No middle ground. No limbo.

"She'll be resting now, but in the afternoons she works over there." The waitress raised her podgy hand and pointed – she motioned over my shoulder, through the glass and out onto the street. I followed the imaginary line made by her broad, stiff finger. All the way to the first floor massage parlour on the other side of the street.

Surely it couldn't be this easy.

"She's a working girl?"

The waitress laughed. She wiped down the counter with a grubby blue cloth. The surface was already clean. The motion was like a nervous twitch. "Of course not, deary. She works on the top floor – *above* the knocking shop. Immaculee is a psychic."

My head went cold; my brain froze. My heart turned to ice. I felt it dripping, dripping, and beginning to thaw.

The dead; it always comes back to the dead.

The waitress laughed again, and then she began to sing along to the old man's whistled tune:

"*...and I'm feeling good.*"

I wished that I could join in, but any attempt at harmony would have been a lie.

SEVEN

As a rule Sarah rarely drank anything stronger than cranberry juice before lunch – and then only sparingly, because she'd heard somewhere that too much of the stuff rotted your insides. Today, however, she was drinking whisky. She needed it just to get through this task.

She stared at the floor, frowning at the pile of creased paperwork she had pulled from the drawers: faded envelopes and dog-eared manila folders, all making her wish that she could set fire to the whole fucking lot. Yes, that would be good; send the old bastard's legacy up in flames. But she wouldn't, of course. She could tell herself that destruction was the way to go, but the reality of the situation was that she needed to know what was in there. Those photographs had piqued her interest; they had triggered her mental twitch and the only response was to investigate. After all, didn't she want to be a detective?

The backbone of any case, as her father had said many times, was the careful sifting of information.

Somewhere outside a dog barked. The sound was snappy, incessant, and before long it began to play on her nerves. The familiar sound of a police helicopter flying overhead drew her focus. She wondered who they were after, and had to restrain herself from going to the window to take a look outside. She was off duty: let the others deal with whatever was happening out there. She needed a break from other people's problems so that she might concentrate on her own.

Slowly, she began to play her fingers through the grubby folders and loose sheets of paper, flipping the edges. There were receipts from restaurants she'd never heard of, and from towns she had never visited. The dates on the scrappy tariffs were ancient – going back decades. For an organised officer, her father's personal files were chaotic. She remembered that he'd been in some kind of blues tribute band when she was a kid, playing rhythm guitar to ease the stress of the job. He'd given it up when she was aged about ten, and she knew that he'd continued to miss gigging for the rest of his life.

Freedom, he had always told her, was when the people you loved couldn't be with you. It had sounded like an insult, but her mother had always just laughed. Well, at least her mouth had: her eyes never quite seemed to get the joke.

"What were you hiding in here?" The question, spoken aloud in that way, took her by surprise. She had not expected it. Despite the fact that it must have been on her mind, she had no idea where such a blunt query had originated.

"Hiding…" The word tasted bad, like bitter spices in a day-old curry. Deep down, even when she was much younger, she had always known that her father enjoyed a hidden life – an existence even more degraded than the one he let her see at home. Did the evidence of this other life lie somewhere within the stuff he'd left behind, stashed away like the bent evidence of a forgotten crime?

Sarah closed her eyes. She drank a mouthful of whisky. It burnt her lips; she felt her cheeks flush hot with blood. She savoured the feeling. It made her feel close to being alive.

The phone rang but she ignored it. The sound went on for several rings, and finally stopped. Sarah didn't move. She was staring at the pile of her father's paperwork, and thinking about the rest of it that was stored around the big old house – in drawers and cupboards, the space under the stairs, the loft rooms, and the cellar. It was everywhere, the complicated evidence of his existence, and who knew what story might be sitting there just waiting to be told.

She reached out and picked up a creased folder. Inside was a sheaf of bills and receipts taken from motorway service stations, trucker's cafes, roadside diners and nameless burger bars. Her father had kept everything; he was the quintessential hoarder, a man who knew more than anything the value of detail. It must have been the detective in him. He'd always said that crimes get solved either because the perpetrator threw something away he should have kept or kept something he should have destroyed. The only sure way was to control everything: keep it close, and know when to burn it.

But he'd died before he could burn anything of his own hoard, hadn't he? Also, his enormous hubris had conspired to make him believe that he was completely untouchable.

Pride was another error he had always told her to be wary of. It was ironic, then, that he had succumbed to that very sin himself.

She put back the folder and picked up an old cardboard Kodak wallet. The photos inside were disgusting: her mother and father in various sex acts, and wearing an assortment of weird costumes. In some of the shots other men had joined in the fun, but they were all wearing masks. Her mother's paper mask did nothing to conceal the woman's terror. It was there, in her exposed eyes, for all to see.

"The bastard," she said through gritted teeth, confronted by physical proof of the depths of the man's disregard for his wife. "What else did he do to you?"

Sarah felt moisture on her cheeks. She had not cried for years – not since her mother had been put in the home. She certainly had shed no tears when her father died. All she had felt was a sense of release. And even deeper, down where the shadows lived, she had also felt a surge of satisfaction.

Before she went any further with this she had to see her mother. She had not visited the woman since the funeral – Sarah's mother had been too sick to attend, but it had been a psychological ailment rather than physical.

The time had come to reach out, to reconnect with her family and her past. Maybe then she could unravel the puzzle of her father's life, and finally understand what it was he had done. Because she knew he'd done something – something more than what had been done to her, and even to her mother. Her twitch was telling her so, along with the scant evidence she'd already seen.

A man this depraved would not have stopped with his immediate family. He would have kept the best – or the worst – for those who could not talk back.

She stood, her legs aching, spine creaking, and walked over to the telephone. She picked it up and dialled. Despite rarely ever using it, she knew the number by heart.

"Hello? Yes, my name is Sarah Doherty. My mother Helen is a patient there. Yes, that's her. Room number 12. Alzheimer's." She stared at the wall above the phone. There was a crack in the plaster, and a tiny spider squeezed out. It seemed to have too many legs, but Sarah knew that was impossible. She reached out, extended her thumb, and crushed the fucker, leaving a dark smear on the wall.

"Sorry? Yes, I'd like to come over and see her later today, if that's OK. Thank you. Yes, I'll be there around–" She checked her watch: it was now 10.30am. "How does one o'clock sound? Thanks. Bye."

She stood for a while with the receiver gripped tightly in her hand. Her palm began to sweat but still she felt unable to put it down. "Come on, you," she whispered. "Be cool. Be strong." She put down the receiver and backed away from the telephone table. His phone. His telephone table.

His house.

"You twat," she muttered. "I should burn it all to the ground." But then she would destroy everything; all the evidence would go up in smoke, even before she had gone through it. She couldn't have that. There was a mystery here, and something inside her – the same instinct which had recognised its presence – was desperate to unearth whatever it was her father had only half-buried.

The phone rang again. Instinctively this time, she walked back over and picked it up.

"It's me." Benson's husky voice always calmed her down – it was only when he was physically with her that she began to feel uncomfortable: only when he was in her bed, if she was honest.

"Hi. How's it going?"

"I couldn't sleep, so thought I'd call you. Were you in bed?" She could hear music in the background; some kind of bass-heavy rock.

"No, I was just sitting around in my pants and thinking about my father."

He laughed. "Pants, you say? How about I come back over and help you out of them?"

She ignored the banter. "Listen, I'm going to see my mother this afternoon. At the home." She waited; the silence began to grow and mutate into something rather frightening. A thing which, if she allowed it to fully form, might wear the face of her father. "You know – the nursing home."

More silence.

"Oh." Finally he broke it. "I see. You don't talk about her that much. When did you last see her?"

Sarah swallowed but her throat was dry. She coughed. "Ages ago: when he died. I could use some company this afternoon, if you're not doing anything." Now why the hell had she said that? It was always the same: his voice, his manner, slipped behind her defences and made her think that she cared about him more than she actually did. That she cared about him at all. It was ridiculous.

"What time should I pick you up?" His tone had become deadly serious, just like it did when he was on the job. He was an impressive copper; she had always thought so.

"Be here for noon. I'll have coffee and sandwiches waiting, and then we can go."

"It's a date." He paused again. "Listen... I'm glad you opened up to me about this. Sometimes..."

"What? Sometimes what?" But she knew what he was about to say; she'd been waiting for it for quite some time.

"Sometimes there's, like, this wall that I can't get behind – you know? It's like you've built it to keep me out. I can only see parts of you, through the gaps in the wall."

"I know. Sorry." But that was a lie; she wasn't sorry at all. "I've always been like that. There are things about me you don't know. I might tell you about it some day. Then again, I might not. Let's just wait and see. OK? Let's take things easy."

"I hear you. No problem. We'll take it day by day. I'll see you at twelve." He hung up the phone.

God, why couldn't she feel more affection towards him? Benson was a catch by any measure of the word; he was a good and sensitive man, but also a *real* man – one who would protect her with his fists if it ever came down to that. She knew other women who would kill to get hold of someone like Benson. But not her. No, she was compelled to keep him at a distance, to build that wall and let him walk around it, only ever catching glimpses as she stood behind the battlements. An arm, a leg, the back of her head as she walked away...

Maybe, she thought, if he ever sees the whole thing it might scare him off.

It was now almost eleven, much too late to start rooting through her father's things. She needed to have a shower and get herself sorted out. Put on some lipstick, have another quick shot of whisky. She walked to the drinks cabinet and took out the scotch. Half a bottle left; it had been full only two days before. Then there was the bottle of wine she drank after every shift just to unwind – unless Benson was there, of course, and they would share the wine before she tied him up to fuck away the stress.

"You have a problem, my girl." She smiled at herself in the mirror above the cabinet. She was still young enough, and pretty enough, to carry it off. But before long the bags would form under her eyes and her flesh would begin to sag and wrinkle. The skull would show beneath the skin. She knew enough from her mother's habits that once a woman hit thirty, thirty-five at the most, the bottle started to whittle away her looks.

Hopefully by then it would be too late to matter. She'd either be tethered to a man or, well, tied down or dead. It was a nasty thought, but one which was never far from her mind. It was part of the job, a fear you had to befriend and call your own. It could happen any day out on those streets, and in any given situation: a robbery call, breaking up a fight outside a pub, riot duty, a drugs raid.

There were a million ways to die in any city, and Leeds was up there with the worst of them. She had known two people who had been killed on duty, and her career was only just two years old.

They never told you about that in training, and her psychology degree had been a bit too detached from the urban grime of reality to even go near such a topic. None of her old University friends had remained in touch, not when they heard that she was a copper. It did that to you, the job: it stripped away your old life, making you anew, turning you into a brand new being. And wasn't that exactly why she had been drawn to it? To remake herself in the image of another?

The trouble was, other officers tried to cast her in her father's image, and that was something she certainly did not desire. In fact, it was the last thing she wanted.

She looked again at the pile of paperwork. "Who were you really?" There was no answer forthcoming. "Who the fuck were you, Detective Inspector Emerson Doherty? And, more to the point, who the fuck am I?"

It wasn't the first time she had asked this question, but she had never before said it out loud. Only in a whisper, in the dark, in the night: in the moment just before sleep when even she could not hear the words.

"Who am I?" This was the real reason behind her quest to uncover her father's secrets. Because if she found out enough about him, then surely answers to the questions of her own identity would follow.

She had to believe that. She needed to cling to it, if only for the sake of her sanity, because whatever happened from now on, she didn't want to follow her mother into the nuthouse.

She would rather eat a bullet.

She went upstairs to the bathroom and turned on the taps. She'd changed her mind about the shower: a quick soak would be better, more soothing.

Undressing slowly, she watched the tub fill with water. Then she opened a drawer and took out a bottle of bath oil. She poured the fluid into the water, enjoying the smell of eucalyptus. The stuff never failed to relax her, and these days she actually hated to bathe without it.

A short time later she turned off the taps and eased herself into the hot water. As usual, she tried hard to ignore the faint cross-hatching of scars on the inside of her thighs, but was unable to keep her gaze from them. The scars were faded now; barely there at all. But she could see them as clearly as if they were open wounds. Her father had caused them, when he used to hurt her to stop himself from fucking her. So many times when she was young he had come into her room after dark and stood over her bed, swaying. He had always smelled of drink, and his voice was throaty.

But he had never touched her, despite wanting to. She could feel his desire like a dry heat, even then. Instead he had cut her; lightly, but often, and with a sharp blade. A thin medical scalpel.

Sarah touched the scars with her fingertips.

When he was finished he would leave the room, locking the door behind him. Then, shortly afterwards, when she had treated the wounds, she would hear muffled screams from her parents' room. Trapped there, her head filled with the sounds of abuse, she had always been dragged into sleep by nightmares. The bedroom door remained locked all night, but when she woke in the morning it was always open, as if he'd returned and stood over her, perhaps even inspecting her wounds as she slept.

Maybe doing something else she did not want to imagine, even now.

Sarah felt her eyelids drooping. They were heavy as stones, or the pennies placed on a corpse's eyes to weigh them down.

She remembered:

This one time, when she was nine or ten years old, he had come again into her room. He moved with the usual slouched gait. In his hand he held the scalpel – a new one; it was shiny, even in the dark. He said nothing, just pulled back the bedclothes and squatted by the side of the bed. She knew enough to pull her nightdress up over her thighs, exposing the pale flesh. It was pointless fighting: the door was locked and he was so much stronger than her.

Lately he had started wearing the costume. It was strange, almost monkish: a long, black smock-type thing, with a white gauzy hood covering his features. There was something ritualistic about the outfit, and it made her think of prayer.

Is that what he was doing? Praying to his god?

She slid down in the bath, the hot water cradling her, keeping her safe. The water level rose around her ears, containing her within a quiet world. Her life receded, drifting away. Another scene took its place:

The scalpel blade flashed, catching gleams of light from the streetlamp outside her window. She did not scream; she would not give him the pleasure of hearing her pain. She had learned not to scream a while ago. It ensured that the ordeal was short. He carried it out like a duty, as if it were a job of work. By now each tiny cut was perfunctory, as if there was no passion behind the act. It had gone on for so long that it had almost become a chore.

Then, the beast once more quietened, he left the room. The door clicked shut. The sound of the lock echoed in the cavernous dark.

She waited... waited... and then came the muted screaming. Then she took the cotton wool balls and antiseptic lotion out of her drawer and began to dab at the cuts.

When she woke, mere moments had passed. She checked the clock on the wall, and it told her that she had simply been drowsing. The water suddenly felt dirty, contaminated. Her father did that: he blighted whatever he touched. Even now, after his death, he was able to cast a shadow and cause a stench.

The bastard was dead, but he would not rest.

He was dead, but he was watching.

Watching over the people he owned.

EIGHT

It was gloomy when They stepped off the bus. The air was wet and heavy and the sky trembled as if machines thrummed behind the heavy grey clouds, generating the weather. Drizzle fell like insincere kisses; it was light, almost waxy, and promised nothing but more of the same. They stood at the side of the road and watched as the bus pulled away, an unstable outline in the murk. They could not remember boarding the vehicle – Their consciousness had emerged at some point during the journey and the first thing They had been aware of was the sight of a city approaching.

Cities. They loved cities, despite never before being able to enter one. These places were Their playgrounds and Their workplaces. Wherever people massed, and the energy of mortal men and women was strongest, Their designs flourished.

A city, then....

Oh, yes; They loved it here.

Traffic was heavy. The rain and the scant daylight conspired to fill the road network with harried drivers. Couriers hurried here and there: in small white vans, on bicycles and mopeds. Workers emerged from tall buildings to consume brief lunches before tunnelling back into the communal hive.

The evidence of their designs was everywhere. They smiled. They were happy. To see the designs in action was such a gift; They rarely got to examine the results of Their work at such close quarters. Moments like this one were to be savoured.

They walked slowly from the spot on the pavement, enjoying the feel of two spindly limbs skimming above the surface. They clenched Their hands into fists and then relaxed. Over and over: a succession of empty threats on the end of two skinny white arms.

They caught sight of Their body in the mirror of a shopping quadrant window – a lovingly restored Victorian arcade. The body was small, almost invisible within the greater mass of flesh and movement. It was clad in scruffy rags. Torn jeans covered the legs. A thin shirt encased the fragile torso. The face was partially hidden by long, lank hair.

They scanned Their memories for the particular design – if any – allotted to this form, but found nothing. Perhaps it was free of Their interference. Not everyone was lucky enough to be a subject, a framework, for the perfection of Their duty. Some people spent their entire lives without being blessed by a design.

A tall man in a smart suit brushed against Them as he passed by in a hurry. A design trailed from him like webbing. The complex nature of its construction was a joy to behold, and They paused to admire Their handiwork.

Such complex patterns; a veritable labyrinthine structure clung to the man. There were so many placements, such a vast array of conceptual pathways in evidence, They wished They could simply follow him and observe as the design evolved.

So that's what They did: They stalked the man from across the street, enjoying the way that several older versions of the design fell away like skeins of dead flesh then drifted on an unseen breeze, floated up into the air, and dissipated in the upper levels of the atmosphere. Even once they had been installed, the designs kept growing and mutating, becoming things which adapted to the person who carried them.

The discarded raw material might find its way back and be re-cycled for another design; some of it might even attach itself to a design already in action, snagging on an outcropping and changing an existing shape and process in the beautifully or-ganic way They had only ever witnessed in Their imaginations.

The man jumped into a taxi outside a large, contemporary public house. His face crumpled, and then reformed. The design was changing him, re-contextualising his basic role in the human race, simply because of the matter which had drifted away. No one else could see this, of course. No one but Them.

They watched him for as long as They could; until he was no longer visible. The air moved around him, making room for his ever-changing design.

They knew:

when he got home he would find the key he had misplaced a week ago and as he bent over to retrieve it he would concuss himself by catching the edge of an occasional table with the side of his head and in the hospital he would be treated by a nurse he had dated in his school days and they would later conduct an affair and he would leave his wife and then a year from today a year exactly from this moment a year and not more not less the nurse would bend over to pick up that same key in the lounge of their rented flat and be killed instantly as her temple connected with the edge of a small occasional table the same table he brought with him from the house his wife would keep in the divorce

Such was the beauty and simplicity and sheer mathematical im-possibility of the design. His design. The one They had created for him, and which was changing with every second he re-mained alive.

They crossed the road, enjoying the sound of car horns and the yelling of drivers who stuck their heads out of side windows to shout abuse. The screech of tyres. The song of the city.

They stood outside the public house – a bright, cheery building with lots of glass along the frontage and huge swinging doors. They once again saw Themselves reflected in the glass, and They tried to smile. But it did not work; the expression was alien to Them, a thing They could not even begin to rationalise in the context of Their designs.

After a short while They crossed the footpath to the door and pushed it open, walked inside. It was warm; music was playing; people drank and laughed and ate salty snacks from shallow bowls at the bar. Hardly anyone noticed Them, so They stepped lightly across the room, looking for something – looking for *someone*.

They had sensed a familiar tension in the air. It told Them that there was at least one soul present who had been touched, or breathed upon, by the lost one. He had breached the external barriers protecting Their designs, entered it, and then sealed it behind him. He had interfered in a way which had always been forbidden.

He had made himself part of the designs, and by doing so had caused a mess. That was why They were here: to clean up the mess, stitch together the tattered holes in whichever designs the lost one had damaged.

They scanned the room. There were so many auras; They could see them all now. Their vision was improving. Most of the auras They saw were torn and frayed, but the specific one They sought would be slashed and trashed, hanging in frayed tatters from whoever carried it. The designs were visible to Them like the exoskeletons of certain insects; they enveloped the bodies of the subjects, fusing with their auras to create a sort of scaffolding for the energy held within.

Then, at last, They saw it. Several of the separate links of the small design were coming apart at the seams; some of them had broken away and dissolved, leaving behind only seared stumps. This person had been touched only briefly by the one they had come to find, and possibly several times removed, but still he had been touched. The damage to his design, however minimal, pointed to this fact. He had come into the lost one's orbit, and his design had trembled.

They began to cross the room, approaching the man. He was young, and he was very drunk. In his hand he held a shot glass; the liquid inside was golden, fiery. He finished it in a single mouthful, and then motioned to the barmaid for more – and that was when They were spotted.

"Get out of here, kid." Another man had approached Them from the side, his hands held out away from his body. "What the hell are you doing in here? You're underage: go back home to mummy."

Laughter. Shouts. An unseen woman singing.

The man grabbed Them by both shoulders and steered Them back the way They had come, towards the door to the street. The crowd parted; people smiled; a large woman with a big shiny face pointed and began to giggle.

Once outside the man knelt before Them, his face creased into a gentle smile. His entire demeanour changed. His design was small and fragile; an incomplete element hung from his back and left to wither. They were sad. "What's up, son? You in trouble? I know someone who might be able to help. I can take you there. He... he takes in young kids like you, gives them a job. You can earn good money."

They knew exactly what he meant, what he wanted. They knew it all. It was part of his pathetic design. As was a possible future outcome, one which might change with the slow flexing of his tired design.

later after his shift he would go to sammy's place and spend some time with one of the chickens sammy kept locked up in the back and there would be blood and tears and that was just how he liked it and then he would wipe himself off and pay sammy to keep his mouth shut before going home to where his fat wife and her drunken sister would brag to him about the men who bought them drinks and the drugs they kept

*from him and then he would surf the internet for old school photographs
and masturbate and get angry because he couldn't come and he'd beat
up his wife while she laughed again in his face and then he'd get some
drugs of his own and several months later an old ex-chicken from
sammy's place many years before would see him later that night and follow him along a dark alley and cut his throat and laugh in his face like
his wife and his sister and then the boy would flee vowing never to return
to sammy's but weeks later he'd run into this man's wife and her sister
and he'd fuck them both and the wife would choke to death as he stran-
gled her because he could no longer get it up with a woman just a man
an older man a man who called him chicken and he'd miss the man and
the other men just like him and that would be the end of his design*

They shook Their head. They could not yet speak – this
mouth; it refused to work properly – but They could grunt. They
could moan.

"Hey, kid, what's that? What's wrong with your head? You been
in an accident?" The man reached out for Them again, his fingers
grasping. "Hey, come here. Let me help you." When he pulled his
hand away his fingertips were red.

They backed away and left the man there, crouched on the
sidewalk and thinking of chicken – his pet name for all the boys
he and Sammy recruited from the streets to service their clients
in the basement room of Sammy's Hi-Fi shop in Bestwick...

They knew this, because it affected the designs of those who
passed by on the street, making them flutter. Serendipity knew
no moral boundaries; it was free to all. As long as it was designed
for them.

They walked to the corner and waited. The young man
They'd spotted inside the pub would have to come out at some
point, and when he did They would be sure to follow. They
would trail him wherever he went, because eventually he
would lead Them to the lost one.

And then Their work here could be completed.

NINE

The sky was dull grey, the colour of sorrow, as they left for the Stoneville residential home. Benson took the wheel while Sarah sat in the passenger seat staring out of the window at the drizzle, which seemed to form fuzzy grey clots in the air. She was trying not to think too hard about where they were going, just clearing her mind and allowing the greyness to saturate her perceptions. She hoped that it might even drown her thoughts.

"How long has she been in this Stoneville place?" Benson stared straight ahead as he spoke. She glanced at the side of his face, at the scars, and wished again that she could bring herself to love him. "Before your dad died, wasn't it?"

"Yes. She's been in the home for over ten years. He drove her there, with his unreasonable behaviour. But she would never have left him. She wouldn't jump, so her pushed him." She looked back out of the window and saw a small girl standing at the side of the road. They were travelling through a grotty sub-urb to the south-east of Leeds – a cluster of grimy housing estates bordering the M621 – and heading towards the motor-way. The girl stared at the car, a strange smile on her pale face. She was wearing a T-shirt and jeans, with battered running shoes on her feet. No socks. Her long, tatty hair was soaking wet.

Sarah smiled back at the girl, wondering what she was doing out there in the cold and the wet. The girl raised a tiny hand and waggled her fingers, and then she ran along the street and vanished around a corner into a gloomy looking alleyway.

"I'm starting to realise just how badly my father treated her," Sarah turned back to Benson. He was frowning. "I found some photographs..." But she could say no more, not yet. She did not want to describe to Benson what she had seen in the photographs.

"What kind of photos?" He turned his head. His eyes were shining; his teeth were pressed together beneath the thin covering of his lips. She saw a momentary flash of his skull, like an image of death superimposed over his scarred features.

"Oh, nothing. Just some of his old shit, that's all. Nothing important, anyway." Lies, all lies. Why was she unable to tell him about her suspicions, her fears? Why could she not just tell the truth?

They remained silent for a while, listening to the thrum of the wheels on the wet tarmac as they briefly joined the M1 motorway, gaining speed. Traffic was light: there were a few trucks clogging the slow lane, with bored drivers leaning across oversized steering wheels. Benson stayed in the middle lane – something she hated – and undertook the cars to his right.

"How do you pay for the home? I mean, it must be expensive to keep her there, in such a good place. How do you fund it?"

Sarah closed her eyes and tried to focus. Her vision was swimming. She felt queasy. "My father was well insured, and his police pension helps. There's also, well, the slush fund."

Benson flicked the indicator with his middle finger and moved the car over into the slow lane in preparation to leave the motorway at the A650 Wakefield exit. "The slush fund? What's that, then?"

"He was a heavy gambler, and he used to win a lot of the time. I'm sure you've heard the rumours. He used to treat gambling like another job, a secondary career, and any money he made went into what he always called the slush fund. There was a lot of cash in there by the time he died. More than I had ever thought possible."

For a moment she thought that Benson had not heard her, then she realised that he was ignoring what she had said, probably because he was unsure how to react to the information.

"Where exactly is this place? I'm not sure where I'm heading." He slowed down the car and his hands flexed on the steering wheel. Sarah was unsure if he was tactfully changing the subject or simply distracted by the unfamiliar geography.

"Just head for Pinderfields Hospital and I'll tell you when to turn."

"So you're loaded, then? A little rich girl?" He smiled, the scars making tiny white replicas of the forced expression across his rough cheeks. "Does that make me some kind of gold digger?"

"Turn right, then keep going and you'll see the sign for Stoneville."

They fell again into an uneasy silence. She thought that Benson might assume he'd offended her, but couldn't bring herself to care. She craved a drink – more of that whisky from earlier in the day. Her throat itched and her stomach was churning. She was beginning to sober up. Maybe they could go for a pub lunch after they'd seen her mother. And Benson could pick up the tab, just because she knew she could make him.

Before long the Stoneville residential home came into view, rising above the road as if it were reaching out towards her, drawing her into its skewed orbit. Sarah swallowed but her throat was dry; she coughed, attempting to produce at least some moisture, but failed. Her teeth ached. She felt utterly forlorn – yes that was the word. There was no other that could do justice to her feelings at this precise moment in time.

Forlorn. For some reason the word held a strange resonance, as if it were a place on the map and not an emotion.

"You look pale. Are you OK?" Benson reached out a big hand and grasped her leg, squeezing lightly to reassure her. It hurt, just a little, but he left his hand where it was, just above her knee. Sarah fought back the urge to scream. She didn't want this, not any of it: her pain was her own, and she would suffer it alone, just as she had always done. It was not something to be shared, like a fucking takeaway pizza.

"I'm fine," she said, tersely. "Don't worry about it. Just drive."

He took away his hand.

Benson slowed the car and turned into the large parking area at the front of the building. There were a lot of vehicles there already, and Benson's beat-up Ford Focus looked out of place amid the Porsches and the Mercs and the shiny 4x4s owned by middle-class housewives visiting their fucked-up mother-in-laws.

"There's a lot of money here. Loads of new wealth."

Sarah nodded. "Don't I fucking know it? They charge a fortune just to feed and keep the residents clean – that's what they call them: 'residents.' Like it's some kind of holiday camp." She stared at the hulking Victorian structure, hating it in a way that she could barely explain, even to herself. Her mother was well looked after here – no matter how hard she tried to convince herself otherwise – and the money used to pay the bills wasn't even hers anyway.

No, it wasn't about the money. She just loathed the fact that her father had sent the senile old bitch here, and then practically forgotten about her – or at least pretended to. Just left her to rot.

"So this is it?" Benson turned off the engine. They were parked next to a large black four-wheel-drive with tinted windows and a private number plate. Someone had scratched the side of the vehicle; to Sarah's trained eyes it looked deliberate, as if they'd used a key or a penknife blade. She smiled.

"How about you wait here in the car? I'm not sure I can handle you coming in there after all." She turned to face him, feeling sorry that she'd let him drive her all the way here only to be told to wait outside like the hired help.

"Well... I was kind of hoping I could meet your mum. You know, at least it would mean that I knew a little more about you." His dark eyes glimmered and his mouth twitched. He didn't know whether to smile or to grimace. She actually admired his self-restraint – if their positions were reversed and it was Benson telling her to wait here while he conducted business, she'd be screaming at him.

It was another reason why she should have feelings for him, and another reason why she didn't. How could such a strong man be so weak?

She softened: "You're right. It's cold of me to even ask you to wait outside. Sorry. I'm just, well, you know. It's tough." She reached out and placed her fingers against his forearm, allowing herself to enjoy the contact. The skin of his arm prickled, as if he had gooseflesh. That was the moment she realised that he truly loved her. She was certain; there was no mistake. Benson was in love with her, and she didn't give a shit, *couldn't* give a shit, even though she wanted nothing more than to love him back. Just a little.

"Come on," she said, nodding. "Let's get this over with." If she had a heart, it would be breaking right now. If her bastard father had left her with even a scrap of human emotion, she would be fighting back tears.

Instead she winked at him and opened the door.

They got out of the car and crossed the gravelled car park, heading towards the domineering main entrance: huge wing-shaped doors situated at the top of a set of wide stone steps flanked by tall fern bushes in expensive-looking pots. Sarah linked her arm through the crook of Benson's elbow, and he responded by sliding his hand over hers. For a moment there, she felt as if they were a real couple, perhaps visiting some estranged family member.

It was a pleasant sensation, so she tried to hang on to it for as long as she could, feeling deflated as it began to fade.

If only such fantasies could be made real. Maybe then her nightmares would recede and the darkness of her world would lighten a shade, promising daylight.

"You OK?"

She didn't realise that she'd stopped walking until he spoke. She looked up at him, the weak sunlight glimmering at his back, and felt that all of a sudden he represented some other world – a distant place where she could be normal. She squeezed his hand; he squeezed her back. Neither of them uttered a word. Many miles yawned between them, an unbridgeable gulf, and Sarah experienced the sensation of falling – but not into him, or towards him: she was falling down, away from everything Benson stood for.

Benson's silhouette became something grand, a sort of representation of a strength she could never know. His buzz-cut hair, the slope of his broad shoulders, the line of his neck; he assumed in her imagination the ideal of an ancient warrior, a man more fiction that fact.

Just for a moment: and then it was gone. He was a man again, just another man who wanted to fuck her.

They resumed their journey, climbing the stone steps and pushing through the double doors to enter a large, airy reception area. A long wooden desk was situated along the foot of the staircase, and a rather large Chinese lady sat behind it, speaking quietly on a telephone. There were leaflets scattered artfully across the polished surface of the desk and fresh flowers stood oddly erect in a vase. A huge leather-bound guest book lay open beside the computer terminal into which the Chinese lady was staring, examining data on the small, gently flickering screen.

"Yes, that's fine." Her voice was pure Yorkshire, which seemed incongruous when coupled with her strong Oriental features. "We'll see you then, Mr Jones. Thanks, bye." She hung up the phone, flicked her painted nails at the computer keyboard, and turned to face Sarah and Benson. Her hair was short and black.

Her ears were tiny. "Good afternoon. Can I help?" The woman's smile was almost a challenge; it set fire to rather than lit up her small, round face.

"I'm here to see my mother. My name is Sarah Doherty."

"Ah, yes, Miss Doherty. We spoke earlier on the phone." She smiled again, this time conspiratorially.

"Oh, that was you. OK. Yes. Well, I'm here as promised. Can I see her, or is she still having lunch? We don't mind waiting." Sarah pressed up against the desk, dropping her shoulders and placing her hands on the shiny wood. She felt tense but for some reason did not want this woman to witness it, as if to reveal that tension would be construed as a weakness.

"I'll just check for you. One moment, please. Take a seat if you wish." She motioned with a hand towards some leather sofas by the doors, and then whisked out from behind the desk and moved swiftly and quietly towards another set of double doors, behind which she vanished from sight. Her smile seemed to remain behind, hanging in the air like that of the Cheshire cat from *Alice in Wonderland*.

Snap out of it, thought Sarah. Focus!

"Odd woman," said Benson.

Sarah nodded. "A real fucking weirdo, if you ask me. They all are: like little plastic dolls, afraid to show any real emotion in case the shell cracks and all the bile leaks out." She was surprised by the venom in her tone, and raised a hand to her mouth as if to block the words that were spilling from between her lips.

Benson did not reply, but she could tell that she'd unnerved him. It seemed like she was always doing that, even when she wasn't trying – *especially* when she wasn't trying.

"This was a bad idea. I'm sorry." She turned away from the reception desk, looking towards the main entrance. "Maybe we should go... before she comes back."

Benson laid a hand on her arm. She looked down at it, peering as if it were an alien object that might burn her flesh. "Come on, Sarah. You wanted to ask her something, didn't you? About your father?" His grip was strong, grounding her, tethering her body to the earth in a way that she could not possibly deny. He was like a part of the landscape, and all she needed to do was bind herself to him.

Sarah nodded. "Yes. But she probably won't be able to answer. She barely even remembers who I am. It's taken her. The Alzheimer's. There isn't that much of her left." Her eyes prickled but she refused to cry. She would not allow Benson to see her like that, not now, not ever.

"Just try, eh? What have you got to lose, really? Ask her what you came here to ask and then we can go home and have a drink."

Sarah sucked in a breath, held it, and then let it go. Her head felt light, as if the skull were as thin as an eggshell and held nothing within it but air. "Yeah, yeah. Fuck it. It's pointless anyway, but I might as well try."

Footsteps sounded loudly on the polished floors, but when Sarah looked around there was nobody there; the reception area was empty. She heard movement upstairs, and in other rooms on the ground floor, but there was not a single person in view. Benson stood rigid at her side, a statue, a cold presence that had slipped between the cracks of her life.

She felt as if the world had suddenly backed away from her, like a bystander retreating from an armed drunkard. Tiny steps, a smile, a nod: open hands raised in an attempt to calm the gibbering psycho.

"Where is everyone?" She spun on her heels, grabbing Benson's hand. His fingers were cold; his skin was dry as paper. He said nothing.

A tall, broad shape shifted slightly in a doorway under the stairs, pulling slowly back into shadow before it could be examined in full view. Sarah caught sight of dusty dark clothes, pale hands, and a small white towel or blanket covering the face. Just like the vision of her father in her bath-time dream-memory,

the figure was dressed in some kind of ritualistic outfit. A de-
mented holy man on a fool's crusade: a shabby demon in her
view, but retreating, forever backing away, just out of sight...
Who the hell was it over there, and what did they want?

The figure slipped gradually away, the covered face shrinking
to a single white point in the darkness. Although she could not
make out the features beneath the white covering, she felt certain that it was smiling.

"What? I don't get you." Benson's mouth moved out of synch
with the words, as if he were a character being badly dubbed in
a foreign film. "What do you mean?"

Then, like air rushing in to fill a vacuum, the room was once
again teeming with life. People moved across her line of sight,
doors slammed, voices were carried towards her on the still,
stale air.

The doorway was empty.

Reality...

Reality was empty.

"Sarah?"

She looked up at Benson, and then down at his hand. For a
moment, she thought that he was someone else, a person she
had never met before in her life, and that he was restraining
her. But the feeling passed and then she knew who he was, of
course she did: he was the only solid thing in her life, and she
resented him for his strength and solidity. She hated him for
being weak enough to love her.

Then, in a moment of clarity, she realised why she could
never truly care for him. Benson would always be denied her,
standing forever out of reach, because she had never really
loved herself.

TEN

I stood outside the grungy-looking doorway opposite the café staring at the handwritten flyer that was pinned to the right of the door, just below a row of battered stainless steel buzzers and a horizontal grille.

Model/Massage

If it wasn't so depressing it might have been funny.

But somehow I had lost my sense of humour regarding the world; somewhere along the way it had been eaten up and spat out into the gutter.

People brushed against me as they passed by, some of them glancing at me disdainfully as I waited outside the entrance to the knocking shop. A woman sucked air through her teeth, averting her gaze; a couple of teenage Asian lads laughed and called out to me. I ignored them all and stared at the door. It was painted pillbox red and the old paintwork was bubbled and blistered, like diseased or badly sunburned flesh.

Immaculee Karuhmbi. It was an odd name; poetic and strangely beautiful. Foreign, obviously: perhaps African. There was a singsong quality to the name that made me think of tribal songs and the wide-open spaces and scrubland of a far-away veldt.

I turned my head and looked at the café I'd just left; it felt a million miles away, as if the main road were in fact an ocean separating me from that other place. The neon sign was bent and hung down further on one side, and the bulbs in the accent above the letter *e* had burned out. The owner didn't seem to mind such inattention to detail regarding his premises. It was just another thing that went wrong at some point, and nobody cared enough to put it right.

Turning back to face the scarred old building I was about to enter, I let out a small breath and wondered what the hell I was doing here. Why had I not just stayed in the stupid haunted house, sat tight, and ignored that damned clockwork voice on the telephone?

But I knew why – of course I did.

A small, quiet voice located somewhere at the back of my head, where all the primal hopes and fears were curled up into a tight little ball of anxiety, spoke softly to me, prodding me onwards.

It might be her, said the voice. *It might be Rebecca.*

The voice on the phone had sounded nothing at all like that of my dead wife – it had barely even sounded human: more an approximation of human tones. But still, there was always the chance, however slim, that it was her.

Rebecca.

My wife.

And wherever Rebecca was, I would also find Ally, our daughter. Wasn't this the only reason I was still alive, the single thing that had stopped me from ever ending my own life? The narrow hope that one day, in some way, I might see them again?

Recent betrayals of their memory aside – and even older ones craftily ignored – it was still the thing that drove me, the carrot I dangled ahead of myself just to help get me through the dark. Hope. That's what it was: blind hope. I had nothing else to cling to.

"Moron," I whispered under my breath. "Fool." It was true.
But what's more powerful than a fool's logic?

I stepped forward and rang the buzzer for the top floor. There
was a burst of static, as harsh and unforgiving as a murder victim's scream, and then a voice cut through the din: "Hello?"

"I've come to see Immaculee Karuhmbi. Is she available?"

Again, there came a short explosion of static before the voice
continued. "Do you have an appointment? Appointments only,
I'm afraid." I could not tell if the voice belonged to a man or a
woman, but it was polite and direct and sounded like its owner
would not take any crap.

"I..." I remembered the clockwork voice, and how it seemed
to know everything – or even to be orchestrating things from
the other end of a dead line. "Just tell her that Thomas Usher is
here to see her. If she still won't accept my call, I'll go away."

This time the pause was longer, and it took me a few seconds to
work out that the clicking sound I heard was probably the speaker
being silenced as the person upstairs passed on my message.

I closed my eyes. My head ached. The world was like a giant
bruise, gently pulsing.

"Come on up." Then, before the static could be heard again,
the communication was ended and the door lock clicked loudly,
allowing me to enter. I pushed open the old red door and stepped
into a dimly lit passageway, with torn wallpaper on the damp
walls and no carpet on the burnished floor. The floorboards
creaked as I walked over them and the door eased shut behind
me with only the slightest nudge from my hand.

The air was dense. Dust hung thick and heavy in the passage;
a phantom cloud. The skirting boards along the base of the walls
were coming loose, there were holes in the plaster and the floorboards had wide gaps between them. The place felt derelict, but
I knew that people dwelled here: both the living and the dead,
standing side by side like soldiers in some weird war against a
common enemy yet to be identified.

Straight ahead was a closed door. There was a hatch set into the door at eye-level, but with no way of opening it from the outside. The door handle had been removed and the door had been hung in such a way that the hinges were hidden.

I hadn't noticed at first but in the wall at the foot of the stairs was a strange little cubby-hole, a sort of built-in cupboard with its door removed and with a tatty dining chair shoved into the space. Across the doorway, attached to each side of the frame, was a makeshift shelf or counter positioned at midriff level. Behind the shelf, sitting on the chair, was a wiry old man with badly drawn tattoos on his face. Behind him were crude shelves piled high with hand towels.

"Hello." I took a step forward, unsure at first if he were alive or dead.

The old man grinned, flashing several yellow teeth and a lot of gaps in his blackened gums. "Fanny or phantoms?" He laughed, finding his question – which he had no doubt asked hundreds of times – hilariously funny.

"I'm here to see the psychic." I didn't even crack a smile.

"Top floor," said the old man, squinting at me. He licked his lips. His tongue was coloured an interesting shade of green. "Just keep climbing the stairs until you see a door covered in a load of African shit – that's the one you want." He laughed again. Spittle flecked the air in front of his wizened face. He raised a hand to scratch at his inky, monkey-like features. His fingernails were obscenely long, with dirt caked behind them.

"Thanks." I moved past him, keeping my distance. I felt that if I even entered his orbit I would be stained for life, dirtied beyond the hope of ever feeling clean again.

The man's laughter followed me up the first flight of stairs, and then suddenly stopped when I reached the narrow half landing, where the stairs turned abruptly to take me to the first floor. It was as if an invisible hand had reached out and snatched his mirth away, silencing him forever.

I passed a series of doorways on the first floor landing, giving them not much more than a cursory glance. I'd been to places like this before, in my former role as a paid guide to the departed. Once, a few years ago, I'd helped rid a Bradford massage parlour of a particularly nasty spirit – an unknown murder victim who claimed to be an early study of the Yorkshire Ripper, when he was still not much more than an inchoate serial killer.

I climbed the stairs to the upper level, noticing that the décor improved as I made my way up through the building. The second floor landing was blocked off by yet another door, with another grille set into the wall. I reached out and pressed the button. This was clearly the door to which the old bastard downstairs had referred: the wooden surface was decorated in attention-grabbing African designs, probably hand-painted by whoever took up residence on the second floor. Some of the motifs were gorgeous and some were scary and brutal.

"Yes." It was the same voice – odd, sexless, yet good-humoured.

"It's Thomas Usher again. I'm inside."

A buzzer sounded; the door mechanism clicked and the door popped open an inch. I pushed the door wide and passed through, then shut it quietly behind me. The air was fresh and breezy; there must have been a window open somewhere. I could smell freshly cut flowers.

"This way, please." Now that I could hear the voice first-hand, I realised that it belonged to a young woman or girl. She stepped out of an open doorway to my left, and smiled. She was young – not much more than a teenager – and breathtakingly pretty. Coffee-coloured skin, remarkably pale eyes, bright white teeth. Her long, plaited hair was partially covered by a brightly-coloured scarf and she was wearing what looked like some kind of tribal dress. It was all earthen colours and swirling patterns. Beautiful.

"Hello." I smiled. It felt good to smile. Natural. I realised that I hadn't smiled like that in a long time.

"Hello, Mr Usher." She stepped forward and held out a thin brown hand. I took it, and almost kissed it before realising that all she was expecting was a polite handshake. The girl's beauty had knocked me for six.

"Miss Immaculee has been expecting you. They told her you were coming." Her teeth were so very white, like shards of bone, and her strange eyes were... *hypnotic*. "Please come this way."

"Who told her I was coming? I don't understand?" I was now speaking to the girl's back as she led me through the doorway and into a large, dim room. She was walking barefoot, and for some reason that seemed incredibly erotic.

"Why, the voices of course. Always the voices."

The walls of the room were hung with thin drapes, and each one depicted some kind of African scene. They were marvellous examples of tribal art, and I wondered if they were simply there for show or held some kind of mystical association.

"Hello, Mr Usher." The voice which beckoned me deeper into the room was low and husky. I expected to see an aging male blues singer and not a middle-aged psychic woman.

The young girl left my side, walked to the door, and exited the room. She closed the door silently behind her; it seemed like a practiced move. The darkness quivered; the low lights trembled.

"Step closer, Mr Usher. I'd like to see you."

The woman sat in a high-backed chair at a highly polished table. She too had her hair wrapped up in a scarf, and several black tendrils hung down over her shoulders. Her eyes were large and deep and almost black. Her lips were full. Her cheeks were narrow, showing off her delicate bone structure. Her skin glowed. She had no arms.

"Come. Sit by me." She twitched her head to invite me to her table.

She had no arms.

I didn't want to stare, but what else could I do? She was wearing a white open-necked blouse with the arms pinned back and had an elaborate necklace at her throat. Her breasts were large and her shoulders were broad. And she had no arms.

I sat down at the table, facing her across its shiny surface. There was a glass set in front of the woman, with a long straw sticking out above the rim. She bent her head and took a sip. The drink had no aroma that I could detect; I thought it might be vodka. "Can I get you anything, Mr Usher?" I liked the way she said my name. Her eyes widened; she drank me in like the vodka, plucking me from my seat and examining what she found, rolling me around on her tongue.

"No. Thank you. I'm fine."

"What brought you here, if you don't mind me asking? Did someone give you my name, or was it a dream?" Her direct manner was alarming in some ways yet comforting in others. At least I didn't have to play games with this woman.

"What shall I call you?"

"My name: Immaculee."

"OK… Immaculee. It's rather beautiful, you know."

"Yes, I do know. I have been told that many times." She smiled. Then she took another sip of her drink.

I decided to get to the point: "Somebody spoke to me on the telephone and told me to seek you out. I have no idea who this person was – or even if it *was* a person. Do you understand what I mean by that?"

She nodded once. Her eyes caught the light. They shone like dark stones brought up from the depths of a vast black lake.

"I was told to come here but I don't know why. I'm being as honest with you as I know how. Can you help me? Do you even know what I'm talking about?" I leaned forward and into the edge of the table, pressing my elbows against the wood.

"I lost my arms in 1994, Mr Usher. Do you recall, by any chance, the Rwandan Genocide? I was – I *am* – a Tutsi. My village was attacked by Hutus armed with knives and machetes. They did not think us worthy of wasting bullets." She paused;

I waited. A clock ticked loudly somewhere in the room. I hadn't noticed it until now. "They hacked to death my husband and daughter, right in front of me. They raped my daughter first, as I watched. Then they chopped her to pieces."

I didn't know what to do, what to say, so I just listened.

"Do you know what it is to lose someone, Mr Usher? Do you know how that feels? I think you do."

I nodded. "I know a little, yes, I've lost people, too."

"I thought you must have – that's why the voices chose me to deliver the message. Because we are joined in a way, by our loss."

I was afraid to interrupt her, so I just sat there in the gloom and waited for her to finish.

"Those *men* – those Hutu murderers – they raped me amid the remains of my loved ones. Then they urinated on me. Finally, they cut off my arms and left me to bleed. They thought I would die there, surrounded by pieces of my family. I remember their laughter as they walked away, drinking beer and boasting of how I'd enjoyed it."

The clock had stopped; all the clocks had stopped. I could hear the screams of the murdered and feel the tears of the innocent. My skin burned; fires raged around me. My tattoos danced. There was a ringing in my ears that could only be a distant scream.

"But I didn't die. Oh, no; I survived. They took my family and they cut off my arms, but what I got in return was *the voices*. They come back to me – my loved ones. They come back and they tell me things, but only when I am asleep. Only in my dreams…"

I felt like screaming. This woman had been through so much. It wasn't fair, wasn't right. Why must she continue to suffer?

"I sleep a lot. Young Traci tends to me. She gives me gin and vodka to ease my nerves and cooks me wonderful meals I rarely eat."

I realised that the glow I had noticed earlier on her skin was the radiance of death. It was not far away now; she was preparing and praying for it to arrive quickly. Her intense bright-burning presence, the torn and ragged voice. Was it cancer? In her throat?

"Two nights ago another voice entered my dreams. One I had not heard before. It was... mechanical, somehow. Like a wind-up toy. It told me to pass on an address." She leaned forward, her motion smooth and silent and horrific. I hated myself for being afraid, but I was. I was terrified.

"She said you must go to the river. There is a place, a ware-house: number 3, Dock Side. I don't know where exactly, but it is in London." She gasped for breath, but when I reached out to her across the table she pulled away, baring her teeth. "Not to touch. You mustn't touch – no one ever touches me again." Then, as if nothing had occurred, she smiled. It was a sweet smile, almost ethereal in its delicateness.

"Was there anything else, or was it just the address?" I blinked rapidly, feeling tears that would not come. My eyes were dry, but they were aching. I wished that I was able to cry, just this once.

"Yes. There was another thing – something important. She told me to repeat it word for word." The psychic bent forward at the waist, sipped her drink.

"Yes, Immaculee? What was it?"

She straightened in her chair, and I experienced the full force of her savage dignity, her refusal to break. Here was a proud woman, a strong woman, who had refused to give up. Yes, she was damaged and she drank too much, but she was alive – she was *present*. She was not a ghost. Not yet.

"Tell me. Please."

"The voice said: 'Stay away from her. Even if she finds you, stay away. You cannot help. She is lost to you, even though you think you have found her.'" She slumped in her chair, as if by speaking the words she had exhausted herself. "That is all." She looked down at the table. I stared at the small mounds of her stumps under the shirt; they were like absurd misplaced breasts.

I stood up, feeling nauseous, and backed away from the table. Fumbling in my pocket I produced a few notes and threw them onto the tabletop. "Thanks," I mumbled. I could barely even speak.

"No charge," she said, without looking up. The room seemed darker now, as if a veil had been drawn across the window.

I turned and I hurried out of the room, leaving the money were it had fallen. The young girl, Traci, was sitting cross-legged on the landing, a dented stainless steel bowl held between her bare knees, and skinning some kind of root vegetable with a small knife. She was humming a strange tune as she worked, and when she looked up at me I finally realised that she was blind.

ELEVEN

It had been a while since Sarah had seen her mother, and the woman looked older than ever. It was upsetting that she seemed to have aged so much in such a relatively short period of time – it wasn't exactly years, just a few months since her last visit – and Sarah felt herself stumble as she walked through the door and into the quiet sun room.

"I'll wait here," said Benson, hanging back in the doorway. "Call me when you're ready for me to come through." He smiled; his scars crinkled.

She looked down at the floor. Her running shoes were dirty. One of the laces had come undone. "Yeah. Thanks." Looking back up, she turned her gaze towards her mother. For a moment, she thought that someone was standing behind the seated woman, but when she blinked the image faded.

Sarah took a breath and walked towards the large bay window, where her mother was sitting in a wicker chair staring out at the beautiful but rain-swept garden at the rear of the home. Slivers of hazy sunlight somehow managed to make their way through the wet glass, forming a bright pool around her mother's feet. Her legs, beneath heavy stockings, looked swollen. Specks of dust hung in the air, painted by the light.

"Mum?" She approached the chair and placed a hand on her mother's shoulder. "It's me, Mum. It's Sarah."

The woman did not stir. She just kept looking out of the window, at the short, yellowish grass and the sagging flowerbeds. Once spring came, those beds would be so pretty, and bursting with colour. Right now they were resting, the plants and flowers waiting to be brought back to life by the turning of the seasons.

The sun room was bright and airy, despite the weather. The windows were all closed, to keep out the chill and protect old bones, but the weak sunlight seemed to gather there, focusing on the bright little area. A frail old man sat in an armchair by the wall, his eyes glued to a television set. He was watching a news programme – reports of a tornado in Texas – with the sound turned down. On his lap was balanced a newspaper, its pages open to the sports section. He was drooling. His eyes were unfocused.

"Mum? Can you hear me, Mum?"

The woman stirred in her seat, her head twitching slightly to one side, as if she were straining to hear. Perhaps she heard her name being called as if from a great distance – the immeasurable distance between sanity and dementia.

Sarah pulled up another chair and sat down, her knees pressed together and her bottom perched on the front edge of the seat, as if she were poised for a quick getaway. And wasn't that exactly right? Wherever she was, whoever she found herself with, the thought of escape was never far from her mind. He had made her this way: her father, the bastard. He had trained her for constant flight.

She reached down and opened her handbag, taking out the cardboard folder with the photographs inside. She'd selected just a few from the collection, and found it difficult to look at them again so soon. But she had to. If she wanted to know the story behind them, she had to push through the mental wall and confront these uncomfortable truths.

"Mum. Look at me, Mum." She made her voice hard, and stared at her mother's tired face. A nerve twitched in the woman's cheek. Her eyes were moist, as if from the constant threat of tears.

"Look. At. Me." It felt wrong to be so stern – like speaking harshly to a child – but what else could she do?

Slowly, her mother turned to face her. One side of her mother's mouth was twisted downwards, as if she'd suffered a mild stroke. Her lips were wet. "Sarah…" Her voice was a low, drawn-out sigh.

"Yes, Mum. It's me. It's your Sarah."

Recognition flared in her eyes. She tried to smile – she clearly did – but it was more like a silent snarl. "Hello, Sadie-baby."

Her mother had not called her by that pet name for many years. She had forgotten how good it sounded, how full of love. Sarah took a deep breath and clenched her fist. Then, realising that she was crushing the photographs, she released the pressure. She blew out air through her nose. "I need to ask you something, Mum. It's important. Can you stay with me for a minute, just while I show you something?

"Of course I can. I'm not busy." Sarah's mother's eyes were dead; there was hardly anything of her personality remaining behind them. Just a spiky darkness, like a black pit lined with pointed black teeth. If Sarah did not take care, that darkness might just turn and bite her.

"Look at these, Mum. Tell me about them." Carefully, she took out the photographs and laid them in a row on the table before her mother, smoothing out the creases with her hands. There were five photographs in all, and each one showed a different stage of some kind of sex game. Sarah watched her mother closely as she placed the photos in a line, and it pained her to see the woman flinch at the sight of each one, as if from a blow.

"What's the story with these? Come on, Mum. He's dead now – you can tell me. I know you protected me when I was a girl. You don't need to do that anymore."

Her mother's eyes – large, moist and rheumy – flickered upwards, staring into Sarah's face. There was a silent plea there, a
request that she pursue this line of enquiry no further. But she
could not hold back. She was, after all, her father's daughter,
and despite his many flaws the man had been a fine and instinctive detective.

"Sadie-baby..."

"Don't fucking call me that. Tell me. What about this one?"
She held up one of the photographs: it depicted her mother
being sodomised by a naked man in a leather gimp mask while
she fellated another whose face was covered in what looked like
a floral patterned tea towel tied in a knot at the back of his head.

Her mother sighed, and then spoke. "They made me take
part. The photos were so I'd keep quiet... not speak about the
other stuff."

Sarah felt her heart break, but it had been broken too many
times before to even count. Heartbreak was a feeling with which
she was familiar, and often she took a strange form of comfort
from the fragile pain in her chest. It felt like a tiny bird pecking
at her ribs. "Why, Mum? Why did they need your silence?"

Her mother's head dipped. Tears fell from her red-rimmed
eyes and dirtied her gaunt cheeks. "They did things that nobody could know about. They took... criminals; people they
thought might commit even more vicious crimes. They took
them and..." She glanced about the room, as if looking for
spies. Her hands gripped the arms of the wicker chair and her
feet skittered on the smooth floor. "They took them and they
did things to them. I don't know what – I never knew that.
But I know those things they did were awful." She began to
rock in the chair, her eyes flickering closed. Then, oddly, she
began to hum a wordless tune, a meaningless doggerel she
clearly used for comfort.

"Mum. What else, Mum? Is that it? They kept you quiet so
you wouldn't tell?"

But the old woman was long gone. She had retreated back into herself, where the things she had been forced to do could no longer reach her. Inside, she was clean and untouched. Inside, she was pure and bright; she knew nothing of the darkness in which she had been held captive for so many years of her life.

Sarah reached out and gripped her mother's shoulder. The bones, through her skin, felt tiny and fragile, like those of a bird. "What else did they do, Mum? What did *he* do? I know there's more. I'm certain. He did worse things. Tell me what they were." The threat of violence in her voice unnerved Sarah; she felt capable of causing real damage to her frail and ailing mother, and the realisation was enough to make her afraid of herself.

"Oh, they took me all ways." Her mother's voice sounded like a fading echo. It was small and distant, yet held a terrible power within the words. "They did me, all of them. Some of them I didn't even know, had never met. They put things on me and in me. They used me like a doll and laughed about it afterwards."

Sarah relaxed her grip. She felt sick. "But you protected me, didn't you? At least you did that. You kept me safe."

Suddenly, entering another spell of lucidity, Sarah's mother glanced sharply up and to the side. This time her eyes were dry; they were sharp as broken glass. There was a subtle slyness in her features. "No, I didn't keep you safe. He did." She smiled, but her lips were parched, cracked.

"Who? Him? Father?" Sarah took an involuntary half-step backwards. "Protected me from his own filthy hands?"

"No, not that stupid shit. The angel. It was the angel who told him never to touch you. Never to hurt you. Not to kill you. The angel protected you." Then, thankfully, her gaze went blank and she slumped backwards into the chair, her energy spent. She started humming again, but the sound was barely as loud as a series of heavy breaths.

"Mum... Mum?"

Nothing. No response. Just that awful toneless humming.

Then, a slight movement: her mother's hand scurrying like a small animal across her leg. She reached down to the floor, where she kept her handbag – she was always afraid of someone stealing her things. Long white fingers fumbled with the catch, and then they popped the bag open. She took out something – a small package – and held it out to Sarah, not even looking in her direction, still humming, distracted by whatever vision had taken up residence inside her head.

Sarah took the package. It was a folded envelope, and inside it was an old-fashioned audio tape. She unfolded the paper and read the label. Written on it in black ink, in her father's neat, graceful handwriting, there was what looked like two initials and a date:

D.T.
1984

Sarah felt like she was floating; her feet lifted from the floor and the jerky motion tipped her, tilted her over to one side so that she was leaning towards the window. She righted herself, and then realised that it had all been a trick of perception. She was still standing upright, clutching the cassette tape, and staring at the top of her mother's head.

Looking at the thin grey hair and the skull beneath the skin.

The thin, imperfect curve of her skull. Beneath the papery skin.

Hair and bone; a thin and fragile covering to protect the shattered dreams that writhed beneath….

Even as Sarah watched, two or three holes appeared in the top of her mother's cranium, thick blood bubbling up from the fissures. The holes appeared as if they were being drilled, but no apparatus was visible. The small, round holes filled up with blood and the blood ran down her face, baptising her in red. The woman did not even register the wounds. She just sat and stared at the rain-smeared window, at the sun-starved and wilting garden beyond, and hummed that silly fucking tuneless dirge.

Then, abruptly, the holes began to close up. The blood re-treated, vanishing, running backwards into the rapidly healing wounds. Sarah's mother's head was undamaged.

Behind her, Sarah sensed someone moving into the shadows; but when she turned around to look there was nobody there. Benson still stood outside, with his back against the door. No-body else had come near.

The old man in the corner chuckled softly, but it was only because there was now a comedy show on television. The sound was still muted; figures capered across the screen, dancing as if they were being shot by automatic weapons.

"What is this, Mum?" But there was no answer. Of course there wasn't. "What's going on? Has he come back? Is he here?"

What a stupid question… but was it? Was it really so absurd?

Benson, behind the door, moved away from her line of vision. Through the small square of glass she caught sight of a reflection skipping away into the room. She spun around, trying to catch sight of whatever was causing the illusion, but there was only the old man and the television, the figures convulsing on the screen.

"That's it," she said out loud. "It's the fucking telly. Mind's playing tricks… the TV." She tried to smile but it didn't sit right on her face; the muscles around her mouth felt too tight. The fact that she was talking to herself made her feel afraid.

"Get away from me," she said.

The old man chuckled again, and when Sarah glared at him he was sitting in his armchair with a thin silken hood falling softly over his head, billowing as it swallowed his motionless features. His body was covered in a long black robe, and his arms were folded neatly in his lap. The edges of the white hood fluttered down the front and sides of his face, covering his neck and throat, and finally came to rest, as if a breeze were dropping. He turned his head and watched her, examining her through the threadbare hood.

"Get away," she repeated, and it was just an old man again,
his toothless mouth grinning at the funnies on the television.

There was no black robe, no diaphanous white hood.

Sarah raised a hand to her face and felt tears on her cheeks.
She glanced once more at her mother, but the woman was no
help to her at all. She was rocking backwards and forwards, her
hands gripping the arms of the chair, her tiny old-woman feet
rising and falling on the floor, making soft little tapping sounds
against the boards.

Sarah reached out and touched her mother's head. There
were no wounds; that vision had passed. She rubbed her
mother's dry, rough scalp. "I love you, Mum. I always did. I'm
sorry I never told you."

Then, knowing that there was nothing more for her here, in
this dry, dead place, Sarah turned away and headed for the door
so that she could rejoin the living.

But each step of the way she felt trailed by the dead.

PART TWO
BACK FOR MORE

TWELVE

Trevor was lying on his back in the bedroom, coming down from his last high. He wasn't even sure why he kept taking the drugs – they had stopped blotting out Michael's face a long time ago, and even made it stronger and clearer in his mind. He turned his face sideways on the pillow, his eyes coming to rest on the photograph of his brother. He was a small boy with a tentative smile, but dead behind the eyes.

I did that, he thought. I killed whatever once lived there, in his head.

Dead. Behind the eyes.

It was dark. The lights were out but the blinds were open. The moon looked small, as if it were moving away from the Earth, fleeing the scene of so much horror and degradation. Trevor stared up from the bed, out of the window, and wished that he was up there, on the surface of the moon. He often imagined himself as an astronaut, skulking on a moon rock and leaving the world behind. Taking off his helmet and finding that he could breathe. He would sit there, looking up at the stars, and be glad that he was finally alone. Nobody could touch him there, on the hard grey surface of a fossil planet, and he was unable to touch anyone else.

Touch. Touching.

Dead behind the eyes.

This combination of words seemed to create a monster; a thing that had chased him all his life, and was now gaining fast.

What was that boy's name again? Oh, yes, Derek. The young man who'd fled in the night. What had he been saying about getting someone younger? Thoughts swarmed like stinking flies; Trevor's head was filled with them. He felt them climbing across the inside of his skull, felt the horrible vibration of their buzzing wings. As if he, too, were dead behind the eyes: nothing there but rot, dry and black and loveless.

Blinking, Trevor sat up on the bed and glanced across the room. He was naked. His flaccid cock lay against his thigh, useless and unwanted: a short-range weapon whose ammunition had long ago been spent.

He looked at his jeans, cast aside on the floor by the wardrobe. He'd been drunk last night, but wasn't there a vague memory of taking the boy's number – taking *Derek's* number – when they'd first met in that horrible club? He recalled a scribbled sequence of digits on a skinned beer mat, which he had then thrust into his back pocket. They had both known that the number would not be required, that the night would end with them leaving the club together. But certain social customs must still be maintained, rituals needed to be carried out and small gods appeased.

Trevor was sweating. His naked torso shone when he glanced down at it. The drugs. They always caused his body to react in this way, raising his core temperature. Any drug: booze, dope, speed, heroin. They all did the same thing to his system, turning up the heat, burning out the badness...

He swung his legs off the mattress and stumbled across the room, his bare feet dragging in discarded clothing and magazines. Bending down, he picked up his jeans and fumbled through the pockets. He found the beer mat right where he'd suspected it would be, in the left rear pocket. The soggy cardboard had curled at the edges, and spilled alcohol had caused the numerals to smudge, but the number was still legible. Still useable.

Trevor glanced at the clock on his nightstand. It was still early: just after 9 pm. No self-respecting night owl would be asleep at this hour. In fact, Derek would probably be at home preparing to go out on the prowl, preening himself to present his wares to the night.

He sat back down on the bed and picked up his mobile phone, keyed in the number and put the phone to his ear.

It rang five or six times, and Trevor was on the verge of hanging up. Then, thankfully, someone answered.

"Yeah." It was the same voice, but subdued by the digital miles which lay between them.

"Derek? It's Trevor… from last night." He let that one hang, trying to gauge the boy's mood.

"OK. I'm listening."

Trevor smiled. "Listen, I'm sorry. I acted like a prick. I… I have things on my mind. Life's been a bit messy lately. But…"

"But what? Life's full of butts, and there are several awaiting my attention this evening."

"But I like you. You seem nice. I was wondering if we could meet up again. This evening, perhaps. I could take you somewhere. Somewhere decent. Somewhere expensive."

"Well, well, well…" How obvious. How predictable. The promise of a pricey meal and everything changed, the edges suddenly smoothed out. "That does sound nice. By way of an apology, you mean?"

"As a starting point, yes. Then we can talk. About something I'm interested in."

The line buzzed. Those flies, they had left his head, exiting through his ear, and somehow got inside the mobile phone.

"OK. You book a table and I'll meet you in an hour. Where did you have in mind?"

"How does the Atlantic Grill sound?"

"Fuck me. That would be great, but I doubt you'd be able to reserve a table for an hour's time. They have a six-month waiting list. As a minimum." There was a hint of desperation in his voice. High-class restaurants, expensive tastes – these were things to which the boy aspired, part of a world he desperately wanted to infiltrate. Sometimes people were so easy to read.

"I have a table there whenever I want. I once did the owner a favour. He's a friend of mine." Trevor was smiling. He thought the boy could probably hear it in his voice, but he didn't care. He had snared his prey.

Was that really how he thought, in terms of the hunter and the hunted?

"I like you more and more each time we speak." The boy's voice was a soft purr.

Yes. Hunter and hunted. That was how the world worked – this world, at least. He could barely remember how the other world functioned, the one he'd been able to glimpse through the hot glare of theatre lights as he strutted across the stage. Night after night after night. Speaking to the dead. Flirting with the departed.

"I'll see you there in an hour. The table will be in my name. I'll tell them to expect you, Derek." He ended the call, his thumb sliding over the hang-up button. There was no need for any more: this was already a done deal.

Trevor felt much better now. He knew what he wanted, and Derek knew too. They had avoided the issue, letting it stand there between them like a dusty stage upon which wonders would be unveiled. It was part of the act, just another line of the script. They would eat and drink, and possibly even kiss, and then they would discuss the real reason for Trevor's call.

He remembered the boy's voice before he had left last night, his words hanging in the air like birds of prey: *I can get you someone younger, if that's what you need.*

What he needed… what *did* he need? That was the big question, wasn't it? It always had been. What exactly did Trevor desire? An interesting word, desire: so strong, so meaningful, so full of potential. He looked at the pillow, at the old photograph. He picked up the photograph and held it to his face. He kissed it. His lips stuck briefly to the image before pulling away.

"Oh, Michael. I need *you*. Of course I do. I always did. I needed you in a way that you didn't want, couldn't handle. You were everything to me... everything."

The room went darker, just a fraction but enough for him to realise that he was no longer alone – if he ever had been. His gift was slowly returning. That bastard Thomas Usher had stolen it from him, taken it and shattered it like an empty bottle, but now it was on the rise. He could feel the presence of others. Their breath filled the air beside his face, their bodies jostled for position in whatever room he entered. They were waiting for him to come back to them, forming an orderly queue for the time when they could speak to him again.

The dead always had so much to talk about. They were lonely, most of them, and they craved company. He had been a good listener, back in the day, and the dead never forgot one who listened. They respected him in a way that the living never had.

"I'm coming," he whispered. To the dead. To Michael's memory. "I'm coming back."

His gaze drifted to the full-length mirror. It was an antique, something he'd picked up when the money was good and the bookings were flying in. It was said to be haunted; a famous mirror with a story to tell. But he had not seen anything odd or strange in the mirror until last night, when things had turned sour with the boy, Derek. The hand. That cold, wet hand. It had been reaching out to him, drawing him in... or at least trying to.

A hand to hold.

He walked over to the mirror. The surface was no longer reflective. It had begun to fog over in the early hours of the morning and continued that way throughout the day. He could no longer see himself in its smooth, flat surface: all he could see was grey, like a slab of mist cut from the world and set on a stand in his bedroom.

"Who are you?"

There was no answer. His gift was still too weak; he could not yet hear the dead.

"Why have you come to me?"

A drum began to beat, slowly, rhythmically, like an ancient tribal summoning. The sound only existed inside his head; he knew that. But still, it was sad and beautiful and haunting: a haunting sound from a haunted mirror heard by a haunted man. He blinked back tears. He thought about Michael, and how Michael had hated Trevor's attentions, had been so scared of him. But Trevor had been unable to stop himself; he was not strong enough to resist.

Never strong. Never strong enough. Not to resist.

So he had acted upon his compulsions, not even thinking about the hurt he was creating, the damage he was causing. His little brother had been physically weak, and unable to fight back. Trevor had told himself that it was just an expression of his love, a way of making things special between them, but deep down inside he knew that he was lying to himself, lying to his brother, lying to them all.

Lying all the time. And still lying now, even when there was no need.

The truth was something he could never quite reach – even the truth about himself, about who he really was and what he was able to do. All those years performing, faking it for an audience, and the bitter truth was that he had been gifted all along. He had always been able to hear the dead speak, but it was easier to ignore them and put on an act, give the people what they wanted rather than what the dead needed them to know.

"Come to me. Here. Now. Show me that you can hear me."

The pale hand appeared again, pressed against the other side of the glass. Up close, Trevor could see that it was cut, ragged, the skin was peeling away from the bone. It seemed human, but there was something not quite right about the way it looked. Like an imperfect imitation; the battered hand of a ruined mannequin.

"Yes, that's it. That's right. I'm here for you." Trevor could feel a power in the room, a force that was coming to him from beyond the mirror. It was his old gift returned, but also something new, something different. Before, whatever he had been able to do had originated from deep within him, at his core, but this... this was from somewhere else, an external point towards which he was being drawn.

The hand clenched into a fist. Knucklebones popped through the pallid flesh. They were sharp, white, more like teeth than bones. The fist began to writhe against the glass, smearing it with strange clear ichors – the thing's blood?

Did ghosts bleed? Did they weep real tears?

"What are you?"

Slowly, by inches, a pale orb appeared through the thick mist, like a weird vessel breaking the surface of a still, grey sea. It was spherical, or perhaps oval. It took several seconds for Trevor to realise that what he was seeing was the top of a head pushing through the grizzled gloom. A large bald head.

Once it cleared the veil of grey, he began to make out the cuts and slashes in the skin, the small hollows in the skull. It was the top of a head: the pate of some strange being heaving into view, and then pressing oddly against the glass.

The skull was soft; it flattened as it was forced against the glass.

Thankfully, the head did not twist and enable the being to look up, into the room. It remained in the same position, pushed up tight against the glass.

Another fist rose and slammed silently into the glass. The figure was certainly humanoid, even if it was a shell, a disguise (and just what had prompted that thought?).

A shell. Yes, that was it... Trevor realised that he was looking at a husk, a man-shaped suit containing something else. The tattered flesh, the bloodless pallor. The malleable bones. It all added up to a costume.

The head was now moving across the glass, the bones pressed flat. It looked like some kind of dance, a manoeuvre choreographed from the movements seen in bad dreams, and Trevor was fascinated and repulsed in equal measures. How could bones be this soft? How could those fists make no sound against the other side of the mirror?

"Tell me who you are?"

The drumming. He had been so distracted by this vision that he had forgotten all about the drumming sound. It had increased in volume, threatening to spill from his head and out into the room. It was the soundtrack of the strange creature, the song of its arrival. The beat of its birth. The thing was dancing in rhythm, moving to the beat, and Trevor was drawn to its perverse motion.

Then, like sweets being snatched from the clutching hands of a child, the figure pulled back from the glass. The fog closed in, filling the space where it had been. The drumming stopped.

"Come back to me!" Trevor fell to his knees and placed his own forehead against the glass. It was cold, like ice. His own skull felt soft, as if it might cave in with the pressure.

"Please come back."

For a moment – a fleeting moment that felt like a snippet of dream – he was sure that he heard laughter. But then it was gone, not even an echo remaining. Not even a vibration left in the air. Gone. Gone.

Gone.

THIRTEEN

Sarah had found the telephone number in her father's old note-book, the one he had not stashed away but kept in plain view, in a drawer with his old warrant card. It was his police-issue book, where he recorded the names and dates and essential information of people who might help him. He called it his Snitch Book. Back when Sarah had lived here, in the family home, he had shown her the battered cover of the book often, telling her that good, reliable informants were as important to a police-man's job as deductive reasoning.

A good snitch or informant, he had said, could solve a crime for you. If you knew what to ask, and how to ask it.

Like everything else in police life, her father had claimed that it was an art form. Everything was an art form according to him: the questioning of suspects, the breaking-in of doors, even the quiet words spoken in a silent lounge or back room to inform a loved one of their father/lover/brother's death.

It was all art, or so he claimed. Art of the highest order. Like a fucking Van Gogh.

Sarah glanced at the blinds, seeing darkness at the window through the gaps. It was late enough that she should be tired, but too early to try and force sleep. Benson had wanted to stay with her after they had visited her mother, but she had convinced him to leave. His attention had been cloying, and she wanted some space in which to think, to process what had happened in the rest home. He'd been crestfallen when he walked out of the door, but she didn't care. Let him have his little huffs and sulks; she had more important things on her mind. She had business to take care of.

Sarah was aware of the fact that – just like her father – she was in danger of becoming obsessed, but she had never been able to turn her back on a mystery. It was a defining characteristic, and one which had got her into a lot of trouble throughout her life. When she was a kid, she earned the reputation as a pest, someone who would never let a thing lie. She had unearthed a lot of secrets, and it had always cost her friends. This niggling skill of hers was part of the reason why she was so alone.

She turned the notebook over in her hands, feeling the dried sweat and the threat of violence held between the bindings. There were many names written down in there, and an equal amount of numbers, but only one of her father's informants had been respected enough to also be called a friend. His name was Erik Fontana. That was not his real name, of course – it was a stage name. Fontana was a club singer. He had played the circuit for years, making friends, forging contacts, being Johnny-on-the-spot whenever something nefarious went down, or was planned or gossiped about.

She picked up the phone and dialled. The number could have been for anything – a house, a flat, a squat, a nightclub – so she just let it ring out, hoping that it was still current. Finally someone picked up at the other end.

"Yeah." A female voice. Low, throaty, gruff.

"I'm trying to contact an Erik Fontana. Do you know him?" She waited, her fingers picking idly at the telephone cord. It was coiled like a thin serpent around her wrist. The plastic was cold, alien to the touch.

"Fuckin' hell, that's an old name. Yeah, I know him. Goes by his real name now, though. Has done for years. It's Eddie. Eddie Knowles." The woman sounded like she smoked forty cigarettes a day. Her throat was ruined.

"Is he there? Can I speak to Eddie?"

"Listen, pet, I don't know who you are, but he's my husband. If he's been fucking you, that's all it is. A fuck. So do yourself a favour and do one, yeah?" A sharp intake of breath: she was apparently sucking on a cigarette. The fact that the woman was still on the phone led Sarah to believe that the man she wanted was there, probably listening to one side of the conversation from another room.

"No, you don't understand. It's nothing like that. Erik... I mean Eddie. He was a friend of my late father's." She licked her lips. She didn't want to offer any more information, not until she knew the man was actually there, on the premises.

"Who's your dad, then? Is he a booking agent, a club owner? Does Eddie owe him money? Cos if he does, that's just another kind of fucked." She cackled loudly, like a witch. Then she sucked again on her cigarette.

Sarah sighed. "My father's name was Emerson Doherty. He died almost seven months ago." She inhaled softly, amazed by the sudden surge of emotions which threatened to overpower her. Darkness boiled within her belly, churning up her insides. She felt sick. The world seemed to wobble for an instant. The room swelled, and then shrank back to its proper proportions.

"Oh. Doherty. You his kid? The girl? I met you once, when you was little. Cute. I... I'd like to say I'm sorry for your loss, but I ain't. Not one bit."

"Don't worry about it. I'm not sorry either."

Again, that hideous cackling, like a Shakespearean sorceress: *Hubble bubble, toil and trouble. By the pricking of my thumbs...* "OK, pet. Eddie's in the back room, having a wee smoke. I'll go get him. He always had time for your old man, although no fucker else did. For what it's worth, you don't sound like him. Not one bit. And you can take that as a compliment."

"Thanks..." But the woman had already thrown down the phone. Sarah could hear her receding footsteps, stomping away across what sounded like bare floorboards but was more likely to be a cheaply laminated kitchen floor. She strained her ears and made out distant voices, laughter, and then different footsteps – these ones much softer – as they moved towards the phone.

"Yeah. This is Eddie." His voice was less damaged than the woman's yet it still held the grizzle of tobacco and alcohol abuse.

"My name's Sarah Doherty. I believe you knew my father."

"Yeah. I knew him. We were friends, him and me, as much as you can be in this game. In this life. We respected each other." There was the hint of a smile in his voice, a sliver of humour that wasn't particularly healthy.

"I'm ringing... well, I'm not exactly sure why I'm ringing you. I found some photos today. Of my dad. Weird shots of sex parties. I remember you always used to go to the same parties he did, and mixed in the same circles. I was wondering if you could tell me anything about a club or something he might have belonged to."

"A club? I don't know what you mean, not really. We went along to sex parties back in the day, yeah, there was plenty of that. Sex and gambling and all kinds of naughty stuff." He laughed. It sounded like the gurgling of a blocked drain. "I wouldn't go talking freely about this, except that the old bastard's dead. I suppose nobody cares what he got up to in his private life. Fuck, they all knew about it anyway. Most of his gov'nors was there, too, in them stupid masks. We all had a fine old time." He seemed to revel in telling her this. It was as if he were trying to shock her, to draw out of her some kind of reaction with his words.

"What about the other stuff you mention. The other fun and games. Did any of that involve vigilante activity?"

"Fuck me, girl, you aren't backwards in coming forward, are you? How the fuck do I even know who you are. A voice on the phone. A few pretty words down the line. I mean, you could be anyone." He laughed again. It sounded like the promise of an assault.

"I have money. If you meet me tomorrow I can pay you for the information. I just want to find out about my father." Her mouth was dry. "I want to get to know more about how he spent his time, even if I don't like what I find."

There followed a lengthy silence, as if Knowles were thinking about something. Sarah heard a clock ticking – not in her house, but on the other end of the line – and something about the sound was hollow, false, like an imitation. She waited.

"Listen, love. Ask yourself a question. Ask yourself this: 'How much do I want to know? How deep should I get?'" He coughed, spluttered, and then regained his composure. "Your dad was into some pretty heavy stuff. I knew about some of it, but not all of it. We rolled together for a while, were pretty tight in fact, but he started getting too intense. His position on the force gave him access to plenty of privileged information, and made it possible for him to hide a lot of evidence."

"OK." She shivered; an involuntary reaction. The heating was off. The house was cold. But this physical reaction was not a result of the low temperature, or the inactive radiators. "I want to know. As much as I can."

"Meet me tomorrow morning, then, at ten thirty. I'll even buy you brunch. Bring two grand and I'll tell you what I know. It ain't much – God knows, he kept his cards close to his chest, that fucker – but it's more than you have." He paused here, but not for long. "You're a copper too, aren't you?"

Sarah nodded, slowly. There were no secrets, not really. "How did you know?"

His sudden laughter took her by surprise. She pulled the phone away from her ear, wincing at the volume and intensity of the unpleasant sound. Finally, once it had faded, she returned the receiver to the side of her head and listened. The line crackled, surged, crackled again.

"Because the apple never falls far from the tree, love. You might think it does, but you'd be wrong. Some things are in the blood. They run deep."

Her ears were ringing. There was a pressure building inside her skull, a hard, dense shape growing, building, and forming like a tumour. "What do you mean by that?" The pressure grew. It was immense.

"See you in t' morning, love. Meet me where your dad used to – if you're who you say you are you'll know exactly where I mean. Bring the money, or I'm leaving."

The money wasn't a problem. Her father had left her well provided for with his slush fund, and she wanted nothing from him. It would be a pleasure to give some of it away. He could have the lot, if that's what he wanted: every fucking penny.

She held onto the phone for a few moments, her grip tightening on the plastic casing. She tried to hear something behind the white-noise crackle of static, but there was nothing to be heard. Just dead noise. The sound of emptiness. No matter how hard she tried to convince herself that there were voices wailing, trying to be heard, there weren't. She was wrong. She was always, always wrong.

Sarah crossed to the armchair and collapsed into it, sliding her legs over the padded armrest and sitting sideways. She was back on day shift tomorrow, and would no doubt pay the price for losing so much sleep. The pressure in her head had dimmed, the bones no longer threatening to break apart. She didn't know anything – all she had were a few photographs, some garbled rubbish from her mad mother and a cassette tape. She reached down, into her bag, and took out the tape.

D.T.

1984

It meant nothing to her. Initials. A date. What did it signify? The handwriting was certainly her father's, there was no doubt about that. But what had he been trying to indicate upon the grubby sticker, and what was recorded on the tape?

She struggled to her feet and went to the coffee table, where she'd placed one of his old tape recorders next to the whisky bottle. Sarah only owned CDs, so she'd been forced to rake around in a cupboard to locate the ageing machine.

Her father had always loved his music, and had always created mix tapes, consisting of his favourite songs. There was a shelf downstairs, in his cellar office, which contained nothing but similar cassettes with only a year scratched on each sticker to identify the contents: collections of songs from that particular year, with no track listing. After every tenth cassette there was another one, made up of his favourite songs from the previous decade.

The tapes went back to the 1940s. Obviously, the early ones were retrospective, put together long after the fact, but it was just another indication of her father's obsessive pathology.

Even music was not safe from his madness.

She slipped the tape into the machine and pressed play. There was a lengthy gap before the first track began – inexpert, amateurish – and she frowned. He was usually so careful, so *exacting*, in everything he did. Why the long delay?

The first track was by Aztec Camera (or so her memory suggested), and Sarah was disappointed to realise that it was a song she actually liked. She hated having anything in common with her father, even something as superficial as a pop tune.

It took her three or four songs to realise what was wrong with the recording.

Just as she'd noticed at the beginning of the compilation, the gaps between each track were slightly too long. It didn't sit right, not with what she knew about her father and how he operated. He would never make such a shabby mistake.

She reached out and turned off the tape. Then she hit the rewind button.

Darkness bled through the windows; the meagre light from the desk lamp did nothing to hold it at bay. To Sarah the shadows felt like a subtle invasion, as if something unnatural were creeping up on her, waiting for her to acknowledge its presence in the room. But still she made no move to turn on the main lights. She was far too engrossed with the task at hand, and nothing could swerve her from her course. Again, she despised the parallels between herself and her father. They were both single-minded bastards, refusing to stop until the job was done.

She listened to the odd pause at the start of the tape seven times before she heard the sound. It was small, slight, barely even audible. So she turned up the volume, pushing it up right to its limit. The tape's hiss and crackle almost covered up the sound, but not enough for her to make out that it was a voice.

A voice she knew.

Her father's voice.

"*Danny Tate. Nineteen-eighty-four.*"

Written on the cassette tape:

D.T.

1984

Of course; now that she'd heard the name and the date, the connection was obvious. This tape, it was some kind of soundtrack and her father was whispering an interstitial message, a cipher meant to be decoded only by himself. Did it relate to a case he'd been working on, another investigation with which he had become obsessed? Had he been on the trail of someone, locked in a hidden war against an unseen nemesis? She could imagine him doing this in his spare time: choosing a criminal to become the focus of his obsession.

Sarah didn't recognise the whispered name at the beginning of the tape, or the year: they meant nothing to her.

None of it meant anything. Not yet.

FOURTEEN

I was sitting on the threadbare sofa drinking whisky straight from the bottle. After leaving the Rwandan psychic's place, I'd gone over the road to a grubby little off-licence and stocked up on booze. I knew I should be trying my best to remain sober, to work things through in my mind, but the call of the bottle was much too strong, so I filled two blue plastic carrier bags with bottles of the cheapest and strongest stuff I could find.

Only when I was drunk could I stop myself from caring; somewhere in the depths of oblivion was a place where I could rest, and be unafraid.

Fear. That was the real problem – or a large part of it.

I'd spent years trying to convince myself that none of this was scary, that it was just an aspect of the greater map of existence: ghosts, spirits, phantoms, they were all just slivers of us all, roaming lost and confused and slipping between realities like water through cracks in a great damaged jug.

But that wasn't true. It *was* frightening. In fact, it was terrifying. All of it. The more I experienced, the more afraid I became, and the harder I tried to pretend that I could take it all in my stride, like a man hurrying along a dark alley and keeping his eyes locked straight ahead.

It was dark outside, and the lights in the house kept flickering. The electrics in grey zones are prone to trickery; the phantoms interfere with the current, making it oscillate, breaking the connection.

I stared at the main ceiling light. It was surrounded by an original plaster ceiling rose. I wondered if the adjoining houses had the same problem with the electrics, but there was nobody to ask. The council had bought up the neighbouring buildings a couple of decades ago, when some chitty or purchase order had come down the pipe from central government. Most of the houses on this side of the street were empty, near derelict. Boarded windows, security shutters across the doors. Danger signs pasted to the walls, warning of a demolition process that would never happen, not in a million years.

I lived in a world of lies and half-truths, of pretence and fakery. Nothing was solid; everything shifted all the time, quaking, breaking, and reforming before my eyes. Even reality could not be trusted.

I glared at the old Bakelite telephone, daring it to ring. If the clockwork voice tried to contact me tonight, I would tell it where to go, and what to do. It could fuck off and fade away into the ether, leaving me in peace.

The whisky was doing its job. I was beginning to lose interest, to forget that I really did care about this stuff.

I'd tried to eat a sandwich earlier in the evening, some prepacked crap I'd brought back from the shop. It was supposed to be tuna fish on wholemeal bread but had tasted like cardboard filled with a layer of pulped bone. Gritty. Unappetising. Even the whisky offered more sustenance, at least to my ailing soul.

The soul: there was something else that couldn't be trusted.

I slid my legs off the sofa and managed to sit upright. My head was fuzzy; it was a pleasant feeling, that sensation just before you start to get properly drunk. I felt like I could take on the world and win, if only I cared enough to bother.

I realised that I was giggling. Something in the corner – a shadow within shadows – moved away from the wall. It had too many limbs, and dropped to the floor and sort of scuttled across the room. I turned away, not wanting to see. As long as they left me alone, I would pretend that they weren't really there. The ghosts, and the things that were ghosts of creatures I did not even want to imagine.

Not all ghosts are human. Some of them – the ones who have become so lost that they will never find their way – are the spiritual remains of other things… things which are *other*.

I drank more whisky. Giggled again. Then I entertained the notion that I was going insane – or perhaps I already had done, months ago when I first encountered the being that went by the name of the Pilgrim and lost the second love of my life in the process.

But I didn't want to think about him – that fucking Pilgrim. I had sent him away, banished him from my life.

So instead I thought about loss.

Everyone I had loved, everything I held dear… I lost it all in the end. There was nothing left to cling to, to hold close to my breast. No warmth; no humanity. No love.

It took me several seconds to realise that someone was knocking on the front door. The door led straight out onto the street, just beyond a tiny patch of concrete and a low brick wall. It could be anyone, if anyone were foolish enough to wander along this street, and pause outside this house. This haunted house.

"Go away!" My voice was only slightly slurred. I took another swig of Famous Grouse.

The knocking sound persisted. Whoever it was meant business. They were not going to leave without a fight.

Awkwardly, I got to my feet and staggered across the room. The space between sofa and door suddenly seemed to stretch for miles, as if the closer I got the greater the distance became.

I closed my eyes, paused, and when I opened them again the room was the same size it had always been.

A haunted room in a haunted house on a haunted street.

Through the crinkled glass panes in the front door, I could make out a small, slender figure. I placed my hand on the door, tickled the handle. Then, feeling slightly giddy, I grasped the handle and pulled open the door, revealing the young girl who was standing on the doorstep.

"Hello," I said, not immediately recognising her. "Can I help you?"

She was wearing a long green parka that stretched down to just below her knees, and the fur-lined hood was pulled up against the cold to cover most of her face. She was turned slightly sideways, but pivoted to face me when I spoke, and that's when I realised who it was.

The girl from the psychic's place. Immaculee Karuhmbi's helper. What was her name?

"Traci," she said, as if she could read my thoughts. "It's Traci. Traci, with an *eye* not a *why*. Remember me?" Her blind eyes burned into me, and I could barely understand what was happening. *"Tee. Are. Ay. See. Eye."*

"Yes. Please, come in." I stepped back, unprepared for such a visit. My hand pushed the door closed as she crossed the threshold, and it felt like I'd let a trickster spirit into my life.

"I'm sorry to bother you." She shrugged off the hood and then removed the coat. Then, calmly, gracefully – as if she could see so much further and clearer than I ever had – she passed me the coat.

I reached out and took it, my fingers brushing against her hand. Her cold, cold hand. My mouth went dry. "Take a seat. I'll just hang this up." I went to the staircase and draped her coat over the banister, wondering how long she'd stay. Wanting her to leave. Needing her to linger.

"Immaculee sent me. She was worried about what happened earlier today. She feels… odd. She feels odd about passing on a message from a voice she's never heard before." She said this as if we were discussing the weather. It was nothing to her: a mere trifle. She even picked at her fingernails, distracted. Her grey eyes were hard and soft all at once. She was beautiful.

"Believe me, I feel as weird as she does. I haven't followed through on the message. Not yet. I don't really know what I should do with the information." Why was I being so open with this girl? I sat down in the armchair, my hands spread flat against the dusty material.

"She also sent you some food. She says you aren't eating." Traci offered up a small package I had not even noticed. It looked like some kind of leavened bread, along with cheese and meat, all wrapped up in cellophane. "She worries about people. About everyone. She worries about us all."

I stared at the girl, taking in the thin short-sleeved shirt with its top two buttons undone, the skin-tight black jeans, and the smooth, dark skin of her arms. She was like a creature from a fairytale: a dark, sinuous temptress painted in the colours of innocence. I was beguiled by her presence in the room.

"Thanks," I said, making no move to take the package. So she put it down on the cluttered coffee table, next to the empty glass. "Can I get you a drink?"

She stared at me. Even though she was blind, I could feel the heat of her gaze. "Some of that whisky would be nice." How did she know? How could she see what I had in my hand?

"Yes. Of course. I'll pour you some." I reached out and grabbed the glass. My hand was shaking. I spilled whisky as I poured her three fingers of the stuff, and instead of handing her the glass I put it back on the table before her. It was a test, a silly little trick just to see how she responded.

Traci smiled. She reached out and picked up the glass with her dainty little fingers, the nails painted black and with tiny silver stars. "Thank you," she said, before taking a sip.

"How old are you?" I'm not sure why I asked; perhaps I already knew what was about to happen, and I was scared and alone and filled with a desire that felt dirty.

"I'm nineteen. Twenty in a few months time. Why do you ask?" She paused; sipped. "Are you planning on seducing me?"

The house seemed to lurch, but gently, cautiously, in case it ruined the mood. "No. Of course not."

"What a pity," she whispered, smiling around the rim of the glass. She was toying with me and I loved it. This game, this pretence, it took my mind off everything else. Perhaps, I thought, that was why she'd been sent here: to distract me, to stop me from acting too hastily. A beautiful diversion.

Immaculee Karuhmbi knew more than she was letting on. She was much deeper into this situation – whatever the hell it was – than she might care to admit. Was this girl a relative, a daughter or a niece? Had the psychic lied to me about losing her family in the massacre?

Or was Traci simply a temptation, like something from the Christian bible? Was this to be my time in the wilderness, when I would be approached by the devils of my desire?

Shit, the drink was affecting me more than I had thought. I wasn't a messiah, or some kind of roaming prophet. I was a drunken loser in a grotty house who used to think that he could make a difference.

"Why did you come here? Why did she send you?"

Traci smiled. The tip of her tongue poked out between her small white teeth. "I came here because I wanted to. It was my idea to check on you, and nothing to do with my mistress. When I told her my plan, she gave me the food and asked me to pass on a message. I listen closely and I do the things she wants but I don't ask for reasons. Traci with an eye not a why."

I leaned forward in the chair, half smiling. The timber creaked, the joints complaining. "Tell me this message, Traci with an eye not a why."

Traci put down her glass and turned to face me square on. Her cheekbones were razor cuts in the dark sculpture of her face. Her eyes were like a glimpse of another reality – one I had not yet encountered. "She says that you must follow your heart, whatever your head might tell you. The voice cannot be trusted – pick and choose the information you act upon, and never go against your instinct." She sat back, crossing her legs. Denim whispered conspiratorially in the gloom.

"Is that it?" I was biting my upper lip, breaking the skin and drawing a spot of blood.

"That's it. She tends to speak like that, my mistress. She sometimes talks like she's in a soap opera, or a bad costume drama. She likes to be melodramatic." She laughed, and it was not an entirely pleasant sound.

"Why do you call her mistress?"

She stopped laughing. "Because that's what she was, until recently, when she became very ill. I shared her house and her bed. These days I just clean up after her, and wait for her to die." She uncrossed her legs. This time it made no sound.

"Tell me why you're here." I leaned even further forward, resting my elbows on my knees. The lights flickered again, as if trying to set the scene.

"I came here to fuck you. That's all. Just to fuck. You interest me, and I like to get closer to interesting people… to men and women who can teach me something."

Her smile was like a knife.

"I can teach you nothing. I don't know anything." There were tears in my eyes; my joints had all locked stiff, becoming rigid.

"Let me be the judge of that." She stood without moving, or so it seemed. I was so tense, so out of it, that she seemed to swell out of the chair and hover before me. Her hands fluttered to the front of her shirt and unbuttoned it all the way down. She was not wearing a bra. Her skin was perfect. That's the only word I can use, the only one that fits.

Perfect.

So perfect... like a ghost of herself, a spark of energy caught between the folds of reality. Because all ghosts are immaculate; they all represent a sort of perfection, even the bad ones – the ones who do bad things.

Her shirt dropped to the floor and she reached down, reached out, reached inside me. I took her hand and she pulled me upright, as if I weighed no more than an empty paper bag. She led me to the bottom of the stairs, and I followed close behind. She took me up to my room, and I closed the door. When I turned round to face her, she was standing naked on the bare boards, with her legs set slightly apart, her arms raised up, and her hands held open like wonderful black flowers. Her beautiful blind eyes shone, but they were dark too: it was a dark light that bled from them, filling the room and enveloping me, drawing me towards her, dragging me in.

I went to her, I went to her and I let her strip off my clothes and rub me down with her perfect hands. I was drunk, I was empty, and I was falling into her as she opened up like a vein, like a ventricle, like a heart.

This is what she did: she reached inside me and cupped my heart, squeezed it like a piece of rotten fruit, making it bleed. She squeezed so hard that I was pouring my heart out.

I slid urgently between her legs and she took me in, offered me shelter from the storm, and kept me safe from my demons for a little while. We fucked beneath the cold eyes of phantoms. They stood there, all in a row along the wall, as if they were lost deep in prayer. The figure in the black cloak and white cowl sat on the floor by the door, its legs crossed and its palms held flat against its thighs. It was an avatar, a threat, a shape of things to come. I looked away, not prepared to receive its message until I was ready.

I watched them all watching me, and I did not feel afraid.

I was not scared.

She had given me succour, and I was home: right at home with the dead.

Much later, when we were both spent and sweating in the darkness, we lay on the mattress locked together like conjoined twins. One of Traci's legs was folded between both of mine, as if it were boneless. She stirred at my side, her lips making a smacking sound and our sticky skin snapping apart like sheets of paper torn from a waterlogged book.

"How do you do it?" her voice was soft, part of the darkness.

I blinked, wondering how I could even begin to answer. "How do I do what?" Playing dumb was the only ploy I could think of, but I knew it wouldn't deflect her questions.

"You know what I mean. How do you make contact with them – the dead? The ghosts. How does it work?"

I pushed myself up into a half-sitting position, my head resting on the pillows. The mattress felt like a small boat cast adrift on a dark ocean. There was no land in sight. "I have no idea. Honestly. All I know is that I was involved in a car accident that turned out not to be an accident at all. After that, I started to see them."

The dark swam before my eyes.

"What do you mean, it wasn't an accident?" She shifted on the mattress, her slight body sliding against mine. I felt her ribs, the meat of her thighs. She was dark upon dark.

"Someone made it happen. I found out about six months ago, after believing that it was an accident for a very long time. This person – this thing – he made it happen as part of some plan I can't even contemplate. I think it was some kind of game. He said he wanted what was inside me, the thing that makes me able to make contact with the dead. But he's the one who made me that way. Isn't that ironic?"

"This world..." she paused, as if gathering her thoughts. "This place where we live, pretending that it's all there is. Things happen that can only be part of some bigger plan, or maybe it's just chaos. A massive chaos that hovers at the edges, pressing against all our lives." She couldn't complete the thought. It was too big, too fearsome for her to continue.

"You're closer to the truth than you might imagine." It was all that I could add. There was nothing more to say.

Traci curled into me, her soft, lean body adapting to my own hard edges. "You know why I really came, don't you?"

I looked down at her, the top of her head, her vulnerable scalp. "No. I'm confused by all of this. Tell me."

She spoke without looking at me; her face was buried in my shoulder, muffling her words but not enough that I was unable to understand what she said. "I came because I'm frightened. Immaculee... she isn't herself lately. She's dying, and I think that's allowing other voices inside her head – ones that can't be trusted. For a long time now she's believed everything she's been told, and it's all come to pass. All the predictions and the hints of events. It all happened just like they said. But this is different. It isn't right. This new voice – she doesn't even trust it herself."

I kissed the top of her head. Her hair was damp and kinky. "So why does she listen to it?"

"Because she has no choice. She's terrified. I've never seen her so afraid. I've been with her for several years now, since she took me from the massage parlour downstairs. She took me in, taught me things, and made me into a whole person. Before I met her, I was servicing fat old men with sweaty bodies and hard hands. It made me glad that I couldn't see them."

I said nothing. It was not my place to interrupt, or to judge.

"So it hurts me to see her like this: on the verge of death and terrified. She's wanted to die for a long time, just to be with her family. I was the only thing that kept her going, but now even that isn't enough. And this new voice – this fabrication – it lies to her. It's deceitful."

"How do you know? Maybe it's telling the truth. How can you even know?"

She shifted position again, this time bending her neck so that she could pretend to look up at me, into my face. Her eyes were not grey but black: it looked like they'd been scooped out and replaced with darkness. "Because she told me. She told me that it lies. But she's too afraid to ignore it, because it told her that unless she does what it wants she'll never see her family again." She blinked, but the dark patches remained. They saw right through me. She was blind but she could see me as I really was: alone and helpless in the dark, the cold and endless dark…

I could understand completely Immaculee's fears. The only thing that had kept me going for many years was the hope that I would see my family again, if not in this life, as ghosts, then in the next one, in the next reality. The thought that someone, or some dreadful thing, could take that sense of hope away from me and use it as a threat made me freeze inside.

I couldn't blame Immaculee Karuhmbi for passing on a message that she knew might be some kind of trap. In her place, and confronted by the same fears, I would have done exactly that.

Traci slept in my arms, her small body quivering occasionally, as if in the grip of bad dreams. Sleepless, unable to even doze for a second or two, I stared into the darkness of the room, watching the shadows of the dead as they drifted in and out, passing to and fro, and wondering what was in store for me.

I glanced down at the girl, at her skin and the bones beneath, and knew that I couldn't trust her.

I could trust no one.

I lived in a world of lies and half-truths, of pretence and fakery. Nothing was solid; everything shifted all the time, quaking, breaking, and reforming before my eyes. Even reality could not be trusted.

FIFTEEN

They watched the house. Their patience was infinite. They had no need to rush things, to force a confrontation when one was not required. They simply watched and They waited. They had all the time in the world – this world and all the others They had not yet seen but knew of.

All the time. Everywhere.

Their influence was felt in every world imaginable, and in some that could not be imagined even by the most insane of men.

When They had left the pub earlier, the young man had not reappeared. They had waited a long time, but to no avail. He had moved out of Their reach. So They followed the other man – the one who had escorted Them from the pub and spoken to Them outside on the street. He interested Them. His design was threadbare, a frail and dying thing, but it held traces of... *something*. There was a hint of the lost one, a whisper of his passing just about visible within its folds and niches. The man had been touched by someone who had been touched by the one They sought. Their severed companion, Their long lost brother.

They had followed the man through identical streets of dull, squat buildings, and then when he had boarded a bus They had lost him for a little while. They walked the streets, sniffing out his design. It was difficult, because there was not much there, but in the end They picked up his scent. They walked and They walked, and finally They came to this street.

And now They were waiting, watching, keeping Their eyes on his house. It was a small, narrow terraced house in a forgotten area of town. Not an old house, with history between its walls, but one made of new materials – it was perhaps twenty or thirty years old. They did not even know the name of the place where the house stood, but there was nothing here except a sense of despair. A deprived area; a place bereft of dreams. There was not much evidence of Their designs here, only fragments.

This puzzled Them for a moment. They had never before questioned the nature of Their designs, or even wondered about Their purpose as They tweaked the fortunes of these beings. They simply created the seeds, the beginnings of potentially great things, and then let them slip away and drift towards wherever they might land. There was an element of Fate in what They did, although They did not deal in Fate. They dealt in chance, serendipity. Coincidence.

They were, for all intents and purposes, the Architects of Serendipity.

They had been called many names across the centuries, and hailed as both demons and angels. The ancients had called Them evil, but more enlightened civilisations had prayed to Them, even built temples in Their honour. Their image was buried deep within the hidden tombs of the Pharaohs; They were mentioned in the Bible, but in Their true form. The Book of Revelations had Them caricatured as Satan's servants, but that was just another made-up story, a fiction that had utilised the notion of Them rather than the reality.

Religions tended to do things like this; make fiction of the facts, and create monsters to be feared.

They were far more complex than any mortal ideology could fathom. They were beyond religion, inaccessible by faith.

They were the Architects, and this name above all others fitted Them well.

The man left the house after nightfall. He was wearing a long coat and carried a small sports bag over his shoulder. His design fluttered like a trapped bird, eager for escape. That was something else They had noticed: sometimes the designs were eager for release, and they struggled against their captive forms.

It was something else for Them to think about: more information to process.

The man walked along the street, and They followed him from the shadows. They kept well behind him, and made Their footsteps silent. Nobody else moved along the quiet street. The houses were all locked up tight against the darkness, doors barred, windows sealed. This was a neighbourhood where people were afraid to leave their secure little castles at night: a place where human evil dwelled.

The man turned the corner, jogging across the road and onto a patch of waste ground. They followed. He resumed a walking pace, pushing headphones into his ears and hunching his shoulders against the chill. They felt no cold; despite using a human body for transport, They had no real human feelings. This thing – this child – was a vessel, and nothing more. They had taken the abandoned corpse and raised it, squeezing inside, inhabiting the cold meat and shifting around in the soft, sticky innards.

Even the lost one, who was much more comfortable in these regions, was forced to travel this way. He had used the same body for quite some time, but had been known to exchange his mode of transport when it grew old or decrepit or simply ran out of juice. That was when They could almost see him, when he emerged for a moment, like a thing from a pupa, to swap skins.

They had left him to his games for decades, but now it was time for him to return to Them, to come home. His designs were out of control. He had begun to return to his work after it was done, like a dog sniffing its own vomit, and meddle in a way that was forbidden. The Architects served no master, but there were certain rules They had to follow. For even the Lords of Chaos must follow rules...

The lost one had broken those rules. He coveted something he was not allowed to have. He wanted to become something more than his station allowed – he sought to be godlike. He had been planting the seeds of this transformation for some time, hitching a ride on fanatics and cultists, utilising the ancient energy of long-banished witches and warlocks and bad spirits. None of it had worked – he had been thwarted so many times, mostly by his own ambition.

But now things were different. Now he had discovered a potential new source of energy – or had he in fact created it?

There was a man. A man who might possess something unique, a power that could crack open the shells of realities, allowing them to bleed. And if the layers between realities filled with the blood of time and space, there would be nothing left to hold on to.

Even the Lords of Chaos must follow rules.

And the only rule that mattered was that everything must remain fluid; reality was whatever it was shaped to be. But all realities must remain separate; if they came together, stalled and collided and cracked open, they would cease to exist. Belief must be single-minded, and if an alternative source of belief appeared, the old model would then become useless.

This was what They understood: there was no guiding force, no single being who oversaw some grand cosmic project. All there was, all there could ever be, were the realities shaped by those who lived within them. If belief was suspended, and reality was forgotten, even for a second, it would all fail like a row of candles in a storm.

They followed the man for several miles, watching him closely. Not once did he notice Their silent pursuit; nor did he pause to glance over his shoulder. He was oblivious to Their presence, even though he had already touched Them.

Soon he came to an area that was even worse than the one he had left behind. The buildings were dirty, their walls covered with spray-painted obscenities. Youths stood on street corners, or lounged in dark parks, drinking from bottles or smoking their primitive drugs.

They passed among this disenfranchised populace, noting the scant presence of Their designs. But whatever evidence there was of Their work, it was shabby and flyblown; minor tatters hanging from forgotten husks of humanity like flesh stripped from a kill.

The man approached a shop: Newsome's Electrics. The windows were protected by blocky security shutters and the door was barred by a sturdy steel grille. The man knocked, rang the bell, and waited.

"Who is it?" The voice was crackly, barely audible, and came from a speaker by the door.

"It's me. It's Don."

There was no reply, but a buzzer sounded and a mechanism clanked loudly in the door frame. Don pushed the door open, finally glancing back – if only to check that nobody noticed as he went inside.

They chose that moment to step out from the shadows.

Don paused. He looked confused for a moment, as if something did not quite fit into the scene he was viewing, but then he smiled. His teeth were stained. His gums pulled back from his incisors. There was something of the animal about this man, and They knew that They had done the right thing in following him.

"Fuck me, it's you. From earlier today. I am right, aren't I?"

They nodded. Their head was heavy. Something shifted awkwardly inside the skull.

"Come here. Come on, out of the cold. My friend lives here – the one I told you about. Sammy. He'll see you alright. Sammy will sort you out." Again, he smiled. It was hungry, filled with avarice They could easily understand.

They moved forward. They nodded Their heavy head.

"Don't say much, do you? Cat got your tongue?"

They grinned. It felt wrong. Their teeth were loose, the dead gums losing hold on the enamel.

"Doesn't matter. In fact, it's better if you don't talk. Nobody will listen to you, anyway." Don laughed. His whole body shook. He was large, muscular even, but he had a big gut. He must lift a lot of weights, to enhance his strength, but he was not a fit man.

As soon as They got close enough, he grabbed Their arm, His grip was tight; he did not want to let go. "Come on. Come up. Let's go and meet Sammy." Hunger flared more intensely behind his eyes.

They allowed Themselves to be manhandled through the doorway and along a short, narrow hallway. It was dark, the walls were damp and peeling and the stairs ahead were steep.

"Up here. That's where Sammy is. His flat is above the shop." The stairs also led down, into a basement area, but there was a closed door at the bottom. The door was heavy-duty, a specialist item; it looked thick, as if the room beyond might be soundproofed.

They knew what went on behind that door.

It was Sammy's "Chicken Hut": the place where he kept his chickens, and took his paying customers to have their fun. Sex was an alien concept to Them. They did not understand it beyond the need to procreate, to continue the species. Sex as pleasure, as a way of venting human emotions, was not something They could fathom.

The idea of sex as an outlet for anger and self-loathing was even less clear. They did not understand that at all. Perhaps it was something They could learn, and then incorporate into Their future designs. Anything that might improve Their designs was to be welcomed, embraced. All information could be utilised. It was all part of the raw material.

"Come on, now. Don't be shy." Don pushed Them in the small of the back. "Jesus, that head of yours looks bad. Did somebody mug you, were you attacked?"

They raised a hand to Their head and explored the wounds. There were two of them, small holes bored right into the skull, almost to the surface of the brain, which had then been cauterised by a hot iron. They had not been present when the damage occurred; They had entered this body after the fact, when it was already cold and inert and lonely, lying on the floor in an abandoned warehouse near a derelict multi-storey car park. They remembered it now: the small dead body hidden away under a tarpaulin, and the ease with which They had been able to slip inside. It was yet another connection to the lost one, but one They did not understand.

The wounds were dry, but there was crisp blood caked in Their hair. It was amazing that no one had noticed before, and They had been allowed to move through the city freely. But They had the impression that these beings – these human beings – did not care enough for each other to intervene in such matters.

That was why Their designs flourished so well. Why the designs grew and grew, virtually unmolested, becoming like party costumes on the backs of these odd, loveless creatures.

It was… interesting.

Such knowledge could only improve Their work.

"That's right, keep on climbing. Nearly there."

They stepped onto a landing and waited, allowing Don to overtake Them and push open yet another door. Light spilled out; rock music was playing at a low volume. A fat man with his dark hair pulled back into a greasy ponytail was sitting on a bicycle before a long table weighing white powder on a set of kitchen scales.

"Don, how the fuck are you?" He spotted Them a second later, this man, and his attitude changed. He became almost loveable, reaching down into himself to produce a demeanour that was clearly meant to inspire trust. "And who's your little friend?" He had uninspired tattoos on his forearms – a bulldog wearing a Union Jack vest, a swallow, a flag upon which was etched the word LOVE. His eyes were small and squinted. His belly was big and soft, and his design was enormous.

His design.

It was immense.

The biggest They had yet seen.

It enveloped him, like intricate wings, plummeting into his flesh and back out the other side, hanging above him in a glass-like nimbus, curling and coiling, decorating the room with its splendour.

They smiled at this man. At this Sammy. They smiled at him and They saw that Their work was good.

"What's your name, little man?" His smile was a pit without end, a depthless void in his face.

"He doesn't speak. I think he might be a mute." Don glanced down at Them, and he was smiling too.

"Oh, bravo. Nice one, Don." Sammy stood, pushing the bicycle back and away from the table. It had the word "Chopper" stencilled along the main bar on its frame.

They laughed. It was the first time They had made a sound since entering this body, and it shocked Them to hear it filtered through Their new lips.

"Funny little fucker, aren't you?" Sammy was now standing before them, his fleshy arms outstretched. He was smiling, smiling… always smiling. That hole in his face seemed to suck in the light, neutralising it. His design glimmered. It was bigger than him, bigger than all of them. It filled the room.

"Would you like something to eat, son?"

They nodded. They did not feel hunger, but it was the right thing to do in the circumstances. Sammy would expect Them to be hungry. They were entranced by Their own handiwork, and momentarily all thoughts of the lost one, and Their mission to find him, left Their mind.

"Cheese on toast suit you? I haven't much in, but I'll rustle you up a few slices."

They followed Sammy deeper into the room. Don closed the door behind Them. Locked it.

Beneath the floor, down the stairwell, and in the basement, They sensed the presence of others. Battered young boys, all of them kept locked up tight in that basement room. The chickens; the cash cows; the poor abused souls Sammy Newsome had acquired from the streets, with the help of his good friend Don.

They knew that They would soon be joining those boys, those chickens, but the idea did not trouble Them. The longer They could be around these characters the better.

They remembered Their purpose here, the reason why They had come to this reality, and once again They felt the touch of the lost one – he was close, he was hovering at the edges, prowling the periphery of this story. If these men had not yet met him, they surely would make his acquaintance soon. All They need do was be in the right place at the right time, and be on hand to intervene.

They could see it in the designs.

The lost one had been meddling; he had tampered from afar with the outcomes of these two spoiled lives. They could see that now, oh so clearly.

They stood in the room, under the roof of abusers, and waited for bad things to happen.

SIXTEEN

Derek had clearly made an effort. He sat there all clean and tidy in an expensive black silk shirt and skin-tight black trousers, with a self-satisfied smile on his face. His pretty, pretty, lineless face: his smooth and lovely face, which Trevor wanted to slap.

"That was delicious." Derek sat back in his chair, rather expansively for such an effete young boy. The material between the buttons on his silk shirt bulged slightly, ruining the illusion of untamed youth.

"Good. I'm glad." Trevor smiled at his guest. He picked up his glass of merlot and took a large mouthful, then refilled it from the bottle that stood on the table between them. "How about we have another bottle of this nice red to enjoy with our dessert?"

Derek's eyes lit up. He was impressed by extravagant displays of wealth. He probably came from a deprived background and judged success in terms of money and acquisitions. Trevor knew the type well: he was one of them. His childhood had been devoid of compassion; his father had deserted the family when the boys were young and his mother had been forced to take on two jobs just to provide for them. His mother... she was such a cold-hearted woman. That was why the boys had clung together –

more specifically, why Michael had needed so much attention from Trevor.

But they were all dead now. His father had been murdered in London many years ago. His mother had suffered a fatal heart attack a little while before her eldest son had found fame as a psychic. And Michael – poor, poor Michael – had, of course, been the first to go. He had taken the hard way, the bloody way, out of his own personal nightmare.

Trevor remembered his mother coming to him at night sometimes, after a late shift at the hospital where she was an auxiliary nurse (when such a role still existed). After cleaning up the blood and piss and shit and vomit, she would come to him, freshly scrubbed, and demand that he hold her, caress her. She always wore her dressing gown, and it always gaped at the throat, revealing her cleavage. She would moan as he embraced her, and it was only much later, when he was old enough to understand such things, that he had realised his mother was taking sexual gratification from his attention.

She never had another man after Trevor's father died.

She didn't need one. She had her sons.

"I can't believe you know the owner here. That's very impressive." Derek licked his lips. It was unclear whether he was trying to be seductive or just cleaning food from his mouth.

"Oh, no it isn't, friend. I know a lot of people… I *knew* a lot of people, anyway, before the scandal. Some of them turned their backs on me, but a few others stayed on my side. When you put people in touch with their loved ones, they often feel that they owe you a great debt. They don't realise that I do it – I did it – because I had no choice."

Derek nodded, fascinated. He could not take his eyes off Trevor. It was such a turnaround from the last time they'd met that Trevor had to bite down his laughter. He raised his hand to attract a passing waiter, and ordered another bottle of wine. The waiter glided away, as if on castors.

It was nice here, he thought. Civilised.

There was a family at the table closest to theirs. A husband, a wife, a little boy – the boy was eight or nine. Trevor glanced at him, and the boy caught his gaze. Trevor stuck out his tongue. The boy began to giggle, and hid his mouth with a crisp, white napkin.

"Steady on," said Derek, noticing this brief exchange. "You're being a bit blatant, aren't you?"

Trevor looked away from the boy, and directly into Derek's face. He hadn't even realised that he'd been flirting. But Derek had: Derek picked up on this stuff. "I didn't even think. But, yes, you're right."

Derek grinned.

The waiter brought the wine, opened it, and waited while Trevor tasted it. He nodded. "Thank you, friend. That's lovely." The waiter smiled and floated away.

"I hope your associate – is it Sammy? I hope Sammy is a little more discreet than I just was." He was starting to feel excited. His stomach tightened. His crotch was warm.

"Don't worry." Derek leaned forward, affecting a conspiratorial posture. "Like I already told you, I've known Sammy for years. He's very trustworthy. He has to be, the people he gets at his place. Police, politicians, celebrities: all kinds of top people. You wouldn't believe it."

"Oh I'm sure I would," said Trevor, recalling some of the clandestine parties he'd been to back in the day, and the so-called big names who'd attended alongside him. At the height of his fame, he'd been part of an inner circle that met up in different locations three times a year and kept young boys on ice. Literally, on ice: huge ice cubes at the centre of a room, with naked boys in chains balanced on top. When he thought about it now, the whole thing was surreal, like something out of *de Sade*, but at the time it had felt like nothing special. Just another way of having fun.

But now all that was out of his reach. The circle had been sealed: he was no longer welcome inside its perimeter.

"Yes, I would believe it." He sipped his wine. It tasted wonderful, even better than the last bottle.

"I've spoken to Sammy already, and vouched for you. He says he has some new stock – a couple of chickens fresh from the roost, as he put it." Derek watched as Trevor refilled his glass. The boy's eyes never strayed from Trevor's fingers, as if he were trying to pin them to the table by force of will alone. "He's happy for you to go along, once I've given you the address. You see, my word can open a lot of doors. I can get you into places you didn't even know existed."

Trevor put down the bottle. He clenched his hands, unclenched them. His fingers were stiffening. The alcohol was affecting his circulation. "And what's in it for you? I realise you aren't doing this out of friendship, or as a favour; certainly not after the way our last meeting ended. So what do you want? What is it that I can do for you, friend? Money?"

Derek placed his hands on the table, palms down. He took a deep breath and paused before letting it out. His eyes were large and full of something Trevor could not quite recognise but thought that he should. Was it fear, hope, or something more obscure?

"It isn't money, then?"

Derek shook his head. "No. Money is nice, of course, and if you want to offer me some I'll take it. But that's not what I want in exchange for introducing you to Sammy. I'll give you his address if you do something for me – something important."

Trevor waited. He wasn't sure what the boy was about to say, but for some reason it made him afraid.

"I want you to contact someone for me. A person who died a long time ago. I want you to get in touch with my sister."

Well, he certainly hadn't seen that one coming. "OK. You've taken me off guard. I was expecting a more... conventional method of payment." He tapped his fingertips on the table top, trying to halt the momentum of the situation so that he might gather his thoughts and decide how best to proceed.

"There's the deal," said Derek, his hand shaking as he picked up his glass. "That's what I want. You help me and I'll help you. I have a slip of paper in my pocket with Sammy's address and a code word written on it. You do this for me, and that paper is yours."

Trevor could do this; he knew he could. As the evidence of the strange presence in the mirror proved, his gift was returning. The fakery and deceit, all the years of pretending, had been stripped away and he had discovered at their core the remnants of his true ability. He could see the dead, speak with them, and perhaps even be heard by them. He knew he could. Ever since that day in his fifteenth year, when he had become aware of a spirit alongside him, reaching out to him for companionship, he had known. And now it was all coming back, at last. It was coming back to him.

"OK, I'll do it." The words came so easily. He was surprised that he felt no trepidation as he spoke them. He was no longer afraid.

The family at the next table got up to leave, and the young boy stared at him, smiled. Trevor grinned back, but it was not a friendly expression. The grin contained all the hunger that had been building up inside him for such a long time, and he felt it spreading across his face like a stain.

The little boy burst into tears and hugged his mother's leg. The woman held her son tightly, and glared about the room in search of what could have provoked such an extreme reaction from her son.

"I'll do it," said Trevor, knowing that, yes, he could, he really could. "With great pleasure."

"Now," said Derek, his eyes shining, so bright and clear. "How about ordering us some dessert?"

They shared a tarte au chocolat. It was a huge portion, easily enough for three, but they left nothing on the plate. Trevor felt Derek watching him as he ate, but whenever he tried to catch the other's gaze, his eyes flickered away to look at something across the room. A strange atmosphere had developed between them. The position of power had shifted. Trevor was now in control – he had once again assumed the position of authority.

Trevor signalled for the waiter and asked for the bill. Neither of them wanted coffee or a liqueur.

"So. What now?" He stared at Derek, pushing him, teasing him. "Fancy going for a drink somewhere?"

Derek sat up straight, his back held rigid. He looked pensive. His former arrogance had faded. "If you don't mind, I'd rather go straight to your place. I mean, can we do it now? Or do you need to prepare. Is there some kind of... I dunno, some sort of ritual you need to go through?" His hands fluttered in the air as if trying to catch his words and put them back in his mouth.

Trevor sat back. He smiled, softly. "No, it's nothing like that. This isn't something I turn on and off. I'll be honest with you: I haven't been able to speak with any departed friends for quite some time, but since I met you my gift has come back. It's been a slow process, but now I feel strong again. I feel... capable." he knew that he was lying – his returning powers had nothing to do with Derek; it was all down to the figure in the mirror, who-ever he might be. But there was no harm in flattery. Indeed, it might even grease the wheels of commerce, so to speak.

Derek looked pleased. He seemed to inflate before Trevor's eyes, as if he'd put on weight during the meal. "Wow. That's a nice thing to say. Maybe... maybe I'm helping you, then?" He was regressing, becoming younger the more he spoke. "Like an inspiration or a muse."

"Perhaps." Trevor caught sight of the waiter returning with the bill. "Perhaps not. Who can say?"

He paid the bill and stood, pushing back his chair. Derek fol-lowed suit, deferring to Trevor and allowing him to lead the way. The power shift was complete: Trevor was fully in charge, in control. He liked it better this way.

"There's a taxi rank outside. We'll grab a cab." He spoke over his shoulder, not waiting for his eager guest to keep up, but trusting that he would.

Outside there was a queue of taxis waiting at the kerb. It was too early for people to be heading home, so Trevor opened the rear door of the black cab at the front of the line and climbed inside. Derek followed him, maintaining a short distance between them, as if he had discovered some new respect for the psychic.

It was a short journey to Trevor's flat, and the fee was low. He tipped the driver heavily – another show of wealth for Derek, who was by now almost foaming at the mouth. Trevor was enjoying this; it made him feel like a big man, a king, just like he'd been when he performed on the stage. He had even stopped hating Thomas Usher, the man who had taken it all away. Just for a while; for tonight. Tomorrow he would hate him all over again.

"Come on up. We can let the mood develop. There has to be the right mood, you see. I'm a bit rusty, so can't just jump right into this." He unlocked the main door and climbed the stairs. Then he let them both into the flat.

He left the lights off. Darkness was best. It helped.

"This way," he led the way. "My bedroom. It's where all my old stage stuff is stored, and I'll probably make a better connection in the place where I'm most comfortable." He had a vague idea of what he was doing, but nothing more. He knew that this was all for show, and that the real reason for using the bedroom was something else entirely – a reason he wasn't yet ready to fully embrace.

The mirror was in the bedroom, and as soon as they'd stepped out of the cab he had felt the figure behind the glass tugging, urging, wanting him to bring Derek into the room.

If he'd been asked at that very moment, he would have sworn that he intended to at least try and contact Derek's sister. But afterwards, when it was all done, he realised that he'd had no such intention at all.

"Follow me, but keep quiet. I'm trying to grab hold of something... a vibration. A mood. A feeling. If your sister is anywhere near you, I'll find her. I'll bring her forward and get her to speak."

The mirror was right where he'd left it. Of course it was; it was unable to move, and the figure trapped inside could not yet impact upon the world this side of the glass. The mirror's surface was dark; it looked fluid, as if it were composed of water. It rippled as he watched. Shapes passed beneath it – a hand, an arm, a bald head? It looked like a figure was swimming, darting and coiling beneath dark waters.

"Just a moment," said Trevor, opening one of the large wardrobes at one end of the room. His old stage outfits were stored in plastic. He selected his favourite – a pastel green number – and slipped the suit jacket over his shirt. It felt good, like a comeback.

"That's nice. It suits you." Derek was sitting on the bed. He had one leg crossed over the other and his hands were flat against the mattress.

"Thank you, friend," said Trevor, feeling like the show was about to begin.

The room had darkened further, as if a great shadow were falling. Trevor looked up, at the light fitting, and then back at Derek. "Is your sister's name..." It came to him in a flash, and a slender presence stepped forward, away from the wall. "Is it Suzie?"

Derek stared in disbelief. He nodded slowly, incapable of words.

"Suzie... she's here, aren't you, friend?"

The washed-out suggestion of a female figure drifted across the room, towards the bed. She stood beside Derek, arms hanging by her sides, and waited. She was dark – almost black. Smoke curled from between her lips. "Did she die in a fire?"

"Oh, God. Oh... Yes. Yes, she did." Tears shone in Derek's eyes. He looked like a different person, someone Trevor had not yet met. "Yes. My Auntie Jean's place. An ember popped in the

grate, and burnt the place down while everyone was asleep."
He began to sob. His shoulders shook. He clenched his fists on
the bed.

At Derek's side, the mirror was black, like oil. Something
moved erratically in the darkness.

"Suzie, friend. Can you hear me? Can you give me a message
for your brother?"

The figure bent at the waist, as if leaning in for a smoky kiss.
She raised her hands, and tried to clasp Derek's head. She
seemed annoyed, as if she were trying to hurt him. Or warn him.

The surface of the mirror boiled; something was raging within.

The female figure straightened at the waist, her head turning
to face the mirror. Then she began to back off, to move away,
her hands in the air and her mouth gaping in a silent scream.

"It's OK, friend. Just take your time." Trevor stared at the
figure.

Derek, noting the source of the psychic's interest, turned
around on the bed to face the empty spot in the room where
his sister now stood. "Suzie? It's me, Suzie. It's Little Delly...
your baby brother."

The mirror bowed inward, as if under great pressure. The glass
had become elastic; it bent and stretched, sucking the air towards its concave centre. The bedclothes began to shift on the
bed, the loose covers drawn towards the mirror. Derek, oblivious, was pulled along with them.

"That's right, friend." Trevor was no longer speaking to the
ghost of Derek's sister. He was communicating with the man in
the mirror.

Derek, finally understanding that all was not well, started to
whine. "What's going on? What is this? Is it Suzie?" He was
pulled backwards, towards the mirror. Even as he fought back –
too late; much too late – the mirror sucked him in, hungry for
whatever he could give.

"Just relax," said Trevor, smiling. "Let it all happen."

By now Derek was trapped within the energy whose source was the mirror – or whatever hid behind it. His skin trembled, vibrating on the bone, and as Trevor watched the boy's face began to bubble and lift from his skull, as if long, fat fingers were burrowing under his flesh to sever the connection from bone.

Derek tried to scream, but when he opened his mouth his head was spun around and his lips were tugged free, like a sock being pulled from a foot. It happened that quickly: both lips, mostly undamaged, simply left his face and vanished into the big black mirror. His teeth were bared like bone; his new smile was hideous.

Trevor wanted to look away, he really did, but he was unable. The sight was hypnotic. The same drumbeat he'd heard before was sounding in his head, threatening to break his skull.

As Derek was dragged towards the mirror, his clothes were torn from his body, leaving him naked. His skin bubbled, blistering on the bone. It was as if someone was pumping air into his body, and it was separating the flesh from his skeleton. His mouth worked, still trying to scream, but the mirror had his tongue: the free end was held somewhere inside the mirror while the root was pulled taut at the back of his throat.

Trevor was awestruck. He had not expected anything like this. Deep down, he knew that his guest was an offering, a sacrifice to whatever dark entity was trapped in the mirror, but he had hoped for a cleaner demise.

Skin, muscle, tendon, blood… it all went into the mirror. The boy's musculature was exposed for a second, as the skin was peeled away like the rind of an exotic fruit, but then there were only the bones: his skeleton sat, quietly and politely, like an unexpected visitor on the bed. Then, abruptly, it toppled onto its side, the bones rattling like dry sticks.

Trevor stared at the mirror. The motion had stopped. It was just a mirror again; a simple reflective surface. Except for the fact that it was not reflecting anything of the room in which he stood. Instead, there was a figure, and behind the figure a ruined landscape of broken buildings and charred earth.

The figure was bald, and he stood wrapped in Derek's skin. He wore this skin-suit casually, as if he were modelling it for a mail order catalogue. He stood with his head bowed low, his arms raised slightly at his sides and his hands open.

"Who are you?" Trevor stepped forward, closer to the mirror. "Who?"

The bald head tilted upwards, revealing dark eyes and a wide grin. The face, like the head, was completely hairless: no eyebrows, no lashes, no stubble. Smooth, clean. Pure.

"Who are you?" he repeated, standing now in front of the mirror – and before the figure, which barely resembled Derek at all. He fought against the urge to kneel.

The bald head tilted slowly to one side, as if its owner was carefully considering his reply. The grin twitched, forming words:

"I'm the Pilgrim and I'm here to save you."

PART THREE
NO EXIT

SEVENTEEN

The phone call came early, around 5.40am. Sarah was still asleep in the spare room – she hadn't yet been able to face her old room, the one where all the worst memories were kept. Her dreams had been uneasy, restless, as if the confusion making such a mess of her waking life was mutating into phantoms which had seeped in through the holes in her skull – her eyes, her nostrils, even her gaping mouth. Natural holes, rather than ones someone had bored into bone with a primitive hand drill.

She reached out and tried to find her mobile phone, her eyes refusing to open even a millimetre. She felt the weight of a book against the side of her hand as her fingers pushed it off the night stand, and then she tipped over a glass of water. Finally her hand fell upon the phone, and she grasped it like a weapon, dragging it across the crumpled bed sheets and towards her face.

"Yeah. Hello." Still she was unable to open her eyes. They were sealed, glued shut during the night. She imagined old copper pennies balanced on dead men's eyelids.

"It's me. Are you awake?"

"Benson? What? Where the fuck are you?"

"I asked you if you were awake. Wide awake." His tone was dour. He sounded angry, as if she'd pissed him of in some way – and she probably had. "I need you awake right now."

At last she could open her eyes. Light seeped in through the fluttering lids, but not much. The room was dim, musty, and the heavy curtains were drawn tight across the windows. "I'm awake." She sat upright, her senses kicking in. Her copper's instinct told her that something had happened – probably something bad. "Tell me."

"OK, I don't have much time so listen carefully. I'm at Roundhay Park. In the Arena. An early morning jogger found two bodies. Young boys. Both of them have holes drilled into their skulls, and the wounds have been burned. You need to get here if you want in on this. Do you understand me?"

Sarah blinked into the shivery darkness. She felt sick and light-headed, as if she had just downed a bottle of strong liquor. The room seemed to shudder, the walls trembling, and it came to her in a flash that she was trapped – they all were: trapped inside a plot they could barely even understand. Stuck in a moment that might just last forever.

"You hear me, Sarah?"

She nodded. "Yeah. Thanks. Who tipped you off?"

"A sergeant I know – murder squad. He was the first officer on the scene, and knew that we'd found that kid in the dentist chair. He's doing us a favour – doing *me* a favour, actually. Just don't say I never give you anything, eh?" Then he ended the call, leaving her hanging.

She hated that. It took away her power.

"Thanks," said Sarah, swinging her legs off the bed and lunging for the wardrobe. "Thanks a lot, you prick." But she was actually pleased that he'd called, of course she was. Sarah was not the kind of police officer who liked to be left out; she wanted to be in on everything, right to the last. She and Benson had found the first dead kid, so it was only right that they maintain an interest in the case as it panned out. She silently thanked Benson's friend for the tip-off, acknowledging the fact that he did not have to let them in on anything and she owed him one, whoever he was.

She showered quickly, and put on her uniform without even opening the curtains. She knew the clothing well enough to dress in the dark. These clothes were like a second skin – or perhaps they constituted her *real* skin.

It wasn't far to Roundhay, and she knew all the back roads and rat-runs by heart. There were very few pedestrians around at this hour apart from returning night-shift workers or early commuters on their way to catch the first buses of the day. Those few people Sarah did see all had the same shambling demeanour, whether they were heading home or towards distant offices or factories. She knew how they felt; it was the weight of the world, the early-morning dead load that pressed down on you and didn't go away until later in the day, when everyone else was up and about to take on their share of the invisible burden.

Sarah was on site before 6.30am. The rain had stopped. It was still dark, of course, but the promise of light hung in the air like a diffuse vapour. She left her car in the parking spaces behind the *Deer in the Park* public house and walked through a gap in the bushes at the rear of the building. Even from here, a hundred or so yards away, she could see uniforms milling about at the top of the rise, most of them staring down into the wide, deep bowl of the Arena and studying whatever was down there.

At one point, when the huge park was first created, the depression was intended as the location of another lake. Something happened to prevent this, and the indentation was left in place; nobody bothered to fill it in. During the summer months, bands and actors performed there, in the makeshift Arena. It drew the crowds; it entertained the masses.

Right now Sarah was drawn to another kind of entertainment: the thoroughly modern spectacle of recreational homicide.

She nodded at a few familiar faces as she descended the side of the incline, her eyes locked dead ahead and her boots scraping on the packed earth. Three police vehicles were parked with their noses pointed towards the dip, their doors open and their lights on. She ignored the stares from other officers and carried on down the hill, spotting Benson where he stood near the centre of the Arena.

The two bodies had been covered with white sheets. Scenes of Crime Officers were yet to arrive to carry out their technical duties, so nobody was going near the two small mounds. Someone had taped off an area around the corpses, and Benson was standing by the flapping red barrier, looking her way.

Sarah smiled. He nodded.

"Thanks for calling," she said as she drew near.

"It's OK. I figured we should both be here, just in case we spot something that might make a difference later on." He seemed more relaxed than he had on the phone.

Sarah stared at the sheeted bodies. "How old?"

"As far as we can make out, they seem to be aged around twelve years old. Just a couple of kids."

She looked at his scarred face. His eyes were hard, like pieces of granite. He gave nothing away – that's why he was so good at this part of the job. Benson calmly calculated everything, detaching his emotions from whatever was going on around him. He was the master of this kind of thing: it was second nature to him. "Is it the same as before?"

He turned to her, his mouth twitching. It was almost a smile. "Yeah. Several holes drilled into the skull, and then something like a hot wire pressed into the holes to stem the flow of blood." He turned back to stare at the covered bodies, his hands flexing at his sides.

They stood there in silence for a few moments, infected by the stillness of the early morning and the hushed awe of the other officers who for some reason seemed unwilling to approach the location of the bodies. Birds began to sing; distant traffic noise filtered through; up on the hill, somebody gave out a short, embarrassed laugh.

Then, after what seemed like the longest moment Sarah had ever experienced, someone did finally wander over to join them.

"This is Sergeant Reynolds." Benson nodded at the other man. "He's the one who called me."

Sarah looked at the man. He was tall – well over six feet – and extraordinarily handsome. She'd never seen him before: she was sure that she would have remembered such a striking individual. "Thanks, sir," she said. "I mean, for letting us know about this."

Reynolds nodded. "Benson and I go way back. I owe him more favours than I can ever repay." The two men exchanged a glance containing levels of meaning that Sarah could not even approach let alone penetrate. It was an odd moment, and one that lasted just about long enough for her to be certain she hadn't imagined it.

"All the same… thanks. We really want to be kept in the loop on this one. Is there anything more you can tell us?"

Reynolds sighed heavily, as if he was already tired of talking about the case. "At five o'clock this morning a local solicitor was out taking his usual daily run and he found them like that, laid out like slabs of meat on the grass. We estimate that they couldn't have been there long. All kinds of people wander round here at night, so if the bodies had been left earlier someone would have found them and we'd have been informed. The sight of a dead kid melts the hardest of hearts." He smiled, and suddenly looked ugly.

Sarah glanced at the shapes on the ground. She felt a dizzying wave of sadness wash over her and through her. "So what does it mean? Is this some kind of display?"

Reynolds put his hands in his pockets and bunched up his shoulders. "I think so. It's like he's showing off… maybe even taunting us. He's set these boys out like trophies, showing us what he's capable of. Whoever he is, he's getting more confident. The first one – the one you found – was hidden away. These two are out in plain sight, like a gift."

They fell into an uneasy silence. Benson scanned the top of the rise, looking for someone. Reynolds watched Sarah, and she held his gaze.

"We have a mutual friend, by the way," said Reynolds, buttoning his overcoat against the chill. His breath was a faint white phantom in the air before his face, dispersing as quickly as it appeared. "DI Tebbit. I used to work under him, before I was transferred to the murder squad."

Sarah nodded. "How is he, sir? I haven't heard anything for a while."

Reynolds looked down, and then raised his eyes slowly back to Sarah's face. He blinked; a strange, almost mechanical movement. "He's bad. He slipped into a coma late last night. They don't expect him to come out of it, either."

The news hit Sarah hard. She'd known DI Tebbit for a couple of years and liked him a lot. More than a lot. He had looked after her since their first meeting, when she was a fresh face on the force. Tebbit had known her father, and disliked him with a passion, but he had been taken with Sarah for reasons she still could not define. She'd always suspected that the man had a crush on her, but the notion had never offended her.

"He's a good man." Reynolds was staring her down, almost like an obscure challenge.

"One of the best," she replied, narrowing her eyes and setting the muscles in her jaw. Was he testing her? If he was, she failed to see why and for what purpose. They were all on the same side here.

"I knew your father, too..." Ah, there it was: the kicker to this subtle confrontation. The silence after his words was filled with questions, but ones he was clearly unable – or unwilling – to ask.

"Yes? Well, a lot of people knew my father. Most of them knew him better than I did. Or at least they liked him better." She set her stance, legs held slightly apart. This was getting weird, like some kind of mental warfare.

"He was a great copper. He trained me... showed me what's what." Reynolds glanced over at Benson, and her boyfriend (that word – it still made her feel uncomfortable, like trying on a hat which she knew didn't suit her and never would) gave a slight shake of the head. When he realised that Sarah had seen the gesture, he tried to cover it by raising his hand and coughing into his fist.

The old boys' club was at work again. It never failed to disappoint her.

Sarah felt suddenly trapped between the two men. They flanked her, their limbs forming the boundary of a human cage. She entertained the eerie thought that if she suddenly decided to run they might chase her, and if they caught her away from prying eyes they might do something unimaginable.

Now where had that thought come from? She was growing paranoid; things were getting to her.

The Scene of Crime Officers finally arrived, breaking the strange spell. Several figures in crumpled Hazmat suits drifted down the sides of the incline, drawing in on the locus of the crime. Like mystics, they carried themselves with a grace and confidence that seemed otherworldly. Sarah envied them for a moment: their role in an investigation was defined by rigid scientific parameters, simple scales and rules. Tests could be carried out to discern the truth of a situation, and all emotion could be cast aside. Ambiguity had no place in their lives.

Sarah and the two men watched as the silent SOCOs did their thing. They erected a tent around the bodies and lifted the sheets, carefully combing the area and the corpses for evidence. Their padded white feet moved softly over the hard packed ground; their white-hooded heads nodded, twitched, and occasionally bent towards clipboards to examine raw data.

After a while it became apparent that Sarah and Benson were no longer quite as welcome on the scene. They walked away in silence, each wrapped up in their own storm of thoughts. Sarah was beginning to feel that Benson might be hiding something from her about his relationship with Sergeant Reynolds – or was it something to do with Tebbit? She didn't know what secrets he was holding within, or what they had to do with her, but she sensed his discomfort.

"We need to talk later," she said. "When the shift's over." They walked towards her car, a measurable distance growing between them in terms of both physical space and spiritual empathy.

"OK. If you like."

"Come back to mine? Make it late, though – after eleven. I have a few things to do first. But I think it's time we talked about my father."

Benson stopped walking. He was staring at the ground, at the short grass and the patches of exposed earth between his feet. "Why now?" Finally he turned to face her. His scars seemed to writhe like snakes across his cheeks.

"I've found… something. I'm not quite sure what it is, but you might be able to help me sort through things and get it straight in my head. I need another brain on this, and, well, there's nobody else I can trust."

Benson's lips curled into a slow, cruel smile. "Are you saying that you trust me now? Is this a breakthrough in our relationship?"

Sarah couldn't help but smile back at him. "What I'm saying is that I can't trust anyone else. Not with this, anyway. You're all I have, and that's not much but it'll have to do."

"Oh, such flattery. I feel blessed." He started walking again, long and even strides she could barely keep up with. Sarah seemed to sense an air of relief about him now, as if he had narrowly escaped a situation that he didn't want to face until he was fully prepared.

She slapped him on the arm. "Take it where you can get it, lover. I won't say it again."

They reached the car and Sarah climbed behind the wheel, her hands gripping the cold plastic. She did not open the door for Benson. He could manage fine all by himself, and she didn't want him thinking she'd gone soft on him, like some frail little girly. She would only go so far to meet Benson, not even half way; the rest was up to him.

A show of weakness: that simply wouldn't do. No, that wouldn't do at all. Despite everything she constantly fought so hard against, and all the personality traits she denied had ever belonged to her, Sarah Doherty was still undoubtedly her father's daughter.

EIGHTEEN

Sarah had been given foot patrol that day. A lot of coppers thought it was the short straw, the shitty shift, and preferred to pull a vehicle patrol, but Sarah liked to walk the beat. It made her feel closer to real police work – the old-fashioned kind, where you spoke to people and interacted with the community rather than spending your time filling out computer forms and logging notes onto a central database.

She had struck lucky and landed the city centre beat. It was an easy shift during the day; Leeds United weren't playing at home and there was no sign of the stag-and-hen crowd who packed out the pubs and clubs every weekend, even during daylight hours. No, all she had to contend with was the odd shoplifter, some pissed-up old geezer stumbling across the Headrow and shouting at the traffic, or a minor RTA – a collision at a set of red lights, a harried taxi driver losing concentration at the wheel, a bus mounting the pavement and clipping a parked car.

She was patrolling alone, with an arrangement to meet up with another constable later that morning. They were short-handed, as usual, and Benson – who was usually her partner on foot patrol – had been seconded to the murder squad. His friend, Sergeant Reynolds, had specifically requested Benson's help on the case. He had not asked for Sarah – and again she felt as if she'd failed whatever obscure test he had put her through that morning.

It was just after 10am. She had arranged to meet Eddie Knowles, her father's old informant, at half-past. She knew where the meet was supposed to be – she had guessed immediately, as soon as he'd mentioned that he had in mind the same place he always met up with her father.

As its name suggested, The Vault was located in the old warren of vaulted cellars beneath a decommissioned Church on Clarendon Road. The Vault had been a registered charity since the early nineteen seventies, but had acted as an unofficial homeless shelter since about 1952. These days it served as one of only two recognised care centres for the city's homeless population, and had developed a good reputation and working relationship with the authorities along the way. So successful was the venture that several old residents of the Vault now worked there as volunteers – wardens, advisors, even part-time counsellors.

Sarah's father had contributed a lot of money to the charity. Ostensibly they were police funds raised by charity events but in reality Sarah knew that these legitimate monies had also been mixed up with a substantial portion of winnings from his illicit gambling parties. He had never been that interested in the money – only in the risk involved in winning it.

There was also the religious aspect.

Sarah's father might have been a Grade A bastard, but he claimed to have believed in God. In her opinion it made him even more of a monster – during her relatively short time on the police force she'd already encountered a lot of people who used the cloak of organised religion to cover their tracks and justify their terrible acts, and as far as Sarah was concerned her father was no different to any other self-serving scumbag.

In fact, he was worse than the lot of them. She was only now discovering how much worse that might be.

She walked along the busy Headrow, taking in the late morning sights. Pedestrians dodged traffic as they crossed the road, most of them heading for The Light shopping centre and its multifarious consumer delights. A group of teenagers moved slowly on skateboards along the footpath and onto the paved area outside the art gallery. Sarah paused to make sure that they were not causing any damage, and then moved on towards the edge of the Ring Road, satisfied that she could leave them alone.

Eddie Knowles was waiting for her outside The Vault. She had not seen him since her early teens, but he hadn't changed a bit. He had the same scrawny build, greasy nightclub-Elvis pompadour hairstyle and shady demeanour she remembered from all those years ago. She watched him as she slowly approached, and at first she thought that he had failed to spot her. Then, smiling, she realised that he was spying on her – pretending that he was looking the other way, but scrutinising her every move.

"Hello, Erik." She stood before him, matching his height and easily a couple of inches broader than his narrow frame.

"The name's Eddie these days, and I'll thank you to use it." His grin betrayed the fact that he wasn't really offended, just playing a role for her benefit and no doubt for his own amusement.

"Good to see you again, Eddie."

He raised a stubby hand-rolled cigarette to his lips, sucked on it, and exhaled the thin grey smoke. "Likewise, pet. I hardly recognised you, apart from the fact that you inherited your dad's cocksure swagger." He grinned again, flashing yellow teeth and a small, questing tongue. "Let's hope you don't have the cock, eh?"

"Fuck off, Eddie. Let's go inside and get a cup of tea."

"Aye. Good idea. I'm parched." He moved away from the wall and nodded at the small, chubby woman sitting at the reception desk behind the strengthened glass security doors. She moved a hand across the counter and buzzed them in. Eddie pushed through the doors – no outmoded display of chivalry here – and walked across the short reception area. "Mornin', Sheila. How goes it?"

The woman smiled. She looked bashful, as if she was flattered by the attention of this shabby little Lothario. "Oh, get on with you." She nodded at Sarah, her face now rigid. "Good morning, Constable."

Sarah smiled, took off her checkerboard hat and held it loosely by her side. "Don't worry; I'm not here on business. Just calling in for a little chat with my old friend, Eddie." She cocked her head to the side, indicating the subject of her explanation.

The receptionist looked relieved. The last thing she probably wanted was trouble on her shift. "I'm afraid I'll still have to ask you to sign in – that means both of you, Eddie."

"Aye, aye. No sweat." Eddie ambled over to the desk and signed an open guestbook with an absurd flourish, then turned and handed Sarah the pen. His fingers were dirty; grit was caked beneath the nails. She couldn't help noticing things like that: it was in her blood to tally the finer details, just in case they proved to be of importance at a later date. Her father's training; always her father's training.

After signing in, Sarah followed her host out of the reception area and through another set of doors. They walked in silence along a hallway, and then entered through a set of wide double doors and went into the Vault Café.

The café was quiet at this hour, and everyone was gearing up for the lunchtime rush. They served free meals between the hours of eleven and five, the kitchen and serving area staffed by volunteers and a few ex-residents of The Vault – people who had gained a lot of self-respect from their stay here and wanted to pass forward the good fortune.

A few men, most of them with patchy beards and dressed in clothes inappropriate for the weather, sat around drinking tea. They exchanged words, looked around at Sarah and Eddie, and held great secrets behind their tired eyes. Eddie went to the serving tables and returned with a pot of tea and two cups.

"Thanks," she said, pouring the drinks.

"You want something to eat?" Eddie had stubbed out his cigarette in the lobby, but he looked as if he was already in need of another. His eyes had taken on a suspicious glaze and a muscle in his left cheek twitched every couple of seconds as a result of nicotine withdrawal.

"No thanks, Eddie. I'll eat later. Wouldn't want to take food out of the mouths of the needy."

He let out a single bark of laughter. "Fuck me, pet, that's exactly like something yer dad might've said, back in the day." He clutched his cup with both hands and drank deeply.

"So." Sarah put her own cup down on the table. "Why the name change?"

"Aw, it's my real name, innit? I stopped using the stage name when I left the circuit. Haven't done a turn in years; not since I had some nodules (he pronounced the word *nujoolz*) scraped off me throat." His eyes twinkled, but it was a false glimmer. There was little genuine humour behind his expression.

"And you've turned your back on other things, apart from the name? Is that right?" She leaned forward, resting her elbows on the table.

"Very direct, aren't you, love? That's something else you get from him." He winked. "To answer yer question, yeah I've put a lot of stuff behind me. I settled down and got wed, started behaving meself. After yer dad died... well, he was the only one left who even listened to me anyway. Things have changed on these streets, and not for the better. Back when I was sleeping here every now an' then, and not just popping in for elevenses, I was a *known* man, a bloke everyone respected." He licked his lips. "These days I'm just a sad old joke, a reminder of how things used to be."

Sarah rubbed her hands together. She wasn't sure why she did it, but the motion relaxed her. "Oh, you're not so old,

Eddie. Not so old and not so forgotten. I remember you used to give my old man a lot of tips. He swore by your little nuggets of information – said he'd struggle to solve a thing without you."

Eddie shook his head, slowly. "Flattery, is it? Is that what you think will make me talk? Is that what they're teaching you these days?"

"I'm sorry. That was crude. No, I don't think that's how I'll get you to open up. But I know what might." She reached into her inside jacket pocket and took out an envelope. "There's a lot of cash there, Eddie, and all I want in return is for you to tell me what everyone else probably already knows."

Eddie's eyes lit up – and this time the light was real. "Oh, aye? What's that, then?"

Sarah lowered her voice. "I want you to tell me what he did. About the little club he ran – the card school, the sex parties, and whatever else they got up to after hours and outside the station. I have my suspicions, but I need someone who was around at the time to confirm them."

The room seemed to dim, the lights flickering softly. Sarah glanced up, at the ceiling fixtures, and watched as the bulbs waxed and waned. She thought she could see moths hovering around the light fittings, but the image vanished whenever she focused her gaze directly on that area of the room.

"Maybe they forgot to pay the leccy bill." Eddie's voice was bitter, filled with a tone that was not quite regret but something similar, something that went a lot deeper.

When Sarah looked back down at the table the envelope was gone. She smiled, and then looked up, back into Eddie's eyes. "All I want is info, Eddie. I'm not trying to rake up old ashes, or ruin anyone's reputation. A few weird things have happened, and I just want to put the old bastard's ghost to rest." Only then, when she said it out loud, did she realise that was exactly what she'd wanted all along.

"Alright, pet. I'll tell you what I know, but as I said on the phone you might not like it. You know when a kid grabs a stick and stirs up a wasp's nest? Well, that's what you could have on your hands here. A fuckin' huge wasp's nest. And you could get stung." He refilled his cup but made no move to offer her another drink.

"I'm all ears, Eddie. All ears and eyes." She smiled, to show him: to demonstrate how big her eyes were. Just like that big bad wolf in the fairy tale.

The lights flickered again, but this time it was less erratic, as if they were following a rhythm. It lasted a few seconds, and then ceased. The room now seemed brighter than it had before, as if the power surge had resulted in a greater luminosity within the bulbs.

"Your dad was the best and the most vicious copper I've ever known." Eddie stared right at her, deep into her big, bad wolf's eyes. "He was a bastard, but he was also the best friend I ever had."

"Yes," said Sarah. "People's opinions seem to follow the same lines on this one." She smiled.

"Well, he helped me off drugs back when that was all I cared about, and he helped me get a few gigs – first with his band, and then on my own. That's when I first started on the club circuit, and it gave me the best days of my fuckin' life. The *best* ones."

His eyes misted over, as if he was back there, in his glory days, but then he returned to the moment. The past could not claim a man like Eddie for long: there were too many monsters back there to harm him.

"I knew your dad was into some pretty hardcore stuff from the start, but at first I thought it was just gambling, and maybe a few whores. He arranged those sex parties. I think you already know this – that it might be one of those weird happenings you mentioned – but he got your mum involved. He took her along and bullied her into joining in, just to keep her quiet. I know that. I know because he told me. He laughed about it when he was drunk. He had a nasty side… but I'm guessing you already know that, too."

Sarah held Eddie's gaze. He was testing her, feeling her out. If she looked away, or showed any sign of weakness, he might clam up and decide not tell her the rest. "Yeah. I do know about that. I know about all that. I even have the scars to prove it."

Eddie nodded, satisfied that she could handle what he was saying. "It got worse. It went beyond all that. He had secrets from everyone, even from me and especially from his missus, from your poor old mum."

A chair leg scraped across the tiled floor; the sound was too loud, as if someone had turned up the volume on a sound effects tape. Somebody laughed, and it turned into a whooping smoker's cough.

"He and a few of his friends started taking repeat offenders off the streets and smacking them around. It started, God, back in the early Seventies, before you were even born. They were like a fuckin' vigilante squad, swarming into blocks of flats in Beeston and Bestwick in the early hours and dragging fuck-ups out of their beds. They took them to a place – I never knew where – and they kicked the fuck out of them, showing them the 'error of their ways'. That's what they called it – all formal, like. *'The error of their ways.'*"

He paused here, as if allowing her to take in the full impact of his words.

"OK." She blinked; the lights were still too bright. "So they were, what, trying to clean up Leeds? Get rid of the scum?"

Eddie nodded. "Aye, but they were doing it their way, not using the official channels. It went on for a few years, and then a low-level drug dealer was killed. After that, they stopped. They got away with it, and they counted their blessings and they went back to more *traditional* police work." His emphasis on the word traditional was almost funny: almost, but not quite.

"Then what?" Sarah's throat was dry, but she was pleased to hear that her voice sounded just about normal. She wanted another drink but the teapot was empty – Eddie had finished the dregs. "What happened next?"

Eddie let out a heavy breath and sat back in his chair. He rubbed his limp quiff with his small, bony hands, teasing it out. "Four or five years before you were born he found religion. Said he saw an angel."

Sarah stopped breathing. She stopped and was afraid that she might not be able to start again. "I knew he was always a bit fanatical, but not when it started."

An angel, just as her mother had claimed. Sarah felt cold inside; her gut tightened.

Eddie made a sound deep in his throat: it could have been laughter or simply a snorting noise as he cleared his airways. "I can't be sure exactly when it happened. But he claimed that he met an angel, and this fuckin' angel taught him how to see the evil in people. Well, when I say people, what I really mean is, he said he could see the evil in little kids before it even developed. That he could see what kind of criminal a child would become before they knew it themselves. Like he could read their minds or see the future or summat."

For a moment Sarah thought that she could hear distant music, and then, when she turned around to inspect the room, it faded. As if whatever the source of that music might be, it was now moving away, leaving her far behind. She thought of childhood carnivals, of leering clowns and tamed and beaten animals going through tired routines.

A second set of doors, opposite the ones she and Eddie had entered, banged open but nobody entered the room. The doors hung that way, wide to the wall, for what seemed like well over a minute, and then they slowly closed. Beyond them, walking away, with its back turned towards her, Sarah glimpsed what looked like a robed-and-hooded figure. But no, that couldn't be right. Not here, not now. She must be seeing things.

She turned back to face Eddie, who had gone pale. "Did he tell anyone else about this?"

Eddie shook his head. "No. I managed to convince him that he was talking a load of old shite – he was drunk and stoned at the time, and working on too many big cases than he should've been. He was losing his grip. He never mentioned it again, and I had no reason to bring it up." Eddie was still pale: his cheeks looked as if they'd been smeared in flour.

Sarah pushed away from the table, as if she was about to stand, and then changed her mind. She ran her hands through her hair, palmed her face. "Jesus, Eddie. Didn't you think to tell anyone? I mean, he was clearly losing his mind."

Eddie shrugged. He blew air through his pursed lips. "No. Back then, blokes didn't interfere in each others lives that way. They gave each other space, and they never questioned any-thing. Especially blokes like us, who lived that kind of life, who saw the things we saw and did the things we did. Bad blokes... dead bad bastards like us."

Sarah bit her bottom lip. She didn't know what to say, or how to react. This was all too much; she was overloaded with infor-mation she didn't even want to have inside her head.

The lights flickered again, but this time when they settled the room was much dimmer, nearly dark. It was almost dark in the middle of the day.

NINETEEN

It didn't take me long to locate Dock Side on the map. I braved the outside world again and used a terminal in a small internet place near the football ground, glancing nervously over my shoulder in case Traci had decided to follow me again. I hadn't seen or heard from her since we'd slept together, and even then she had left quietly in the night while I dozed. She didn't leave a note. In fact she left nothing behind but the smell of her sex.

I typed 'Dock Side, London' into an internet search engine and the first hit I got was for a disused riverside warehouse in Rotherhithe, on the opposite bank of the Thames to the old Wapping newspaper plant. According to the link I accessed, the warehouse had once been owned by a company called Pilgrim Products. There was no mention of what that company did, or what it was they supplied or- manufactured, but the name rang bells so deep inside me that I feared they might never be silenced.

The Pilgrim. It seemed obvious that I would encounter him again, even in such an oblique manner as this. He had dogged me all through my life, watching and interfering from the sidelines, until he had finally entered centre stage and taken from me the only thing I had left to care about.

A long time ago he had killed my family, and then he had done the same to my lover.

He was the reason – or at least a large part of it – that I had nothing left in this life but a slim hope, a slender promise of redemption that continually danced out of reach.

I left the café and headed straight for the underground station, feeling as if whatever time I had was slipping away. I had no idea where this sudden sense of urgency had originated – perhaps it was something to do with the Rwandan psychic who had supplied the address; or maybe it was because of the attentions of her ex-lover, who had shared my bed.

And now here I stood, outside Canada Water tube station. As usual, the day was slightly overcast; thin clouds hung like webbing in the sky. I stared up, directly overhead, and wondered what might be watching from above that grey canopy. My senses were going into overdrive. My tattoos itched. All the old feelings were returning; the familiar signifiers that I was on to something. As if I hadn't known all along that dark forces would find me quickly, even in my silly hiding place: a haunted house in a haunted city in a haunted country; crouching in a pathetic corner of a haunted world.

It occurred to me, and not for the first time, that everyone and everything was haunted. And it had always been that way.

I walked down to the river, passing an old pub called *The Mayflower* that sat with its haunches on the riverbank. I remembered that I had been here before, many years ago. There was a ghost on the premises, one that I had been unable to help.

The warehouse looked foreboding even in daylight, but that was probably because of the personal connection I had with the building. It was large and decaying. Exposed steel bones poked through ruined layers of cladding and the roof was pitted with holes. PIL-GRIM PRODUCTS was stencilled in faded white lettering across the front elevation, and I almost turned around and walked away.

But I didn't. I stood and I stared and I began to be afraid – really afraid, for the first time in months. My previous stoical attitude caved in and the childlike fear beneath stared up into the open air, wishing that it could go back into hiding.

It might have been a trick of perception, but the sky above the warehouse was darkening, as if it were being churned up by a storm. Silent flashes illuminated the cloud cover over the roof. Dark shapes that could only be birds circled the place, remaining in the grubby air rather than roosting in the eaves.

I felt like I'd wandered onto the set of a horror film, and I realised that once again I was being manipulated. In reality – *my* reality, the one in which I existed – the day was bright, the sky was a little clearer. But right here, right now, as I stood and watched, a sliver of the Pilgrim's reality was slipping through to stain my view. If he were here, next to me, he would be laughing. He was such a theatrical bastard, and I knew that all of the set dressing was more for his benefit than mine.

It was all just part of the joke.

"I'm not afraid," I said, lying. "I'm not afraid of you." That last part, at least, was true. The Pilgrim himself did not inspire fear in my heart, but the darkness he stood for disturbed me in a way that he could only aspire to and never quite attain. Like me, the Pilgrim knew his limits, and he had to stay within them.

There are levels to human fear, like the landings of an infinite stairwell. Near the top, closest to the air, there are the common and everyday fears: lost love, a ruined career, living on the streets with no one to care. Then one level down there dwell the fears of age, death and the end of your existence. These are the fears that bite. They have their teeth in us from the very day that we become aware of our own mortality.

Beneath even these, on other, lower landings – ill-trodden levels where it isn't wise to venture – the spiritual fears roam. The fear of faithlessness, of vanishing into the void, of everything we ever believed in being exposed as nothing but a lie.

That is where the darkness lives. The shadow between the stars, the spaces between individual souls – the thing we choose to call the Devil.

The Devil lives on the lowest landing, the rickety one with warped boards and no handrail to break a fall. He sits like a bloated corpse in the darkness we all keep inside, trying to smother it with friends and lovers and commodities while he watches from below. It is the place we never get to see until the moment right before we die.

That place, the spot where we are most vulnerable, is where I need to operate. It is part of my calling to dance with the Devil, even when I am uncertain of the right moves.

Breathing deeply, I set off towards the warehouse, noting how much it resembled another similar building, one from my recent past. A steel-framed structure where I'd discovered the hanged body of a pretty young woman and a wailing man on the ground at her feet: the place where all this madness had begun. I tried to imagine if I might have acted differently had I known the events that would follow, but I couldn't be certain. I believe in free will, but it is compromised. With each choice we make in life there comes a price, and sometimes that price is too high to pay. But we must always cough up; we *have* to pay our dues, even if we change our minds. Once set in motion, the transaction must be completed.

I stopped before the building's entrance. There were thick chains across the doors, with huge padlocks binding them together. It looked like they were meant to keep something inside rather than to prevent anyone from entering the place.

The warehouse was a detached steel frame set among other stone buildings, also derelict. At one time the banks of this river had seen monumental trade, but now the old structures had either been renovated or turned into expensive riverside apartments or left to rot. I glanced at its neighbours, aware of the dead eyes of broken windows and the barred mouths of doors.

Nobody but the Pilgrim would have sent me here. The only thing stopping me from walking away was the fact that I no longer cared what happened to me.

Graffiti adorned the warehouse walls, but it was patchy and for the most part incoherent. The material covering the steel members was torn and warped, and the damage had obliterated whatever messages previous visitors had daubed there.

I saw fragments of names, pieces of abusive propaganda, partial telephone numbers and the faint promise of sexual acts carried out by whoever answered the call. Then, drawing my gaze like a spray of blood, I saw the only message meant specifically for me.

Again, it was incomplete, but there was enough of it left in black paint on the grey wall that I understood immediately I had come to the right place. Not that I had maintained any doubts, but if I had done they were now gone.

...ento Mor...

Part of a well-worn Latin phrase I'd been tagged by several months ago: a message, a warning, a reminder. A not-so-gentle admonition to inform me that one day I too must die.

Despite the fear gnawing at my guts, I managed a tiny smile.

"Let's see what you have for me," I whispered, moving slowly and uncertainly around the building looking for a way inside. I did not have to search for long. On the east elevation there was a rent in the cladding just about large enough that I could slip inside.

I took one last look at the sky, and saw a clearing directly above me. It was yet another taunt: a glimpse of forever above the canopy of horror under which I walked.

Then, dropping my gaze, I turned sideways and wriggled in through the gap.

It was gloomy in there – as I had known it would be – and the floor was uneven. Once I was fully through the skin of the structure, past the beams and columns and hanging teeth of metal, I began to notice the smell. The aroma of old sex, cannabis smoke and petrol filled my nostrils. Shards of daylight poked through holes in the walls. Most of the windows were either boarded over with timbers or had steel shutters, but a few of them – those higher up, near the mezzanine level – had only torn sheets of builder's paper taped across their frames. Through these latter minor openings I was allowed enough light to make my way across the large, open space.

Used condoms, empty beer cans and broken bottles littered the floor. The remnants of weird machines stood in shadow, and I wondered if they were real or simply another fabrication, the industrial wreckage of a different version of reality.

Oddly, I sensed no ghosts inside the building. There was an atmosphere, yes, but it didn't reek of the dead. There was a sense of otherness, of difference. It felt like I was walking across a stage, but not inside any normal kind of theatre. I had felt this way before, on several occasions, but rarely had it been so powerful. I could taste something vaguely metallic on my tongue, but it was an alien flavour; my skin prickled; my insides knotted.

Somewhere near the centre of the wide room, I stopped. The steelwork seemed to make a low humming sound, as if it were transmitting a frequency I could not access. The paper across the upper windows fluttered, but I felt no breeze. The gloom deepened, shifting subtly around me like deep water. I was aware of unknown currents, and felt suddenly out of my depth.

Something shifted behind me, and I fought the urge to turn around and look. After several seconds, I could fight it no more and spun slowly on my heels. There was nothing there, but a short distance away, against a supporting column, there was the suggestion of coiling movement, as if a great snake was wrapping its thick body around the steel upright.

I looked away, blinking. This was all shadow-play: a series of cheap parlour tricks meant to unnerve me.

Groping for a connection to the outside world, I looked up again, peering at the chinks of light that bled through the papered windows. This time when I raised my eyes, I saw other things, objects which at first defied logic.

Small plastic doll parts were suspended from strings or wires attached to the ceiling. They spun slowly in the darkness, tiny arms, legs, torsos, and heads. When I saw them indirectly, from the corner of my eye, they began to look real – disassembled children left there to warn away trespassers. But when I looked directly at them they were simply doll parts.

I looked away, and then back at the dangling pieces. They were plastic again, just pieces of manufactured toys. But still, there was something, a detail that didn't quite add up. It took me a while to realise what was wrong, but when I did it hit me like a blow from the shadows.

Each of the doll's faces was the same – a blank pink oval. I strained my eyes to examine them, and even in the meagre light from the holes in the paper across the windows, I could see the blank plastic skulls. I tried to think of the significance of those empty plastic faces, but the intended meaning eluded me. I was left only with the impression that there was a message here, on the end of those wires, if only I had the ability, or desire, to see it.

I moved across the space, going deeper inside. The place where I'd gained access now seemed miles away, as if it were receding. I fought the sensation, but it was stronger than me. It felt like I was leaving the world behind.

"I know you," I said, speaking to whoever was manipulating my reality. "We have met." There was no answer; the dark beckoned, reaching out towards me like a potential lover.

I saw balloons on the floor. They were fully inflated, almost to the point of bursting, so the features printed upon the stretched elastic surfaces were not immediately familiar. As I drew closer I realised that it was my face on the balloons, but mutated, elongated by the air inside them. "Very clever." I sounded confident, but my defences were fragile. My skin crawled; the ink ran and reformed the protective emblems I wore upon my body. The screams of those I had failed were almost audible as they writhed across my back; inked names slowly ripped from my flesh.

I kicked through the cluster of balloons, trying not to look at my own strangely shaped features. I stared straight ahead, at a point on the wall. Then I realised that someone was moving towards me. The figure was thin, crumpled, as if it were a crude amalgamation of body parts rather than a whole. I paused, my feet shuffling, ready for flight. Then I realised that I was staring at my own reflection.

Shards and slivers and squares of mirror had been fixed to the wall. The effect was like a mosaic, but one that reflected reality in a way that was out of true. It was a visual metaphor, another silly trick, and if I had not been so nervous I might have smiled.

There were other things reflected in the piecemeal mirror, and they forced their way into my perspective as I watched. It was like a painting by Goya, or a nightmare inspired by the ingestion of narcotics. If anyone but me had seen this, they would have lost their minds in a second.

Behind me, but not really anywhere behind me (just in the twisted reality depicted in the mirror), a huge man worked a gargantuan pair of bellows in absolute silence. He was naked from the waist up and his legs were wrapped in what looked like bloody hospital dressings. His torso was thin but his arms were thickly muscled, like flesh-coloured oak trees. On his head he wore an odd feathered cowl. They looked like the feathers from various birds of paradise: beautiful colours, all shapes and sizes. The bellows were leathery, as if they were made from dragons' wings, and the bone handles were so thick that he couldn't close his fists around them.

The man worked the bellows as hard as he could, the cords on his body straining, sweat streaking his chest and oversized arms, but they inflated only a little. Like Sisyphus, he had taken on a task that could never be fulfilled, a job with no point other than the allegorical.

Unable to resist, I turned and glanced over my shoulder. There was nothing but that quivering near-darkness. When I looked in the mirror the man was still there, persisting with his task.

I began to examine the scene held within the reflective fragments, and as I did so I reminded myself that I was seeing them through a fold in reality, a spot where some kind of heave had occurred and things were bleeding through. The sights I was only beginning to make out were from another reality entirely – one that I had no desire to enter.

To the right of the man – and over my left shoulder, a huge leviathan lay on the floor. I struggled to understand what it was, and then the familiar asserted its grip, telling my mind what to visualise, and I understood that I was not looking at a real animal. It was a papier mâché elephant, laying on its side, its belly slit open and a very small, very old man sitting on a wooden chair inside its emptied gut. This man had no face: the front of his skull was the back of a head. That all-encompassing head swivelled through three-hundred-and-sixty degrees as I stared. Back of the head was front of the head was back of the head: it was yet another symbol that I couldn't decipher.

The elephant's rear-left leg began to twitch. The movement was quick, jagged, and the little old man with no face moved his own leg in tandem, tapping out a silent beat. The two were linked; they were part of the same image.

I blinked, wishing that they would vanish. Somehow the hollow papier mâché beast and its wizened inhabitant were even more horrific than the man with the dragon-wing bellows.

"Just show me," I said. "Show me what it is I need to understand. Fuck off with the symbols, the puzzles... just show me what you want me to see."

In the fragmented mirror something else began to form. The vision resolved itself from a light fog, becoming clearer and clearer, as if in answer to my words. It was a man – a normal man in a dark suit. He was sitting on a three-legged wooden stool, like a milking stool, with his back to me.

I stepped forward, having to force my legs to move. It was like walking through mud. The man just sat there, staring into space, stiff-backed and unmoving. I approached the shards of mirror, so close that I could see their perfectly smooth shorn edges. The pieces of mirror had not been shattered; they had been sliced, or moulded.

"Who are you?"

The man didn't move.

"Tell me who you are. Is it you I've been looking for?"

He nodded his head, once, a tiny movement in the mirror-mosaic.

"Show yourself. Show me who you are."

Just as the man began to turn around I realised who he was, and for the first time since the accident that had claimed the lives of my family, I experienced a genuinely spontaneous emotion – one that I didn't have to force or fake.

The man turned incrementally, as if his joints were rusted and their motion was restricted. He moved awkwardly, like a clockwork toy. His hands were resting on his knees. His feet remained flat on the floor. He twisted from the waist; a wholly unnatural movement.

I tried to scream but my voice would not come. It was broken: it was busted, like a vandalised machine.

The man turned and I looked at his features. He turned and I stared into my own face, inspecting my wide, watering eyes for signs of deceit.

"So you found me." His voice was the female voice I had heard on the phone at the house in Plaistow, and again on the mobile phone in the café opposite the massage parlour. It was a false voice, a clockwork lie. But this time it sounded familiar. The voice was that of Ellen Lang, my dead friend, my murdered lover.

"Who are you?" I fell to my knees. The floor was hard; it sent shockwaves through my legs. "What is this?"

"You found me. You needed to find me." That voice: it was summoned from old machine parts, ancient cogs and levers.

"I needed to find myself." The truth was so obvious that it seemed almost trite, the tired punch line to an old joke. Was this yet another form of mental torture, or had Ellen come through from another realm to help me, perhaps even to protect me… to save me from myself?

"Stay here. Don't go there. Don't go back. You can't help her. You never could." Words formed on the fractured surface of the mirror, written in breath. A light misty message, one that Ellen's cobbled-together avatar could not possibly hold back. "Don't," she said, and then the figure on the chair – the representation of me – crumpled, fell apart, its dusty clockwork pieces scattering across the floor.

I read the misted words on the glass, even as they faded, and they were in direct opposition to what the figure had told me.

Go Home.

Somewhere far off, probably behind the haphazard mirror, a baby started to cry.

Then I saw something else in the reflective surfaces, a scene broken into scores of separate images. Only when I took a step back, gave myself some distance, could I see what was forming in the silvered shards on the wall.

The wailing of the unseen baby grew louder, as if it were distressed.

I saw the room above the massage parlour: Immaculee Karuhmbi's place. It was a mess. Furniture had been smashed, the walls had been hacked at with blunt instruments, and a body was positioned on the floor, shrouded by detritus.

The corpse was that of the Rwandan psychic. Her armless torso was face-up, eyes open, her mouth was agape. As I watched, the scene jerked into life, like a film roll starting to play. Straddling the psychic's body was Traci (*with an eye not a why*), her factotum, her ex-lover. The skinny little girl I had fucked on a grimy mattress in the grey zone. Traci looked insane: she was naked, her hair was writhing like a nest of vipers, and her thin body was soaked in sweat. She smiled – she *grinned* at me, I'm sure of it. She reached down and tore a chunk of meat from Immaculee's stomach, and then stuffed it into her mouth. I closed my eyes when, slowly and methodically, she began to chew.

The sound of a baby crying began to fade, gradually turning to silence.

As I turned away I knew that there had never really been a choice, despite what Ellen had somehow managed to say to me. If it had even been Ellen at all, and not simply another trick by the one who taunted me from the ginnels and alleyways between realities.

Of course I would return to Leeds; I would always go back, go home. There was nobody left here to cling to, and no other place that would have me.

TWENTY

Sarah pushed slowly through the doors and stood in a narrow corridor, wondering where the black-robed figure had gone. She knew that Eddie Knowles would follow her. He had no choice; he was part of this now, even if he denied it to himself. He was just as much involved in whatever the hell was going on as Sarah, perhaps even more so.

"What is it?" His voice was at her shoulder, hovering like a bird. "What happened?"

"I saw... I don't know. Someone. Somebody's been following me, hanging around wherever I go. If I didn't know any better I'd say it was my father's ghost."

Eddie didn't laugh, and that unnerved her. He was not the type to believe in spooks. Eddie lived in the real world, the hard world of greed and violence, not some soft-centred place where things went bump in the night.

"Say something, Eddie. Tell me I'm being fucking stupid."

"You're being fuckin' stupid." His voice was deadpan – flat and unconvincing.

"Thanks," she said, taking a step forward.

"Any time, love. Any fuckin' time."

She walked forward, moving hesitantly along the corridor.

Up ahead were several doors, positioned on either side of the
tight space. She could hear the faint strains of a radio playing
somewhere in the heart of the building, probably in one of
the dormitories.

"Keep going," said Eddie, still following her. "There's something I should probably show you, now that you're here."

"Where?" She kept moving, her feet scuffing the floor. The
radio fell silent.

"Turn right at the end, and then go through the first door."

Sarah did as Eddie asked, and found herself standing in the
doorway of an odd little room. Low concrete benches lined the
walls, and located at the centre of the room was a sunken area in
which sat a small altar – there was a font, some candle-holders,
and a small framed picture of Jesus Christ holding a bleeding
heart. Assorted paraphernalia of faith: small articles of the divine.

"It's the prayer room." Eddie stepped past her, walked to one
of the benches and sat down. He stared at the altar, his gaze cold
and implacable. "Me and your old fella, we spent a lot of time
in here. It was a nice quiet place to chat." He looked over at her
and smiled, his fringe flopping to cover his lined forehead. It was
a strange expression, and seemed somehow more genuine than
anything else about the man. In that moment he looked vulnerable, as if he were letting down his defences.

"OK. So what did you want to show me?" She folded her
arms, not yet ready to lower her own barriers, not completely.

Eddie shook his head. "You coppers… you can be blind as fuck
sometimes." He motioned with his arms, bringing them up and
out, as if embracing something invisible. "Look at the walls. The
pictures. These people were all regulars here at one time or another – this is how they're remembered. They're all dead now,
but these drawings are like a shrine to their memory, a way of
making sure they're not forgotten."

Sarah let her gaze wander around the room and took in the
delicately chalked portraits that dominated the walls. She had

already noticed them of course, but nothing about them had drawn her interest enough to deserve more than a brief glance. They had been applied directly to the plaster render, and then framed with thin plywood strips. Each one was incredibly well done; the level of detail was breathtaking. She did not know any of the faces, but she guessed that the actual men the portraits were based on looked exactly like these representations. "Yes. They're lovely. But what does all this mean to me?"

Eddie laughed. It was a quiet sound, and slightly creepy. Sarah was reminded of the sounds her father used to make as he prowled the family home, late at night, drinking whisky, talking to himself and laughing at his own dirty little jokes; all the sounds of madness, or at least of sanity that was coming apart at the seams.

"Well?" She didn't mean to sound so angry, but she was unable to hold it back. Eddie, she felt, was wasting her time. She had better things she could've spent that two grand on. She unfolded her arms, letting them hang, her hands making tight little fists at her sides.

"For fuck's sake, can't you see? You coppers… how the hell do you expect to solve anything when you can't even take the time to stop and look at your surroundings? Take another look at the fuckin' pictures." He was angry too; angry and frustrated, and, yes, even slightly disappointed. And there was a tone of sadness in his voice that she had not noticed until now.

Sarah looked again at the walls, puzzled yet eager to discover what Eddie was talking about, what he so desperately wanted her to see. Most of the men depicted in the drawings had beards or stubble, and they all sported dark rings around their eyes. Even in these idealised pictures, the men (no women: just men) looked tired, worn out and drained by the harshness of their lives. Then, finally, she saw it. She felt like an idiot for not noticing it at once, but it wasn't something she would have expected, not here, in this place.

One of the drawings was of her father.

Stern and unmoving, he stared down at her from the wall, his eyes blazing like embers. Even when he was happy he had looked aggrieved. It had held him back, that inability to express anything other than an inner rage. His superiors held him in awe, his peers suspected he was always on the edge of a burn-out, and everyone else was afraid of him. His family feared him most of all.

"Oh, shit. It's him. What the hell's he doing up there?"

"Well done." Eddie stood and took a step away from the bench, then stopped, as if he was uncertain what to do now that he was on his feet. "Congratulations, you can now call yourself a detective. Have a badge." Beneath the humour, there was a thinly disguised note of bitterness, even contempt.

He laughed again, but this time the sadness was held at bay – or perhaps she had imagined it after all.

Eddie walked over to her, moving slowly, with tiny steps. "He was a hero to a lot of people, you know. If you think you can change that, I'd think again. Nobody wants to hear about him doing anything but solving crimes, giving money to his pet charities, and maybe fronting a few sex and poker parties. People like their heroes tarnished. It makes them more believable. What they don't like is to have their heroes ruined."

Sarah turned to face Eddie, her shoulders sagging. She felt weak, almost ready to give up. "Like I said before, I have no intention of dragging anybody's name through the mud. I don't want to damage his reputation – this is just for me, for my own piece of mind. I feel like I'm going mad, and I need to find out why. I want to *know*, damn it!" Her strength returned as she spat out those final words, and she clung to her rage as if it might help her continue her search.

Eddie nodded. Then he turned back to face the room, slipping his hands into his trouser pockets. There was the quiet jingle of loose change, the music of a man's meagre possessions.

When Sarah looked back at the drawing of her father, he was wearing a white cowl over his head. His shoulders were draped in black. His eyes were hidden. She blinked, and then she saw his face again, uncovered. The hood was no longer in place. She could have sworn that this time he was smiling.

"Come here," Eddie moved back towards the bench he'd only just vacated. He moved quicker now, as if he were nervy and on edge. "Sit with me for a while. I think we understand each other now."

Sarah followed him and sat down. The bench was cold and hard; the cold seeped through the seat of her trousers and into the meat of her buttocks. She wriggled her backside on the concrete, trying to get comfortable. "Yes. Yes, I think we do, Eddie. All I want is a little truth, you know. No more lies. No more bullshit. Just some honesty, so I can put that bastard and what he did behind me."

Eddie was staring into her eyes. His face was open and appealing; in that moment he looked kind and generous, as if he really cared. "A little truth," he said, mulling over her words.

"He used to hurt me, Eddie. He cut me – slashed my legs to stop himself from doing other things, sex stuff. And he beat and raped my mother. Now you tell me that he abducted and kicked the crap out of criminals, and maybe even killed one of them? Can you appreciate why I need to know – *what* I need to know? He was my father. What if... what if, like you said back there, the apple doesn't fall far from the tree?" She lowered her head. She had the impression that Eddie was reaching out to her, his hand hovering close to her head. Then she felt the hand move quickly away, as if he had relented and dropped it into his lap.

"OK." His voice was low, husky. She liked it this time; she liked it a lot. It sounded like hope. "OK, I'm going to tell you something. Just let me speak, and then don't ask any questions. I'm about to tell you all I know – everything. I'm keeping nothing back, I swear it. Not this time." He sounded as if he were speaking to someone else and not to Sarah; perhaps even to her father's portrait watching them from the wall.

She was afraid to look up in case Eddie changed his mind. Perhaps if he saw her face, looked into her eyes again, he might lose his nerve and withdraw his offer of honesty. So instead she watched her hands fidgeting between her knees. Her fingers looked long, pale, as if they belonged to someone else. She could barely feel them.

"Your mum couldn't have children. Not many people knew that, and those who did kept the information to themselves. Especially after you came along."

A clock began to tick somewhere just outside the prayer room: the sound was loud, regular; it sounded strange, false, like a cheap prop in a bad film. Sarah tried to focus on Eddie's voice, on the words that were circling her like flies around a corpse. Time seemed on the verge of stopping. Eddie's revelation held the power to do that, to alter her world.

"You're not a stupid girl, so I'm assuming you've picked up my meaning. One day your father brought you home. You were a newborn. He said that he'd taken you from some fuckin' junkie scumbag who was going to sell you on the streets for a fix. Nobody questioned him: he wasn't the kind of man to be questioned."

The sound of the clock faded. She felt like she'd heard that same idle ticking before, at several points during her life. *Déjà vu* flooded her, making her dizzy.

Eddie continued; his voice was so low now that she had to strain to hear him. "He pulled some strings and called in a lot of favours. The paperwork went through easily, and he made sure that it went missing afterwards, burned in a small office fire."

He paused, breathing deeply.

"This all coincided with a spell when your mother had to stay indoors for a few months. He'd hurt her badly and she was healing slowly. Next time she stepped outside she had a kid. Everyone called it a miracle, but they just called you Sarah."

Sarah was crying but she felt nothing. Her mind and body were empty. She was like a deep well whose contents had been drained, a dry riverbed in the middle of a massive drought...

"So there's no need to worry about apples and trees." The expansion was unnecessary, but she was glad to hear him say it, just to prove that she had not misheard or misunderstood his story. Until he said those words, forcing them home, she was unsure if this was some kind of hallucination, a daydream brought on by too much stress and irresponsible daytime drinking.

Sarah turned her head and looked at Eddie Knowles. He was staring at her, and had clearly been doing so for some time. All the time it took to tell her the truth – or at least this version of it. For the truth, she knew, was always, always relative. Nobody ever knew it all; they just possessed fragments, like the separate parts of a body seen through a torn shroud.

"That's it. That's all I know. I don't know where you came from or how he got you. It wasn't something you could ask him, even when he was drunk. He told me once that the angel had given you to him, but I didn't dare ask him to explain what he meant. I was too scared. We all were. Everyone was scared of the man, but at the same time we felt safe that he was on our side."

Sarah nodded. She understood completely. "That's how I felt, too. Even when he was hurting me, or when he beat up my mother. He still made me – made us *both* – feel safe. He protected us from the greater horrors of the world. He was like... I dunno, like some kind of buffer. But lately I'm starting to think that he might have been responsible for all those other horrors, the ones he pretended to save us from."

Eddie reached out and she took his hand. He squeezed, and she sensed a thousand apologies and a million regrets being sent through his fingertips and into her body, heading for her heart. But she was probably imagining it. Apologies – even unspoken ones – did not come easily to people like Eddie.

"I know," she said. "I know, Eddie, and it's OK. Really it is. You've told me now, so you can let yourself off the hook. You've let your secret out of the box."

He turned away and gazed at the small altar, and smiled at the tatty picture of Christ. "I'm not a religious man, but I always felt good here. Comfortable – you know? I've kept all this inside for so many years that it's been eating me up like a cancer. He was a cold, callous man, probably a murderer and certainly an abuser… but he was my friend. And you don't rat out your friends, especially if you're terrified of them." Eddie made a choked sound in his throat, as if he were holding back some kind of grief.

Sarah nodded. She looked again at her father's face on the wall. This time, when she met his gaze, he was not smiling, but she refused to look away. She glared back at him, challenging him to react. His mouth was a tight line drawn across the bottom of his wrinkled face and his eyes were burning – blazing – but it was a cold fire, a flame created by hatred.

Come on then, you fucker, she thought. Show yourself to me now. Give me a glimpse of you in that stupid hood, and I'll chase you right back to hell.

The unseen clock was no longer ticking. Somewhere, loudly, a door slammed. Laughter chased its own tail through the corridors, fading gradually to silence.

The shade of the man who had called himself Sarah's father remained hidden, as if it were now his turn to be afraid of her.

TWENTY-ONE

He was floating again. Drifting from up high and falling slowly back down towards the bed. The drug was wearing off and he was remembering who he was, where he was, and what he had been doing. The room came into focus around him; the walls, the ceiling he was moving away from, and the bed that clasped his body in a soft, padded embrace.

"Michael?" He wasn't sure why he'd said his brother's name, other than the fact that he felt as if the boy were close by. His scent hung on the air. The ghost of his voice vibrated like the memory of a scream in the atmosphere.

"No, Trevor. Michael isn't here. Your brother is dead, remember? You killed him."

Trevor sat up, rubbing the side of his head. The good feeling was gone now. He needed more of the heroin to retain it every time he took a little trip. In the past he had used drugs as a recreational pursuit but now he needed them to keep the world at bay.

"Come on, Trevor. Come back to me. You've been gone for a while, you know. I've waited patiently but now it's time to talk."

Who was that? Was there somebody else in his room? Trevor looked around, but there was nobody there. The wardrobe door was open and the plastic packing around his stage outfits had spilled out onto the floor, creased and torn. He recalled taking out some of the suits and trying them on, parading before the mirror and reciting some of his old show spiel. He had been performing for someone, that was clear – but for whom?

"Oh, come on. Pull yourself together."

Trevor turned around and looked at the mirror by the side of the bed. The man clothed in poor, trusting Derek's skin – the one who had called himself the Pilgrim – was sitting cross-legged behind the glass. He was naked. His body was smooth and hairless. Between his legs, which he now uncrossed, was just a flat area of pink flesh. He had no belly button.

"Oh, God..."

"Why do they always have to mention that name?" The Pilgrim smiled; his teeth were as white as bone. Derek's teeth had not been that clean, which meant that they possibly were shards of bone that had ruptured through the gums. "I mean, every time I meet one of you people you call out the name of God, as if it's real. As if he *exists*. Please, give me a break. There is no God, and I'm the closest thing you have to the Devil." He laughed. It sounded like drains backing up, or like the final rattling cry of someone choking to death.

"Who are you?" Trevor was now sitting upright, his legs hanging off the side of the bed. He realised that he was wearing a silly gold suit with no shirt beneath the jacket. The collars were wide and black; the buttons were gold-plated. The suit had cost him a small fortune.

"I told you, I'm your saviour. I'm the Pilgrim. How do you do."

Trevor blinked, but it did nothing to improve the view: the naked figure was still in the mirror, a roiling blackness stretching out behind him. Then, instantly, the blackness dispersed to reveal a view. The flat, empty landscape was littered with burnt machine parts, and in the distance something squatted part way up a slight rise. It was the hollow remains of a partially demolished concrete tower block, the windows empty of glass and the doorways yawning like black mouths. The walls were shattered, and pocked with gaping holes. The tower block looked like it had scaly legs, but that could have just been an illusion caused by the immense destruction of the building: maybe there were a couple of large trees crushed underneath its concrete bulk.

"That's my old place. It's kind of run down. I could do with some-where nicer." The Pilgrim's voice had no accent; it held no tone other than that of mild amusement. It was like a cartoon voice, something fake and contrived. Trevor had the distinct impression that the Pilgrim was merely a façade, and his words were toys.

Behind the broken-down tower block, with its slumped upper floors and spilled insides, the land rose to form a hill. At the summit of the hill there stood a smouldering tree. The spindly outline looked as if it had recently been burning and somebody had only just put out the fire. A long, slightly bulky shape hung in the branches, torn and twisted and unrecognisable. It looked like a dead monkey.

"I used to know her," said the Pilgrim. "She promised me a ride but when the time came she wasn't quite up to it."

The view faded, turning to grey. Empty space surrounded the Pilgrim, and Trevor stared at the figure as he began to rise. Derek's skin hung slack on the Pilgrim's bones and it shifted like a loosely wound sheet when he moved. The skin didn't quite fit; it was baggy on his form, slightly too large to contain him.

"What do you want from me?" Trevor remained seated on the bed. He was too afraid to move, yet something told him not to be. Some inner feeling convinced him that he would not be harmed.

"It's more a question of what we want from each other, my dear, dear friend." Another smile: a flash of those bone teeth. "I mean, we do both want something, don't we? And I believe that we can work together to achieve those needs. The thing is, you see, we want similar things. We both desire the end of Thomas Usher."

Trevor twitched at the sound of that name. Even now, after months of trying to rid himself of the hatred, he could not bear to think about Usher. The bastard had ruined him. He had turned up at a show in Bradford and revealed the truth about Michael's death – that Trevor had driven his brother to suicide; that his sexual demands had been so great they had consumed his little brother's sense of self-worth and destroyed him.

"I hate him," said Trevor. "Hate. Him."

The Pilgrim nodded. "Oh, yes. As do I. But he has something I want – something I *need*, actually. If I promise to help you kill him, you have to help me first."

Trevor inched towards the edge of the mattress, the soles of his feet settling lightly upon the floor. "What do you mean?" he stared at the unreflecting glass, at the naked man preening himself behind it. "What exactly do you want me to do?"

The Pilgrim stalked the short width of the mirror, running his hands along his body and swivelling his hips in an elaborate motion each time he turned to pace in the opposite direction. He made no sound as he walked. His step was light, and his movements seemed fluid and unnatural. Finally he turned to face Trevor. His lower half spun around first, followed by the upper part of his body. He grinned. His bald head shone, the skin wrinkling like wet tissue paper.

Trevor waited.

"I need you to get me out of here. Our mutual friend, Mr Usher, somehow managed to trap me here, in the space between mirrors, and I am unable to escape without the help of someone on your side of the glass." He shrugged. The stolen skin of his shoulders crept along his wasted muscles.

"Hang on… this is, well, it's crazy. You're telling me that there's a space behind all the mirrors in the world?"

The Pilgrim nodded. Then he sat back down on the ground, once again crossing his legs, calf over shin. "Clever boy."

"And," said Trevor, "and you're trapped there, behind the glass, inside the mirrors?"

Another slow nod; his eyes glistened. They changed through blue to brown, and then settled on a peculiar shade of grey. "You catch on fast." The sarcasm in his voice was practically hostile.

"I can't believe this."

The Pilgrim inhaled, his nostrils flaring. His features were bland and forgettable. "But you're seeing it now. Here I am, right in front of you, inside the mirror. You can't doubt that fact, can you? I mean, your eyes are showing you the truth of the situation."

"I've been on heroin," said Trevor. "Strong stuff, too. This could all be some kind of hallucination." He didn't even believe what he was saying, so why should this strange creature even listen to his feeble excuses?

"Oh, please..." The Pilgrim threw back his head and laughed silently. His narrow shoulders hitched and his chest inflated. This lasted for several minutes, and then he looked forward again, right at Trevor. He was not smiling. The laughter was gone; it had died. "Let's not get silly, now. I'm trying to remain calm, to keep you fully informed. Don't make me threaten you."

Trevor scuttled backwards, across the bed. "What do you mean? You can't hurt me. Not from behind there."

The Pilgrim nodded his bald head, slowly, deliberately. "And what, pray tell, did I do to your little friend?" This time when he smiled his teeth were pointed, tiny white triangles set into his pale pink gums.

"Listen. OK, just listen." Trevor pressed his body against the headboard. He felt stupid, helpless, and he wanted this to end. But he knew that he had started something he must now see through and nothing he could do or say was enough to halt the momentum. "You said something about getting rid of Usher for me. Killing him. Did you mean that?"

"Oh, that's better. Much better." The Pilgrim held out his arms, opened his hands, and showed Trevor the tiny mouths that had opened up on his palms. The two mouths were lined with identical white triangular teeth, just like the ones in his mouth. "I'm in the habit of drawing deals, making bargains, forming pacts." The three voices spoke in unison, the sound emanating from face and palms. "The deal I'm offering you is simple: you get me out of here and I help you to get Thomas Usher. As I've said, I want him too, but I promise that you can deliver the killing blow. Now how does that sound, Trevor Pumpkiss? Tell me how it sounds to you."

Trevor got to his feet and walked around the bed. He pulled the gold suit jacket tight across his chest, feeling confidence flooding through him. There was power here; he could feel it. Power to control, to conquer. Power to destroy. "That sounds good," he said, smiling. His fear was fading. This man – this Pilgrim – could be a valuable ally.

"Good, good." The Pilgrim stood, rearing up in a way that suggested he possessed no bones beneath that borrowed skin.

"Tell me what I need to do to get you out of there. Do I need to break the glass, or is it something more complicated? Rituals? Prayers? A sacrifice?" Trevor stood directly in front of his new friend, staring into his ever-changing eyes. "Tell me what I have to do to help."

"Oh, it's something more complicated than that. Yet it's also very simple." The Pilgrim reached out a hand and pressed his palm flat against the glass. The small mouth had vanished. The palm flattened against the glass, and then it grew and stretched until it was covering an area of mirror three times its original size.

"OK," said Trevor, placing his own palm over that of the Pilgrim, seeing it dwarfed by the other's giant hand. The glass felt cold; it was like ice. "So tell me."

"To put it crudely, I need blood. The living energy in human blood will allow me to become strong enough to break through. I have grown weak; my form has withered. I'm tired, so very tired. I have been stuck here for a long time – a span of time that isn't tied to your world's measure of days and years and centuries. Time doesn't exist on this side of the glass. I hear the constant ticking of clocks, but they are meaningless. They taunt me." He tilted his head to one side, narrowing his eyes. "Blood will replenish my resources. I only need a little. The blood of one person should just about do it, but without that I haven't quite got the strength to break out of here."

Trevor took his hand away from the glass. "Are you… are you a vampire?"

"What?" The Pilgrim roared with laughter. He staggered backwards, vanishing for a moment into the grey folds of nothingness, and then stumbled back towards the mirror. "Oh, Trevor. Bless you, Trevor. A vampire? No, they don't exist, you silly man." Slowly he managed to control his hysteria. Then, looking forlorn and regretful, he moved his face close to the glass. "I'm something much better than that."

Trevor couldn't move. His body was rigid, the muscles and tendons locked, fused together. "What are you, then?"

The Pilgrim stepped back, swiftly and theatrically. "Why, I'm an angel of course." He fluttered his eyelashes in a hideous caricature of seduction. A long, pointed tongue flicked out to moisten his lips. "I'm an angel who's come to help you."

Trevor stared intently into the mirror, trying to make out something else within the grey background. He could no longer see the littered landscape, or the fallen building, or the hill with the smoking tree. He did have a sense that there was something more here, behind and beyond the Pilgrim, but he was unable to discern what it was.

Reality, he thought in a momentary insight, was something that could be shaped. This was not a conceptual notion; it was true, it happened. This creature was the proof of it, and if Trevor stood at the Pilgrim's side he might be able to learn the magic and start to redefine his own reality.

The idea appealed to him greatly. It would be something to cling to, a dream to hold. And even if the dream in time proved to be a nightmare, at least it was something he could call his own.

He waited for nightfall, and then he prepared to leave the house. He had fixed up the last of his gear and taken the lot: one big hit, mainlined right into a fat vein. He felt good, invincible. He felt detached from it all.

"Be careful," said the Pilgrim, sitting beatifically behind the mirror. He looked like he was hovering above the ground; a perverted Buddha. The grey area above and below and around him was nothing but empty space, the grubby back-end of the universe.

"Don't worry. I'll bring you something back. Something good."

The Pilgrim raised a hand and flexed the tips of his fingers in a tiny waving gesture. The fingers did not bend at the joint.

Trevor left the house and drove to an area where prostitutes and rent boys prowled, canvassing the kerb for business. He trawled the infamous cluster of three or four streets, choosing the least popular stretch, the low end of the scale that was populated by junkies and fetishists and people who had long ago sold their basic humanity.

He pulled up at the kerb and waited with his lights on.

After five minutes someone approached, stepping casually out of the darkness. It was a boy, aged about sixteen or seventeen, and he was smoking a short hand-rolled cigarette. The boy had a skinhead haircut and was dressed in a tight black T-shirt and dirty blue jeans. He was too thin, malnourished; his ribs stuck out through the material of his T-shirt and his knees were like billiard balls covered in denim.

Trevor rolled down the car window and stared straight ahead.

"You looking for business?" The boy was leaning towards the window but not quite poking his head inside. He was canny, this one; he had street smarts.

"Depends what's on offer." Trevor was flying. He could barely control himself and felt like he might giggle at any minute, spoiling the act.

"Depends what you want," said the boy, nobody's fool. "This is entrapment, you know."

Trevor turned to the boy. He was grinning. His teeth were yellow and there were a few gaps in his gums. He had once been pretty, before the drugs had taken hold, and there still remained a sense of innocence behind his wasted features, even if it was badly corrupted. The boy's eyes were tiny, with dark shadows beneath. His cheeks were hollow, his skin sallow and waxy. He looked haunted. Or hunted. Perhaps both.

"Well?" The boy winked. It was a gesture that aged him, cracking open the carapace of youth to offer a glimpse of something darker, and in that moment Trevor made his decision.

"Back to my place. I want the lot: full sex, blow job, tromboning, a bit of rough domination." The words tasted like vomit. "The whole works."

"That's better." The boy walked around the front of the car, sashaying his pathetically narrow hips, and then opened the passenger door. He climbed in and placed his hand directly over Trevor's crotch. "That's much better. So drive on."

The journey lasted only minutes but it seemed to last forever. The boy worked his hand in Trevor's lap, making him hard, and with his other hand he turned on the radio. There was a cheesy pop tune playing and he sang along, his voice high and fragile, like that of choirboy. It was a beautiful voice, and its wavering notes made Trevor begin to doubt what he was about to do. Then he glanced down, at the boy's fingers in his zipper, and he regained his composure.

"We're here." He stopped the car and stared straight ahead, through the windscreen and into the bleak urban darkness. "We can get out now."

The boy removed his hand from Trevor's trousers, and he

wilted. It was an instant reaction, and Trevor knew that his erection would not return, not tonight.

They walked up to the house and Trevor paused on the stone steps. "Are you sure?"

The boy laughed. "Don't be daft, man. This is what I do for a living. But I can pretend to be unsure, or a virgin, if that's what you like. You got any drugs?"

Trevor took him inside and closed the door.

The house closed in around him. He was acutely aware of the mirror upstairs and the presence behind the glass. Hunger crawled along the hallway, creeping into the rooms and rolling across the walls and ceiling.

"Upstairs," he said, taking the boy's hand. "In my room."

The boy allowed himself to be led. "You got drink up there? I'm feeling a bit too sober."

"Yes. I have everything you want up there. Everything we need." He led the boy up the stairs, along the hall, and into his room.

"Wow," said the boy. "This is a nice place. Cool mirror. How does it do that? Is it a trick?" he walked straight to the mirror, slipping off his T-shirt and dropping it to the floor. His body was painfully thin, like a doll's torso. There were faint scars on his back; a black rose tattoo was pasted onto his left shoulder. His collarbones were sharp as cleavers.

"Yeah, it's a trick." Trevor stood at the door, afraid to go any further.

"You a magician or summat? Those suits are fierce." He motioned towards Trevor's gold jacket, and then the open wardrobe door and the stage outfits that lolled from the gap like drunkards. "You famous? You been on telly? I've never fucked anyone from telly before." The boy began to undo his trousers, slipping them down his thin legs.

"Hello there," said the Pilgrim, appearing in the black glass. "And what do they call you, my boy?"

To give him his due, the boy reacted fast. He pulled up his

jeans and turned to flee, all in a single motion. He did not scream. Even in extremis, he realised that it would be wasted energy, that there was nobody around to hear. He took a step – just one – and then he halted. The skin of his face went tight, as if someone had clamped a huge bulldog clip onto the back of his head. The flesh began to slough from the bone, but unlike Derek's flesh it came away in chunks. Blood sprayed and hung in the air, clogging into globules like fluid spilled in zero gravity.

Trevor could not bear to look but he was unable too look away. He stared at the boy, at the clots of blood dangling in the air, and he felt more alive than he had in years.

The human body holds eight to ten pints of blood, and Trevor watched in awe as every single speck of the boy's blood was drained from his body. The blood gathered above him, forming a surreal crimson reflection, and then it moved sluggishly towards the mirror, dropping down as the boy's exsanguinated corpse flopped to the floor.

The Pilgrim opened his arms. His eyes were closed.

The blood-image spread and flattened and pressed against the glass, and then was slowly absorbed into the Pilgrim's world. It smothered his body, writhing against him like a dark red sheet caught in a strong wind, and then it entered his body through the pores in the flesh he wore.

This last part of the process took only seconds, and when it was over Trevor could barely believe what he had seen.

"Ah, that's better." The Pilgrim opened his eyes. They were deep red, like orbs of blood. He licked his lips, and his tongue was also red, stained dark from the boy's juices. "That's much better." The skin seemed to fit him now, perfectly; it clung to his form as if he had been born wearing it.

"What now?" Trevor's voice was weak and raspy as he struggled to gulp down air.

"One more thing." The Pilgrim shuddered. "Just one more thing."

"Anything," said Trevor.

The Pilgrim smiled shyly, shrugging his shoulders. "This might sound trite, but you need to believe."

"What?" Trevor took a step back, opening his hands and shaking his head. "What do you mean?"

"I'm like Tinkerbell," said the Pilgrim, grinning. His mouth was as wide as that of a shark. His bone teeth shimmered. "I need you to believe."

"I already believe in you." Trevor stepped forward, occupying the space he'd just vacated. "How could I not?"

"No," said the Pilgrim. "You misunderstand me. You don't have to believe in me. I already believe in myself. I need you to believe that I can step through this mirror and enter your personal reality. *Believe* that I can come over there and join you. You see, my friend, it's all about belief. Everything is about belief. Without it, we have nothing. Belief is the glue that holds the universe together, and I need some of that glue from you. Believe that I can come through the mirror, and I will. It's that simple."

Trevor was shaking. His eyes were filled with tears. "I do," he said. "I believe."

"Are you sure?" said the Pilgrim. "Are you really, really sure? I need you to be certain."

Trevor nodded. He couldn't speak. His face had turned to stone.

"Thank you, friend," said the Pilgrim. "Thank you very much." He sounded like a low-rent Elvis Presley impersonator. He even did a little shimmy, shuffling his feet and grinding his pelvis in a tight little circle. Then he flicked out his hands at waist level, waggling his fingers as if he were playing the piano. "Uh-huh, huh, huh."

"I believe," repeated Trevor, staring at the amazing being before him. And he did; he really did.

Then, without further preamble, the Pilgrim stepped casually through the mirror and into the room.

TWENTY-TWO

Benson wasn't due at her place until after eleven, but Sarah already felt fidgety and restless. The events of the day were weighing down on her like a sack of offal and the news she'd received from Eddie Knowles stunk at least as bad as what was crammed inside that proverbial sack.

So Detective Inspector Emerson Doherty wasn't her real father. The thought made her feel weird: not exactly relieved, yet not unhappy either. It just sat there, the truth, like a dead elephant in the room, rotting away before her eyes. She could handle it, just about, but what she failed to balance was the corresponding realisation that her mother had not given birth to her.

Sarah loved her mother. She always had done, and this wouldn't change a thing regarding how she felt. It was simply a matter of adjusting, of redefining the boundaries of their relationship in a similar way to when her mother had been put in the rest home.

Sarah didn't even want to start thinking about who her real parents were. That way there was only madness. That road led only to despair and disappointment, and maybe even tragedy. No; she didn't want to think about that at all.

She sipped her tea, tasting the whisky she'd poured into the cup along with the brew. It warmed her, made her feel comforted. But wasn't it the people in your life who were supposed to do that for you, and not alcohol? She was aware that she was starting down another bad road, one lined with the corpses of drunks and losers. She didn't want to go there, not ever. If she did, it meant that her father – God, she had to stop thinking of him as that: he was just Emerson now – had won the battle for her soul.

Now there's a melodramatic thought. She smiled, wondering what had prompted it. Sarah wasn't given to hysteria: she usually tried to keep a lid on things and react calmly and realistically. She didn't even believe in the concept of a human soul, and she certainly had no time for God.

"Fuck you," she said, to the empty room, to the walls her father – no; *Emerson* – had decorated, to the entire house he had left her, just to ensure that his cold, dead fingers were still stuck in her life. "Fuck you, old man." She drank her tea. It was hot. The whisky burned her throat.

Sarah had already been hard at work. When she'd returned home from her shift she'd changed into some old jeans and a stained shirt and pulled everything out of the bureau in the living room. There were bundles of envelopes with red elastic bands around them, tattered cardboard Kodak photo wallets, more bills and receipts and hand-written chits from her father's time touring with the band. Then, tucked away inside an old Swan Vestas matchbox she had discovered a small key. It was silver, with a looped handle, and looked more like a decorative pendant than a key that might work in an actual lock.

She held the key in her palm now, as she finished off her whisky-laced tea. It was cold; the metal refused to warm up, even to her body temperature. That fact alone was pretty weird, and it made her feel like Emerson was still holding on to the key, from beyond the grave.

"OK," she said, standing. "Let's do this."

Sara left the room and walked along the hallway of the old period house. There were a lot of rooms in the property – the roof
space had been converted decades ago so that her mother could
inhabit the entire upper floor; Sarah's old bedroom was located
on the first floor, along with the master bedroom, the guest room
she currently slept in, the family bathroom and a small sitting
room; the ground floor contained the main reception or living
room, a small toilet and washroom, and the enormous kitchen.
Then, down a further set of stone stairs, there was the cellar.
Emerson had loved to spend time in the cellar: it was *his* space;
a combined den and office facility.

The rest of Emerson's stuff was stored down there. Dusty files
pertaining to old cases that he'd managed to copy and smuggle
out of the station, his personal files, which he ran concurrently
with the official ones; his notebooks and other scribbled mus-
ings; his old guitars and harmonicas. It was Emerson's lair: three
separate underground rooms divided up by thick stone walls,
with bare bulbs hanging from the dusty ceiling.

Sarah stood at the top of the stone cellar steps, feeling like she
was invading his space. She had never been allowed down
there, into his personal space, when she was younger, and even
now, as an adult, she was afraid to descend. She had been hoping to put this off indefinitely, but circumstances had dictated
that she visited the bastard's hole. "Just a little look, Emerson,"
she whispered, pleased at how well she was growing accustomed to using his name rather than the false title of father. "A
wee peek into the belly of the beast."

The lights were on in the hallway but it was still dim. Outside,
the night was deep and dark and threatening; inside, the weak illumination did little to stave off the feeling of being observed. The
lights flickered. He was there, alongside her, trying to scare her.

"Oh, no, she said. "No you don't, big man. I don't scare that
easily – not anymore. You'll have to do better than that.

She reached out a hand and pushed the door at the top of the steps. It swung inward, slowly, stirring up thin streams of dust that hung in the air like fine webbing. The door was a cheap timber item with flimsy central panels. Its construction was lightweight, and it felt light as balsa wood in her grip.

She leaned over and flicked the light switch. The bulb in the ceiling, halfway down the flight of stone steps, did not respond: it was dark down there. Of course it was. The house, along with its dead owner, was toying with her, trying to spook her, probing for a reaction. It was obvious.

The steps led down into darkness. The stairwell was narrow, barely wider than her body, and she knew that she would have to go down in the dark if she were to go down there at all. Alone. In the dark. Under the house.

Towards the very centre of the spider's web.

She blinked. Then she peered downwards, picking out each individual stair in the gloomy little passage.

Right there, on the bottom step, sat a figure. Sarah could only see it from behind, but the figure was wearing a long black robe. There was a flash of white above the robe, a loose silken hood worn over the head.

Behind her, the lights flickered again. "Not scared, Emerson," she said, lying to him. Lying to herself. "Not even close." She took a small step forward, dropping her left foot onto the second step down.

Below her, shrouded in gloom, the figure slowly began to turn.

"Fuck. Off." She took another step, heading down, ready to confront whatever sat there, waiting so patiently for her to pay a visit.

The kitchen lights flickered one more time, and then they went out for what must have been less than a second. When they came back on, the figure was no longer there. The bottom step was empty. Yet, strangely, Sarah still felt that she was not alone in the narrow, cramped stairwell.

She moved down the steps a little faster than she had done so far. She had the feeling that someone was behind her now, following her, and perhaps even reaching forward to shove her between the shoulder blades, causing her to fall. She hurried, trying to throw off the sense of paranoia. Then, at the bottom of the steps, she finally allowed herself to turn back and look. At the top, beyond the open door, the light was bright but barely made it over the threshold. It was as if the light was unable to penetrate some kind of invisible barrier; that it was not welcome down here, in the depths of the house.

She turned to the second door. It was unlocked. The key was in the lock. With admirably steady hands, Sarah reached out and turned the handle. It clicked loudly, and then the door swung silently open. She remembered that it used to scrape on the stone floor; that was how she always knew that Emerson was down here, and it had allowed her to breathe more easily. Perhaps he'd planed half an inch of wood off the bottom of the door, or was this yet another little trick?

She stepped inside, reaching around the opening to turn on the lights. The electrical connection was allowed to work: the lights came on, the naked bulbs shedding harsh illumination onto the old, scarred stone.

She pushed closed the door behind her: this time its bottom edge scraped loudly across the stone floor. She smiled. "Very clever, Emerson."

The cellar was cluttered with old furniture – free-standing shelf units, battered chests of drawers and other assorted items that her parents had been either unwilling or unable to throw out. Tall filing cabinets stood along the walls like waiting officers. Some of the wall shelves were fixed high up near the ceiling, and whatever had been stored there was now covered in a thick layer of dirt. The place looked like it hadn't been cleaned for years. When she was a girl, Emerson had always seemed to be dragging cleaning apparatus down here – bucket, brush and mop, vacuum cleaner, assorted rags for polishing – but it seemed that his old habits had died long before him.

"Messy boy," she whispered. "What happened to all that fastidious neatness? Did it vanish when your mind snapped completely? Did you find other things to obsess over instead, you mad bastard?"

In one of the corners something stirred. It sounded like a wet length of rope being pulled slowly across the stone floor, but when Sarah glanced in that direction there was nothing to be seen. More games; more tricks to try and scare her. But it wasn't going to work. She was onto him, and his pathetic distractions were just so much smoke and mirrors.

Sarah passed through the first cellar – the main underground room – and into a secondary chamber. This one was smaller, narrower, and even more cluttered with objects. She saw what she wanted immediately. Against one wall (the rear external wall) was an old writing desk. Its top was crammed with stuff: pens, notepads, an old rusty tin cup, some kind of sports trophy and another model from Emerson's vast collection of out-of-date twin cassette players. Above this desk, on a wooden shelf bolted to the wall, there was a row of audio cassettes.

"There you are." Sarah walked over to the desk and pulled out the chair. She leaned over and selected a few tapes. Most of them were Emerson's yearly compilations, containing his favourite songs from the particular year noted on the sticker, but between these tapes, every fourth or fifth, cassette, were tapes similar to the one she'd been given by her mother. Rather than a year and subtitle, each of these other tapes had a year and two initials written on the faded, peeling labels.

"What did you do?" But Sarah had a feeling that she already knew.

She plugged in the old player and sat down at the desk. The first tape she slipped into the machine held the identifying information, A.M. 1977.

She pressed play.

Again there was a long gap before the first track began. Beneath the hissing of static and the muffled sounds from within and outside whichever room had been used to make the recording, Sarah could make out something else. Just before some up-tempo stomping anthem filled her ears, she heard what sounded like someone coughing.

Sarah rewound the tape.

She pressed play.

She turned the volume right up, so that the static was almost deafening.

The sound she had heard was a voice. It was whispering, and the words were bleeding into each other, but she knew it was her father – she knew it was *Emerson* speaking into the microphone. Not her father. Emerson, just Emerson.

"Manchester. Small, underfed, blonde hair, brown eyes. Easy."

Sarah's throat was dry; she felt sick. The cellar seemed to become smaller, the ceiling lowering and the walls closing in. The air was mouldy, it stunk of old decay.

She played the intro again.

"Manchester. Small, underfed, blonde hair, brown eyes. Easy."

She remembered what Eddie Knowles had told her about her father's vigilante activities. How he and a handful of friends had taken career criminals off the streets and dealt out their own brand of old-school justice. Then, Eddie had said, things went too far. Someone was killed – did he say a dealer, or a junkie? She couldn't recall, but the detail wasn't important. What mattered was the fact that things had... escalated.

Eddie said that the group had stopped after that. They had gone back to their card schools and sex parties. But what if Emerson had been unable to stop? What if he liked it too much to even consider calling time on his out-of-office activities?

She imagined him walking the streets of some quiet town late at night, after playing a gig with his band. The other members would have gone somewhere to drink – a pub, a club, or back to some grotty digs in the rough part of town. But Emerson went for a little walk. Then, Sarah thought, had he picked someone up? A prostitute, a junkie, a housebreaker? Had he walked with them back to his rented van – there were a lot of receipts from van rental companies in the bureau upstairs – and taken them somewhere?

Then what happened? What did he do after that?

How had he killed them?

And later, after he had met his angel, had he then turned his attention to children, having tired of preaching to the converted? Had he seen their criminal futures laid out before them, then taken them from the streets and opened up their skulls to let the evil he had seen there out into the open air?

She thought about the words at the beginning of the tape.

Then she played the tape again. This time she played it all; she fast-forwarded through the songs and listened to the spaces between, the interstitial moments between numbers. She found a pair of headphones in a crammed drawer and put them on, and the sound came through even better, clearer.

Her father's voice. No! Emerson. It was *Emerson's* voice.

"Manchester. Small, underfed, blonde hair, brown eyes. Easy."

A song by The Sweet.

"Back of the van. Back of the head."

The Sex Pistols.

"Empty shop. Straight-backed chair.

Bread.

"The hood. The blood.

Emerson, Lake and Palmer.

"The blood, the blood, the blood, the blood..."

Sarah's hands were shaking now; at last they were shaking. She turned off the player and ejected the tape, sliding it back into its plastic box. Then she put all of the cassettes – every single one – back on the shelf and sat back in the chair. She looked around, at the gloomy little cellar space, and wanted to cry – but who would she cry for? Unrepentant criminals who had been murdered by a jaded, possibly insane copper? The copper himself, twisted so far out of shape by the job, his inability to father a child, and the fact that all of his friends were either bent coppers or thieves and killers?

Who could she cry for?

The little girl who had been rescued, then subjected to a life of torment? The little girl with no daddy, who desperately wanted to please the substitute daddy she fucking hated, loathed, despised with a passion that made her feel as if she, too, were losing her mind?

Across the room, on the far wall, there was a framed photograph. It was black and white, held behind a dusty frame. Emerson – the figure she'd been seeing for days now, stalking her, keeping an eye on her progress, guiding her to this place, here and now: sitting on a kitchen chair with his hands resting flat against his thighs, wearing a long black robe and a delicate white hood.

She thought about all the things. All the things he had done. To her, and to her mother. All the dirty, rotten fucking things he'd done to them both, saying all the time that he loved them and wanted only to protect them from the filth of the world, the terrible things people did to one another outside these walls, these old stone walls cemented in blood.

All the bad things…

The dead bad things the broken world had to offer.

Then, as she watched, and that phrase resonated deep inside her head, the figure in the picture stood and walked away, vanishing off the edge of the photograph.

The frame was empty. It had never contained a photograph.

Sarah turned around, her eyes aching, and watched as that same figure – the one she'd seen reflected in the dirty glass in a cheap frame – walked out of the room and through the main cellar. She heard the scraping of the door across the stone floor. Then his footsteps sounded on the stairs. She held her breath while he walked across the ceiling directly above her: through the kitchen, then on into the hall, and finally stopping in the living room. He chuckled once, cynically. Just like he always did when he was alive.

Suddenly, drawing her attention from the ceiling, a drawer slid open in the desk. It banged against her right leg, and when she looked down she saw that the compartment had been hidden until now, disguised by the design of the desk.

Hidden; like so much else it was hidden from view.

A secret drawer.

A secret place.

A secret.

Inside the draw was a wooden box about the size and shape of a toaster. The paint had all flaked from the box, and it was old and weathered. The box looked very old.

Sarah picked up the box and placed it on the desktop, staring at it. She ran her hands across the smooth, ruined surface of the box, and then tried the lid. It was locked, sealed up tight.

Without even pausing she took the little silver key from her other hand. She had been gripping it all along, and had almost forgotten that it was there.

The key fitted the lock perfectly.

She turned the key and the lock mechanism slowly went into action. It stuck a little, but she jiggled the key and finally the teeth bit. The lid popped open half an inch. Leaving the key in the lock, Sarah opened the lid fully. Inside, on a lining of white silk – like that hood, that horrible white hood – were several objects.

The first object was the upper part of a human skull, with two smooth-edged holes in the frontal lobe.

The second object was actually a bunch of other objects tied up with string. Human finger bones: ten of them, the small bones of eight fingers and two thumbs.

The final object Sarah at first thought was an old-fashioned wooden-handled drill. The type of thing people had used, long before the advent of power tools, to put holes in various building materials. On further perusal, once she took the object out of the box, she realised that the drill had been modified. It looked *different*, unlike any kind of conventional construction tool she had ever seen. It was not something a workman would use to build a cabinet or make a hole for a screw or a plug in a hard wall.

The handle was wide; it had a large wedge-shaped top end. And the drill bit was thick with just a corkscrewed tip rather than the full length.

It looked… well, to Sarah it looked *lethal*. More like a weapon than a tool.

The drill, she realised, had been tweaked for a purpose other than the one for which it had been originally intended.

This drill, she thought, with her heart thundering in her chest and hot, burning bile rising at the back of her throat, had been used to put the holes in the portion of human skull she'd found nested alongside it in the old wooden box.

The drill… This drill…

It was a device used for amateur trepanning.

TWENTY-THREE

Trevor was cracking up; he was losing his mind. That was, if he hadn't lost it already, over the last few months. Since his life had fallen to pieces.

He was standing outside, on the corner of his street, just trying to get some perspective on what had happened over the last few days, during which he'd seen some unusual sights: a malevolent presence had murdered his pick-up, consumed the blood of a rent boy, and then stepped blithely through a mirror and into Trevor's room.

Things like this were not normal; they didn't usually happen, not to people like him. Men like him did not usually hide skinned bones and drained bodies under their beds and converse with fallen angels.

People like him... and what, exactly, did he mean by that? Ex-stage show psychics with a penchant for little boys? An ageing queen so repressed, so held hostage by his own desires that he could barely even function like a proper human being? A rapist who was responsible for the tragic death of his own brother? Is that what he meant? Is that what he was? The ultimate definition of *people like him*?

Did he even deserve to be called human at all, or was he a lot more like that fucking creature, the one who called himself the

Pilgrim, than he would care to admit? Was he really just some kind of monster?

He held his mobile phone loosely in one hand, trying to decide whether or not to use it. The phone was a modern, lightweight model but it felt heavy, like his guilt. He looked at his other hand, the one formed into a tight fist. Did he dare open it and make use of what was held inside?

He'd taken the folded piece of paper from Derek's discarded clothes; it had been in his rear trouser pocket. After the Pilgrim had stolen Derek's skin, the clothing remained in a heap on the floor. Trevor had bundled it up and taken it out of the bedroom with the intention of burning it somewhere, but Derek's words had sounded inside his head, taunting him:

I have a slip of paper in my pocket with Sammy's address and a code word written on it.

A code word, a safety word: something to inform whoever answered the phone when he rang that Trevor was OK, that he was legit, and Derek had vouched for him. It was a good idea, really, and Trevor applauded Sammy the scumbag's attitude towards keeping his business under wraps. This was heavy stuff; if anyone found out it could mean a lot of people went to the wall. Trevor had moved in these circles before, so he knew the kind of high-ranking officials and media high-flyers with whom he shared his particular fetish.

No, that was wrong. It was more than a fetish. That word belittled what he felt. It reduced it to the level of a mere sexual peccadillo. Trevor's desires were intense; they had formed him, making him the man that he was. He had gone through the fire because of them, and walked out the other side with the soles of his feet smoking…

He opened his hand.

The slip of paper was crumpled into a ball, but it began to loosen even as he watched. He helped it along, opening it up with his other hand. A small paper flower, a bloom of damnation…

He smoothed out the paper onto his palm, where it curled up at the corners like one of those silly fortune-telling cellophane fish he and Michael had loved to consult as boys, and read the telephone number. It had a local area code: it couldn't be too far away. He could make it there and back in an hour or two, and then return home to face the Pilgrim with his mind emptied of the turmoil that now bubbled away beneath his skull.

Trevor tapped the number into his mobile and waited. The ringing sound echoed in his ear, sounding like it was miles away.

"What." The voice was quiet, and it held a subtle note of threat.

"Hello… my name's Trevor. I was given this number by Derek."

"I don't know any Derek." The words were anything but final: they were an invitation to prove himself.

"He told me to call. He said that you were expecting me."

"I said I don't know any Derek." Again, the man did not hang up the phone. He waited for Trevor to continue.

"He gave me a code word."

Silence.

Trevor looked again at the piece of paper. The word was scrawled untidily beneath the number and a partial address: *Newsome's Electrics*. It was an odd word, but no doubt it meant something to somebody. Unless it was just a phrase chosen at random, perhaps from a book or newspaper that might have been lying around at the time.

"Hummingbird."

The silence stretched. Then, just as Trevor was about to give up, the man spoke: "OK. So you're Trevor. When do you want to come?"

"Well," said Trevor. His throat was dry, But it was not with fear; oh, no. It was dry with passion. "How about now?"

Again there was a lengthy silence. Trevor listened to the emptiness on the other end of the line, trying to make out noises in the background. He heard what sounded like a door slamming, then music from a radio. He couldn't identify the tune, but it sounded familiar.

"OK. You got lucky. I'm free right now, so you have a window. An hour, that's all, and it'll cost you double because of the short notice."

Trevor had no idea what the going rate might be, so could not even guess what it would be times two. "That's fine. Money isn't a problem."

"As a customer recommended by Derek, you can set up a tab. We like our people to come back, so we're good to you the first time." There was humour behind the voice; the man must be smiling.

"Where do I go? I can come right over."

"The Bestwick estate. You know it?"

Trevor nodded, then realised that the man couldn't see him. "Yes. Yes, I know it."

"Newsome's Electrics. It's a shop on the Precinct – the only one that isn't boarded up. The recession, you know. Only our kind of business is recession-proof." Again, Trevor detected a lightness of tone, and he half expected the man to start laughing.

"I'll be there in about twenty minutes."

The man hung up the phone.

Trevor called a taxi firm located a few streets away and told the controller to send a car to pick him up on the corner. In less than five minutes it arrived, the sullen driver staring through the windscreen and paying little attention as Trevor climbed into the back of the vehicle.

"Bestwick," he said. "Drop me off at the Precinct."

The driver grunted and pulled away from the kerb, his meaty hand reaching out to press a button on the digital meter. Voices faded in and out of audibility on the in-car radio; the controller back at the office giving out instructions and calling out for the occasional fare. Traffic was quiet, so they reached their destination in less than fifteen minutes.

"Thanks," said Trevor, passing his money through the toughened Plexiglas partition and pressing it into the driver's sweaty palm. The driver grunted again. "You were great company." He got out and watched the cab drive slowly away.

It was dark at the Precinct. Most of the street lights had been vandalised and a lot of the nearby houses and flats were empty, with their windows boarded over and metal security shutters bolted across the doors. The only obviously occupied building on the short row of derelict shop fronts that formed the Precinct was the one with Newsome's Electrics painted in crude lettering below the eaves. The shop was tiny, stuck between an empty Chinese takeaway and what had once been a hardware shop (remnants of faded posters in the shattered windows advertised power tools and timber treatments).

"Fuck," said Trevor, thinking that he might have been foolish to come here. This was a dangerous area. Anything could happen. Nobody knew where he was, and there were no friends left to care about him anyway.

Glancing around, taking in the dark houses and the broken-down shops, he shuffled towards Newsome's Electrics. High-security wire mesh had been installed over the window glass. The door was barred by a sturdy iron gate with an intercom fixed to the wall at the side of the entrance.

Trevor approached the door. Light spilled down from a room above the shop, but the lower floor was in darkness. He reached out and pressed the buzzer, not allowing himself time to think, to back out and run. He needed what was being sold here; he needed it like never before. He hoped that one of them might look just a little bit like his brother, like Michael. That would make all the risk worthwhile.

The intercom buzzed with static, and then a voice cut through the storm: "Aye."

Trevor leaned in close, suddenly bashful. "Hummingbird," he said, slowly, enunciating each syllable so that he would not have to say it again.

A buzzer droned and then there was a loud clicking noise. "Pull on the gate." Then the intercom went dead.

Trevor reached out and gripped the metal uprights of the security gate. He pulled lightly, then harder when there was no initial response to his pressure. The gate snickered open. He pulled it further and stepped onto the lower of two concrete steps that led up to the front door. The buzzer intonated a second time and the main door popped open. Trevor, glancing over one shoulder, pushed open the door, and stepped inside. He pulled the gate shut behind him, and once he had moved into the dark hall beyond the entrance, he did the same with the front door.

Ahead of him was a set of stairs. Along the short hallway was a doorway, which he presumed led to the shop. He was unsure of what he should do, where to go, so he just stood there for a moment, caught between two worlds and feeling slightly absurd about his predicament.

Light bled down the stairwell as a door on the upper storey was opened. "Up here." It was the same voice from the phone and the intercom: it even seemed to contain the same static hiss. But that was silly. Trevor knew that his mind was playing tricks and if he wasn't careful he would come close to a state of panic.

He started to climb the stairs, heading towards the open door. Yellow light spilled onto the worn carpet and down the steep staircase, lighting his way. It was like following a trail of dull fire, or a pathway formed by embers. Again, Trevor tried to clear his head of these silly thoughts. He was romanticising the situation, and if he continued to do so he would ruin it. Part of the fun, after all, was the seediness of the encounter. He was self-aware enough to know that, and honest enough to admit to his weakness.

His fear evaporating and his confidence growing, blooming like a flower in his chest, Trevor stepped onto the landing and walked through the open door.

"Hi there." A large man sitting on an old Raleigh Chopper bicycle smiled at him. He was smoking a joint. A thick cloud of smoke hung in the air; evidence that the roll-up was not his first of the evening. "Nice jacket. You must be Trevor. I'm Sammy."

"Hello, Sammy. Yes, that's right. I'm Trevor. Thanks for seeing me at such short notice."

The man grinned around his spliff. "Oh, that's OK. Isn't it, Don?" He turned his head and looked at a battered leather sofa that was pushed up against the wall near the wide entrance to a small kitchenette, his greasy ponytail swinging like a fat rat's tail.

"Aye," said the tallish, well-built man on the sofa. He was holding a beer can and blinking as if he'd only just woken up. "No bother. No bother at all."

"Thanks," Trevor said again, set off kilter by the men's lazy attitude. From the telephone conversation he'd had he expected them to be more defensive, perhaps even to put on a clichéd hard man act. But they were just a couple of dopers, getting high on their own gear.

"So," Sammy held his joint between his fingers. He stared at Trevor. "What do you need this evening? What can we get you to dampen your fire?"

The man on the sofa – Don, was it? – giggled softly.

"I was told... Derek told me that... well, that you could supply something to suit my needs." His lips were moving but they felt awkward, like rubber: two water-filled condoms glued to his jaw.

"No, no, no," said Sammy. "I need you to be more *specific*. You have to tell me what you want, mate. That's how it works, you see. I don't know you, even though our mutual *fiend*," – he laughed here, proud of his little quip – "Derek has introduced you. That's why you have to tell me up front what you want. Let's just say I'm paranoid." He smiled. His teeth were yellow, the gums receding. His cheeks were bruised with broken capillaries. "I'm sure you understand."

They were a suspicious lot, these people. But Trevor could understand their reticence; perhaps if he'd been more circumspect himself, he might not have been exposed as a fraud and a child-molester by that bastard Usher.

"Well?" Sammy wheeled the Chopper backwards and forwards across a small area of floor. He pretended to rev the handlebars, like a small child playing motorbikes.

"I'd like some chicken. Some young chicken. I want to have a little boy." He licked his lips. "Is that honest enough for you? Do I pass the fucking test, friend?" Anger surged through him for an instant, but then faded. He was too horny to maintain his rage.

"That's *lovely*," said Sammy, revving his bike handles. "That's just too fucking perfect." He grinned, flashing his dirty teeth.

Don, over on the sofa, began to laugh. It was a soft sound, almost like weeping. Trevor glanced over just to check, and saw the man's face shining beneath the cheap lighting in the cramped room. He winked at Trevor, shaping the fingers of his right hand to resemble a gun and cocking the trigger of his thumb.

Trevor looked away, feeling like he needed a shower. The sense of collusion between himself and these men was making him feel sick.

"This way," said Sammy, hauling his bulk off the bike frame. "Downstairs. We keep them in a nice basement room, where they can be all safe and sound. They're my chickens, and I like to call it the Roost." He waddled towards the small kitchen area, where there was another door Trevor had failed to see until now.

Trevor followed. He glanced again at Don, but the man had slumped over onto his side to sprawl on the cushions, stoned.

"Just through here and down the other stairs," said Sammy. His huge backside was barely contained by his torn, faded jeans: an acre of buttock cleavage hung out above the beltline.

Trevor was led through the door and down a flight of wooden stairs, these ones seemingly constructed by some cowboy builder who had no clue regarding the nature of structural stability. Trevor clung to the banister as they descended, and as Sammy's bulk caused the whole staircase to twist and shudder, he prayed that he would make it to the basement level in one piece.

At the bottom of the stairs was a large open space with a concrete floor and soundproofed walls. Along a narrow corridor Trevor could just about make out the edge of what looked like a steel cage. He could hear quiet weeping. Somebody was singing – it was a traditional nursery rhyme: *Three Blind Mice*. The effect created by the combination of crying and the high-pitched singsong voice was eerie, as if Trevor had stepped into an obscure antechamber of hell. He fought a brief but intense battle between fear and desire.

Desire won. It always did.

"It's along this way, Trevor." Sammy waddled towards the corridor. At first it looked like he would be too big to make it but to Trevor's surprise he managed to fit through the gap. "Keep coming."

Trevor walked across the concrete floor. His hands were flexing, making fists. His mouth was bone dry. He followed the big man along the short corridor, glancing to the side and into an unoccupied cell. There was a single bed shoved against the wall, and a coil of rope on the floor.

The singing stopped abruptly.

At the other end of the corridor the room opened out. There was a huge plasma television screen with an inbuilt DVD player mounted on the main wall. *Spongebob Squarepants* was running with the sound turned off. A low table beneath the huge screen held an array of video equipment: several monitors, a computer keyboard, some kind of control box. Trevor glimpsed the inmates of the cells in fuzzy monochrome before he saw them in the flesh, but as he properly entered the large room he turned and stared at them through the bars.

As far as cells went, these ones at least gave a nod in the direction of comfort. Each one contained a double bed with silk sheets, a table and a chair, a recliner, a wash basin and toilet, and a double wardrobe. There were framed paintings of nudes hanging on the concrete walls and the steel bars were draped with what looked like Christmas streamers. There were six barred cells built against the wall, with a boy in each. The boys were relaxing. Some of them were watching the television, staring blankly at Spongebob's undersea antics, and others were lying on their beds looking up at the ceiling. One of them was reading a book – Trevor stared at the cover and saw that it was a Roald Dahl novel.

"Welcome to the Roost," said Sammy, spreading his arms wide and smiling at the boys.

None of the boys smiled back. They ignored the two men in their midst, allowing the moment to wash over them. They were used to this, these boys, these chickens; it was just another day in the terrible prison cell of their life.

"Take your pick. It's quite a varied collection; the united colours of Benetton. I pride myself on diversity." Sammy, smiling, stepped to the side and approached the bank of monitors. He pressed a button on the control panel and the upstairs room, with his friend, Don asleep on the sofa, appeared briefly on one of the small screens.

The boys were beautiful. They were immaculately clean and dressed in expensive clothes. No two of them looked the same. There was a blonde one, a dark one, a vaguely oriental one, a black one, an Asian one and a strange pale one who just stood in the corner staring out through the bars.

This last one unnerved Trevor. The boy stepped forward as he watched, moving close to the bars. His small hands came up and gripped one of the bars, the thin white fingers snaking around it. His hair was mousey brown, his eyes were bland, and he was very thin. He looked blank, a clean slate, as if nothing in the world had touched him. There was nothing behind his eyes, just a vast indifference, and Trevor found himself backing away from his infinite gaze.

"Our newest acquisition," said Sammy. "You don't like him? He doesn't say much, I'll give you that. But he's pretty."

Trevor shook his head. "I like that one," he said, pointing to the slight blonde boy in the end cell. The one who – if Trevor squinted and looked at just the right angle – looked a little like his dead brother. "Yes, that one will do me just fine, friend."

The boy smiled like he was obviously taught to. His slack lips curled up to reveal white teeth, a small, moist pink mouth. But his eyes... his eyes were terrified.

"You have an hour," said Sammy. He walked to the cell door and opened it. The boy stepped back, not quite cowering but clearly wanting to curl up into a ball on the floor. "He's good, this one." Sammy's bulk blocked the entrance to the cell. "He's one of our most popular chickens. He cries at the right times and he likes to call you Daddy."

"I don't want that," said Trevor, moving across the room. He was aware of the pale, silent boy watching him. Those dead eyes were upon him, creating a cold spot at the small of his back. "But I would like to call *him* Michael."

Sammy stepped to the side and Trevor walked into the cell. The door clicked shut behind him and Sammy turned the key before pocketing it.

"Hello, Michael," said Trevor, almost in tears. "It's been a long time, brother. A very long time."

"Back in an hour," said Sammy, heading for the stairs. But Trevor didn't even hear him.

TWENTY-FOUR

Sarah was sitting motionless in the dark, trying to make sense of things, when she heard someone ringing the door bell. She knew who it was; it could only be Benson. She glanced at the clock on the mantelpiece but it had stopped hours ago. The hands were frozen at 9pm. What the hell is it with these fucking clocks, she thought. If I'm not hearing phantom ticking then they're stopping on me, halting time.

She stood and crossed the room. Behind her, the clock started ticking again. When she glanced back at the clock's face the hands were poised at 11.15.

Even time was turning against her, trying to spook her.

She walked to the front door and opened it. Benson was standing on the steps with his head bowed. The air was heavy with the threat of rain. It was cold. Benson looked up, unsmiling. He looked tired.

"Hi," she said, stepping back, into the hallway.

"Hi, yourself," he said, following her inside.

"How was your day with the murder squad?" Try as she might, Sarah could not keep the mocking tone from her voice. She wanted Benson to know that she felt cheated, deserted. That she should have been included in the investigation.

"Yeah, sorry about that," he said as they walked along the hall and went into the living room. "I tried to convince Reynolds to bring you onboard but for some reason he wasn't having any of it."

"I don't think he likes me," said Sarah, lowering herself onto the sofa. She flexed her bare feet on the carpet and then swung her legs up and slid them beneath her bottom.

"I think you might be right." Benson sat next to her. His hand moved reflexively to rest upon her leg. "Sorry."

"It's not your fault. Because of my – because of Emerson – I seem to have a lot of baggage with certain people on the force. Most of it I don't even understand." She placed her hand over his, a subtle show of solidarity. The problem was she didn't think that it was a genuine gesture. She felt apart from Benson in a way that she never had before in their short relationship. He'd been different from usual at the crime scene in Roundhay Park that morning, and she'd been given a glimpse of a side of him that she didn't like. It made her wonder how much more of himself he was keeping hidden from her, and if those other parts of his personality were just as unpleasant.

"We didn't get anywhere, if that makes you feel any better."

She glanced at his face. At the scars on his cheeks and his dull, flat eyes. The room was still dark; she hadn't bothered to turn on the lights. "What do you mean?"

"The lab boys have turned up nothing on our original body – the one in the dentist chair. We still don't know who he is. The other two, from this morning, are still being examined. We have fuck all to go on here. No prints, no residue, no traces of DNA. The bodies are clean." In the gloom, with the shadows pressing in from the corners, it looked like Benson was smiling.

"Want a drink?" She got to her feet and went to the drinks cabinet. The whisky bottle was half empty and she couldn't even remember when she'd bought it. Taking Benson's lack of response as an affirmative, Sarah poured two large measures and carried the glasses back to the sofa.

They sipped in silence, and then Benson put his glass down on the floor and turned his body slightly towards her. "So. What was it you wanted to talk to me about?" He licked his lips. The darkness made his face look flat, like a mask.

"I've found something out. Something about Emerson Doherty."

Benson tilted his head to one side. He looked like an inquisitive dog. "So tell me – if you want to, I mean. I know how you are with this family stuff, so don't feel under any pressure. I know I've been pushing you a bit, but it's just because I want you to include me more in your life."

She nodded. Then, something occurred to her. "It cuts both ways, you know."

Benson reached down and picked up his glass. He held it against his lips for a second, and then took it away. "How do you mean?"

"You've never really told me much about yourself either. I mean, I know very little about your background, where you grew up, the things that shaped you. I might be the one who plays my cards close to my chest but I've actually shared more with you than you have with me." She was right. It had passed her by before, because she was so caught up in her own problems, but Benson rarely talked about his own past.

"You never thought to ask." He took a drink, emptying the glass.

"OK," said Sarah. "I'll accept that. I have been a bit self-involved, but you've hardly volunteered much information. Neither of us has, so let me start this off." She took a deep breath. "Let me tell you what I've found out, and we can go from there."

Benson adjusted his position on the sofa, sitting up straight with his back pressed against the cushions. He nodded. "I'm listening."

"I found some photographs in his stuff. Nothing much, just a few snapshots of him at these sex parties he used to organise. You know about those, right? Every fucker else seems to."

Benson shrugged. His powerful shoulders rolled high in the darkness. "I had heard rumours... everybody has."

Sarah bit her bottom lip, and then blew a burst of air out through her nose. "Well, it turns out that he made my mother go along with him. He forced her to join in, even though she didn't want to. He needed to keep her quiet, you see, so he used the photographs of what was done to her as a threat. If she ever betrayed him, he would show them to her family, her friends... anyone he could, just to hurt her."

The words were streaming from her like water now. She couldn't stop them.

"I also met up with an old informant of his, and it seems that he was doing a lot more than throwing kinky parties. He was involved in all kinds of criminal activity – gambling, drugs, whores, God knows what else – and laundering the money he made through various police charities. He was good. The only people who knew were the ones who were in on the whole thing. Nobody else heard as much as a whisper."

Benson wriggled on the sofa. He looked uncomfortable. "Jesus, Sarah. I didn't know... I mean, everybody's heard stuff about the card schools and him and his mates skimming a few quid on the side, but not at that kind of level."

"It gets worse."

Benson said nothing.

Sarah leaned back, stretching her legs at an angle and resting her feet flat on the floor. "I'm not sure who else was involved in this, but there was some vigilante activity. Emerson and some of his buddies on the force started to abduct criminals and 'teach them a lesson'. They kicked the crap out of a lot of people and warned them off whatever it was they were doing. My theory is that these fuckers were interfering with Emerson's sidelines. So he took it upon himself to get them out of the way."

Benson was staring at her. Even in the darkness, he looked pale.

"A drug dealer was killed. I don't know how, but they murdered him, possibly by accident, possibly not. I don't know. The whole thing was covered up and they stopped their little games. Well, most of them did. Only Emerson carried on."

Benson jerked to his feet, taking a few steps away from her. Sarah was shocked by his sudden movement, but she hid it well. "Is this all true? Can you trust your source?"

"Yes," she said, refusing to elaborate further. "Sit down. I haven't finished."

Benson collapsed into the armchair opposite the sofa, rubbing at his eyes with the palms of his hands. He looked like he was about to cry.

"The old bastard got religion. He claimed to have been visited by an angel who gave him the ability to see the future crimes of certain children."

"What?" Benson shook his head. "This is fucking crazy. Can you hear yourself, what you're saying? It's nonsense."

"I know," said Sarah. "I know it is, but it's what *he* believed."

Benson was breathing heavily. He sounded ill. "And what did he do with this... with this knowledge? Did your snitch tell you that?"

Sarah shook her head. "No. No, he didn't. But I found something down in the cellar – some evidence that made everything click into place." She paused then, wondering if she'd gone too far and said too much. How well did she really know Benson after all? Enough to offload this onto him, or was she clutching at something that wasn't really there?

"I'm still listening." He sat back, composed now, getting used to the madness of what he was being told.

"I found a box down there, among his personal stuff. Inside was a bit of human skull with holes drilled in it." She paused; there was no sound from Benson. "And a device that looks like a drill but was clearly used to make those holes." She paused there, lowering her head. "Sounds familiar, doesn't it?" She looked at her hands and waited for him to speak.

Benson shifted in the chair. He coughed once. "I don't know what I'm supposed to say here. This is some weird shit, it really is. I assume you know what it would mean if you went public with the information? What it would do to his reputation and to the force in general?"

Sarah nodded. "That's why I'm telling you. I can't carry this alone. I need some help." She looked up, at his mouth, his eyes, his twitching scars. The face that suddenly looked like it belonged to a stranger. "I might be going mad here, but I'm starting to think that his ghost has come back to kill more kids."

There was tension between them, strung out like a fine wire. Sarah felt it stretch, stretch, and then it threatened to break. She didn't know what to believe; this stuff sounded as crazy to her as it obviously did to him.

"OK, now it's my turn." Benson's voice sounded different from only seconds before. He was calm now; he had it all under control. "I've wanted to tell you this for a long time but thought it might interfere with what we have. I didn't want to spoil things."

Sarah kept her gaze steady. She began to prepare for bad news, tensing her body against imaginary blows.

"I'll come right out with this: I knew your father. I knew Emerson." The words hung in the air, unmoving.

"What are you saying here, Benson? What the fuck are you telling me?" She clenched her fists. Her entire body was rigid.

"I never told you exactly what happened when I got these scars." He raised a hand and brushed his fingers against his right cheek. "I used to run with a few lads. These days it would be called a gang but back then we were just a group, a bunch of bad lads with too much time on our hands. One night, when we were stoned, we nicked a car. I was driving. We went for a joyride, out on the moors, and then when we got bored we drove back into town. I dropped off the others and kept the car – thought I'd get another hour's worth of fun out of the thing before dumping it. I crashed into a parked van in Chapeltown.

Your dad was out on patrol and found me. My face was slashed. I was bleeding badly."

Sarah wanted to hit him. She felt like smashing in his skull with a blunt object. He had been lying to her all along.

"He saw something in me – some good, or maybe something similar to what was inside him. So he took me to hospital and told them that I'd been run over and the driver of the car had left the scene. They stitched me up and sent me on my way, but your dad – Emerson – took me home. Then he took an interest." He paused, reached over for his drink and sipped it.

"What does that mean, 'took an interest'?" Sarah could barely believe what she was hearing.

"He... well, he guided me, I suppose. It was down to him that I finished school and got some grades, then took my A-Levels. He convinced me to apply to the force and spoke up for me at the police entrance interview, and gave me a personal reference. He was retired by then, of course, but his name opened a lot of fucking doors. You of all people should know that."

Sarah bristled; she resented the implication. "Fuck off. I did this all on my own. I deliberately chose a route where I'd have minimal contact with his old flunkies."

Benson chuckled softly. It was a frightening sound. "Come on, Sarah. Even if they didn't say it to your face, they all gave you a little helping hand somewhere along the line because of who your father was. Even your good mate, Tebbit, but he did it to get back at Emerson rather than help him out."

She stood up in a rush; it was a sudden and involuntary reaction. Once she was on her feet she didn't really know why, or what she had meant to do. "He wasn't even my fucking father. He found me. He adopted me."

Benson looked stunned. Sarah was pleased by his reaction. "No... who told you that?" His mouth was gaping.

"The man I talked to, Emerson's old pal. He told me all of it. The old bastard brought me home one night and they adopted me in secret. I'm not Emerson Doherty's daughter. And thank *fuck* for that."

Benson went to her, his arms opening. He rested his hands on her waist, leaning in close. "It looks like we both have a lot of secrets, then. Maybe this is the breakthrough we've been waiting for. What do you think?" His words were empty, bereft of genuine meaning.

Sarah pushed him away, taking two steps backwards. Her thigh bumped against the fireplace. "I *think* that you're a lying cunt, that's what I think. And I think you should leave. Now."

But Benson wasn't looking at Sarah. His eyes were fixed on the wall behind her, somewhere in the corner of the room. Slowly, hesitantly, Sarah turned her upper body so that she could follow his gaze.

A familiar figure was sitting against the wall, his legs bent as if he were occupying an invisible chair, his hands resting flat on his thighs. The long black robe fell all the way to the floor, the plain hem covering his feet. The thin white hood fluttered slightly in a breeze that Sarah could not feel.

She turned back to face Benson. He was still staring at the figure. "You can see it, too?"

He nodded.

"All along? Right from the start?"

He nodded again, his features slack. There was a look in his eyes, something that resembled awe.

"You've seen him all along and you kept coming here, right to the centre of all this. You were coming to see him, weren't you?"

Benson's eyes were shining. They were no longer flat and dead; they were practically bursting with life. "Yes," he whispered. "I've been coming to see him, to pay my respects."

Sarah began to move backwards at an angle, away from Benson and from the figure resting against the wall. She kept her eyes on Benson's face, but he barely even registered that she was there. He was staring at the figure like a love-struck suitor and his entire body was as limp as a bundle of sticks.

Sarah knew exactly what she was doing. She'd always known about the gun. It was all wrapped up in Emerson's mystique, and had always been a major part of the reason that she and her mother had been so afraid to cross him. He had never threatened them with the gun, nor had he handled it in front of them. The idea of the weapon had always been enough to keep them in check, and it had crossed neither of their minds to pick the thing up and use it against him. His grasp had been too strong; the mental bonds too tight. And he hadn't told them were the bullets were kept anyway.

He would never be that stupid.

Sarah calmly opened the top drawer of a tall varnished unit that stood near the fireplace. She took out the small handgun and aimed it at Benson. Still he did not react. She spread her legs and assumed a professional firing stance, bending her arms slightly at the elbows, just like they'd been taught in training.

Benson blinked.

"Get the fuck out of my house." Sarah's voice was cold; her words tasted of steel and they made her tongue tingle. She fought the urge to turn around. She was pretty sure that the figure had vanished but the urge to check was almost unbearable.

Benson blinked again, like a man slowly coming out of a trance. He turned his attention to Sarah, and to the gun. "What are you doing?"

"If you don't leave now I'll shoot you. I'll shoot you in the head and tell them you tried to rape me." She took a single step towards him. "I'm not fucking around."

Benson tensed for a moment, as if he was considering rushing her, but then he relaxed again and held out his hands, the palms facing forward. "OK, OK. I'm leaving. I'll call you later, when you've had a chance to calm down."

"Don't bother. Just go. Don't come back. Don't ever come back."

Benson walked backwards and she followed him, using the threat of the handgun to force him out into the hall and to the front door. He fumbled behind his back and opened the door, then stumbled out onto the front steps, almost falling down them. "We really should talk about this some more."

Sarah shook her head. She forced a smile. "Piss off, Benson, you scar-faced prick." Then, moving purposefully, she slammed the door in his face and slid the bolt into the frame.

She gripped the handle of the gun, wishing that she had some bullets. If Benson had called her bluff, he would probably have overpowered her in less than a minute. She fell against the wall and slumped to her knees, dry-heaving, tears burning her eyes.

Then, when she had herself under control, she walked around the house and checked that all the doors and windows were locked. When she looked out at the street from an upper window, she saw Benson standing on the corner watching the house. He stayed there for an hour, not moving as much as a few feet from the same spot, and then he walked away when finally it started to rain.

When Sarah went to bed she was unable to sleep. She kept the gun under her pillow, just in case. Even though it was unloaded, its presence made her feel safe. She was desperate for help but there was nobody she could turn to, not one person in the world she could trust – apart from DI Tebbit, who was currently lying comatose in a hospital bed at Leeds General Infirmary.

There was no one else. He was the only one. The only person she could go to.

It seemed like the ultimate irony that the only man who could help her was so close to death that he was barely even present in the world. He was as much a phantom as the man who had falsely brought her up as his daughter; just another phantom in the vast ghost-house of her life.

TWENTY-FIVE

Trevor was crying. He tried to hide it from the boy – the boy who wasn't Michael, but who was trying so very hard to be him. He closed his eyes and whispered his brother's name: a chant, a litany, a prayer meant to summon his essence.

"Michael, Michael, oh, Michael…"

But the incantation wasn't working. The boy's body was different; it was bonier, less supple than Michael's had ever been. The meat was too loose on his bones and his skin smelled like vanilla. Michael had never smelled of vanilla. He had stunk of terror, and Trevor was finally acknowledging the fact that Michael's terror was the thing that had aroused him more than anything. Not his unquestioning love, despite what his older brother did to him, or his silent acquiescence. No, it was his fear, always his fear.

In that moment Trevor hated himself more than he had ever thought possible. He hated Michael, too, for being so beautiful and so afraid and so willing to let himself be used. He hated the world. And most of all, he hated Thomas Usher, the man who had finally forced him to face his own grinning demons.

The boy lay beneath him, loose and unflinching. His arms were positioned straight down by his sides on the bed and his face was turned to the side, away from Trevor. The boy's legs

were splayed apart on the mattress, and Trevor was slotted between his skinny thighs. He was turgid; he could not get hard.
The ability to perform the act he most desired had deserted him.

He had lost it all. Michael had taken it with him when he died.

"I'm sorry, Michael... but I'm not sorry. Not really."

The boy shivered.

"You never really loved me. Not the way I loved you."

The boy whimpered softly, trying to bite back the sound but
unable to stop it from issuing between his clenched teeth.

"I love you and I hate you and I want you and I need you and
I *never want to want you again...*" Trevor felt his sense of reality
sliding away, like the rotten flesh from a corpse. Madness began
to leak through the cracks in his skull. He had always been
aware that insanity lay on the other side of a thin crust of scar
tissue, but it was only now that he realised how close it really
was. So near that he could almost reach out and touch it.

Perhaps madness was the answer. If he were insane, the appearance of the Pilgrim in his bedroom mirror might make
perfect sense. And what was madness anyway but a different
way of seeing things? It was just a small shift in perspective, allowing you to view reality from another angle, like looking into
a room through a window you had never noticed before – a
canted window with a twisted frame and stained glass. Or a dark
mirror containing a beckoning, hairless figure.

He shifted his weight, pinning the boy down. He tried to
make it work, he tried so very hard, but in the end all he could
manage was a limp shudder and an empty moan. That was it:
all he had.

Trevor got up off the bed and stared down at the boy. He was
only half naked. Trevor pulled up his trousers and kept his eyes
on the boy's pale belly. He imagined sinking his fingers into that
soft flesh, piercing through the thin layer of tissue, and grasping
whatever he found there. Ripping it out and throwing it on the
floor, then stamping on it.

"Useless," he said, not knowing if he meant himself or the boy on the bed. "Fucking pathetic." He kept staring at the boy, wondering what he should do. He was paying for this – a lot of money – so he demanded satisfaction of some kind, any kind. He just wanted to feel better than he did right now.

"What next?" The voice was soft, a gentle burring sound. It was more like several voices in one, all saying the same thing at exactly the same time.

Trevor turned around in the small cell and looked through the bars. The boy from the other cell – the one who had been staring at him – was standing there on the other side, his face a blank mask.

"Who are you?" Trevor shifted closer to the bed. His leg brushed against the boy's dangling arm. Finally, and much too late, he became aroused.

"Who are We?" The other boy did not move. He kept staring at Trevor through the gaps in the bars. "Who. Are. We."

"I didn't do anything. I couldn't." Trevor was scared but he didn't know why. This pale, calm, utterly empty boy terrified him. "I couldn't. I'm not able, not anymore."

"Who is Michael?" The boy pushed his face forward, closer to the bars.

"Somebody I loved." Trevor realised that he was crying. He raised his left hand to his face and wiped away the tears, rubbing his wet fingertips together. "Somebody I loved more than I could ever love myself." And wasn't that the truth, the real and only truth? Only now, confronted by something slightly unreal, could he admit to himself how he really felt. How he had always felt. About Michael. About himself. His brother had contained all the good, even Trevor's share; and he had wanted to possess that goodness so much that all he could think to do was rape it.

"Where is the lost one?" The boy took a step forward and the bars of the cell buckled slightly, as if some invisible force were pushing them inward.

"I... I don't know what you mean." Trevor's hands were shaking.

"Oh, but you do. It's written all over your design, like a map to a place We have never seen before. You need to show Us how to get there, to him."

Trevor's legs were shaking. His joints failed and he dropped to his knees, as if worshipping the boy. "Please. I don't know what you're talking about."

"The lost one," said the boy. And the bars of the cell began to bend, curving like bows. Then, as Trevor watched, they twisted and sagged and created an opening large enough for the boy to step through.

"Leave me alone. I haven't done anything." Before the arrival of the Pilgrim, the sight of the bars turning to rubber and the boy approaching him might have destroyed Trevor's sanity. But now, after everything else that he had experienced, he simply accepted what was happening.

The Pilgrim. Was that it? Did the boy mean the Pilgrim?

"I know where he is." Trevor shuffled backwards on his knees. The boy on the bed remained motionless, staring at the wall. Perhaps he had retreated inside himself, or had passed out from the shock of the events going on around him.

"Take Us there." The boy tried to smile. His lips twitched like scraps of meat. His eyes were flat, like old coins. His hair was in disarray and matted with dried blood, and now that he was close Trevor could see that there were small, round wounds in his skull.

"I will. I'll take you to the Pilgrim." Trevor was practically begging for mercy. He would have told this weird boy anything to be spared. Despite the boy's slight build and tender years, he had about him an aura of raw power. Jagged energy bristled in the air, like the electricity gathering before a storm.

"What the fuck's going on?" Sammy Newsome – poor, dumb Sammy Newsome, the terrible mother hen – had returned to the Roost. "Fuckin hell!"

The boy turned around in a single swift motion, as if he barely needed to flex a muscle. He moved like water, or like air. Instantly.

Sammy was standing by the desk with the monitors. His mouth was open and his hair was hanging loose from his ponytail. His wobbly cheeks were pink. His eyes were wide. His friend Don stood slightly behind him, holding a baseball bat and breathing heavily.

"Run," said Trevor, but nobody heard. It was too late for running anyway.

"Get back in your cell." Sammy was grinning but he looked unsure. This wasn't mean to happen: the boys never disobeyed him.

Don stepped out from behind Sammy's bulk. He hefted the bat. "Do as he says."

The small boy lifted his hand. It moved perhaps three or four inches, nothing more.

Don stopped dead in his tracks. The right side of his face bowed inward, as if some massive pressure had struck him there. One eye popped from the socket and hung down his cheek. He opened his lips but before he had the chance to scream his mouth caved in, the teeth shattering in a fine spray of powdered porcelain that clouded before his wide, disbelieving eyes.

Sammy, noticing what was happening to his friend, began to scream. The boys in the cells joined in, a deafening chorus of horror.

The pale boy, still standing in the same spot, twitched his hand again. This time the movement was more pronounced, as if he were swatting at an annoying fly.

Don's head imploded instantly. One second it was still recognisably a head, if a little battered, the next it was a fist of crushed flesh and bone bobbling on his tattooed neck. His body slumped to the floor, his legs kicking meaninglessly against the stone.

"*Noooooo....*" Sammy tried to run. It was the last thing he ever did of his own volition.

Trevor wanted to look away, he really did, but he was unable to turn his head or close his eyes. He had to watch: there was no choice now but to see how this all played out.

Sammy's legs went first, his trouser legs seeming to knot and tremble as the flesh beneath tore from the bone. He fell forward, onto his face, and then turned onto his back as he bucked in agony. He was still screaming. His elbows shattered and his forearms went jack-knifing across the room. Then his ankles and kneecaps did the same. One foot remained where it was, detached from the limb; the other one shot off and hit the wall with an audible wet thump.

Trevor realised that he was screaming too. He had joined in the song.

Sammy's body was changing shape as his bones jinked and popped out of joint. It looked like he was being kicked by unseen feet; his flesh dented and rippled. His face had become concave. Trevor was reminded of an old WWI photograph he'd once seen in a magazine, of a man who'd taken a shell full in the face. The front of his head had vaporised, leaving behind a sort of bowl of healed flesh.

Sammy's Newsome's face had done the same, as if a huge boulder had been dropped from a great height and mashed his features into an awful half-moon.

There was no blood yet, just evidence of massive trauma. The man's large body was taking so much abuse that his skin began to tear. At first the wounds were dry, but then his insides started to leak out, and a pool of thick red fluid pooled around him. His flailing body transformed the bloodstain into the shape of wings, like a child making a snow angel on the ground after a heavy snowfall.

He had stopped making a noise. His mouth was fused shut, the lips pummelled so hard that there was no longer an orifice to scream through.

Trevor vomited down the front of his gold jacket, but he barely even noticed. The first thing he was aware of was the smell, but that was soon covered up by the stench of Sammy Newsome voiding his bowels on the cold basement floor.

The rest of it didn't go on too long. Soon there was nothing but a mound of compressed flesh and bone on the floor, next to a headless corpse. Trevor watched as all of these human remains slowly curled up, like slugs coated with salt, and before long all that remained was a series of dark stains on the grey floor of the tawdry basement room.

The boys were no longer screaming. They all cowered in their cells, too afraid to even move in case they drew attention to themselves.

"What did you do?" Trevor could barely believe he was asking the question. He didn't want to know. He didn't care, just as long as it didn't happen to him.

The boy turned to face him. His face was smooth, pale, and he wasn't even perspiring after all that mental exertion. Because it had indeed been a mental force he'd set upon the two men, rather than anything of physical origin.

Trevor licked his lips.

"We unravelled their designs," said the boy, as if it meant something to Trevor. As if he knew what the fuck they were even talking about. "We've never done it before, but the result was rather spectacular. Don't you think?"

Trevor nodded. What else could he do?

"Now." The boy seemed to float towards him. "Take Us to the lost one. Show Us this Pilgrim. We can see by your design that he has influenced you greatly. And he is still manipulating you."

Trevor didn't know what to say. "OK. I'll take you there. Just... please, don't do that to me. Don't kill me."

"We have no interest in killing you." The boy tilted his head. For the first time Trevor realised that the boy wasn't breathing – he had not once taken a breath. "We did this to save you, so that you could help Us."

It was the first time that Trevor could say someone had saved his life, but it was not a feeling he enjoyed. In fact, it felt more like violation than salvation.

TWENTY-SIX

Eddie Knowles was scared. He wasn't quite sure what he'd done, telling Emerson's daughter that she was adopted, but it felt like something had been set in motion, that huge wheels were beginning to turn somewhere behind the scenes of their lives.

He was standing outside his flat in Bestwick, smoking a roll-up. Tanya didn't let him smoke indoors so he was banished out here whenever he had the urge. He didn't mind – it kept the flat free of the smell of smoke.

There were a lot of things Tanya didn't like him to do, but these days he was glad of her guiding hand. He was getting too old, and he was out of shape. The life he had led was catching up on him, like a slavering hound at his heels.

"Fuck," he said, blowing out hot smoke. "Fuck this shit."

A dog began to bark somewhere out in the night. A plane flew overhead, leaving a smeared white contrail in the dark sky. He wished he was up there, flying to somewhere exotic, rather than stuck down in the mud with the rest of the losers.

Depression bit him. He had struggled against black moods for decades, and usually came out on top. But lately he felt close to defeat, like a boxer on the ropes.

The dog stopped barking. The plane had moved on, leaving a gap in the heavens. Drizzle hung in the air, making him feel oppressed.

Eddie finished his ciggie and mashed the butt against the wall, watching the tiny sparks fly and batter against the brickwork. He thought about Sarah Doherty, and the things she was discovering. She didn't know the half of it; all he had told her were the things he could no longer live with. There was more – so much more – but that was all between him and his maker.

Eddie recalled past nights like this one, cold, wet, dark and endless, when he'd cruised with Emerson Doherty, picking up whores and torturing them in derelict buildings. He'd had some fun back then – they both had. But all fun must one day come to an end, and there was always a price to pay. Always. You could never dodge what you owed, or who you owed it to.

Emerson had paid his price when his heart failed, giving him an undignified death. Eddie was still waiting to pay his dues.

He walked a little way along the street, enjoying the cold, damp air against his skin. He suffered with the heat and Tanya always kept the flat too warm. Often he would find himself walking about at night, trying to cool down. Maybe it was the fires of hell he could feel, those eternal flames heating him from a distance, preparing him for the time when he would be called to walk right into them.

A car alarm was droning a few streets away, filling the night with noise. A police helicopter passed over the tops of the houses near the Precinct, shining down a light onto the grubby streets below.

It was a few moments before Eddie realised that he was being followed.

He stopped and glanced behind him, but there was nobody there. When he faced forward again there was a figure waiting up ahead, on the street corner.

"So here it is," he whispered. "At last it's time to pay the piper." He knew that he could have turned and fled, perhaps even escaping into the flat to live another day. But the figure would always be there, biding its time, waiting for payment.

Eddie walked on, heading towards his destiny. It had been a long life, and he had reaped many rewards from the deeds he had carried out. He knew that he could never be called a good man – that was far beyond him now – but in recent years he had tried his best to make amends for at least some of the terrible things he had done. It was not enough, of course: it was never enough. But it was better than nothing.

He remembered with a guilty fondness the screaming of the prostitutes he and Emerson had played with, and the weeping of the junkies they had tied up so that Emerson could practice his technique. It had been Eddie who found the trepanning device, when he had broken into an antique shop in Blackpool. He was going to throw it away (because who the hell would buy such an item?), but Emerson had stopped him, snatching the thing right from his hand.

The awful device had spoken to Emerson, just like the angel he later claimed to have met – it had called and Emerson had answered.

Eddie had always known about the kids, and sometimes that hurt him more than anything. He should have done something to stop the brutal murders, but by then Emerson had too much dirt on him, and if he was honest with himself he had always been too scared to turn against his old friend.

So he had ignored it. The fact that none of the bodies had been found and he didn't have to read about what Emerson was doing made it easier to forget what he had helped to begin. But that didn't mean he never dreamed about them, or he didn't see their poor trepanned skulls and feel the sticky blood on his hands – a regular Lady Macbeth of the sink estates, that's what he was: no matter how hard he scrubbed, the fucking stains would never come out.

The tall figure stepped out into the centre of the footpath, moving directly into his path. There was nobody else around.

The streets were quiet now; even the car alarm had quit its racket. It was just a short lull before the next storm.

"Hello, Eddie." The voice was different but the figure had the same build, the familiar height and width, and up close there was no mistaking the floor-length black robe and the white hood. Emerson had loved to wear that costume; he had claimed that it made him feel like a priest. The world, he had always claimed, was his church, and the blood of the children who would become evil if they were allowed to grow up was also the blood of the angel. A sacrament, an offering: blood flowing to blood.

"You're dead." It was a statement rather than a question.

"I suppose so," said the figure, stepping forward now and raising its hands. One of them held a large hunting knife.

"A ghost."

The figure laughed, and it sounded more alive than anything Eddie could have imagined. "Yes, Eddie, I'm a ghost. And I've come to haunt you."

"Just make it quick." Eddie closed his eyes. He screwed them shut but still he felt the sharp blow to his throat when it came, and he knew that he deserved to experience every ounce of the pain that would follow.

Blood flowing to blood...

The pain: he embraced it like an old friend, and it welcomed him in the same way.

The pain, the warm rush of blood down the front of his shirt, the ground rushing up to meet him...

He felt it all, keeping his eyes shut tight.

And the last thing he heard was that eerily human laughter as it followed him down towards the fiery furnace of his death.

PART FOUR
ENDGAME

TWENTY-SEVEN

The sun struggled to illuminate that cold, bright morning, but despite the dawning of a new day Sarah knew that the darkness was winning the fight. Yesterday's rain had cleared the air; the sky was wide and high and smudged with skeins of white vapour. Sarah looked up at the webby clouds and wished that she had never started any of this. If she had refused Emerson's house when it was left to her after his death, or had put it on the market sight unseen, she might have prevented the horror that was slowly unfurling like great black wings to engulf her world.

She wasn't quite sure why she'd come to the hospital. Last night she had decided that DI Tebbit – her old mentor, her one true friend – was the only person she could talk to about what may or may not be happening, but now she wasn't so sure. He was in a coma anyway, so would be unable to hear her. But the visit was more about vocalising her fears than it was about anyone actually listening to what she had to say.

Not for the first time that morning she thought about turning around and going home.

Earlier she'd considered ringing Benson to give her a lift, but the memory of their last meeting – his strange confession and the weird way he'd been acting – made her want to keep him at even more of a distance than usual, so instead she had used a black cab from a firm she trusted.

Benson.

Had he really been trying to get close to her just because of Emerson, or was his interest more ambiguous? And what of his claims regarding seeing the old man's ghost?

Nothing was simple any more; it was all angles and edges, like she was walking along a narrow alley lined with knives.

And there was another thing that she was trying not to think about. Her twitch, the inherent intuition that had served her so well, was telling her that there was more – and possibly less – to Benson than she could ever imagine. His motives might be unclear, but she was now certain about one thing: she never wanted to see him again.

"Mornin', love." An old man was smoking outside the main entrance to the LGI. He was standing with his back to the wall, staring at the busy road and the concrete expanse of Millennium Square beyond. His face was creased; his eyes were tiny slits above the folded leather of his cheeks.

"Morning." She made to walk past him but he turned towards her, flicking his cigarette across the paved footpath. She nodded, smiled, and changed her course to dodge him.

"They're after me, constable." The man's voice was dry, throaty. "They want to keep me in here."

Sarah raised a hand and backed away. "Listen, sir, I'm here on official police business so unless you have something important to say please step out of the way."

The old man smiled. He had very few teeth left in his head. "I came in here to visit a mate. He has cancer. Not long left. But they say they want to keep me in. Do some tests." His hands were shaking.

"Then I suggest you take their advice." As Sarah hurried past him, she caught the whiff of alcohol on his breath. The man was just another piss-head wasting his time until he reached the grave and had suddenly realised that now there was no time left to do anything worthwhile.

Sarah walked through the reception area and headed for the lift. Tebbit was in a private room on the fourth floor. The Cancer Care Unit. Even the words sent fear shooting through her body, making her short of breath.

She pushed the button and waited for the lift. When it arrived two porters wheeled out a couple of old ladies in wheelchairs and pushed them towards the entrance. The ladies chattered like geese, saying nothing of interest but talking a lot. One of the porters exchanged a glance with Sarah, rolling his eyes upwards and shrugging: *You know what it's like.*

Sarah smiled and entered the lift, then pushed the button for the fourth floor. The lift doors closed, and Sarah was filled with a sudden and intense fear. For some reason she no longer wanted to see DI Tebbit. He was, in fact, the last person on Earth she wanted to face.

For a brief moment, she hated him for making her feel so scared.

The feeling passed, but Sarah was left with a sense of confusion. Why had she been afraid of the man who had always spent so much time and energy on making sure that she took the right path?

Before she could make sense of things, the lift came to a halt and the doors slid open. She stepped out, into a quiet corridor, and turned right. She knew the way. She had been here before, when Tebbit was still conscious and capable of receiving family and friends. They had even organised a group trip from the station.

But now that Tebbit was close to the end, none of his old colleagues wanted to make the journey to see him. It was as if they were afraid that signs of his imminent death might rub off on their skin and mark them out as the next to go.

There was a nurse's station half way along the corridor and Sarah told the man behind the desk why she was there and who she wanted to see. He checked her name on a clipboard, wrote something beside it, and told her that she could have twenty minutes with Tebbit. Normal visiting hours had been abandoned regarding this patient because they didn't expect him to last much longer.

Twenty minutes. It wasn't much, but it was better than nothing.

"Thanks," she said, turning and approaching the door to Tebbit's room. The last time she'd been here the man had been out of bed, sitting in a chair by the window. This time he was lying on his back and waiting to die.

Sarah paused outside the door, reaching out to touch the window hatch located at eye level. She looked through the glass and saw the end of his bed. His feet were small pointed shapes under the thin covers.

She pushed open the door and stepped inside.

Tebbit was flat on his back, with tubes coming out of his mouth and nose. A heart rate monitor beeped softly at his side, attached to one finger by what looked like a small clothes peg. His eyes were closed. His cheeks were pale. The side of his neck was fluttering as the pulse there kept its rhythm, the silent chanting of the blood in his veins.

Sarah stood at the end of the bed, not taking her eyes from Tebbit's frail form. He had never been a large man, and always kept his body trim and fit, but now he was achingly skinny. His scrawny arms rested above the covers, the veins sticking out like cords. His fingers were fleshless, like claws. It broke Sarah's heart to see him this way, but she held herself in check.

"Everybody ends some time," she whispered. "Some day you too will die."

"But isn't it so unfair?" The voice came from behind her. "So *very* unfair."

Sarah turned around, adopting an instinctive fighting stance. She glared at the man who was slowly stepping away from the wall, challenging him to try something.

"I'm sorry," he said, trying and failing to smile. "I didn't mean make you jump."

Sarah relaxed. The man was not a danger. He was small, thin, and looked as if he'd blow over in a strong breeze. She recognised him from somewhere but wasn't sure why. Nothing about his face stood out; he was average.

"My name's Thomas Usher." He approached her slowly, as if he were still afraid that he might startle her. "I'm a friend of Tebbit's."

"Ah, yes. I know you." She shook his hand. It was cold, so very cold.

"Have we met?" He twisted his mouth and looked at her more intently, as if trying to trace her features in his memory banks.

"Once, several months ago. It was during the Penny Royale case, and DI Tebbit asked me to come to your house and collect you. You probably don't remember."

Something flashed across Usher's face, lighting him up from the inside. "Oh, but I do. Yes, I do remember you. As far as I recall, you were a bit huffy." This time he succeeded in smiling. It altered his entire face, showing Sarah how handsome he was underneath the mask of melancholia.

"Yes, I'd just lost my father. I was... troubled."

"I do remember that," said Usher, putting his hands in the pockets of his slightly shabby suit jacket. "I believe he was following you. Unless I'm mistaken, you didn't like me telling you."

Sarah shook her head. "No. I didn't like that at all."

"So you know who I am? *What* I am?" He clenched his jaw. He needed a shave; the stubble growth was short but dark.

"Our friend here told me about you. He shared a few details with me regarding how you've helped him over the years. He has a lot of time for you, Mr Usher."

"Call me Thomas," said the man, walking towards the bed. "Please. No one else does, not anymore, but somehow I'd prefer it if you did."

"OK, Thomas. I'm Sarah. Sarah Doherty."

"I remember that, too," he said, not looking at her; his gaze was fixed on the bed, and the face of his dying friend. "We go back a long way, me and Tebbit. Me and Donald. He's a fine man, a great friend. A brilliant policeman." Usher bowed his head over Tebbit's bed, closing his eyes. He looked like he might cry.

"I can leave you alone if you want. I didn't know anyone else was in here, or I would've stayed outside." She started to leave.

"No. That's fine. I sneaked in here anyway. Nobody knows I'm back in Leeds. Tebbit told me to stay away, but something happened to bring me back. I thought it best if I kept my arrival as quiet as possible." Usher reached down and placed the palm of his hand on Tebbit's forehead. He left it there, like a benediction. "I just wish he was still here to see me. I have things I'd like to tell him."

"Me too," said Sarah, surprising herself with her candour. "He was the only one left who might listen, but now even he's gone."

Usher turned his head towards her. His eyes shone with tears. "Oh, he's not gone. Not yet. He's still here, in this room – in this world, this reality. He hasn't moved on quite yet. But he will do soon, and we'll all miss him, won't we? You and me more than anybody, I'd imagine."

Sarah nodded. She was crying too; tears rolled down her cheeks and onto her chin. She didn't bother wiping them away. There was no point in hiding her grief: it was personal, yes, but it felt right to share it with this man. For some reason she felt a connection between them, and she was certain that the feeling was reciprocated. It wasn't sexual; she was not attracted to Thomas Usher. It went deeper than that, right down to the bone, and inside the genes.

"Do you feel it, too?" he was staring at her: his gaze was… naked. That was the word that came into her mind, the only one she could think of to describe it.

She nodded. "Yes. Yes, I do. But what is it?"

Usher looked down at Tebbit. "I think it's him. He wants us to talk. Does that make sense to you? If it doesn't, I'll go away and never bother you again."

Sarah was aware that she stood on the verge of a pivotal decision. This was a defining moment, something that would resonate throughout the rest of her life. Whatever she said here, it mattered: it meant something beyond this room and the two of them standing over a dying man. "Don't go," she said. "Let's go and get some coffee."

"That sounds good," said Usher. "I can't even remember when I last ate, so I might even get a sandwich." He smiled again. "I could really go for a sandwich right now." His stomach growled, lightening the moment. "Sorry." He lowered his gaze, like a guilty schoolboy.

"Come on, Thomas." Sarah was laughing now; the tears had dried on her cheeks. "It's my treat... I hope you're a cheap date."

They rode the lift in silence, each of them content that a bond had been made between them over the body of their dying friend. Sarah felt instinctively that they didn't have to work at it, this blossoming friendship. It felt more natural than the sunrise, as effortless as strolling in the rain.

They walked across to a small café just off Millennium Square that served all-day breakfasts. Usher ordered a full English and Sarah had a coffee and three rounds of buttered toast.

"Sorry if I'm being a pig, but I'm starving. I can't remember the last time I was this hungry." Usher tucked into his meal, shovelling in huge mouthfuls.

"Knock yourself out," said Sarah, nibbling at her toast. She wasn't really hungry but she didn't want Usher to eat alone.

After he'd cleared his plate Usher asked for another cup of sweet white tea, and then leaned back in his chair. "OK, I'm going to tell you everything. I have nothing left to lose."

Sarah pushed her plate across the table, clearing some space. "You and me both."

"After Penny Royale, Tebbit sent me away. I've been living in London for over six months, locked away from the world and trying to make myself invisible. A few days ago I was sent a message, and I knew that I had to come back."

"What kind of message?" Sarah leaned forward, resting her elbows on the table.

"I'm not quite sure. It was garbled, just a series of images. Like watching an art-house film that I knew meant something but couldn't pinpoint what that meaning was. All I knew was that I had to come back, and right now I'm thinking that you're the reason I was meant to return." He sucked on the inside of his cheek. His eyes went wide. "So, what do you think of that, Sarah Doherty?"

A waitress brought over his tea and scurried away to another table, where someone was asking for the bill.

"It should sound fucking stupid," said Sarah. "But it doesn't. A lot of weird stuff has been happening lately, and this is just the latest piece of a puzzle that's too big for me to see." She took a sip of coffee. It was growing cold. "All I know is that I've needed help and now you've fallen from the sky and offered me some. Maybe this is some kind of message, or fate or destiny or something. I don't know. I really don't know. I *do* know, however, that Tebbit trusted you more than anyone he ever knew, and that's more than good enough for me. I trust you, Thomas, even though we don't know each other. I've never trusted anyone before in my life. How fucked up is that?" She laughed, but even to her it sounded shrill and unconvincing.

"You know what I do – that I communicate with the dead. I don't have to tell you about that. I do need to ask you something, though." He looked paler than before, and his hands were restless on the tabletop.

"OK, just ask. Whatever it is, I'll do my best to answer." She picked up a teaspoon and started passing it between her fingers like a cheap trick, a sleight-of-hand.

Usher let out a long breath. He closed his eyes and then opened them again. "If this sounds crazy just let me know. OK. Does this mean anything to you: the image of a man in a black robe and a white hood?"

Sarah dropped the spoon onto the table. It clattered loudly, making her twitch in shock. "I can't believe you just said that."

Usher looked scared. His cheeks were gaunt; his neck was too thin, the flesh almost translucent beneath the shadow of his stubble. "So it does mean something? Tell me. Tell me who it is."

"It's my father."

"Your dead father. The one who's been following you around." These were not questions: they were simply a confirmation of the facts.

Sarah nodded. "Only I found out recently that he wasn't my father... not my real father. DI Emerson Doherty adopted me, illegally. I'm a Jane Doe. I'm a woman without a name or an identity. I'm whatever it is he made me into."

The café was emptying. Breakfasters were making their way to offices or meetings or the teaching hospital across the road. The waitress was doing the rounds, clearing the tables. She looked tired, like she was at the end of her tether.

"Where are you staying?" Sarah took out her purse and laid a ten-pound note on the tablecloth.

"To be honest, I haven't a clue. I own a house out past the airport, but it's been closed up for months. I'm not exactly keen to go back there, so I was thinking about checking into a hotel here in the city. Can you recommend anywhere?"

Sarah thought about it for a second or two, and then decided that she had a good plan. "Yes, I can. How about my place?"

Usher frowned and twisted his mouth. He looked comically surprised, like a character in a silent film.

"Don't worry; I'm not trying to seduce you. Sorry, but you're *so* not my type. And I never did see the appeal of older men."

Usher smiled, but it was tentative, as if he were still unsure of her motives.

"Seriously, I have that huge old house with just me rattling around inside. You can take your pick of the rooms, and stay with me until you feel ready to go back home... or until this thing gets wherever it's going."

"This *thing*?" He raised one eyebrow.

"This thing, whatever it is."

"It feels like the last part of something," he said, abruptly. "Like something is drawing to its conclusion."

"I know," said Sarah, astonished that he was able to verbalise her own muddied thoughts in such a succinct manner. "That's exactly how it feels: it feels like the end."

TWENTY-EIGHT

Back at Sarah's large, high-ceilinged town house, the girl almost
had to coax me inside.

"Come on, Thomas. I promise not to bite. I've already told
you that I find you deeply unattractive. What further assurances
do you need?"

I shook my head and walked slowly through the front door,
dropping my small sports bag onto the hall floor. My smile was
relaxed now; I felt more comfortable in her presence. I didn't
understand why or how, but somehow she had managed to put
me at ease. Not many people could do that. In fact, most people
– most *living* people – put me on edge.

She turned gradually towards me, scratching at a spot on her
left forearm with her bitten fingernails. "Anyway, as I said in
the taxi, I have selfish reasons for this, too. If Benson comes back
I want some muscle around to give me a hand."

I took off my coat and hung it on the newel post at the bottom
of the stairs. She had told me all about her boyfriend and his
odd behaviour during the journey from the café. "If I'm your
idea of protection, you are well and truly without hope. I could-
n't throw a party never mind a punch."

She smiled at that, enjoying the joke – or at least pretending to. I began to think that this might be a good idea after all. As random and impulsive as her offer had been, it felt right somehow that I should accept the invitation and stay with her. At least for a little while, until things played out to their climax.

I realised that I hadn't thought about my dead family – Rebecca and Ally – for quite some time: ever since the episode in the Pilgrim Products warehouse on the south bank of the Thames, in fact. The message I'd been given was still beyond my ability to work out, but this whole meeting with Sarah Doherty felt like another part of some epic saga. I wasn't sure if I was being mentally slow or if the situation was simply too complex for me to contemplate. My thought processes were blurred; all I could focus on right then was the fact that my friend, Donald Tebbit, was dying.

The young girl who stood before me represented a link to Tebbit that I was yet to understand. Whatever her sudden presence in my life meant, it had been foreshadowed in London, during what I was beginning to think of as my exile in the urban wasteland.

What was it Ellen Lang's clockwork voice had said in that haunted warehouse? *Don't go back. You can't help her.*

I had no idea what the warning meant, not literally. But I decided to ignore it for now. I felt that I could help this girl, and she was certainly in need of my aid. Perhaps if I could work with her to solve her mystery, a light might shine down on my own affairs and reveal a little more about what was unfolding around me. And that was exactly how it felt: like something was unfolding, a giant sheet twisting and unwinding and slowly uncovering what was wrapped up inside.

"Come on," said Sarah. "Let's get you settled in and I'll pour us a drink."

I nodded and followed her along the hallway and into the lounge.

Sarah poured us both whiskies – large glasses, filled almost to the halfway point. It was a bit too early for that kind of drinking, but I took it anyway. I needed the help to bring my emotions under control. The visit to Tebbit's bedside had affected me more than I'd expected. I'd known the man for long enough to call him a close friend – perhaps my only friend – and it hurt to see him like that, unconscious in a single bed and connected to machines.

I'd known for a long time that Tebbit was meant to die of his brain tumour. His wife's silent ghost had shown it to me, a bizarre kind of mime performed to let me know the manner of his demise. She was there in the room when I'd arrived, standing at his side and staring down at him. That's why I'd been standing against the wall when Sarah walked in, watching and waiting for Tebbit's beautiful guardian to allow me the space to approach him. Despite being in a coma, he'd known that his wife was there. I could tell by the way she was smiling, and the tenderness with which she touched his pale, slack skin.

She had been there to guide him. All she had to do was wait for him to slip away and join her.

Would my loved ones do the same when it was finally my time to leave? Was that when I'd see them again, my beloved wife and daughter? The thought had crossed my mind too many times over the years, but I was too afraid to test the theory. What if I killed myself and they didn't come? That would be the worst horror of all: taking my own life to find that I was alone on the other side of the curtain, and doomed to continue my search beyond the confines of the reality I had left behind.

No; that was not the way I wanted to go. I'd been close to ending things on several occasions – one of which was soon after I'd arrived in the grey zone in Plaistow. But I was stronger than I thought, and had not yet weakened enough to take that most desperate of paths. I would survive; I would endure. It was what I did.

When my time came I would go with grace, but until then I had to rage against the dying of the light and use what I had to help others come to terms with their own transition from one reality to another.

The dying of the light: Dylan Thomas. He was another man who knew more than he had ever let on, other than between the lines of his work.

Sarah and I sipped our drinks, staring at each other, conscious of the space between us. It was not the literal space inside the room, but the gulf that sat between us in another sense: the terrible distance created by what we didn't know about each other and the situation in which we found ourselves.

"You mentioned your father – or, more precisely, the fact that he wasn't your father." It felt like a dance. We had to perform the right moves to prevent us from falling on our backsides and spoiling the routine.

"Yes. That's right. I don't know if you knew Emerson Doherty, but he was well-respected on the police force."

I nodded. "Yes, I met him a few times. I can't say that I knew him exactly, or that I liked him, but we came across each other occasionally during the course of my work with Tebbit and others. I got the sense that he didn't like me at all, and he certainly wasn't happy with the reasons I was helping out the police."

Sarah put down her glass on the floor next to her chair. "Yes, for a supposedly religious man he was very mean and closed-minded regarding the idea of belief. It was a case of his way or no way at all. He was even like that here at home – more than he was elsewhere, if I'm honest. He… he wasn't a nice man." Her lips were pale. Her face looked drained of blood.

"What did he do, Sarah?"

She blinked and it looked like she was fighting back tears. "I keep seeing him. Is he here? Can you sense him, I mean? Is he in the house?"

"I think so." I closed my eyes and waited. Something moved downstairs, under the floor. In the cellar? I didn't hear anything, not really: it was more like I sensed movement down there, in the darkness. "He's under here." I pointed at the floor.

"That was his office space," said Sarah. She looked down at the floor. "He was down there yesterday, when I found his secret stuff. I was looking through his things, rooting around for information, and he was watching me."

I leaned forward in the chair. "Did you see him, Sarah?"

She nodded again. "Almost... yes, I think it was more like a glimpse of him. He was there, I know he was there. He wanted me to find something."

The words of the disabled Rwandan psychic came back to me: *You cannot help. She is lost to you...* I remembered her bloodied body on the floor, and the small girl who sat on her chest, eating, eating, partaking of her damaged flesh.

"What else, Sarah? What else have you found out?"

When she looked at me her eyes were moist, shining. Her cheeks were lily-white. "He used to kill children. He said that an angel taught him how to see the evil inside them, to see the terrible adults they would grow up to be. So he took them and he drilled holes in their heads. He used an old trepanning device to... to let the dead bad things out."

The room seemed to be spinning, but slowly; it was a fairground ride I was unable to get off. "Are you sure?"

"Yes. There's no doubt, it was him. He even left messages on his mix tapes, between the songs. It was as if he needed to speak to somebody but could only trust himself, so he put it down on the recordings. The thing is, it's happening again. I found the body of a kid in a dentist's chair, and then two more were found in Roundhay Park. All killed the same way. All with holes drilled in their heads. To let them out – the dead bad things Emerson claimed to have seen inside them. That was one of his phrases: dead bad things. It was his favourite way of describing human evil, the general badness he thought was buried deep in the soul of humanity."

The room was still moving, and I had to adjust myself to the slow-spin of its motion. It felt like we were moving towards something, a home truth or a fundamental piece of whatever puzzle we were locked into. "Do you think his ghost is killing the children? In all the time I've been mingling with the dead, I've not known many of them do that. Not to kill the living. I've known plenty of spirits who've manipulated people into doing it for them, but only a handful who've done it themselves, with their own dead hands. Not ghosts. They don't really like to operate like that. Other things, yes, but rarely the spirits of the dead."

Sarah stood and paced the room. She kept sticking her hands in her pockets and taking them back out again, unable to settle upon a comfortable position. "I don't know, Thomas. None of this makes any sense. I never used to believe in ghosts, but now I don't know what I believe in. If I'm honest, I'm struggling to believe in anything right now."

"Just relax. We'll find out what's going on here, I promise. I think your situation is linked with mine. We were supposed to meet and have this conversation. Even he's gone quiet." I nodded towards the floor.

"OK." Sarah stopped moving. She stood with her back against a book case. "You're right. This feels like it was waiting to happen – like we've both been moving towards this point. I think we can help each other somehow." She ran a hand through her hair. Smiled sadly but tenderly. "Listen, do you mind if I have a quick shower? After that I'll show you your room and we can get some food sorted. I'm tired. I feel dirty. I just need to get clean."

I raised a hand and waved her away. "No, please, you go and do whatever you need to do. Don't worry about me. I'll just enjoy this fine whisky and wait for you." I smiled, lifted my glass in a small salute.

"Thanks, Thomas. I won't keep you long. Just make yourself at home and feel free to have a wander, use the phone. Anything you like." Her smile was faint, and she shuffled out of the door looking drawn and tired. The room finally stopped spinning. It was time to get off the ride, and probably hop right onto another one. That's the thing with fairgrounds: there's always another ride to grab your attention.

I had no doubt now that Sarah was the one both Immaculee Karuhmbi and the clockwork voice had warned me about. The real question was: why had they been so determined to keep me away from her, and from the city I called home?

The strange sounds and images in the Pilgrim Products warehouse haunted my mind: hanging, severed doll parts; the man with the bellows, working so hard to produce so very little; the hollowed out papier mâché elephant and its wizened inhabitant; the incessant wail of a crying baby; the sight of myself in that haphazard mirror; the contradictory message *Go Home* appearing on the glass.

I wish I knew what it all meant, but the truth was I'd probably never find out.

Before I knew it Ellen had come back into the room... but no, it wasn't Ellen, was it? Ellen was gone. She'd been gone for a long time. It was Sarah. Sarah had come back into the room. She had a white towel wrapped around her head to dry her hair and was wearing a tight white muscle vest and a pair of cut off denim shorts. She looked young and sweet and pretty and athletic, and I couldn't help but smile.

"What?" she said, clearly much more relaxed. "What is it?"

"Sorry, was I staring?"

She was still smiling. "Just a bit, Thomas. You old pervert."

I laughed. It felt good; it felt real. "It's just that you remind me of someone. Just there, the way you walked into the room, you were the double of her."

"Tell me who?"

I hadn't realised until now, but she did look like her. "An old friend of mine. Ellen Lang. She's dead now, but she was a wonderful woman. For a minute there, you looked just like her. I had a little flashback to better times."

"I'll take that as a compliment." She took the towel from her head, rubbing at her brown hair, and turned to close the door. That's when I saw it: the tattoo.

The room started spinning again. I was back on that same ride, the one I wanted so desperately to get off.

I stared at Sarah's back, between her shoulder blades. It had been done in Old English lettering, and was small enough to fit between her jutting bones.

I stared and I stared and I tried not to see. I wanted the words to vanish.

But they didn't.

The words stayed right where they were, taunting me with significance.

Even when I closed my eyes I could see them. The words were burned onto the backs of my eyelids.

Memento mori.

A Latin phrase: a terrible reminder of my own mortality. And now of Sarah's, too.

I remembered the hanged girls, the burning tree, the Pilgrim in his weird domain between realities, stalking the alleyways of night and hatching his unfathomable plans. He had followed me my entire life and he was following me still, even here, even now. No matter how fast I ran or how far I went, he always tracked me down. His influence was like a stain, a mark, a blemish. It would not wash off.

The Pilgrim was back – in fact, he had never really gone away.

"Where did you get that tattoo?" I heard myself speak but I could not feel my lips forming the words.

"Sorry?" Sarah turned around to face me. She had Ellen's eyes. Ellen's arms. Ellen's smile. Why had I not noticed that before? The smile: it was Ellen's. And it was beautiful.

"Your tattoo."

"Oh, I've had that since I was about sixteen. Got it done in town." She was rubbing her hair dry with the towel, rubbing it out, rubbing it away. But some things you can never wash out.

"Do you know what it means?"

She smiled, nodded. "Yes, it's a reminder of all our deaths. Some day, and sooner than you might think, we are all going to die. I was going through a bit of a miserablist phase; it seemed like a good idea at the time." Still she was smiling. She had no clue; she didn't know what it meant, not any of it.

I put down my drink and stood, pulling my shirt out of the waist of my trousers. I stared at Sarah, at her lovely, familiar blue eyes, and I wished that I could tell her what was going on. I didn't know myself, not really: all I had to work with was a kind of gut instinct, a deep, vague feeling of unease that wouldn't shift.

I pulled the hem of my shirt out of my waistband and I lifted it over my stomach, exposing the faint scar. The marks left by my last encounter with the Pilgrim. You could barely see it, unless you knew it was there. A light embossment made by hot ash: a not-so-gentle reminder. I tilted my body into the light, hoping that she could make it out and at the same time praying that she couldn't. "Do you see?"

Sarah walked slowly across the room, stopping when she was right in front of me. The smile had slipped. There was nothing beneath. She had not taken her eyes off my face as she approached me, but now she looked down, unblinking, at my belly. I felt her hand as it traced the outline of the scar, the shapes of the words, and then I watched her lips as she spoke the phrase out loud:

"*Memento mori.*"

TWENTY-NINE

Sarah woke up in the dark. The room felt smaller somehow than it ever had done before, as if the walls and the furniture had crept towards her as she slept, stalking her like prey. The old single bed was uncomfortable; its old-fashioned sprung mattress was way past its sell-by date and it hurt her back to use. She had given the guest bedroom to Usher and moved into her old room. This bed was the same one she'd slept in as a child, waiting for Emerson to enter her room and watch her, or to take out the scalpel and cut her legs.

She hated the bed. It would have been better if her parents had got rid of it after she left home. They should have cleared her room and redecorated, changing it all to erase her personality from its interior. But instead they had left everything the same, like a container for the mementos of her childhood. The same girly wallpaper, dotted with ponies. The same posters on the walls of pop stars she could barely even remember and film actors whose names and roles she'd forgotten. Even the books and magazines she'd read back then remained inside the room, stacked along the shelves Emerson had bolted to the walls.

It was as if her childhood was still here, waiting for her, and now that she'd returned to the family home she was regressing, going back to a point in her life when she had been most vulnerable.

She blinked into the darkness, wondering what had woken her. Was Usher walking around, sleepless and worrying? When he'd caught sight of the tattoo on her back something had changed between them. His face had drained of colour and his body had slumped. Then, when he had revealed the matching scars on his belly a strange thing had happened: the bond that had been forming between them became more solid, as if the words decorating both of their bodies were yet another link in a chain that stretched so far back in time that neither of them could see where it began.

In that moment, when Sarah had touched his scars, she felt closer to him than she had to any other human being in her life. Their skin fused; their lives interlocked, like two lost pieces of a jigsaw that had been found again and slotted into place. But still the picture remained incomplete: there were so many other pieces missing from the whole.

Sarah didn't know what any of this meant, but it felt... profound. Something had changed at a fundamental level: a transformation had begun deep inside her, perhaps within the hidden chambers of her heart.

She listened to the house, trying to pick out individual sounds. Timber creaked, the pipes in the walls rattled. The cantankerous boiler breathed like an asthmatic old man. She had grown accustomed to these noises during her stay back in the house – they reminded her of old times, of days and nights she wanted to forget. The heartbeat of the house was the same as it always had been. Nothing had changed, not here: everything had stayed the same.

The curtains were drawn tightly across her window so it took her a while to start seeing properly in the dark. Gradually her vision grew accustomed to the lack of light, and she was able to pick out the familiar objects in the room: the wardrobe in the corner (her empty uniform hanging like a shed skin from the door), the chest of drawers behind the door, the rocking chair near the window where she had used to toss her blazer after school.

There was somebody sitting in the rocking chair.

It was him: Emerson.

As usual, he was wearing his long black robe and the delicate white hood – the hood that resembled an old woman's doily. His features were swathed in white; cruel contours concealed beneath the square of pure silk. He was rocking slowly in the chair, his hands gripping the varnished wooden arms and his toes pressed against the floor. The motion was disturbing, almost too slow. He was looking in her direction, staring at her beneath the hood.

"I'm not scared of you," she said. "Not any more." She sat up on the mattress and slid her hand under the pillow, looking for the gun she'd taken from the drawer downstairs.

The gun wasn't there.

The figure moved one of his hands and placed it in his lap, picking up the gun that rested there, between his knees. "You should be," he said. "You should be terrified." He waved the gun in the air, making small circles with the barrel. "It isn't even loaded."

Sarah watched the gun. It was useless anyway, against a ghost. So why had he gone to the trouble of taking it from under the pillow while she slept? Why not just leave it there, if only to toy with her even more than he was right now?

The figure stood, pushing itself away from the chair. "Did you sleep well?"

That voice… it didn't sound like Emerson, not how she remembered him. It wasn't deep enough; the timbre was all wrong. "Who are you?"

The figure drifted closer to the bed, but stopped short of touching the covers. It stood there, dropping the gun onto the floor. The weapon fell with a gentle thud. "I'm your ever-loving Daddy."

Sarah shook her head. "No… you're not him. Not Emerson."

Behind the figure, in the rocking chair it had just vacated, something materialised. It was another figure, wearing the same ritualistic attire. This one did not move; it just sat there, its head cocked to one side like an inquisitive dog.

"Who are you?" Her mouth was dry and her tongue felt swollen, filling her throat like vomit.

"Who do you think?"

Realisation hit her like a blow to the solar plexus. For a moment, she couldn't speak, couldn't think. She felt staggered by his words and the implication behind them. The truth was cruel; it was yet another punishment heaped on top of all the rest.

She took a deep breath, composing herself. "Benson. What are you doing?"

The figure nodded – Benson nodded. She could imagine him smiling beneath the hood. "I told you I'd been coming to see him."

The figure on the chair shifted slightly, silently. It held up both hands, palms outwards, and waggled its fingers. It was waving at her.

"He's been guiding me, telling me what to do. Showing me the path he chose for me. I don't have the same gift as him, but he's helped me along, pointing out the way I should follow."

Sarah backed up along the bed until her back pressed against the headboard. "What the fuck are you talking about, Benson? Tell me what you mean."

He rolled his head on his neck, as if he were limbering up for some kind of exercise, warming up the muscles before commencing a tough routine. "He told me which ones to take… *the kids*. He saw the bad things inside them, just like he always did, and I took them and hid them and carried out the ritual. He pointed the way and I followed, and together we opened their minds to let out the dead bad things."

Sarah let out a small whining sound, like a stifled scream. She felt trapped, pinned to the bed. Everything was moving fast now, playing out towards the end game, and the best she could hope for was not to be killed by this fucking lunatic.

"You're ill, Benson. You're not well. Let's talk about this and maybe we can get you some help." It sounded pathetic even to her, like lines from a script that should have been rewritten long before the first act began.

"I killed the first one over a year ago, while Emerson was still alive." Benson was ignoring her, carrying on with his monologue as if she wasn't even there. "I hadn't perfected the technique – didn't realise I had to burn the holes afterwards to seal the exit and keep other bad things out. So I hid the body in a warehouse near an abandoned car park and waited for my next instructions, but Emerson died and I was left not knowing what I should do. I was lost for a while... didn't know what to do."

He paused, remembering. The figure behind him nodded.

"Then, after his funeral, he came to me. Just like the angel had come to him He told me to get close to you. He showed me what to do, where to go, and I did the next one in the dental chair, just for show. It was my own special touch, just to stamp my personality on the act."

Benson giggled. It was not a pleasant sound, nor was it a wholly sane one.

Behind him, Emerson's ghost was laughing too, but silently. His shoulders were hitching up and down in undisguised mirth and his body rocked back and forth on the chair.

"He might have been your father, but I'm his only real child. He gave birth to what I am, what I've done. I'm his one true son." With these words Benson seemed to come back to her, re-membering that she was there, cowering on the bed.

He reached up and took off the hood, exposing his scars. His face glowed in the darkness, as if some internal light had been switched on. "These scars... my ruined face. *He* did it to me, marking me out. I wear them like a badge. That story about my face being cut in the crash, it was all bullshit. Emerson did this to me, scarring me as part of a ritual, an induction, to set me apart from the herd."

He smiled, and it was an awful sight. There was nothing behind the expression – nothing but deep darkness, endless night: a forever made up of scars.

"I wear his mark with pride."

Sarah's gaze kept flickering between Benson and the ghost in the rocking chair. She didn't know which one to be most afraid of. Then she remembered something that Usher had said earlier, about ghosts hardly ever hurting someone with their own dead hands. They used someone else, he'd said: they manipulated the living into carrying out such corporeal deeds.

That was when Sarah realised that the living were so much more terrifying than the dead.

Ghosts won't hurt you, she thought, but they can harm you through the vessels of the living. They can kill you indirectly, controlling damaged and willing people like puppets.

"Don't do this," she said, drawing herself up to her knees. "Don't... just remember what we had, what we've shared. What we could have been if we'd both worked hard enough to make it happen."

Benson's smile slid away; rotten flesh slipping from a leering skull. "We had nothing," he said, deadpan. "We shared nothing. All I ever wanted was to be in this house, close to him." He turned and motioned towards the rocking chair, but Emerson's phantom was no longer there. The chair was empty, but it continued to rock gently, as if someone had just stood up and walked calmly away from the scene.

Sarah was edging back along the length of the bed, towards the door, using Benson's momentary distraction to gain some ground. She kept her gaze locked onto him, willing him to look the other way for just a moment longer. But Benson turned around, and his face was like a white sheet of paper in the dark room: vast and blank and deathless.

"Where the fuck do you think you're going?" He moved along the side of the bed, matching her progress. From the folds of his robe he produced a long-bladed knife. Sarah recognised it; the knife had belonged to Emerson, a tool he'd used whenever he went fishing. Ghosts didn't need weapons; only people needed weapons, along with the will to use them. Emerson had kept the blade downstairs in the cellar. Before he managed to get hold of the scalpels, he had even used it on Sarah, carefully carving the insides of her thighs as he tried his best not to rape and then kill her – fighting his urges to remain true to his angel.

"Let me go, Benson. If you're still in there, please let me go." It hurt her to beg; it was not in her nature to ask for mercy. She was a strong woman, an independent person, and resented the fact that she had been reduced to crawling on a mattress on her hands and knees.

"Leave her."

Sarah turned and looked at the door. It was open and Usher stood in the doorway, his face grim and his eyes as hard and cold as chips of ice.

"He's crazy," she said, somewhat unnecessarily. "He killed them all... those kids. It was him."

Usher stepped into the room. Sarah remembered his admission that he was not a fighter, but he looked intent and dangerous. In his hand he hefted a large meat cleaver, which he must have grabbed from the rack in the kitchen. He adjusted his grip on the handle and raised it to waist level. "Don't make me use this," he said. His voice was low. He meant business – or was at least giving a convincing performance.

"Don't be silly, ghost-man." Benson forgot about her for a moment and turned to face the interloper. "I know all about you – Emerson told me, and the angel told him. You're evil. You're responsible for the dead bad things being in the world. You're the doorway they use to come through from whatever hell they call home." He moved forward, reducing the space between the potential combatants.

Sarah slipped off the bed. She was behind Benson now; he had moved far enough away from the bed that she could manoeuvre herself into a good position to strike. She realised that Usher was bluffing – of course he was: he had already told her that he'd be useless if things got physical. She shifted her weight and prepared to strike, scanning the area for a weapon.

"Just get out of here," said Usher. "I'm not who you think I am. I'm not who anyone thinks I am. Whatever is leaking into this place, it isn't because of me. I know that now. I might just be the only thing standing between this world and chaos."

Sarah grabbed the only thing she could think of, a heavy vase, and pushed herself off the floor. She went into an agile leap and brought the vase around in a smooth arc, resulting in the object smashing into the side of Benson's head. She moved silently; a war cry would have acted as a warning, and people only did that in films. He batted at her arms and shoulders as his body lurched sideways from the blow, but she managed to evade his desperate grasp.

Benson stumbled further to his left, and Sarah took the opportunity to dodge past him and run towards the door. On her way there she grabbed her baton from its hook on the wall, where it dangled next to her uniform on its hanger on the outside of the wardrobe door. She spun and extended the baton: it snickered in the darkness. The sound was like muted laughter.

"Bitch!" Benson staggered towards her, his hands like clutching claws as they grabbed and batted at her shoulders.

Sarah acted quickly. She stepped inside and brought the baton up and into his chin, slamming it with all the force she could muster. Benson made a coughing sound and then began to drop; Sarah stepped outside of his reach and swung the baton against his temple. The sound it made upon impact was sickening: a dry crunch as it hit bone.

Benson fell to the floor face first, his weight causing the floorboards to shudder as he made contact with them. He twitched once, and then lay still. Sarah didn't try to fool herself that she was tougher than him. She had only gained the advantage because he had lost focus, because he had allowed his rage and his madness to control him, while she had remained calm.

"Let's get this sack of shit secured and then decide what to do." She opened a drawer and took out a handful of belts, then looped them around Benson's arms and legs, trussing him up like a prize pig in a farm show. "Yeah," she whispered. "That's it, you cunt. Who's in charge now? Who's the fucking boss, eh?"

She was breathing heavily and her arms ached. She was filled with anger. But her training kicked in again and she made sure the knots were tight as she battled to get her emotions under control. She had no idea what she was doing, and what might come next, but she needed to negate this current threat. She couldn't bring herself to kill him – she was a policewoman, and cold-blooded murder went against everything she was employed to protect. No, killing Benson was out of the question – for one thing, it was exactly what that bastard, Emerson, would have done. All she could do was neutralise her attacker, make him less of a danger – bind him so tightly that he was physically unable to get back up and slaughter them both.

She glanced up and over her shoulder, the sweat running into her eyes and making her blink.

Usher stood to one side, blinking back at her. "Amazing," he said. "You're... *amazing*. Just like her." He gazed down at her with what Sarah could only identify as pride.

THIRTY

"...*amazing*. Just like her."

I gazed down at her with a strange sense of pride. She really was amazing, incredible: a woman of such power, such grace... her mother would have been so very proud.

Her mother.

I helped Sarah bundle the bound man – Benson; her ex-lover – across the room and onto the bed, where she tied him to the metal frame with yet more scarves and belts. She moved quickly, professionally, and I realised that she must be one hell of a copper. Her face was stern, the muscles in her cheeks tight as cellophane across her bones.

That steely determination; it was just like Ellen's.

Her mother.

I could barely believe what I was contemplating, what thoughts were speeding through my head. In that moment, as I'd stood confronting that madman with a meat cleaver I'd grabbed from the kitchen work bench, I had been certain. It had all seemed so clear in my mind.

But now I wasn't so sure. Now I was losing faith in the gut instinct that had almost crippled me when I had seen her in so much danger.

I watched as she finished tying up and finally gagging Benson with a strip of tape, and then I went down on the bed beside her. She turned to me, and she looked at me through Ellen's eyes.

Her mother's eyes...

She spoke to me through Ellen's lips.

Her mother's lips...

"We're done here," she said, her damp brown hair falling across her forehead.

Her mother's hair...

Her mother's forehead...

How could I ever have doubted this? Now that I had stopped to think about it, the likeness was terrifying.

This girl, this glorious warrior woman, was Ellen Lang's daughter. I wasn't sure how it had happened, or what had been done to create this situation, but I was certain now that she was Ellen's child.

The Pilgrim's hands had been all over this – it was part of his plan, the events he had put into motion many years ago, before I'd even been aware of my ability to communicate with the dead. I already knew that he had been responsible for the car crash that had killed my wife and daughter – *oh, Ally, Rebecca, how sorry I am for these betrayals* – and that he had simply been trying to kick-start whatever power had lain dormant for so long within me.

That's what this was all about: the Pilgrim and me, or whatever part of me he wanted to own. Was it an organ, like my heart, or something much less simple to define?

The Pilgrim's plans, his weird and complex plans, I could see now that they were just a part of some bizarre long game, a plot to capture whatever energy allowed me to do what I could do, see what I could see, sense what I could sense.

I stared at the majestic young woman before me, and the tears fell from my eyes like scales, allowing me to see, to truly see for the first time.

I felt tired; but I was no longer alone. At last I had someone by my side.

She looked so much like Ellen; like her mother. But if Sarah had inherited her mother's looks, then what, I wondered, might she have inherited from her father?

What exactly had she inherited from me?

THIRTY-ONE

Sarah stood before the mirror in the master bedroom, inspecting the damage Benson had caused to her arms and shoulders. Already she was beginning to bruise, and the injured areas were tender to the touch. She winced, hating Benson all over again.

She realised now that she should have listened to her instincts regarding the bastard. Her twitch – and that feeling she'd had about something not being quite right between them – had been steering her in the right direction all along. Her heart had seen through the disguise of normality he'd worn, even if her eyes were blind to the horror that he had been hiding.

"Fucker," she said into the mirror. She watched her mouth form the word and was puzzled for a moment when the sound of her voice seemed slightly out of synch with the motion of her lips. Like a scene from a badly dubbed film, her voice didn't quite match the movements.

Sarah shrugged off the effect, putting it down to her senses hitting overdrive when Benson had confronted her. Adrenaline was still pounding through her system, and this was probably an after-effect of the violence she'd displayed in the other room.

Benson was still unconscious – at least he had been when she'd left him in her room. Now she was standing in Emerson and her mother's room, and she felt uncomfortable about being surrounded by the same four walls in which the fucker had systematically raped his wife while he thought about fucking his adopted daughter.

It was the first time she'd allowed these thoughts free reign, without couching them in metaphor, and the anger felt good as it crawled around her body, snarling like a wild cat.

Anger was fuel. It could help provide strength.

Feed me, she thought. Feed me and help me end this.

But what was it, exactly, that needed to end? The haunting, certainly: she was sick and tired of seeing Emerson's ghost stalking her as she went about her business. He no longer scared her; she just wanted him gone. Usher had said that he could probably help with that side of things, and she had no choice but to trust him.

Trust. As far as she could recall, she had not trusted anyone in her entire life. This man, this stranger, was the first. But was he really a stranger? And if so, why did she feel such a bond between them, that she already knew him?

Why was there such a strong connection?

Sarah had so many questions and so little time in which to find acceptable answers. She suspected that even the answers she did find, if she could spare the energy to look for them, would provide only more questions. Things were happening here which were beyond her ability to understand: strange things, perhaps even mystic things. Evidence of the supernatural was all around her, like a thick layer of dust, and everything was tainted by its presence.

Her life was dirty; it was filthy with phantoms.

She smiled, aware that behind the smile there lay a form of madness she didn't want to let out into the world. For years she had been strong, not allowing anything from her past to impact upon her present, but now that she thought about things she realised that she had been wrong all along. The past never dies; it clings to you, never letting go. It touches all that you do and everyone you meet, causing subtle ripples in the present that move towards a possible future.

We are our past, she thought. We are formed from the things we have gone through, and if we took them away we would vanish. Like ghosts.

Ghosts. Why did it always come back to the dead?

She thought again of Thomas Usher, and the way that his world was filled with ghosts. How could he live that way, how did he survive without losing his mind? Affection for the man flooded her, bringing tears to her eyes. Now that she had properly made his acquaintance, she could not imagine her life without him. In the short space of time since they had encountered each other at the hospital, by their mutual friend DI Tebbit's bed, Usher had become an anchor in her existence. Without him to hold her in place, to tether her to the earth, she might just float away into the darkness that surrounded her and never return.

Sarah dabbed at a brutal welt on her upper arm with the wet cotton ball she held between finger and thumb, gritting her teeth as the disinfectant stung like a bite. The mirror rippled as she turned slightly to the side, its reflective surface shimmering like the waters of a pond disturbed by a slight breeze.

Sarah stood still, wondering if she'd taken a blow to the head and was suffering some kind of mild hallucination. The mirror continued to ripple; concentric circles moved out from its centre, widening as they reached the mirror's edge. Her reflection moved in the same way, subtly altering. It was like something from a funhouse, and the image chilled her as if a childhood dream had suddenly broken through into reality.

We are our past…

"What?" She reached out and touched the surface of the mirror. It was solid. The ripples were no longer evident. But behind and around her, the room looked somehow different. It was as if the rippling motion had affected the physical space in which

she stood, but when she spun around to examine her surroundings everything looked the same.

She turned again to the mirror, and saw the subtle differences:
pictures hung askew on the walls, the bed was lopsided, the
wardrobe door was open but its leading edge was curved, the
window was frosted over, the carpet moved as if it were a swarm
of insects, the walls were slanted inwards near the ceiling, the
wallpaper was crawling with flies…

Again, when she turned around to face the room, everything
looked normal. The bed, the walls, the carpet, the wardrobe: all
was as it should be.

"*Thomas.*" Her voice was quiet, nothing like the strong yell she
had gone for. She paused, swallowed to clear her throat, and just
as she was about to scream for him again she heard a noise across
the hall. In her room, something shifted heavily across the floor.

Her room.

The room where Benson was lying flat out on the bed, his
hands and legs tied with scarves and belts and whatever else she
had managed to find at short notice.

It sounded like someone was moving furniture about, dragging it across the floor. Then abruptly, she heard the bed
springs squeaking, as if a child were bouncing up and down
on the mattress.

"Shit!" She ran for the door and pulled it open, moving across
the landing. Benson must be trying to escape. She had enough
faith in the knots she'd tied to believe that he could never free
himself, but if he managed to roll off the bed somehow and get
to the door, he could cause them more trouble than they needed
to deal with right now.

Sarah grabbed the handle and opened her bedroom door. The
room was silent. Nothing stirred. The previous commotion had
ceased instantly, as if a switch had been pulled. The curtains were
still closed, so it was dark in there, but she could make out Benson's body on the bed. He wasn't moving.

"If you're awake tell me now, because if I come in there and find you faking it I'll fucking hurt you. I mean it."

No response. Benson was motionless on the bed.

Slowly, carefully, Sarah stepped into the room. She wished that she'd taken the meat cleaver from Thomas, or the knife Benson had been wielding, but the baton would suffice – she had at least been aware enough to bring it with her. She gripped its handle tightly, trusting the weapon to do its job and protect her.

The floorboards creaked under her weight. It sounded like stifled laughter. Had those boards ever made that sound before, or was this all part of some weird joke?

"Talk to me, Benson, or so help me I'll fucking kill you."

Nothing. Not a sound from the bed.

The boards stopped creaking.

"Right, you cunt." She strode more purposefully now, taking long steps across the room and holding the baton like a sword. When she stood by the bed she could see that Benson wasn't faking it: he was out cold. But there was something odd about his appearance, a detail that seemed wrong somehow. She tried to focus but couldn't quite pinpoint what was wrong about the way he looked. He was still bound to the bed, and his breathing was shallow. His hands were behind his back and his legs were pulled up and attached to his wrists, preventing any range of movement other than to gain an inch or so of breathing space.

He had turned onto his side, but that was the only change since she'd left him there.

Or was it?

No, there was something else; something fundamental that she really should be able to spot.

Then she had it: Benson was bald. He'd never been bald in all the time she'd known him, but now his head was completely shorn of hair. Laughter boiled up inside her, threatening to spill out. But this was too weird, too scary, to be funny. In fact, it wasn't fucking funny at all.

What the fuck had happened to his hair?

Benson's head turned freely on his neck. His bindings remained tight, fixing his body in place, but his head swivelled freely. "Hello, Sarah. Long time no see." His lips shone in the darkness. He had no eyebrows. His face was as smooth and shiny as plastic. It was Benson, but it looked more like a copy of Benson: a shop window dummy moulded in his image.

A *non*-Benson.

"What?" Sarah backed away. "What the fuck?"

Non-Benson twisted upright, his arms and legs jinking out of joint. The scarves and belts slackened, allowing him to wriggle free. His limbs looked boneless; they moved like serpents. Before she even registered it, he was standing by the side of the bed, grinning.

"I win," said non-Benson, his voice bland and without even the slightest trace of an accent. It was the kind of voice you forgot immediately after hearing it, but you always remembered what it said.

"What the fuck are you?" Not *who*, but *what*: what the fuck was it?

She was moving slowly, yet still she was terrified that she might stumble due to her backwards motion. The door was only yards away but it felt like miles.

"Me? I'm just your average run-of-the-mill angel." His grin was obscene, like a mutated sexual orifice clinging to the front of his head. His teeth were bone-white and pointed, and they popped up and down in his gums like tiny pistons.

"Oh, fuck." So this was Emerson's angel, the being that had told him to kill. If the situation wasn't so insane it would have made a strange kind of sense. The thing that had moulded Emerson's insanity and used it as a tool for its own grim purpose had now come to claim her, to take back its daughter...

"I'm not yours. I was never his and I'm not yours!"

Non-Benson shook his head. "Oh, I know that. I could never even have sired you anyway. See?" In a flash, he raised the black robe above his waist and showed her an expanse of pale flesh. No hair; no belly button; no meat-and-two-veg.

Again, she stifled laughter. *Meat-and-two-veg.* That had been one of her mother's comedy expressions, and the woman had always laughed at her own outdated word-play.

Sarah knew that she was on the verge of genuine panic. If she didn't get her emotions under control, she was going to die. He would kill her. Non-Benson would gut her like a fish.

There was a loud crash from behind her, across the hallway. It sounded like the big mirror in Emerson's room falling and breaking. Sarah hoped it was Usher, her saviour. She prayed that he was stumbling to her aid and had charged into the wrong room, breaking the mirror in his confusion. It wasn't much, but it might provide a chance of escape, however brief.

"Get the fuck away from me!" She felt her hip brush against the edge of the open door, and she turned and ran out onto the landing. Once there, she almost lost her mind completely. Stepping through the doorway from Emerson's room was not Thomas but a small boy with dried blood in his hair, and staggering behind him was a man in a torn gold-coloured jacket whose flesh was hanging in thick red strips from his bones. Shards of broken mirror were laced into the man's slashed skin, as if he'd been dragged through the reflective detritus after the mirror had been smashed.

Sarah staggered away from the others and half-ran, half-fell down the stairs. "Thomas!" She screamed his name as loud as she could, hoping that whatever power he had control of, he could use it against these… *things*. These creatures from the mirror.

THIRTY-TWO

Trevor's eyeballs were bleeding. That was how it felt; as if the insides of his eyes had turned to flaming blood. He struggled to keep up with the boy-that-was-not-a-boy, the demon-in-disguise, grabbing the doorframe to haul himself out of the room. Minutes ago (hours ago?) he'd been standing in his own bedroom, trying to explain to the boy why the Pilgrim was no longer there. Struggling to find an excuse.

It had all happened in seconds, like some drug-induced vision. One instant he was standing there, before the mirror that had served as his new houseguest's prison and the next he was being pulled into that same mirror by the boy – just like Alice, in his favourite childhood book, he was being taken through the looking glass.

Once there, on the other side of the glass, everything had been different. Not just his surroundings, but whoever he was on the *inside* of his body had also changed. He had become... what? Nothing. He had simply *become*.

Standing in this unfamiliar house, looking over the shoulder of his new master, Trevor knew that he had travelled beyond madness. He had lost his mind and then found it again, on the other side of the mirror. That's what it was, the mirror-side: the discovery of a new way of existing, another state of mind that fell between the cracks of the rational and the irrational and into a brand new reality.

His body had been ravaged by the journey: his flesh had peeled away, exposing white patches of bone, and pieces of the mirror had embedded itself into the bleeding mess of his frame. But Trevor had felt no pain. He was above and below and beyond all of that. Nothing could touch him, not even the angel, the Pilgrim, the lost one... the one who had now been found.

"Thomas!" screamed the strange girl, and then she tripped down the stairs, her head slamming against the wall and her back twisting into an unnatural position. Trevor heard the bones crack. His hearing was hypersensitive now. He had listened to the heartbeat of the universe, and been stunned to find that it matched the rhythm of his own black heart.

But with one major exception: the heartbeat of the universe was not organic; it was clockwork.

On his short/long/real/imaginary journey he had seen and heard many things.

Dragged kicking into the insane alleyways between separate realities, Trevor had seen his brother, Michael, and the boy had teeth like a sabre-tooth tiger. His eyes had burned yellow; golden fur had rippled at his throat. Then Trevor had heard the ticking of an infinite clock, a conceptual timepiece that kept the time of the ages and then turned it backwards, sideways, forward once again.

The heartbeat of the universe...

Drugs paled into insignificance before such experiences as these. Manmade drugs were nothing, a mere trifle. This was the ultimate high, the kick beyond all kicks. Trevor was taken past the nagging, doubting flesh and into a realm of spirit, and all he had to do was believe.

Just believe in the heartbeat of the universe...

"Mama," he said, not even knowing what he meant by the word. "Dada." Blood poured from his eyes, warming his cheeks.

"Bruvva! Bruvva Michael." His gashed lips struggled to form the words, but it didn't matter. Not at all. The words were for Trevor and for him alone – nobody else even needed to understand them. They were his; little gifts to the ghost of his sanity.

"Hummybird!" He half-remembered the safe-word, the one he'd used to gain entry to Sammy Newsome's chicken ranch. Quite why it had come back to him now, in extremis, he had no idea. But it tasted nice in his mouth... like roast chicken.

He began to laugh but it felt and sounded like he was weeping. So what. Who was to know? It was all for him now.

Long pig. He hungered for long pig. But he didn't even know what it was.

But he knew it tasted like chicken.

"Hummy! Bird! Long! Pig!"

His thoughts were alien to him now; he had no notion of what they meant. The words in his mouth, between his teeth, were random and meaningless, but they meant everything in that other place, the wonderful and terrifying gap he'd found between realities. Perhaps this was the language of infinity, and if he learned to speak it well he could return there and join his beloved sabre-toothed bruvva.

Trevor no longer believed in this reality, so it bent and buckled beneath the weight of his gaze – he was slowly unbelieving, unpicking the stitches of his own reality. He watched the walls go rubbery and the stairs flip like a giant tongue, and the girl who had fallen began to sing something beautiful in Latin. He couldn't stop this now, even if he wanted to. He'd come too far to falter.

It's me, he thought. *I'm shaping this*. He was at least sane enough to know the truth of his condition.

I'm making it all... or am I unmaking it?

He wondered if the others saw what he did, but then he realised that he didn't care. Anything he wanted, whatever he could imagine and believe in, would appear before him and be as real as anything else that might be conjured.

If he believed in the heartbeat of the universe...

Dimly, barely enough to make an impact on what was left of his mind, he registered that this belief was what held everything together. Without it, the entire universe would fail, and all the other realities would blend into the same point in space and time, creating a chaotic soup of interchanging nonsense.

The clock – the heartbeat – would stop.

He laughed again, but deep down inside he was terrified.

The world – *his* world – was transforming into a string of sensual non sequiturs.

"Oh, Trevor. What have you done?" The Pilgrim was speaking to him from a wavering doorway. "Why did you bring them to me?"

The boy-that-was-not-a-boy – not really a boy at all – cocked his head. Dried blood crawled along his hairline. Then came the voices, two of them from a single mouth: "When you switched skins, We felt you. We saw you expose your true form, so We followed you though the mirror."

The Pilgrim's face was sad; his bald head drooped and sagged and melted. "None of what you're seeing exists anywhere outside your own little bubble of reality, Trevor." His voice was a swarm of bees. "You've become trapped in a bubble, and now you're no use to anyone."

The boy, the weird little bloody-headed kid, held up both hands to the Pilgrim. "We've found you now. This must come to an end. You've gone too far."

The Pilgrim smiled a liquid smile. He laughed a bubbly laugh. "Just wait and I'll show you who's gone too far. Come and see, and then I'll come with you... if you still want me. I'll return to our designs." His words made shapes in the air: tiny hands with flies' wings for fingernails. *Buzz-buzz-buzzy-fly. Shoo fly; buzz away. Be gone.*

Trevor buzzed too, but in a different way. The scraps of his mind were drifting back towards the shattered mirror, looking for a way back to the other side.

Then, like a vision from some other kind of heaven, Thomas Usher appeared half way up the stairs.

"Shoo fly!" said Trevor, lurching forward – or what he thought must be forward; it was difficult to tell in this buzzing state of flux. "Long pig bruvva!"

Then, thankfully, the boy with the dry-blood hair reached back, reached around, and sent Trevor flying back into the place behind the mirror.

He returned to the heartbeat of the universe, and he was smiling.

THIRTY-THREE

Sarah was in agony. Her lower back felt broken, as if the nerve endings were wreathed in some kind of sticky flame. She was lying in just the right position to enable her to see up the stairwell, and to watch what was going on. She didn't understand any of it, but whatever was happening, it was important. She knew that, at least. She knew it and she *believed* it.

The shredded man in the ripped gold suit who'd been standing behind the boy had vanished. She'd been staring at him, watching his face as it seemed to stretch and warp out of shape, and then he'd smiled, his mouth elongating into an unnatural size and shape, and as the boy had turned slowly and touched his shoulder, the man had slipped quietly out of view.

That was what had happened: he'd slipped out of view. He hadn't gone anywhere physically, not really; he'd just tilted slightly to one side and slipped through a gap into another place. His image was there and then it wasn't, but in truth he had never really been there at all.

Had he been a ghost, too? Sarah supposed she would never find out.

The pain was dimming now; she was losing all sensation in her lower body, becoming numb. That was a bad sign. At least the pain meant that she was still capable of feeling, and that she was still alive. She knew that she had broken something. Something vital. She could only hope that the numbness was temporary.

"Are you OK?" Usher's face appeared in front of her. He had approached her from behind, bending down to her in the stair-well. Her legs were crumpled, her feet touching the wall opposite. Her backside was wedged against one of the risers.

She nodded. "No," she said. Then she shook her head. But it hurt to do that, so she stopped. "No. Something's... busted. Can't feel my legs." Everything below her waist had simply ceased to exist. There was no feeling there, none at all.

"I'll be back in a second." He straightened and began to walk up the rest of the stairs, his hand resting on the banister. He seemed calm, unflappable. There was a strength about him that had not been present before, during the confrontation with Benson. He seemed robust, twice the man he had been before.

Ah," said non-Benson finally catching sight of Usher as he reached the top of the stairs. "Here he is, the man of the hour. So good to see you again, Usher."

The boy, still standing in the bedroom doorway, took a single step back. In that moment, before the boy composed himself, Sarah realised something important: these other two were afraid of Usher. She didn't know why or even how he had achieved such a feat, but they were cowering before him and trying not to show it.

"So bright..." The boy's eyes were wide. His face went slack. "It's so bright. So big and bright and perfect."

For a split second, Sarah thought that she could see an aura around Usher's head, a golden halo of light within which twisted strange veins of some kind of translucent matter. They turned and corkscrewed, those veins, never at rest. They were in constant motion, changing the shape of the brilliant penum-bra. Then the vision was gone and she tried to make sense of the glimpse she'd had, the brief moment when something nu-minous had entered her field of vision.

"I can't ever escape you, can I, Pilgrim?" Usher stood at the top of the stairs, on the edge of the landing. His hands were clenched into fists. He looked bigger than before; his body seemed to take up more space than it should. His outline fluctuated, shimmering like the outline of a poorly projected image. Not for the first time, Sarah felt detached from the situation, like she was watching a film.

"I've followed you since the very start," said non-Benson. "Tracked you from between realities, reaching out to you the only way I could. You were born with something that only we are meant to create. You are unique. A beautiful mutation."

The boy stepped forward, reaching out towards Usher. His eyes blazed. "He was born with this? Born with a design of this magnitude?"

Usher shook his head. "What does this mean? What are you saying? Who the hell are you?"

"We are the Architects," said non-Benson. Sarah felt herself moving away, retreating into darkness, but she fought to remain conscious. She had to see this; she wanted to watch it play out to the very end.

"What?" Usher slammed his fist into the wall. "No more games. Just tell me what you want!" His voice seemed to make the walls vibrate, but surely that was an illusion. Energy buzzed and crackled around his shoulders, making the air fizz like carbonated water.

"We are the Architects, Usher. It's what we are. Our job is a simple one. We create designs, and then we send those designs out into your reality, where they latch onto whatever person attracts them. Serendipity is an illusion: it is all part of our designs. Like bees pollinating flowers, the designs feed from their new owners but they also make them grow, develop their lives along certain routes so that the seeds my brothers and I planted in the original designs may flourish."

Usher fell against the wall, as if he were growing weak. The boy could not take his eyes from Usher; he was transfixed by something that Sarah had merely glimpsed. Was it his "design"?

Non-Benson moved away from the wall, but he didn't quite touch Usher. It was as if he were afraid to get too close. "You are the only person to ever have been born with a design. It has never happened before. But I witnessed such a thing, during one of my forays into this reality. I've kept an eye on you ever since, and tried to... mould your life so that I might take the design away from you, take it away and use it."

The boy staggered backwards. "No! This is wrong. Such beauty... such potential power... It must not be stolen or degraded." The flesh of the boy's face began to wither. His teeth were too prominent and his cheeks sunk as she watched, giving him a skeletal appearance.

Non-Benson ignored the boy. He spoke directly to Usher, holding his gaze. His features wavered, the bones beneath Benson's pilfered face going soft and malleable. "I can't touch it, Usher. If I did, it would destroy me. Why do you think I've not just killed you and taken what you have? I don't understand what it is, or where it came from, but I know I cannot lay a hand upon it... it... is... *untouchable*. I would be torn apart by its power if I even tried."

Usher straightened his back. Power flooded back into his body. Sarah realised that some unseen battle was raging: Usher was fighting off a psychological attack from the other two. "I've always had this with me? This ability. Is that what you're saying?" The veins on the side of his neck bulged, as if filling with air.

Non-Benson nodded. "Yes, that's it. The design was dormant. It had reached its finished form even before your birth. You were born with it, and I arranged the crash to kick-start it, to see what it was capable of."

"And I started to see the dead." Usher looked down, at his feet. He was losing strength again.

"You began to see through the façade, that's all. Instead of your own reality, the one all you silly little puppets believe in, you saw that others exist alongside. You started seeing what we see. You became a little like us – like the Architects."

"This is all… it's all too much. All my life I've felt cursed, and now you tell me that I always was." Usher turned away. His face was deathly white. His eyes were almost black. "I've been cursed from the start."

Non-Benson hovered behind him, clearly desperate to touch him, to take what he had always wanted. Sarah felt nauseous. Sickness burned within her, and then, suddenly, hot vomit spurted between her lips. It tasted bitter. She couldn't keep it down.

"We cannot take this design." The boy had grabbed hold of non-Benson's arm. His fingers sank into the softening flesh beneath his shirt. "You must come back with us, so we can examine the situation. This alters everything. Our designs are no longer simply ours. Don't you see what this means?" His voice was weird; it sounded like an amalgamation of voices.

Non-Benson smiled. His lips skinned back from his face, exposing lion's teeth as they jutted from his skull.

The boy began to shudder. His entire body shook, causing his clothes to writhe. The flesh writhed with them, and his bones began to pop to the surface. There was no blood. The boy was not in pain. Then, in one sudden paroxysm of shuddering, the boy divested himself of both clothes and skin, showing his true form – or forms – at last.

There were two of them; they emerged from the boy's body like bugs from a chrysalis. The first thing Sarah thought was that they looked like conjoined locusts, with huge, chitinous rear legs and pigeon chests that were covered with a crust of black shell-like material. Their hair was long and golden, and slathered in some kind of clear fluid. It fell down across their shoulders as they moved apart: sticky golden tresses, sparkling in the poor light of the landing.

"Oh, God," said Sarah, and her words were not random.

She recalled one of Emerson's favourite sections from the

Holy Bible: Revelations. He had read it to her and her mother often, relishing the descriptions of demons.

And they had hair as the hair of women, and their teeth were as the teeth of lions...

She could barely believe that these things, these beings, were standing above her, still shuddering and rejoicing in their nudity.

Huge dark wings flexed from their shoulders, dripping with more of that viscous matter. They were the giant wings of flies: black, shining, jittering with nervous energy.

...and the sound of their wings was as the sound of chariots of many horses running to battle...

Hanging from their fat rear fat ends, dripping venom, were massive scorpion stings, thick and bloated and twitching. The tails danced in the air as they stretched out to their full length, the thick black wings buzzing around them and disturbing the air with their brilliant motion.

One woe is past; and, behold, there come two woes more hereafter...

Was that what these things were, woe personified? They had called themselves the Architects, the creators of unknown designs, but to Sarah they were the demons of Emerson's worst nightmares. They were things, they were dead, and they were bad, so very bad.

But the worst thing about them was their faces.

...and their faces were as the faces of men...

They were rudimentary, inchoate, but certainly humanoid in origin. It was as if these creatures had once been men, or were striving to be manlike. Sarah could not imagine which of these options frightened her more: the bare scraps of humanity left in their hideous features, or the beginnings of it poking through the horror as if attempting to be born.

She tried to move her legs but nothing happened.

Usher stared down at her, his pale face hanging in the air like a floating mask.

"Oh, it's so sweet," said non-Benson, shed of his borrowed flesh. His wings burred; his stinger dripped; his enormous back legs flexed and bounced. He looked like he was ready to pounce, but he was unable to direct an attack at Usher because of the power within him. So now, instead, he had turned his attention upon the only thing Thomas cared about...

"Father and daughter, together at last."

She had known that he was her father for some time now, but only at the back of her mind. The knowledge had been buried away where it could do no damage. The idea made sense, really: she almost laughed at the symmetry of the situation.

"Your mummy had an abortion, and I took what was left." His voice buzzed, like flies around shit. "And I nourished you in the spaces between, suckling you from the milk of my imagination. I believed... I *believed*, and whatever I believe shall come to pass." His lion teeth gnashed at the air as he spoke, but his voice was now perfectly clear, the buzzing sounds having receded. "The clock of the universe ticks us towards the end of things, and only I know the secret that stops the mechanism." He was ranting now, his human aspect being devoured by the monster he had become.

Just before the thing leapt down the stairwell, the other two creatures grabbed him, drawing all three together in a grotesque group hug. "No," they said, in unison. "This is not how it ends."

The thing Usher had called the Pilgrim turned and began to grapple with the other two creatures, pincers snapping, poison-tipped tail thrashing against the walls in the confined space of the upstairs landing. Sarah once again tried to move, to stand, to crawl... but her legs refused to cooperate.

Usher ran down the stairs and grabbed her by the arms, pulling her up against the wall. "Come on, Sarah. You can do it." His face was contorted from the strain of pulling her dead weight upright, and then he somehow managed to haul her upper body over his shoulder and continue on down the stairs in a lumbering hunched swagger.

Sarah's legs dragged along the floor, hitting the skirting boards, but she didn't even feel the impact – all she was aware

of was the distant motion of her feet, as if she were remembering what it felt like to move them.

Behind them, the creatures squirmed and fretted like boiling
lobsters. Their cries were oddly forlorn, like whale song, and it
seemed to Sarah that they had now abandoned human speech
completely in favour of their natural tongue.

Then, as she lifted her head and blinked through tears, she
saw them tumbling down the stairwell behind them. "*Run...*"
She hoped that Usher could hear her, but her voice was frail and
broken – just like her body.

When she opened her eyes again they were heading down
the cellar steps, and Usher had shut the door at their backs.
Sarah toppled from his shoulders and he was forced to drag her
by her wrists. Behind the cellar door, up on the ground floor,
that eerie whale song had changed pitch. It was beautiful in a
way, but achingly sad. Her fear of these creatures was slowly
being overtaken by an overwhelming sense of pity.

"I'm sorry..." Usher held her face in his hands, stroking her
cheeks with his cold fingers. "I'm so sorry... for all of this."

Sarah smiled – or she tried to; the numbness in her lower
body had begun to creep upwards, and had already reached her
face. Her body felt loose, slack. She had little control over her
muscles. "S'OK," she muttered, her eyes growing heavy. "S'OK,
Dad."

Usher smiled. His eyes, usually hard and sunken into his tired
face, shone like gemstones in the cellar's gloom.

Just as Sarah was falling into a deep, dark place, the cellar
door burst open. Detritus rained down the narrow stairwell, lit-
tering the concrete floor. The sound of something large and
cumbersome descending the stairs was awful, and Sarah's fear
returned, adding to the numbness to nail her to the spot.

Usher stood and turned to face the area at the bottom of the
stairs. His hands were clenched into fists and his feet were positioned shoulder-width apart. "This is where it all stops," he

whispered. Sarah wished that she had the strength to cry out to him, to tell him to be careful.

The first of the creatures hopped off the bottom step and into the cellar. It was ragged, with parts of its anatomy dangling by threads. The chitin breast plate had come apart, flopping open like a door in its chest, and numerous pale, hairless insect-legs twitched as they groped at the air. Flowers sprouted and died from the tips of these appendages, and each one cried out in muted agony as its brief lifespan came to a halt.

"You've been part of my life for so long that I almost don't want this to end." Usher's voice was steady; his body seemed to swell, filling the airless cellar with his presence. "But everything ends, doesn't it?"

The creature – the Pilgrim – shuddered. One of its limbs came away from its battered torso, falling to the floor. Its feet skittered on the concrete. The whole underground room smelled of sulphur and lilies. It was an odd combination, and the resulting feeling of nausea brought Sarah back to her senses.

Behind the Pilgrim, the other two creatures came into view. They moved slowly, and where in worse condition than their brother, but their lethal teeth and scorpion tails remained intact.

"You once told me that the only reason this reality exists is because we believe in it." Usher shuffled his feet. He clenched and unclenched his fists. "Well, I no longer believe in you. I don't believe you ever existed. I. Don't. Believe." Slowly, he turned his back on the creatures. His gaze locked onto Sarah's face, and she felt a warm breeze kiss her cheeks in the dark, dank cellar.

The rest of it was over in seconds. The end came not even with a whimper.

Usher was still standing in position at the foot of the stairs, his eyes fixed on Sarah's face. And behind him the two injured Architects quickly disassembled their distracted brother; pulling off his legs like a crustacean meant for the pot, plucking his wings at the root, biting off his barely human face. They feasted on their kin, absorbing him, bringing him back into the family. Whale-song cries filled the cramped space; they were so loud and sonorous that Sarah could hear nothing else. But she knew that an echo of those cries would remain inside her head until the day she died… and possibly beyond even that.

Then, in a sort of folding motion, the three straining creatures all became one pulsating mass of wings and legs and lion teeth, of golden hair and scorpion tails, of otherworldly pain and forlorn whale-song.

That busy fury, in the form of an unruly storm of woes, rose slowly from the floor and folded even further in on itself, becoming smaller and denser, like a collapsing star drawing energy into its failing orbit: a tiny black hole suspended in the solar system of Emerson Doherty's cellar. There was a loud shattering sound, and a trembling not unlike a minor earth tremor and when Sarah blinked, they were gone.

Up above, in the house, the tremors continued, shaking apart the walls and buckling the floors. After-shocks travelled throughout the structure, creating a storm of brick dust that blinded Sarah. Then even this leftover energy was dispelled, directed into the building's foundations and then deep into the waiting earth.

Usher went down on his knees, exhausted. His hands flailed at the wall, his nails scratched at the dry plaster. He looked spent, and Sarah wondered what part his mysterious power had played in those final horrifying moments of absolute destruction. And what price it would demand of his body.

Sarah was still unable to move. She felt that she might never move again, not without aid. But now, she realised with a warmth at her core, there was finally someone here to help her. Because her father, for whom she had spent a lifetime wrapped up in grief, was back; he was home; he was here.

He was her father. And she loved him, no matter what the cost.

THIRTY-FOUR

When I emerged from the cellar we expected the house to be in ruins, but it still stood. The main walls remained upright, the doors and window frames were intact, despite the shattered glass and broken furniture. The internal damage was extensive, but at least the roof was not going to fall down and crush us – what irony that would have been, to be killed by falling masonry after defeating the Pilgrim and his siblings.

The main thing was that we were safe. I carried Sarah in my arms, like a baby, and walked through the mess of the ground floor. We were both crying, but silently. I'm still not sure exactly what we were crying for.

I set Sarah down on a filthy sofa and used her mobile phone to call an ambulance. I told them that there had been some kind of freak earthquake, and I knew the damage to adjacent properties and terrified accounts from the neighbours would probably make that story stick. Why would they want to consider an alternative reason for the destruction anyway, when a rational story was so close to hand?

Even now, neither of us is clear of the exact details of what happened inside that house. We both saw different things, and for once I suspect that I was the one who failed to see it clearly.

Sarah claims that they were biblical demons, exactly like a description in the King James Bible, Revelation 9 – but from her upbringing her mind is accustomed to Christian imagery and it would naturally shape the sight into something that she could recognise. I have no idea what I saw, but to me they resembled more closely the artist Francis Bacon's *Figures at the Base of a Crucifixion* – austere anthropomorphic creatures writhing in a state of tired agony. They were not ghosts, they were something else. The Pilgrim and his brothers: the Architects of Serendipity. They were something else entirely.

What I think happened is that the Pilgrim's brothers would not let him contrive to take whatever it is they called my design. Either they were too afraid or simply not ready to reach out towards a thing they had called *untouchable*.

At the time I felt as if the design I supposedly possess provided at least some of the energy required to halt the Pilgrim's desperate end game. But in all honesty my final line of defence was naught but a bluff – I'm not sure if it was my disbelief that rendered the Pilgrim powerless or if his belief in my rejection of his reality simply caused him to unravel. Whatever the case, he became the architect of his own downfall.

Or maybe not...

I still cannot understand the true nature and motivations of that grinning trickster demon, and perhaps I never will. Perhaps it is better that way.

Often the things we don't know are the very things that save us. Sometimes ignorance can amount to a kind of salvation.

I don't know if I'll ever see the Pilgrim again, but for the first time in my life a kind of spiritual weight has been lifted. I am no longer afraid; he does not frighten me. The Pilgrim, it seems, is more afraid of me than I ever was of him.

I spent so long under the Pilgrim's gaze that I believed it was normal to endure such intense spiritual scrutiny, and now that he is no longer watching me I feel a sense of freedom that is utterly terrifying in its absence of surveillance.

Part of me misses being the subject of so much attention. The rest of me, the sensible part, is intensely grateful for each and every day that I remain free.

It will take time to get used to this freedom.

It will also take time to grow accustomed to being a father.

Sarah is my daughter, of that fact I have no doubt. She is mine, my flesh and blood. We both know it, by a means that it is beyond our ability to understand. Call it supernatural; call it what you will. It is the bond between father and daughter.

It has been six weeks since the events at Emerson Doherty's old house. The For Sale sign went up a week ago, and there has already been some interest in the property. We have priced it low, as I'm sure can be understood, in order to make a quick sale.

The doctors have told me that Sarah will never walk again. Her lower spine was shattered in the fall; the damage is so extensive that surgery is not an option.

She is crippled, but she is alive. She lives. That is enough for us both.

I have spent so long grieving for my dead family, and hoping that I might see their ghosts, that the very notion of "family" has become something I no longer understand. It is something else that I will be required to learn again.

I have a lot to learn. All over again.

In a few days I can bring Sarah home. I've opened up the old place, the house I bought with Rebecca and Ally, and aired out the empty rooms. I shall wheel her home in the chair, and once I've made some money I will modify the house to suit her needs. Entrance ramps, a stair lift, so many other things that I will have to research and then have installed. Sarah can choose the new décor in every room and I will carry out the work. I have no real style to speak of, and the place will benefit greatly from a woman's touch.

But we have time. We have all the time in this world and the next, as long as the clock of the universe keeps ticking.

Sarah gets glimpses now; she sees things. She calls it her twitch. I am not yet sure how much she has become aware of, but it is her birthright. She got her mother's looks and my... my what? Did she inherit a version of my design, or perhaps just a small piece of it?

I can't be sure. Nothing is certain. Even reality cannot be trusted. Sarah's origin – despite what the Pilgrim told me – is the biggest mystery of all.

All those years ago, when we first slept together, why didn't Ellen tell me that she was pregnant? If she had an abortion, as Emerson's grim angel told me, then why can I find no official record of the procedure?

The Pilgrim, like the devil that lives within us all, on that dusty lower landing of the human soul, is a liar. But couched within a network of lies there is always the shadow of truth. The only truth I care about is that I have a daughter – one that is alive, who I can touch and protect. Little else matters to me.

I will always miss my family, but now I have a new family to share in that grief. I wish Sarah could have known her half-sister, and my wife. I wish we could all be together, if only for a short time...

But I know that will never happen.

Life doesn't work that way.

DI Tebbit is still in a coma. Through all this, he has somehow kept on going, his failing system refusing to give up the fight and go gentle into the night – be it good, bad or otherwise. He is in no state to clean up my mess – not this time – but there are other sympathetic officers who have been willing to help. They have no choice; they are all tainted by Emerson Doherty's madness.

Benson's disappearance has been useful for the police – Sarah showed her superiors the evidence she'd found in the cellars under Emerson's house, and since then his guilt in the old, unheard of killings has been suppressed. Tebbit's superior officers examined the photographs in silence and listened to the tape recordings as the murderer précised his own crimes between songs.

The pay-off we demanded for our silence regarding the matter was that they don't go looking for Benson. He was a killer, an embarrassment to the force, and they are more than happy to pretend that he is just another missing person. They know he's dead; of course they do. But they play the game and they follow the rules, thankful that there are still some pieces left to move around the board...

So many missing people; even those we can see or feel or touch. Sometimes those missing are closer to us than we might like to think.

If my dying friend, DI Donald Tebbit, ever comes out of his coma I will tell him everything we have experienced, but I don't expect that to happen. It is almost his time to go, to become one of the missing himself.

The watchful ghost of his wife never strays from his side. She is there for him, no matter what. Just like Sarah and I will be there for each other, now that we have finally found the remains of our family.

It is enough, for now. In fact, it is more than enough: it's everything we have.

ACKNOWLEDGMENTS

Not too many people to mention this time around, as I kept my head down and went at it like a battering ram. A great debt of gratitude is due, though, to Mark West for being such a great and insightful (and honest!) test reader of this material. I know he found a certain scene hard to take, and I apologise for putting him through the emotional wringer. I'd also like to pay my dues to the great Ramsey Campbell, whose work continues to inspire and astound me. As usual, Gary Fry and John Probert supplied some welcome chuckles along the way (and believe me, with a novel this dark, laughs are hard to come by). Finally, and by no means any less worthy of my humble thanks, I have to say that none of this would have been possible without my amazing wife Emily, and our weird and wonderful son, Charlie.

ABOUT THE AUTHOR

Gary McMahon's short fiction has appeared in numerous acclaimed magazines and anthologies in the UK and US and has been reprinted in yearly "Best of" collections.

He is the multiple-award-nominated author of the novellas *Rough Cut* and *All Your Gods Are Dead*, the collections *Dirty Prayers* and *How to Make Monsters* and *Pieces of Midnight*, and the novels *Pretty Little Dead Things*, *Rain Dog*, *Hungry Hearts* and *The Concrete Grove*.

He has been nominated for seven different British Fantasy Awards as both author and editor.

www.garymcmahon.com

LATE RUNNERS

This short story – written in August 2005 – is the first ever story to feature Thomas Usher. It first appeared in The First Humdrumming Book of Horror *in September 2007.*

It was a long drive to Upper Chinley, particularly at the speed I travel, but my old Volvo managed the journey without giving me too much cause for concern. It voiced the odd groan or stutter when forced to climb one of the many steep inclines we encountered along the way, but for the most part, it soldiered on admirably. I don't like cars as a rule, but this one suited me more than most – although none of them suit me too well.

The village was your quintessential northern English picture postcard scene: shambling cobbled lanes, leaning terraces built of rugged yellowish Yorkshire stone, old people sitting as idle as fading memories in teashop windows, eating Eccles cakes and drinking tea from patterned china cups.

The weather was typically English too: a light smattering of rain falling from a sky the colour of scrubbed slate.

As I passed along the main high street, enquiring eyes intently watched my progress. I was a stranger here, and as such, my business was suspect. It's always this way in small, close-knit communities, especially these days, when even your closest neighbour cannot be trusted.

One quickly grows used to mistrust in my line of work.

School Cottage was located a mile outside of town, and could only be accessed by use of a meandering unmade road that snaked through the edges of a pretty, bluebell-spattered woodland. Trees bent their heads to brush against the roof of my car and animals capered out of sight, rustling loudly through the damp colourless undergrowth. The Volvo's chunky tyres settled into deep runnels worn by the to-ing and fro-ing of other vehicles, and my progress was slow but steady. I would get there in the end; I always did.

Soon the cottage came into view, and I saw the lone figure of a woman standing behind the low front garden gate. As I drew closer, details became clearer, but upon initial inspection she looked as grey as the sky above her; tired, washed out. Like a ghost.

"Mr Usher!" called the woman, waving and limping as she opened the gate and came to meet me as I climbed out of the car. "Hello."

Up close, I could see that she was very old, but her eyes shone with an incongruous youth and vitality. Something here at School Cottage agreed with her, and I feared that if whatever it was ever left she might decline in its absence.

"Ah, Mrs Croft. So pleased to meet you."

She led me inside, and as I followed her, I noticed the heavy bandage on her left leg. She'd told me of her fall when I'd spoken to her on the phone earlier that week; that during one of the manifestations she'd been knocked off her feet and had bruised a bone.

Once inside the neat little house, over hot tea and buttered crumpets at the comfortable kitchen table, Mrs Croft began to tell me her tale.

"It began in earnest just over a month ago, but I've been aware of their presence ever since moving in here thirty-odd years ago – a breeze that shouldn't be there, the sound of distant childish laughter, a sense of being watched whenever I hang out the washing or prune the roses."

"But nothing more... substantial?"

"No, Mr Usher. There's always been a feeling of welcome, even playfulness, here at the cottage. It's only recently that I've started to worry."

I sipped my tea and glanced out of the window above the old porcelain kitchen sink. Opposite was the site of the old school building, long demolished by a stray bomb during the air raids of World War Two, but its essence still rooted firmly in the strong, nurturing earth.

"Lately, there's been a different kind of energy about the place – not exactly bad, just different. Excitable. Uncontrollable. It unnerves me, Mr Usher. I'm eighty-six, and I like a peaceful atmosphere. Anything other than that tends to upset me."

I smiled. Took a bite of warm crumpet, the melted butter rolling over my lower lip and onto my chin. "So you've become afraid – is that what you're saying, Mrs Croft?"

She moved to the window, a stray shaft of weak sunlight catching in her hair and highlighting the grey beneath the subtle blue rinse. "No. Not afraid exactly. Simply concerned."

"Please, tell me more. I need to know everything if I'm to help."

"And how exactly can you help, Mr Usher? I've heard that you can commune with the dead. Is that true?"

Commune with the dead. A nice way of putting it. A coy euphemism for what amounts to some very strange business indeed.

"You could say that." I took another mouthful of my by-now tepid tea. "Several years ago I was involved in a serious road accident, and since that day I've had a certain affinity with the spirit world. I don't know why I was chosen; but I do what I can with the glimpses I'm afforded. I try to help."

Mrs Croft seemed content with that, and she smiled in such a way that seemed to signal the emergence of a tacit trust between us.

"It happens every weekday, at twilight. I hear a faint rushing

sound, like the approach of many running feet, and then comes
the laughter of children. It's concentrated out there, where the
old playground used to be, but sometimes the activity spreads."
She turned to the window, and pointed outside. The rear garden
led on to a flat concrete platform that rested at ground level, a
chipped, pockmarked surface that must have been the school
playground, where countless young bodies had run and played,
hopping and skipping and jumping, beating on the lid of the day.

"Is that where you were when you fell?"

"Yes, I was hanging out some sheets, and behind one of them,
outlined against the dying light, I saw a small figure – a child.
And then I felt fingers plucking at me, tiny hands trying to get
my attention. I fell, but they – or possibly others – raised me up
and set me down again on the doorstep. This is the first time
I've been touched, physically molested, I suppose you might
say... It was thrilling, but also terrifying. I didn't know what to
do... so after the local doctor left, I rang you."

"And how did you come by my number?" I asked, already
knowing the answer.

"A friend of a friend," she said, and poured me another cup
of sweet tea. It's always the way. I do not advertise my services,
but rarely am I idle.

We waited until twilight, passing the hours with a game of
chess. Despite her age, Mrs Croft was a worthy opponent; she'd
played to a high standard in her youth. She told me of her husband's exploits during the Great War, of his sad demise from
what is now termed post-traumatic stress disorder (back then,
it was still called shellshock) upon his return from France. She
mourned him still, all these many years later.

She told me that she had kept all of her husband's things, and
that her bedroom was like a shrine. She smiled coyly as she said
this, and I appreciated that she had been alone in every sense
of the word since his death.

We played more chess, and when Mrs Croft beat me a third

time, we called it a day. The sky outside began to darken, but when Mrs Croft got up to turn on the lights I asked her to wait. I had my reasons for preferring the gloom, and she was happy to grant my slightly unconventional request.

Soon we heard it: light, carefree laughter, riding the wind like wild birds. It was a good sound, a happy sound, and we both smiled.

I moved slowly to the kitchen window, leaving the lights off and being careful not to draw attention to my presence; I'd learned early that it was always best to remain in the background, to watch from the shadows. Dust swirled at ankle level on the uneven concrete platform, leaves and twigs scattering and the air itself corkscrewing like a series of mini tornadoes. They were coming out to play.

As Mrs Croft stood silently by my side – holding her breath in tense expectancy – I watched the vague, finely sketched figures of children appear in the playground; behind them, the silvered outline of a building shimmered into existence – the old school hall.

Most of the children were dressed in quaint Victorian era clothing, others in nothing but rags. These were children of different eras, from different times, but they played well together, as all good children do.

Girls skipped and hop-scotched, threw tennis balls against an invisible wall; boys play-fought, wrestled, and kicked leather footballs between goalposts formed by the piling up of coats and sweaters. The air was filled with layers of sound; screams and laughter, and singsong childhood chants.

A group of children broke off from the rest, and began to run around Mrs Croft's garden. One of them – a small boy obviously chosen to be "it" – chased the others, laughing and shouting as he tried to tag them one by one.

"They're playing catch," I said.

"What?" Mrs Croft was spellbound, even though she was unable to see what I could; she was still able to sense the fun and games beyond the window.

"A game: Catch. It. Tiggy. Tag. One child chasing the runners; he has to catch them all before he is officially 'off', and then another takes his place."

Tears shone in her eyes, and only then did I realise the full extent of what was happening.

The back door suddenly rattled in its frame as something outside clattered against the sturdy timber. I heard the scratching of fingernails on wood, the short sharp sound of a foot kicking the bottom of the door. Mrs Croft tensed against me, her body unconsciously shifting so that mine was in front, protecting her.

"This is what happened last time," said Mrs Croft, panic giving a shrill edge to her voice. "They're trying to get inside."

"No," I said, taking her old, creased hand in mine. "You've misunderstood. They're inviting you outside to play."

She looked at me then, staring right into my eyes, and beyond, deep inside, to the place where all our childhoods collide. And she was a girl again, ten years old and eager to run. Keen to play.

I unbolted the door and stepped aside, allowing her to pass through; she smiled as she sidled past, and once again I felt her hand in mine – this time it was tiny, smooth and unlined.

I watched them play until well after dusk, when the moon and the stars lit their way. Not long after they began to fade, shrinking in on themselves like dying flowers as night fell and the time to play was done. I scanned the edges of the spectral playground, checking the boundary for telltale signs: mobile shadows, coiled, bulky shapes that seemed more solid than the rest of the dark. I saw nothing. This time the darkness was natural.

Mrs Croft was sitting once more at the kitchen table when I finally turned away from the window, her eyes closed and a smile on her slack face. Her wrinkled hands rested on the tabletop, palms flat, fingers splayed. The children had come to claim her, to lead her into the final playtime, and she had responded only with my help. It's what I try to do: I lend a hand; I aid in the crossing from one state to another, pointing out which road must be taken. There are, of course, other necessary aspects to what I do, but this is my primary task, my *modus operandi*.

I am a simple guide, and nothing more.

When I left School Cottage that night it was with a light heart. My work was done and another good soul had been sent on its way, along the correct route and at the allotted time. Sometimes it isn't so easy. But this time Mrs Croft chased happily after the runners; and when she finally catches them she will be home. I can only hope that she doesn't pause in the chase, or run in the wrong direction.

Hashtag

Join in the discussion of this book on Twitter
by using and following the tag **#deadbadthings**

A THOMAS USHER NOVEL

PRETTY LITTLE DEAD THINGS

GARY McMAHON

"I loved it. Subtle, moving and beautifully written." – *Michael Marshall Smith*

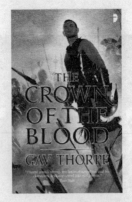

CALL YOURSELF A FAN, MEAT THING?

Collect the whole Angry Robot catalog!